Sign up for our newsletter to hear
about new and upcoming releases.

www.ylva-publishing.com

IRREGULAR
Heartbeat

CHRIS ZETT

Acknowledgments

THIS BOOK HAS EVOLVED DURING the years of writing from a vague idea to a final version I'm happy and proud to share. I wouldn't have been able to create it without the help of many friends and strangers:

The nameless drummer who played so enthusiastically during a concert that I couldn't stop staring.

The friendly staff at my two favorite cafés: November and Stockholm. You have the best tea, coffee, and cinnamon rolls to fuel a writer.

My teachers and fellow students of the GCLS Writing Academy 2016/17. You inspired me to write better and finally finish the book.

My invaluable beta readers who read all or parts of my story and often provided feedback I didn't want to hear but needed to: Bianca, Isa, Jon, Katja, Melanie, Simone, and Trish.

My GCLS mentor, editor, and friend Sandra for teaching and encouraging me. More often than not you knew better than I what I wanted to say and expressed it more eloquently than I could.

The team at Ylva Publishing, especially Astrid, who are not only professional, but super nice too, and published the book in record time with a wonderful cover.

And last, but not least, my wife, Bianca. Thank you for not only tolerating but supporting my mental and physical disappearances into the realm of writing.

Dedication

To Bianca—my real-life workplace romance.

Chapter 1

DIANA STEPPED UP TO THE glass wall and discreetly tried to get a look at her reflection between the large, red letters spelling *Emergency Department*. Neat hair, boring clothes. Not even close to the rock star look she'd sported last year.

She clutched her extra large mocha for a second longer, then tossed the empty paper cup into the wastebasket and wiped her damp hands on her slacks. A glance at her cell phone confirmed she was twenty minutes early. *Well, better early than late.* This was her last chance at a career in medicine, and if she blew it by making a bad impression…

She swallowed. *I won't.*

The electronic door opened with a hiss. Immediately, the clean smell of disinfectant reminded her of her father's practice and calmed her. The entrance area was an empty space designed in imposing granite like a bank, and her echoing steps reinforced that impression. She tried to look confident and at ease as she addressed the woman behind the glass wall at the admission desk.

"Good morning. I'm Diana Petrell, the new resident. I'm looking for Dr. Emily Barnes, if she's here already."

"Hi, Dr. Petrell. We've been expecting you. Here's your paperwork and your ID card. It gets you through here," she pointed to the door in the glass wall, "and into the locker room, cafeteria, and so on." When Diana needed two tries to swipe the card in the right direction, the woman laughed softly. "I'm Stacy. Welcome to Seattle General Hospital."

Diana laughed with her but couldn't say more than "thank you" as Stacy rapidly gave her directions to the locker room.

"Get changed and then find Tony, the day-shift charge nurse." Stacy pointed toward a lanky guy in blue scrubs at the far end of the counter, who smiled and waved. "He'll find Dr. Barnes for you," she added with a grimace.

What's that about? New arrivals demanded Stacy's attention before Diana could find out more about Dr. Barnes.

She headed toward the locker room. As soon as she stepped into the drab beige corridor, a low-level background noise of hurried steps, beeps in various rhythms, and the screech of an uneven set of wheels enveloped her like the hug of a long-lost friend. She hurried past wheelchairs, IV poles, and supply carts to the staff-only area of the ED. When she located the women's locker room, she managed to swipe her ID correctly on the first try and entered the windowless room.

Several of the dented metal lockers stood empty. The walls were painted puke green, but she supposed it might have been a friendly spring color a few years ago. Or probably decades.

A shelf next to the door held neatly folded blue scrub shirts and pants. Diana grabbed a comfortable size to accommodate her white, long-sleeved T-shirt that she planned to keep on underneath. She picked an unused locker and quickly changed. The soft cotton was perfect; she'd missed this.

She removed well-used white running shoes from her backpack and slipped them on. Still comfortable. They had survived the nine years in storage surprisingly well. She had rediscovered them in the same box that held her medical texts, her lab coats, and the dark red stethoscope Henry, her favorite brother, had given her for graduation.

Diana distributed a pen, a penlight, her smartphone, and a black notepad to the various pockets of her scrub shirt. Finally, she slung her ID badge and the stethoscope around her neck. The ritual reminded her of donning armor before a battle, but she wouldn't go so far as to compare herself to a valiant knight. The unaccustomed weight pulled on her shoulders, and she would need several days to get used to it again.

She put on her much-rehearsed confident and friendly smile and went to find Tony. Showtime.

"And here is the staff lounge and Dr. Barnes. Good luck." Tony finished the short tour of the ED. He opened the door for her and left with a wink.

Was he hitting on her, or was this just his normal way of communication? She shrugged it off and turned her attention to the staff lounge.

The middle of the room was dominated by two dark leather couches flanking a large coffee table. Small circular burn marks indicated that it had been here longer than the no-smoking regulations. Mismatched desks with computer terminals lined two walls. Diana was happy to see a kitchenette with an industrial-sized coffee urn, a microwave, and a fridge. All the essentials to surviving a twelve-hour shift.

Diana's focus shifted to Dr. Barnes, the attending who would be her supervisor. She had been unable to learn anything substantial about her from her new colleagues. Everyone had either twitched or frowned whenever Emily Barnes's name had come up.

The slender, pale woman sent out don't-talk-to-me vibes. She was sitting on one of the couches, typing on a laptop. Her strict posture screamed either ballet dancer or military. Or maybe librarian. The neat bun that imprisoned every strand of her light brown hair reinforced this impression.

Should she wait to be acknowledged? That wasn't really Diana's style. A polite greeting had never hurt anyone. "Good morning. Dr. Barnes?"

She looked up, nodded, and studied Diana for a moment with hard gray eyes. "New resident?"

What an unusual eye color and hair combination. "Yes. Hi, I'm Diana Petrell. I was told to meet you here." Diana moved closer and offered her hand.

Dr. Barnes gave it a short, hard squeeze. She didn't stand, and even though she looked up at Diana, she managed to make her feel smaller.

Impressive.

"You're late."

"I thought I was early." A quick look at the clock on the wall confirmed her statement. Five to eight.

"You're not. The morning shift started an hour ago."

Diana bit the inside of her cheek to stop herself from reacting to the cold tone. Instead, she focused on the content of the statement. "I'm sorry. I was told to be here at eight. I'll be on time from now on." She struggled not to ball her hands into fists.

Dr. Barnes took her time moving the laptop to the side. It probably wasn't a coincidence that it aligned precisely with the edge of the table. "I expect punctuality, hard work, and preparation. If you can't commit to our schedule, this residency won't work. It's very unusual to begin your work here halfway through the program and in the middle of the year." She frowned, but the lines were barely visible in her immaculate makeup.

It was difficult to guess her age. Everything between twenty-five and fifty seemed possible. She was probably close to Diana's own thirty-seven.

"I'll evaluate your performance and supervise you until we decide what you can do on your own." Dr. Barnes pointed to the other couch. "Sit. Dr. Wallace emailed me your résumé. What kind of work did you really do?"

Dr. Barnes had a long list of procedures, both diagnostic and therapeutic, to go through. After fifteen minutes, Diana was sweating. This was worse than her job interview last week. Dr. Wallace, the chief of staff, had at least been civil.

Just when Diana thought they were finished, Dr. Barnes presented her a case. "A thirty-year-old male with chest pain. He's pale and a bit short of breath. Vitals are stable. What do you think?"

Was this like a board examination? Diana decided to address the question as if it were. "First, I'd introduce myself to the patient and ask him about the pain and the situation he was in when it started. Then I'd interview him about his history, and then—"

"Skip it. Three differential diagnoses. Now." The tone was sharp enough to make Diana flinch.

Diana bit down any rebellious instincts to answer in the same manner. "Pneumothorax, pneumonia, and intercostal neuralgia. Without further information it's impossible to—"

"Pneumothorax. What do you do?" Dr. Barnes took a sip from her mug.

"If the X-ray confirms it, I'd put in a chest tube." Diana wished she could drink something too. She'd already used up the caffeine from her way to work and her mouth was dry. But she wouldn't give Dr. Barnes the satisfaction of appearing weak by asking for coffee. "Do you want me to explain how it's done?"

Dr. Barnes shook her head. "We'll save that for later. So, did you put in one before?"

"Many. We regularly treated gunshot and knife wounds in LA." Diana wanted to slap herself for bringing up the one topic she wanted to avoid: her last residency.

"Is that the reason you quit? Too much violence?" Dr. Barnes leaned forward. Her gray eyes seemed like lasers, ready to cut through any defense Diana could think of.

Diana squared her shoulders and forced herself to hold her gaze. Yes, she had something to hide, but she hadn't done anything wrong. "During my final year, I had to interrupt my residency for personal reasons. The patients in the ED had nothing to do with it." She had to take control of the discussion and tell Dr. Barnes something about the nine-year gap in her résumé before she asked too many questions. "I couldn't work in the medical field after that, but I regularly read medical journals and visited conferences to stay up-to-date with current standards and new medications." Diana tried to gauge Dr. Barnes's reaction, but her features hadn't moved out of the slightly displeased expression they had been in from the beginning. She continued before Dr. Barnes could interrupt her again. "You'll see that I know how to evaluate patients, treat most of the standard problems, and, most importantly, I know when to ask for help."

Dr. Barnes studied her for a moment, and Diana forced herself not to fidget. If she could bluff her way through contract negotiations with business sharks, she could appear confident now.

Finally, Dr. Barnes leaned back on the couch, but the deliberate movement didn't seem relaxed. "Journals? Conferences? Commendable, but they can't replace real experience. Today we'll work all cases together and see how you're doing. Without my approval, you won't touch anyone or give any orders." She waited for Diana to nod before she continued. "Just pretend you're a medical student, and we'll get along fine."

Student? Was that some kind of a joke? Diana ground her teeth. Her return to medicine after a long absence was highly unusual, but she was no student. She had treated patients on her own before and knew her limits. She fought the urge to tell Dr. Barnes exactly that. It hurt to be on the bottom of the food chain again, but her ego wasn't important today. She unclenched her jaws and faked a smile. "No problem. I'll follow you. Let me know what you want me to do." She would be the perfect demure medical student until she earned Dr. Barnes's trust, and she damn well would be all adult about it.

Just when she thought the worst was over, Dr. Barnes fired more questions. "So, what does *personal reasons* mean? Housewife? Kids? Jail? Drugs?"

Diana laughed until she realized that the last bit hadn't been a joke. Did Dr. Barnes really think she could keep her medical license after nine years in jail? Unfortunately, the chief of staff had forbidden her to talk about the real reason she had spent the last few years out of a hospital. She hoped the story she had come up with didn't sound too weak, but the truth wasn't helpful if she wanted to gain respect as a physician. "No, nothing like that. I...um...I had other obligations. I worked with a friend and had no time for a full-time residency. We lived far from the next hospital...on a farm." Diana suppressed a wince. That sounded even less convincing when she said it out loud than in rehearsal.

She shifted on the couch and tried to think of an alternative direction of this discussion. Her gaze fell on the laptop. "I guess you're doing your charts electronically now. I hope that's an improvement to carrying around the high stacks, like we used to. How many patients have you got this morning? What can I do to help?"

From the look Dr. Barnes gave her, she had seen right through the feeble attempt at deflection, but instead of asking more questions, she hit a few keys on her laptop, then turned it around. "Here, take this one: female, twenty-one years, abdominal pain for five hours in the lower right quadrant, no emesis or diarrhea."

Diana grinned. Appendicitis was an easy enough start. Even her grandma would be able to make a diagnosis. Or was Dr. Barnes tricking her?

Dr. Barnes led the way through another corridor stuffed with medical paraphernalia to a large room where several examination bays were separated by curtains. She pointed to the patient's chart in a metal holder at the entrance of one cubicle. "That's all the paper that's left; the rest is digital. Go inside and examine her. I'll watch, and we'll discuss the case outside before you recommend further diagnostics or treatment. Don't promise anything you can't keep."

Diana swallowed a comeback. Everyone learned in their first week of internship to avoid promises. Convinced that her face muscles would ache terribly in the evening, she resumed her smile and entered the examination room.

As soon as she saw the patient, Diana's heartbeat quickened. *Finally back at work.* She quickly disinfected her hands, using the bottle next to the door. The alcohol helped to hide her clammy palms.

"Ms. Miller? I'm Dr. Petrell. You're here because of abdominal pain, is that correct?"

The young woman nodded and grimaced at the same time. Fear emanated from her in waves.

Diana sat on a stool to bring herself to eye level with the patient. This time her smile wasn't forced as she tried to project calm. "Can you tell me more about it?"

Ms. Miller recounted her problems, and Diana listened intently, asking her to clarify some points and then questioned her about her prior illnesses, medications, and allergies. The familiar ritual helped her to overcome her nervousness.

"You don't take any medication? Not even occasionally over-the-counter pain meds or the pill?" Most patients forgot about those, and Diana had learned the hard way to never take anything for granted.

Ms. Miller shook her head and blushed. "We're careful," she mumbled.

Diana mentally added pregnancy to her internal checklist. Warming her stethoscope in one hand, she stood. "I need to examine you now. Tell me if anything hurts, okay?"

She hadn't done this in years, but the routine was still intact after thousands of patients. She worked her way down until she reached the abdomen.

When Diana pulled up the gown, the patient tensed and put both hands in front of her lower abdomen.

Diana looked up and met her gaze.

Ms. Miller's dark brown eyes were large and gleamed with unshed tears. Her lips trembled, but she didn't say anything.

Diana didn't like that part either, but not doing it wasn't an option. "I'll be careful, but I have to check for myself. I'm sorry." She smiled encouragingly, and Ms. Miller lowered her hands back to her sides. The only thing Diana could do to make it more bearable was to finish it as fast as possible.

First, she checked with her stethoscope for bowel movement and then carefully palpated the patient's abdomen, avoiding the lower right quadrant until last. When she put her hand on the soft skin, the young woman moaned. Diana ignored it and pressed with all fingers as deep into the abdomen as the involuntary guarding would allow. Keeping eye contact with Ms. Miller, Diana ran through the other tests as fast as possible, mindful of Dr. Barnes's presence.

She leaned against the counter on the far wall, arms crossed over her chest. Whenever Diana glanced in her direction, her gaze bored into her.

Diana pulled down the patient's gown without touching her abdomen again. "Is the pain manageable while lying like this, or do you need something?"

Ms. Miller took a deep breath. "As long as you don't prod here again, I'm fine. What's it? What will happen now?"

Diana looked at her with what she hoped was her most reassuring expression. "I'll just discuss this with my colleague, and one of us will be back soon to let you know. Just rest for a minute."

Ms. Miller nodded and closed her eyes.

Dr. Barnes stepped past her and held the curtain open. When Diana followed, she led her to a large counter with a computer terminal. A couple of nurses interrupted their conversation midsentence and scattered in different directions.

Diana looked at Dr. Barnes to find out if her new boss was the cause of their sudden exit.

Her face showed no reaction. "So?"

Diana smiled. "I think it's appendicitis."

Dr. Barnes merely raised her eyebrows.

Couldn't that woman just say what she wanted from her? Diana hated guessing games. "Do you want a more elaborate answer?" When she nodded, Diana continued without hesitation. "The presentation is classical for an appendicitis, as is the age. But she's a young woman with a boyfriend and without regular contraception, so we have to rule out an ectopic pregnancy. A urinary tract infection could cause the symptoms, but the result of the clinical examination isn't really typical for that. She could just have some indigestion or the first manifestation of a chronic inflammatory disease like Crohn's, but I think that's the least likely diagnosis."

Dr. Barnes's expression was still neutral. "What would be your next step?"

Any med student and probably most fans of *Grey's Anatomy* could answer that question, but Diana had promised herself to play by the rules, even the unwritten ones, this time. If Dr. Barnes wanted to quiz her, she'd smile and answer. "I would take blood tests, at least for leukocytes, C-reactive protein, and hCG, and a urine stick. Ultrasound. I'd give her some pain medication while we're waiting for the results and have her fast. And depending on the outcome, I'd inform either surgery or OB."

Dr. Barnes nodded. "We'll do that. Have you performed an ultrasound examination before?"

Diana shook her head. "The radiology department did them."

"Now it's your responsibility." Dr. Barnes twisted her lips in a mixture of a snarl and a grin. "It's a useful skill, but you can't learn it from journals." She started to walk but kept on talking.

Diana clenched her jaw and hurried after her.

"Learn the basics and practice a lot. You can often get a much faster diagnosis than waiting for the lab results." She went on about the different uses of ultrasound in the ED as she grabbed a portable ultrasound machine from an unused treatment room. On their way back to the patient, she stopped a nurse and ordered some morphine for Ms. Miller.

Diana made a mental note of the dosage.

Dr. Barnes set up the ultrasound next to Ms. Miller and pointed out the basic features to Diana. Then she turned to the patient, who watched the machine warily.

"Ms. Miller, I'm Dr. Barnes." Her voice was marginally warmer than before. "I'm going to do an ultrasound examination to see what we've got here. We think it's appendicitis, but we need to check a few things before we can call surgery. You'll get something for the pain."

Ms. Miller flinched at the mention of surgery but lay back as the nurse administered the medication.

Dr. Barnes quickly examined the patient. Appendicitis, as Diana had suspected. She helped Diana to reproduce the same result. She leaned in close to place her hand over Diana's, gently angling the probe in the right direction. Her touch was warm and soft, unlike her demeanor so far.

When Diana managed to find the enlarged appendix with its dilated walls, she grinned with pride. Only an hour into her first day, she had already learned something new and useful. And her aloof boss was actually a good teacher.

Dr. Barnes's explanation of the surgery to Ms. Miller pulled Diana out of her thoughts.

"Don't worry, Ms. Miller." Dr. Barnes smiled and patted the young woman's hand. She seemed genuine, just a little stiff. "It's a routine procedure, and our surgical team works hard to keep pain and scaring to a minimum. You'll be back on your feet soon."

Over the course of the next few hours, they repeated the examination, medical quiz, and teaching routine again and again with different patients. Most cases were as easy as the first one, but Dr. Barnes never seemed satisfied with her performance. Every time Diana thought she had made a favorable impression, Dr. Barnes fired more questions at her. When Diana didn't come up with an answer or an alternative diagnosis fast enough, she had to endure another snide remark. She started to really hate Dr. Barnes's cold gray eyes. Not that they were unattractive or anything, quite the opposite, but they remained the most expressive feature in her artificially smooth poker face.

Finally, the night shift arrived, and Diana was free to go.

"Dr. Petrell."

Dr. Barnes's voice stopped her from opening the locker room door. Diana's hand clenched around the doorknob.

"Don't forget. Seven a.m., sharp."

Did she think Diana was a child who couldn't keep track of her appointments herself? She turned around to tell her that she didn't need the reminder, but the corridor was empty. *Arrogant bitch.*

Diana entered the locker room and closed the door with more force than necessary. At least they wouldn't change at the same time. She needed a minute alone to decompress. Reining in her temper all day had left her shoulders tense, and a headache spread its tendrils from the knots in her neck to her forehead. She sighed as she changed out of her rumpled scrubs.

If only she had brought a comfortable pair of jeans instead of her formal first-day-at-work outfit, which hadn't impressed anyone.

Diana closed her eyes for a moment and leaned her forehead against the locker. The cool metal brought only minimal relief. Her fingers twitched, aching to beat a rhythm on the metal, to convert her tension into music. Instead, she forced herself to turn around and leave.

She had survived her first day. Why should her second chance be easier than her first?

Chapter 2

EMILY WOKE WITH A RACING heart. Had there been a noise? Listening for a minute, she couldn't detect anything. Her bedroom and the rest of the apartment were completely silent; not even the neighbor's dog barked. The predawn twilight cast long shadows without movements. She was alone.

Her heartbeat slowed, but why was she still breathing so fast? Several diagnoses ran through her mind. Pulmonary embolism, panic attack, acute coronary syndrome. *Yeah, right.* She rolled her eyes. More likely, it had been a nightmare. As she untangled herself from the sweaty sheet, she became aware of the throbbing between her legs. *Or maybe you missed the obvious, Dr. Barnes: arousal.*

She groaned. *Not that dream again.* What had triggered it this time? She shrugged; it wasn't important.

Yawning, she rolled over to get some more sleep.

The sounds of passing cars turned into the sea lapping against the shore; the solid mattress transformed into shifting sand, and the soft cotton sheets caressed her skin as the ocean breeze had that night. She took a deep breath. Salt, sweat, and her own arousal still smelled the same. Only smoke was missing.

Don't go there. She moved to her other side, willing her brain to go back to sleep, preferably a dreamless one. It didn't comply. It never did.

When she closed her eyes again, stars twinkled above her, brighter in her memory than they could have been that night. Sparks and smoke from the big fire on the beach flickered through her peripheral vision. The crackling and hissing of the logs, the laughter of the other students, the lingering taste of the rich Merlot on her tongue. Everything rolled over her like breaking waves until the tide threatened to pull her under, and she struggled to escape the overwhelming memory.

Her pulse beat in her neck and temples as if the drums were within her. Some students had been playing for hours around the fire, keeping a hypnotic rhythm, slowly accelerating and decelerating seemingly without direction. Players had been coming and going, drifting in and out without breaking the sound tapestry. A new player wove in and added another layer of rhythm. Emily immediately sensed the difference. It was no longer a soothing background. Suddenly, it demanded her full attention.

At first, she couldn't discern the dark shapes sitting on the big logs until her eyes adjusted to the flickering light. And then she saw her.

She sat with her back toward Emily. The big drum between her legs was barely visible from behind. Broad shoulders and muscular arms drew Emily's gaze. Around one well-defined biceps coiled a sinuous shape, glittering emerald green in the glow of the fire. It snaked over her right shoulder to her back, then widened to a scaled body before getting lost in her black tank top and the darkness enveloping her. The rhythmic movement of her shoulders, arms, and hands was mesmerizing. Muscles and tendons shifted under her skin, taunting Emily to name them, but she had momentarily forgotten everything she had learned in anatomy class.

Emily lost all sense of time as she concentrated only on those hands. Her blood pounded in the same cadence as the drum. The vibrations emanating from it touched her skin. The hands played on Emily now. Her skin burned, and her breasts became heavy beneath the stranger's touch. Or was it her own? Fingers glided over a stomach taut as a drum and buried in the wetness between her legs. The rhythm quickened. The other drummers tried to keep up with her, but failed. The stranger's hands flew faster than anyone else's. Emily's hands flew as well. Hours, days, or only minutes later, her playing climaxed and Emily with it.

Emily woke again with a racing heart, her limbs weak with lassitude. The relief brought by the orgasm mixed with shame and regret. Why would her stupid libido replay that scene on the beach over and over again?

After nearly fifteen years, she had thought she was finally over her eye-opening experience. Periodically, the dream reminded her of the moment she had admitted to herself that she was a lesbian or at least attracted to a sexy pair of arms and a tattoo. Not that this revelation had translated into her everyday life. Work was her main focus; reading came second. She had a friend to spend an evening out occasionally. A lover wasn't part of the plan anymore after her two short relationships during college. The short time with her boyfriend had taught her that she wasn't into men, and her girlfriend had shown her that she didn't need the distraction of a relationship.

The alarm clock startled her out of her musings and compelled her to head toward the bathroom. Without waiting for the water to heat, she stepped beneath the cold spray of the shower, as if it could banish the dream and the lingering feelings of dissatisfaction and loneliness.

After changing, Emily immediately headed to the staff lounge. She needed a coffee. Extra large. She didn't like the bitter taste, but her usual Darjeeling tea wouldn't be enough today. Her trip down memory lane had left her exhausted.

Dr. Petrell was already sitting on the couch, one leg tucked underneath her, studying the screen of her laptop.

Since their first meeting on Monday, Dr. Petrell had beaten her to work every day this week, a feat Emily grudgingly admired. She'd been afraid a resident starting in the middle of the year would be rusty and would slow down the well-oiled machine of her ED. Despite receiving special treatment by the chief of staff, Dr. Petrell hadn't even shown a hint of entitlement. Instead, she had worked hard to get up to speed.

When Emily sat on the couch on the opposite side of the table, Dr. Petrell looked up and smiled. "Good morning, Dr. Barnes."

"You weren't late on the first day." Emily flinched, and the still-too-hot coffee nearly spilled over. She placed her mug on the table, wishing she could lay her head next to it. Why had she admitted this now? She must have been even more in need of coffee than she had thought. Telling newbies they were late was her first-day ritual. Maybe it was her way of passing on her own frustration at being the one who got all the extra assignments, such as playing babysitter for new residents. Whatever it was, it usually felt good. But not this time.

Dr. Petrell didn't question her or demand an apology. She only said, "Okay," with the same friendly tone she used on everyone. Her gaze seemed to want an explanation, though.

Emily blew on her coffee and took a small sip to buy some time. When the taste registered, she almost spat it out. "Ew! Who brewed this?" She went to the fridge for some milk or creamer to make it tolerable.

"It's left over from the night shift." Dr. Petrell laughed and held up her travel mug. "I brought my own, or I'd have warned you. Don't you usually drink tea?"

"Mm-hmm. Sometimes I need more caffeine." Emily sniffed the milk. *Drinkable.* She doctored her coffee and returned to the couch. Time to direct the conversation to work. "What have we got?" She gestured toward the laptop.

"Nothing." Dr. Petrell handed it over. "I'm sure the waiting room will fill up soon enough, but the night shift managed to clear the board."

Emily checked the computer program herself. Every patient in the ED was ready to either go home or to another department. Shit. No work to distract her. Now she had to have "the talk" with Dr. Petrell.

She was a competent resident, never complained, and was always professional with the patients. The first few days Emily had watched her closely and could detect only minor mistakes, nothing life-threatening so far. She had to admit that Dr. Petrell was as good as the other residents she had trained herself. Maybe even better because she brought a maturity to the work that could only be gained through time. The ten or more years she had on the other residents put her closer to Emily's own thirty-six and made working together easier. Why was it so difficult to tell her that?

"The next cases are yours alone. Call me to sign off on them or if you need help. I'll be in my office." There. She had said it all. Well, most of it. Between the lines. Somewhere.

She handed back the laptop, took her mug, and stood. Ignoring Dr. Petrell's open mouth, she fled the room.

Emily clicked *refresh* on her screen for the thousandth time today. She grinned. *Cyberstalking, only completely harmless.* Still nothing new. How long could it possibly take to write a few notes? She reached for her mug to keep herself from checking the digital file again. Empty. Should she go and get another coffee? It would give her a reason to pass the nurses' station to check on Dr. Petrell's progress. But she was one cup short of a heart attack already.

She looked around her tiny office to find another distraction. Her journals were stacked and sorted by publication date; her textbooks were freshly dusted, and the box of pens had been neatly divided into blacks and blues. Her digital to-do list was empty.

Waiting for Dr. Petrell to finish with her patients had been surprisingly productive for Emily. She had answered all her emails, written two case reports, finished an article, and peer-reviewed another. A warm feeling of accomplishment made her smile. Dr. Wallace would be proud of her when she published another article.

Today had been one of the rare days without a real emergency or an overflowing waiting room. Dr. Petrell hadn't needed her help, but she had dutifully reported on every patient before sending them home. Now it was close to the end of day shift, and Emily was bored out of her mind.

Water. She jumped up and squeezed past the desk. She could get a bottle of water from the vending machine in the waiting room. That would get her past the nurses' station.

Just as she reached for the door handle, someone knocked.

She opened the door and came face-to-face with Dr. Petrell. Were those eyes brown or green? That wasn't something she should care about when she looked at a resident. Heat rose to her cheeks. Her stupid fair complexion always gave her away, no matter how much makeup she used. She took a step back and returned to her desk.

"Come in. Sit." Emily gestured to the visitor's chair, concentrated on opening the digital files, and hoped her blush would fade fast.

"I've just finished with the last patient." Dr. Petrell recited the symptoms, the diagnosis, and the proposed treatment.

Signing the discharge order without looking at the patient was a temptation. A simple cold did not warrant the attention of two physicians. But frustration with her extra duties was no reason to do them only halfway, and it was finally something to do. She sighed and rose. "Let's have a look."

"Dr. Barnes! Diana!" Courtney stormed into her office without knocking. "We have multiple victims from a pileup coming in." The second-year resident's voice rose higher with every word in either trepidation or anticipation. Probably both. She turned on her heel and ran back toward the treatment area.

"Don't run!" Emily shook her head. She had told her repeatedly that running around the ED was unprofessional. When would Courtney finally learn some restraint?

Dr. Petrell chuckled but sobered when they followed Courtney. She didn't comment on the news that her evening plans would be derailed.

Emily made quick work of her checkup on the cold victim and joined her waiting colleagues, residents, and nurses.

On the opposite side of the room, Dr. Petrell stood without joining in on in the chatter and speculation of the team.

Emily took the opportunity to study her. Several strands of her dark brown hair had escaped her short ponytail, which, combined with her healthy complexion, gave her a much younger appearance. The wrinkled blue scrubs hung loosely over her long-sleeved shirt and revealed no hint of her figure. Dr. Petrell's lips lifted in a half-smile, and her right hand drummed on her thigh in a complex rhythm, faster than Emily could follow. It was hypnotic, and Emily stared longer at Dr. Petrell's thigh and her long, muscular fingers than politeness allowed. They reminded her of something or someone. The link hovered at the edge of her consciousness.

Dr. Petrell looked up and seemed to notice Emily's gaze on her. Her fingers stilled. "I hate waiting."

Her throat was suddenly dry, and Emily had to swallow a few times before she could answer. "Who doesn't?" She looked around to avoid staring as Dr. Petrell retied her messy ponytail.

The automatic doors opened, and the first paramedics entered with their patient on a stretcher.

Emily sighed with relief. She could return her focus from Dr. Petrell's hands—and the connection she couldn't grasp—to her job. Quickly, she organized the group into teams and assigned each to a patient. She had to suppress an inappropriate smile. Finally, some real work.

Chapter 3

DIANA SHOVED HER HANDS INTO her scrub pockets to avoid fidgeting and giving away her tension while she waited for the ambulance. The adrenaline triggered by the words *pileup* and *multiple victims* had flooded her with energy, and now she fought the urge to move to burn it off. She remembered and relished that feeling of harnessed power from when she was younger, but now something had changed, as if a new note had crept into a familiar song, slightly off-key.

What if she got a patient she couldn't handle?

Shut up. You've done this before. It was true; she had successfully treated polytrauma patients, but that had been years ago. Her recent experience consisted of doing simulations and reading guidelines. She had never suffered from stage fright, but she guessed the dread churning in her stomach was exactly that. How ironic that she developed it now.

When the first patient arrived, Diana followed her assigned team into the trauma room. She knew only Tony by name and Dr. Clarkson, who took the lead. Diana hadn't worked with the attending yet, but she seemed nice enough and, more important now, exuded confidence.

As soon as the paramedics had wheeled the stretcher into the room, everyone jumped into position and started working on the patient simultaneously. One of them recited the patient's vitals and presumably some details on what had happened, but Diana only caught half of it as she fumbled with her face guard. She snapped on her gloves and rushed to the patient to help with transferring him to the hospital's stretcher. As soon as he was settled there, the other staff cut away clothes, attached monitoring, and inserted needles.

Dr. Clarkson systematically performed a quick body check. Everyone seemed to have found their part in the complex choreography without orders, and Diana looked for an opening for her to contribute something.

"Dr. Petrell, get up here and start a central line." Dr. Clarkson moved to the head of the patient and checked his pupils again before turning to one of the nurses. "Let's intubate him."

Happy that she had something to do, Diana exchanged her barely used gloves for the sterile ones a nurse offered and slipped into a paper coat. Awareness of her colleagues' movements receded as her focus narrowed to the small part of skin below the right clavicle. Disinfection, drape, needle, wire, central line, syringe with saline, suture. Everything she needed appeared like magic next to her hands before she could even think of the next step. She had never done this so fast. Proud of her accomplishment, Diana looked up to see what she could do next and met dark eyes glaring at her.

"Finished? I need to get started here." The X-ray tech elbowed Diana out of the way to place a digital detector under the patient, then turned, and shooed her away with a hand motion.

Diana moved back with the rest of the team. Some left the room, but most flattened themselves against the wall, like Diana.

Dr. Clarkson was the first at the monitor. "Pneumothorax."

Shit. Had she pierced his lung during the placement of the central line? Diana glanced at the monitor.

No, the pneumothorax was on the left side and most likely caused by the impact of the car, along with the broken ribs. She exhaled and turned to Dr. Clarkson. "I can place the chest tube."

"Maybe next time. See if you can stop the bleeding up there." Dr. Clarkson had already moved to the patient's left side. "Tony, call radiology for a CT and get him a bed in the SICU. We need to move him along soon."

Suturing a superficial head laceration might be part of the team effort, but it seemed tame in comparison to the real work Dr. Clarkson did in stabilizing the patient.

"Status?" Dr. Barnes entered the room with an older man whose green scrubs and cocky posture identified him as a surgeon.

Without looking up from her work, Dr. Clarkson listed the patient's vitals, his injuries, and their treatment so far. When had she done an ultrasound? Set his wrist? How had Diana missed this?

"Nothing immediate for you, Richard." Dr. Barnes stepped up next to Diana and leaned over her shoulder to check the patient's pupils. Her body pressed into Diana's back, its softness and warmth in drastic contrast to the coldness of her voice. Diana didn't dare to move. "Liz, send him via a CT to the SICU. He can wait there for a spot in the OR if the neurosurgeons don't claim him."

Dr. Barnes left as fast as she had come. When the door closed behind her, Dr. Clarkson exchanged a gaze with Tony, who rolled his eyes.

"Aye, aye, Captain Barnes." Dr. Clarkson chuckled and shook her head.

Biting her lip to keep from laughing, Diana finished the suture. So she wasn't the only one Dr. Barnes checked on constantly. Not even an attending like Dr. Clarkson was safe.

She cleaned the suture site with a wet gauze and put a dressing on it. Good, the bleeding had stopped for now. She checked the patient for something else to do. Nothing else stuck out to her. "Want me to do the paperwork?"

Dr. Clarkson nodded. "Most things should already be logged. But check it and clean up the text, please. I'll see if I can reach his family."

By the time Diana had finished, the transport team had come and whisked away the patient. Dr. Clarkson looked over her shoulder and read the report, pointing out a few things she had missed, then signed off on it. She stood as close as Dr. Barnes had done, but Diana didn't mind this time. Why did Dr. Barnes make her nervous?

As a cleaner swept around their feet, Dr. Clarkson pulled Diana to the side. "Let's have a look at the other rooms. Maybe we can help somewhere."

Finally, after a couple of hours, the digital whiteboard had cleared, and Diana looked for Dr. Barnes to see if she could go or if there was still work somewhere. She found her at the nurses' station, talking to Dr. Clarkson.

Dr. Barnes frowned. "What are you still doing here?"

Why the hell did Dr. Barnes sound so annoyed with her? "Um, I just finished in room three. Do you need my help somewhere else?"

"You know that you have to clear overtime with me. We take work restrictions seriously in this hospital."

Diana hadn't known that, but she was too tired to argue. "I will do that the next time."

Dr. Barnes had been about to say something else when Dr. Clarkson interrupted her. "We just made our round through the trauma rooms. The night shift has everything under control now. You're good to go." She smiled. "And thank you for staying longer. Good work, Dr. Petrell. Have a nice weekend."

Dr. Barnes still frowned but didn't contradict her colleague.

Diana nodded to both of them. "Thanks. See you on Monday."

Her mind reeling, she went to the locker room. It hadn't really been good work. She had been much too slow with their first patient, no matter how it had seemed to her at the time. And she had been so overwhelmed she hadn't seen the big picture. If she had been alone, the treatment could have ended as a catastrophe.

She peeled off her scrubs and wrinkled her nose at the smell of sweat, probably a mixture of her own and that of several patients. Rusty stains and smears covered them, but at least the hospital did the washing for her. She pulled on her jeans but then hesitated. The stains and smell extended to the long-sleeved shirt she wore underneath. No way would she wear that home and risk soiling her favorite leather jacket. She looked around to check that she was still alone before grabbing a fresh scrub shirt to change into.

Just as she had taken her shirt off, the door opened.

Diana jumped back with an undignified shriek and scrambled into the scrub shirt. Maybe they hadn't seen the tattoo. Closing the locker, she sneaked a look at the doorway.

Dr. Clarkson regarded her with raised eyebrows. "Everything okay?"

"Um, yeah. Just my shirt got dirtier than I expected, and I thought it was okay to borrow a scrub shirt. Is it okay?" Great. Now she had turned into a babbling fool.

"Sure. Everyone does that." She opened her locker and quickly undressed.

Diana concentrated on folding her shirt in a way that made sure the stains didn't touch anything else. "I'm sorry I wasn't much help with the first patient, Dr. Clarkson."

The attending had finished dressing and turned around, smiling. "Call me Liz. Everyone does. You're Diana, right?"

Diana nodded. She shoved her shirt into her backpack, wishing she could ball up and stow her problems away as easily.

"Don't worry. We've all been there. It's just your first week." Liz dumped her scrubs into the hamper.

"I thought I could do better." And she had done better, years ago.

"Then you will, the next time. Don't overthink it. If you feel like it, we can talk on Monday and see how we can improve your training. Let's get out of here." Liz held the door open for her.

"Thank you." She didn't just mean the door, and judging by the look Liz gave her, she understood.

Diana's cell phone blared and vibrated next to her ear. Who called in the middle of the night? Her pulse beat faster than the ringtone. Had she forgotten to do something important at the hospital? She grabbed the phone and answered without looking at the caller ID. "Petrell. Hello?"

"Hey, Dee. Did I wake you, old woman?" Mel was difficult to understand over the background of music and voices.

Diana let out a shaky breath. Not the hospital. Only her best friend and colleague. Former colleague, she reminded herself. "Um, yeah. How late is it? And you're older, you know?"

"Midnight. And don't you know that it's impolite to mention a lady's age?" Mel laughed. "I was wondering if you wanted to meet for a beer?"

A few weeks ago it would have been a normal time for her to go out, but now she only wanted to go back to sleep. "Rain check? Work was no fun today."

"That's what I wanted to celebrate with you, your first week as a doctor." The background noise faded as if Mel had stepped outside. "Want to tell me about it?"

"Maybe later." She yawned. "Much later. Why don't you call me tomorrow morning? Or afternoon? If you really want to listen to me bitch about being on the bottom rung of the hierarchy again or my constant struggle to act like an adult or not fitting in with the other kids."

"Sure. At least it's something new and not about your ex making stupid life choices again." Mel sighed. "I wanted to ask you a favor, but it can wait.

Tomorrow evening we go out and party." The last sentence was a statement, not a question.

Diana groaned. "Don't you remember the last time we celebrated my first week as a doctor? We partied for two days, and I ended up going to work with a hangover. I can't survive something like that again. I'm definitely not in my twenties anymore."

"Me neither. We'll just stay clear of hard liquor and tattoo artists this time, and we'll be fine."

Diana rubbed the small rod of Asclepius above her left ankle. "I'll remind you of that tomorrow."

"No need." Someone called Mel's name, and the intensity of the background noise increased again. "I'll let you get back to sleep now."

"Thanks. Enjoy your night."

This time, Diana put the phone on the charger in the kitchen where it belonged before she returned to bed.

Taking a breath of the clear air, Diana stretched next to the entrance of Green Lake Park. Her muscles and tendons protested after a week of neglect. She had promised herself that she would keep in shape and take better care of her health during her second residency. At least she didn't have to nurse a hangover after her evening out with Mel. They had kept the celebration low-key, eating pho in a small Vietnamese restaurant with a couple of beers instead of doing shots in a bar with women much too young for them. She'd had enough of that in LA, and she supposed Mel had secretly enjoyed the change of scenery as well.

Diana tightened her shoelaces, then set off at a moderate pace. Most of the trees around her were still caught in winter's sleep, but here and there a few light green buds had broken free already. She was looking forward to the blooming cherry trees at the other side of the lake.

Diana swerved around a little girl and immediately collided with another woman going the opposite direction. Both grabbed each other and swayed until they found their balance.

"I'm sorry."

"Sorry, I didn't see—" Diana looked up. *Dr. Barnes? What are the chances?*

"Good morning, Dr. Petrell." Dr. Barnes shifted from foot to foot and didn't look directly at Diana. She wore running clothes that looked brand-new. And who put on makeup to go running?

"Good morning. I'm sorry, I was just so eager for my run. I'm looking forward to getting some sun." Maybe this could be a good opportunity to get to know each other and ease the stiff atmosphere at work a little bit. Diana bounced on her toes and smiled. "Are you planning on using the trail around the lake too?"

"No. I've got, um, sensitive skin. I could never run in the sun. I usually go to the gym over there." Dr. Barnes pointed at the other side of the street, then tucked her hair behind her ear.

Diana barely managed not to frown. Indoor running wasn't what she'd consider her favorite workout. She wouldn't exchange a beautiful lake and fresh air for a room full of sweaty people. It was a flimsy excuse; that's why they had invented sunscreen.

Or had Dr. Barnes told her that to prevent an invitation to run together? Welcome back to the world of hierarchy: Attendings didn't socialize with residents. But maybe the reminder was necessary; she'd been about to ask Dr. Barnes to join her.

Offering an empty smile, Diana nodded. "Okay. I'd better get going. See you tomorrow."

"Wait, please." Dr. Barnes swiped at her hair again even though it hadn't moved an inch. "If you have a few minutes, I'd like to talk to you about Friday."

Diana shrugged. This was certainly not the perfect setting for a critique of her work. But she should count herself lucky that it wasn't within earshot of the other residents.

"I watched you handle some of the minor injuries. You were thorough and unhurried—"

"You mean slow. I know." Diana didn't want to listen to the polite paraphrases. She preferred her critique direct.

"It's true. You could have been faster, but what mattered to me more was that you didn't miss anything. That would be unacceptable." Dr. Barnes's voice had turned cold with her last sentence. "Getting overconfident is a typical mistake of residents."

Diana nodded. There wasn't really anything she could say. What was Dr. Barnes trying to tell her? Was it a warning that she was being watched, still on probation? Dr. Barnes could watch her as much as she liked; *overconfidence* wasn't her problem at the moment.

"You're more mature than the others. I guess the age difference shows."

That sounded almost like a compliment, but Dr. Barnes didn't do those. At least that's what the other residents said.

"Thank you."

"Maybe you lost medical experience, but your approach to work didn't suffer from your break." Dr. Barnes tilted her head and looked at her directly for the first time since the conversation had started. "What did you do in those nine years? Didn't you say you helped a friend and lived on a farm?"

Shit. Diana clenched her teeth and swallowed the rising anger. The almost-compliment had only been a prelude to the real question. "It's complicated. And has nothing to do with my work performance." She avoided Dr. Barnes's eyes. Why hadn't she thought of a better cover story? She had to end the conversation before she either lied or went against a direct order from her boss's boss. "Dr. Clarkson offered to help me on Monday to improve my speed. Is that okay with you?"

Dr. Barnes frowned. "Sure. If Liz wants to help you…"

"Great. See you on Monday, then." Diana hoped her tone didn't betray her apprehension.

Dr. Barnes just looked at her for a moment. Her features were carefully neutral, probably the same expression she wore at work when patients told her the weirdest stories. Then they softened slightly. "Enjoy your day off." She waved her hand and left without a backward glance.

Diana inhaled deeply, but the spring air that she had enjoyed earlier didn't help clear her head. She gazed upward. The sun was shining; small fluffy clouds dotted the brilliant blue, and the temperature was comfortable. A perfect spring day. She wouldn't let this encounter spoil her Sunday morning. She started her run, faster and faster.

When she reached the lake and merged on the round trail, she slowed down and concentrated on her heart rate. *This isn't a race. You've nothing to prove.* She chuckled, and an elderly couple sitting on a bench stared at her. Now that her embarrassment and, if she was honest, her anger with herself had faded, she could appreciate the irony of the situation.

In the past years, she had been the one others tried to impress. Too many people had fawned over her. That had been one of the many reasons she had left her old life and returned to medicine. She wanted to be treated like a normal person again. And now that she was, she didn't like it. Dr. Barnes had every right to question her.

Diana's defensive reaction wasn't how she thought she should behave now that she was supposedly all mature and grown-up. She promised herself to keep the next conversations with Dr. Barnes on a more professional level.

On her way back from the gym, Emily passed through the park. She lingered, hoping to meet Dr. Petrell again. *And what would you say to her? Your first talk didn't go very well either.* She didn't actually know where she had gone wrong. As Liz had done on Friday, she'd wanted to let her know that she had done a good job, but Dr. Petrell had reacted as if she had criticized her.

And just as she'd thought she gained some ground, she had lost it all with the question about the nine-year gap in her résumé. She had said before that it was a private matter, and Emily probably should have respected that. But what if she'd done something that could potentially damage the hospital's good reputation?

An icy shiver ran down Emily's spine. She wouldn't allow that.

Why was Dr. Petrell so closed off about her past? And why did Emily even care? Usually, she kept her distance from her co-workers, especially from the residents. They were only temporarily passing through her life. What made Dr. Petrell different?

Emily sighed. Why was it so difficult for her to understand people? Including herself. Sometimes she cursed her parents for raising her isolated from other kids, but it wasn't fair to lay the blame solely on them. She'd deliberately passed on enough chances at school and university to get out more, preferring the company of her books to that of her peers. If Jen hadn't been after her to be friends instead of roommates, she wouldn't even have a best friend.

A final look around the park didn't show her Dr. Petrell among the dense crowd of runners, bikers, skaters, and people out for a casual stroll. The same sunshine that had drawn them all out chased Emily back inside.

If she didn't want to end up with undignified freckles and red blotches, she had to leave now.

She'd talk to Dr. Petrell on Monday. No, not talk, she'd just tell her that she appreciated her work. Direct and easy, no chance of another miscommunication.

Chapter 4

ONLY A WEEK HAD PASSED, but Diana had already relearned her most important skill as an emergency physician: always hunting down fresh coffee. She deeply inhaled the bitter aroma; the scent was almost strong enough to kick her brain cells awake one by one. A shame it was still too hot to drink. She'd need the energy boost to attend a lecture right at the beginning of her shift.

The furniture in the staff lounge had been rearranged so the sofas faced the wall opposite the door, and a large, white screen had been pulled down from the ceiling, covering most of the kitchenette. Diana stood in the back of the dark room, hoping to escape questions.

Someone bumped into her from behind.

She held her mug away from her body to avoid stains or, worse, burns.

"Did I miss something?" Courtney's whisper was not as unobtrusive as she probably thought. Running footsteps had announced her imminent arrival, and Dr. Barnes paused her lecture to glare at her.

Grateful that she wasn't the victim of that stare this morning, Diana refrained from answering.

"Glad you could join us. Why don't you come to the front and help us?" Dr. Barnes waited until Courtney wove her way through the small group of residents and students. "Since you're late, I suppose you don't need to learn any more about chronic rheumatic diseases and can teach us instead."

Courtney winced, and several others giggled.

It was the first lecture Diana attended, but the other residents had warned her to stay below Dr. Barnes's radar if she wanted to avoid humiliation. Being punctual was a no-brainer. She'd arrived fifteen minutes ago and still had been too late for one of the few seats.

A couple of well-placed questions showed Courtney's lack of preparation and sent her back into the fold.

Soon Diana tried to balance her notepad on top of the coffee mug as she jotted down some notes. She looked around for a place to discreetly store the drink. Maybe at the window? Two residents leaned against the sill, and she moved toward them. She had been introduced to the shorter of them, a pasty guy with a prematurely receding hairline and a waist that showed his preferred method of stress reduction probably wasn't sports.

Diana tried to remember his name. Alex, Andy, Alec, or something like this.

"The bitch is boring me to death this morning," he whispered to his taller colleague.

The other resident nodded and rubbed his eyes. The shadows under them were almost as black as his short hair.

She paused. For her, the lecture wasn't boring at all. Was she supposed to already know all this? It was more in-depth than anything she had heard in her last residency. She leaned closer to put the mug on the windowsill.

Maybe-Alec grinned at her. "Coffee? Good thinking. I wish I had been early enough to get some."

"You can have mine. I didn't drink from it yet." She had been too busy listening and taking notes, but it was probably better not to tell him that. If the others all thought this was basic stuff, she didn't want to give away her need to catch up. One of the first things she had learned in med school was that most of her classmates were highly competitive and used every available weapon to move up the ranks. Admitting a lack of knowledge was like swimming among sharks naked and covered in blood. She returned to her former place in the back to avoid further conversation.

An hour later, Dr. Barnes concluded her lecture.

Diana put her pen away and shook out her hand. She frowned at the almost ineligible handwriting. She'd need to transcribe it soon, or she'd lose the ability to actually use her notes for her work.

"Thanks for the coffee. You're the transfer, right? Diana?" Maybe-Alec and the tall resident had come over.

She nodded. "Right. I'm Diana."

"I'm Peter, and this is Alec. Nice to meet you." Peter just waved, but Alec offered his hand. He had the kind of limp handshake Diana had always hated.

"Where're you from?" Several others stopped on their way out and added their own questions. "What year?"

While she wasn't in the mood to get into her history now, this was probably the fastest method to get her story out. She had learned enough about information management, rumor control, and the importance of a good first impression in years of giving interviews.

She addressed each colleague who had thrown in a question with her best PR smile. "I'm not a direct transfer. I used to work in LA but took a few years off. They're still deciding which year they'll place me in. Probably second." That's what the chief of staff had told her. It hurt. She should be grateful they even accepted those two years, but she had been only a couple of months short of finishing the fourth and final year of her residency when she had thrown it all away.

Alec introduced some of the others around him. They all exchanged platitudes and made small talk about Seattle weather, the best bars, and how their work stopped them from exploring those.

Diana deflected a few invitations to show her around the nightlife. The last thing she needed was a night out drinking and bitching about work. "Thanks, but I'm not really new in town. I went to U-Dub."

That comment led from complaining about work to a retelling of the worst memories of med school.

Nothing had changed. Doctors were still like med students, always circling around the same topics of conversation: med school and work. It had gotten on her nerves nine years ago, and her patience was waning now. She was looking for a way out of the discussion when she noticed Dr. Barnes.

She had to pass through the group to leave, and her effect on the chatting students and residents was impressive. They fell quiet immediately and parted like the Red Sea.

"Don't we have patients to see today?"

The question caused the other residents and students to rush away.

Diana smiled. Finally, she was able to hear her own thoughts. "Do you want me to follow you again today, Dr. Barnes?"

She shook her head. "You did well on Friday. You're free to choose your own work, but find me when you need me." She started to leave but turned around after a few steps. Was that an actual smile? "Call me Emily."

It was a smile, completely transforming her features, softening the usually hard line of her lips. Even more surprising, Dr. Barnes—no, Emily—had paid her a compliment. And let her off her leash.

Emily left before Diana could come up with an appropriate answer.

Diana went to the next workstation and logged in to the electronic whiteboard. She grinned as she studied the abbreviations of the complaints, feeling like a kid in a toy store.

On Friday evening, Emily stood at the foot of a gurney and watched Diana insert a subclavian line into her patient. He was unconscious and intubated. The team that would transfer him to the ICU waited impatiently at one side of the room.

Emily wasn't annoyed that she had to supervise her resident; she found herself enjoying watching her. Diana was able to do different things independently with both hands at a time. That was not very common for nonsurgical residents. Emily herself could do it, probably because of the endless hours of piano lessons she'd had to endure as a child. At least something good had come out of it.

"Do you play the piano?" Emily had not planned on voicing her question.

"Yes. Why?" Diana barely glanced at her and continued working. She had already placed the J wire and was threading the catheter over it into the blood vessel. After Diana had volunteered to place every central line in the last days, her speed had improved dramatically.

"Um. Not important. Just a thought." Definitely not a topic she'd go into in the middle of the ED. "Is this your last patient? When you're ready, we can go over the other charts and head home for the weekend." Due to some extra shifts, it was the first time in four weeks Emily would have two days off in a row, and she wanted to make the most of it.

"I'll be with you in a minute. Are you in a hurry to go home?" Diana's tone was a little teasing.

Emily hesitated. Her private life had always been off-limits at work. No one asked questions like this or teased her, ever. Not that she would admit it out loud, but Emily liked that Diana had relaxed around her since she had toned down her own reticence. It helped that Diana was still respectful.

"No. Well, maybe. I'm meeting my best friend, and I can never guess what she has planned." Okay, maybe that had been a little too much sharing for her own comfort, but she was nervous. The last time they had gone out together, Jen had tried to play matchmaker and had tortured not only Emily, but also a very nice and very boring acquaintance of Jen's with an evening of forced conversation. She secretly hoped they'd go dancing at Jen's favorite club instead, something she'd never dare on her own.

Emily stopped her musings and concentrated back on Diana, who had finished and took off her gloves and disinfected her hands. Why couldn't Emily stop looking at them? She abruptly turned around and called over her shoulder, "Come on, don't dawdle."

Not waiting for an answer, she left the room in search of a free computer terminal and never doubted Diana would follow.

The music was deafening, and Emily soon gave up on trying to understand Jen's remarks. They had arrived at the club early. A DJ entertained the crowd before tonight's concert, and the dance floor was already teeming with dancing women. Jen was supposed to be working, covering a new band for one of the music magazines or websites she wrote for. That didn't keep her from checking out the women in the audience and pointing out her favorites. One of them would undoubtedly go home with Jen at the end of the evening.

Emily gestured that she'd go dancing for a while and squeezed onto the crowded dance floor. The bass vibrated in her belly, calling her body to synchronize with the beat. She closed her eyes and relaxed into the rhythmic movement of her feet and hips. She became one with the music, swaying, flowing in the current. Other people were rocks in the stream, guiding the flow, but never stopping it. She touched their bodies, and they touched hers, and she was not alone anymore, submerged in the crowd. She was safe.

The music slowed, and couples took the chance to connect.

She made her way to the bar, desperate for a drink. She nearly bumped into Jen, who stared at a dark-haired woman standing with her back to them.

Emily tried to get a good look at her, but other women kept getting in her line of sight.

"Who's that?" Emily spoke directly into Jen's ear to avoid shouting.

"Dee Dragon. Isn't it great to see her here?" Jen turned and smiled widely.

"Am I supposed to know her?" Emily could never remember the names of all the musicians Jen talked about.

"You know Eos, the band?" Jen bounced on her toes. "She was their drummer."

Emily had heard of them and liked their music; she even owned a few CDs. But the name of the drummer didn't ring a bell. "Isn't that the band with the tiny blonde with the dark eye makeup and the tall, black guitarist? I don't think I have ever seen a picture of the drummer."

"Yeah, that's them. The guitarist is hot." Jen fanned herself. "Dee Dragon wasn't on the covers so much and stayed out of the media most of the time. About a year ago the band separated, and she suddenly disappeared from the scene. No announcement or explanation. There are a million rumors: drugs, alcohol, drugs, brain tumor, drugs… You get the picture. Maybe I can get an interview." Jen turned around again and studied the woman leaning against the bar. "I just need a good conversation starter."

The crowd thinned, and Emily could get her first good look at Dee Dragon, at least from behind. She was tall, and her brown, wavy hair hung just below her shoulder. Her most striking feature was a large tattoo that covered most of what Emily could see of her back. An emerald-green dragon with open wings looked directly at her and spewed fire. Brilliant red flames sneaked over her left shoulder to her arm and wound around her biceps. The scaly tail mirrored the path of the flames on the right side.

Emily's heart rate escalated, and she had trouble breathing. This couldn't be right. It must be a coincidence.

Dee Dragon couldn't be the woman from the beach who had been haunting her dreams for nearly fifteen years. But every detail from that night was imprinted into her memory, and she could recall everything as if it had happened yesterday. The hair was different now, longer, the shoulders maybe a bit wider, and the muscles even more defined. But the tattoo was the same.

"I met her before." *Why did you say that?* Her stomach clenched. Jen wouldn't let it go now.

"What? Dee Dragon? You just told me that you don't even know who she is. Where?" Jen was nearly jumping up and down.

"The beach." The less she said, the better.

Jen made eye contact. It was her patented I-know-you'll-tell-it-all stare. "What beach? What are you talking about?"

Emily tried to look away. "Remember the beach party you dragged me to, just at the end of college? I told you I was listening to the drumming circle all evening. I saw her playing there." Years later, she had admitted to having realized at the party that she was a lesbian. Hopefully, Jen didn't remember that confession.

"Are you sure? That's perfect. I can use this to chat her up." Jen took Emily's hand and pulled. "Let's go and talk to her."

"No." Emily pulled her hand back. "I can't."

Jen studied her. "What's wrong? Why not?"

She would not get into it here, in the middle of a club. "I have to go. To the restroom."

Before Jen could ask more questions, Emily walked in the opposite direction, away from the bar and Dee Dragon and her mesmerizing tattoo. In the bathroom, she washed her hands and pressed the cool fingers to her temples, careful not to smudge the carefully applied makeup. The eyes staring back at her from the mirror seemed unnaturally large in her pale face. Her upper lip trembled. She was hyperventilating and grabbed the sink to hold on. Deliberately, she slowed her breathing. Passing out would be really embarrassing. Maybe someone would call 911, and the paramedics would bring her into her own emergency room.

She snorted, not sure if she already qualified as hysterical or merely panicking. She had never met the woman and couldn't imagine talking to her. What would she say? *Nice to meet you. You've been the woman of my dreams for years.* Or *Hello, you are even more beautiful than in my masturbation fantasies.*

And now Jen had set her sights on her. Emily knew what would happen. Jen would make small talk, invite her to a few drinks and dances, and the evening would either end in bed or with an interview, probably both. She was persistent, resourceful, and usually successful. Dee Dragon didn't have a chance. The thought hurt like a kick in the stomach.

A fire kindled in her middle, slowly spreading through her chest to her head. It burned off her panic and helped her to regain her composure. She looked down at her hands that still clutched the sink. Her knuckles had nearly taken on the color of the porcelain.

Emily released the death grip and deliberately stretched her fingers. She would not go out there to watch her dream morph into a distorted version of her fantasies. She would just leave and let Jen work on her target on her own.

On her way to the door, she had to pass the bar, so she hid behind a large woman with broad shoulders and tried not to look at Jen and Dee. It was like passing an accident on the highway. She involuntarily decelerated and couldn't keep her gaze off them.

Jen stood between the bar and Dee, talking and laughing. Dee's back was still turned toward Emily, and the mesmerizing tattoo caught her gaze again. She forced herself to look away.

Just as she had made it past them, a couple of women carrying a pitcher of beer and several glasses appeared out of nowhere.

Everything seemed to happen in slow motion: A hard shoulder stopped Emily in her tracks. Beer flew out of the pitcher in a golden arch.

Emily jumped back and hit another body, solid as a rock.

"Watch it!"

"Are you blind?"

Emily raised her hands, palms facing outward. "I'm so sorry." She grabbed a few bills from her pocket and shoved them at one of the women to pay for the spilled beer.

She had to get out. Fast.

Before she could hide again, Jen grabbed her hand and yanked Emily over to them.

"Are you okay?" Jen looked her up and down.

Apart from a few drops of beer on her shirt, her dry tongue sticking to the roof of her mouth, and a racing heart, she was fine. Unable to speak, Emily nodded.

Jen stepped to the side and gestured toward the woman she had been talking to. "Dee, this is the friend I told you about, Emily Barnes. Emily, this is Dee Dragon."

Emily forced herself to look up at Dee. Her gaze locked on hazel eyes that seemed as wide as her own.

Jen's voice dimmed to a distant murmur, and Emily's vision blurred for a moment.

She couldn't speak; she couldn't breathe. *Don't faint!* She bit hard on the inside of her cheek, and the pain helped her to focus.

This was literally the woman of her dreams. And she already knew her.

Chapter 5

Why now? Diana had managed to avoid revealing the person behind her stage name for all her years in the music business. *Fuck.* Now that her medical career depended on keeping it a secret, she was found out in her first month—and by her attending of all people!

Diana needed a plan. Fast. Maybe Emily would help her?

She took a deep breath and willed her voice to sound normal. "Hi, Emily, nice to meet you." She tried to plead with her eyes. Was it really possible to communicate that way? Hopefully, Emily got the message.

Emily swallowed several times. "Hi." She was paler than ever and looked everywhere but at Diana.

Why was she so anxious? Because her friend had dragged her to a lesbian club? Diana turned to Jen, who had asked something she hadn't caught.

Jen pointed to the bar and gave them a questioning look.

Great idea. "Another beer, please." She could use something stronger but needed to keep her wits together.

Emily waited until her friend had been swallowed by the crowd around the bar. "Jen says you're a rock star? How's that possible? Are you even a real doctor?" Some color had returned to her cheeks as she progressed from shocked to accusatory.

Diana winced. Had anyone heard her? She looked around for a reaction, but everyone seemed to mind their own business. She took a step closer and leaned in to speak directly into Emily's ear. "Of course I am a doctor. Everything I've told you about my work history was the truth." The accusation hurt, but her pride wasn't important now. "I don't know what Jen said, but yes, I was a drummer in a rock band."

Emily shook her head. "That's just... I don't know what to say."

"Please, don't say anything. To anyone. I can give you a longer explanation, but not here." She looked again in the direction of the bar. They still had time.

Emily frowned. "Does anyone at the hospital know?"

"I told the chief of staff everything at my interview, and he told me not to talk about it at work. Or anywhere. It's actually in my contract that I can be fired immediately if I compromise the hospital's reputation in any way." Diana looked into Emily's eyes. How could she convince her to keep quiet about it?

"Jen is my best friend. If she finds out that I kept this from her, and she probably will, I'll jeopardize our friendship." Emily held her gaze now, and Diana could almost see the internal struggle as she weighed the pros and cons. "I don't know if she told you, but she's a music journalist. She's after the story of Dee Dragon's disappearance from the music scene."

Oh shit. A nosy journalist was the last thing she needed. "Please, I don't want to mix my old life with my new one. If our co-workers knew, they would always judge me for what I was and not for what I actually do. And I don't want the press to have an impact on my work at the hospital. Patients might not take me or our ED seriously anymore."

"I need to think about this for a minute, okay?" Emily closed her eyes and rubbed her temples. "I can't lie to Jen if she asks me directly, but I won't say anything right now."

"Fair enough. Thank you." There must be a solution better than keeping secrets, but at least the immediate threat was banished. She couldn't believe the coincidence. "Did you really see me at a beach party when we were both students? Or was that just a line Jen used to chat me up?"

Emily blushed and avoided meeting Diana's eyes. Her gaze finally settled on Diana's left arm, and the tattoo burned as if the fire were real. "Yes, it's true. I remember your tattoo. But I never saw your face at that party, so I didn't recognize you at work."

Wow. Emily's memory was excellent. Diana wasn't sure she even remembered the party. Her college years were a blur of parties, music, and occasional frantic study sessions.

"Hey, Jen, is this for me?" Emily looked over Diana's shoulder and smiled. She grabbed the beer bottle, took a large swallow, and started to cough.

Diana reached over to help her, slap her back or something, but Emily withdrew and shook her head.

Jen seemed oblivious to the tension between them.

Diana forced herself to focus on Jen's tale about a funny incident at the bar and to keep her mind off Emily. She laughed at the right cues and kept the conversation going, jumping from one topic to the next, hoping to keep away from the music business.

If Emily hadn't told Diana about Jen's profession, she would've interpreted her behavior as flirting. She paid rapt attention and played the enamored fan. Were these kinds of tactics even ethical for a journalist?

Emily appeared to concentrate entirely on peeling the label from her bottle.

"And what are you doing here today?" Jen used a pause in conversation to launch the questions Diana had anticipated. "I hope you're playing. I would love to hear you play." She touched Diana's arm and smiled up at her.

Diana lifted her beer to her mouth so that the lingering hand dropped away from her arm. "I'm actually playing in a bit. Friends of mine have lost their drummer for the evening and have asked me to help out. Their new album—"

"Isn't that a bother to come here for just one evening? Or are you living somewhere close? Are you working on a project here?" Jen interrupted before she could steer the conversation back to safer ground.

Emily looked up, and her gaze seemed to bore into Diana.

Did she regret her promise not to say anything? Diana put down her empty bottle on a table behind Jen to gain time. She willed her hands not to shake. "No, no project right now." She took the cell phone from her jeans and checked the time. "Listen, it was nice meeting you both, but I have to go. We'll play soon." She risked one last glance at Emily. Was it safe to leave them alone to talk?

Emily stood slightly behind Jen and answered the silent question with a nod. She would keep quiet—at least for now.

Behind the small stage, Diana leaned her forehead against the cool brick wall and hit it several times with her palm. "Fuck, fuck, fuck!"

Someone cradled her neck and rubbed it gently. She recognized the familiar calluses of a professional guitar player.

"What's wrong, Dee?" The soft voice belonged to Mel, her reason for being here today.

Diana turned around. "I just met someone, a reporter. She asked too many nosy questions." That covered only half of the problem, but Diana didn't want to get into it before the concert. Later she'd tell Mel all about the weird coincidence of meeting Emily.

Mel frowned. "Nothing here indicates what you're doing for a living. Nobody knows about," she lowered her voice and looked around, "the hospital. I haven't told the girls. They just know you're an old friend and have nothing better to do this weekend than to rescue the poor drummer-less newcomers."

Diana snorted. "You're hardly a newcomer. You're what, five years older than me?" She hugged Mel. "But thanks for the support. I hate hiding who I am. I guess the closet must feel like this."

"So you finally get the complete lesbian experience. Congratulations. If this reporter comes back to bother you, point her out to me. I'll find a way to keep her occupied, away from you." She hugged Diana back and then stepped away from her and slapped her playfully on the shoulder. "Five years older? Do I look too old to play with the new kids?"

"No, no, of course not." Diana made a show of looking her up and down.

Mel did look good, as if the fresh start with a new band had rejuvenated her. Or maybe the move back to the city where they'd spent their youth together. Even if the fine lines in her face hadn't magically disappeared, her skin was smoother than it had been the last couple of years, only a shade lighter than her chestnut eyes that shone with enthusiasm.

Diana laughed; she had missed the easy banter that came with belonging to a band, a group of friends. "Come on, kid. I'll show you how to rock."

They made their way onto the stage, and Diana settled behind the drums. She put in the earplugs, stretched her arms a few times, and tested each part of her instrument with a flick of her drumsticks. The familiar routine settled her. She waited for the others to take their places and play a few test notes.

Studying the audience, she wasn't quite sure if she hoped or feared to see Emily. Stage lights flickered over the mass of women. And there she was, her turquoise shirt gleaming in the bright light. Emily looked sexy in the tight shirt and skinny jeans. Nothing like the prim and proper attending she knew at work. She smiled at something Jen said, and in that one unguarded moment, she transformed from a colleague into a woman. A beautiful woman who stirred something inside Diana. *Stop it. She's off-limits, and really what is it with the sudden attraction?*

Mel gave the signal, and Diana started to play. Loud, hard, steady. She closed her eyes. This was not a time to think, only to feel. Her head nodded; her hair fell over her face. She let her body take over, swinging with the rhythm, legs bouncing, her drumsticks a part of her arms like her hands. She felt more than heard her opening in the song and segued into her first solo of the evening. The music was all she had to care about now, and it was enough. It had always been enough, and for this evening it became the center of her world again.

Emily studied Jen, who kept her gaze on the band. Maybe Jen would let the story go. Emily sighed. Not very likely. Jen would probably keep on hunting for clues and information until she discovered everything. She worried that keeping this secret could hurt their friendship. And what would such story do to the hospital's reputation? Their ED would be a laughingstock. Emily's stomach hurt as if the loud base beats were actual hits to her core. Her work meant everything to her. She'd always admired Dr. Wallace for keeping the house scandal-free, and the least she could do was to help keep Diana's past under wraps.

Between songs, as the singer told a winding story about the origin of the next one, Jen turned around and grinned broadly. "Isn't that fucking fantastic? We met Dee Dragon, and she was really nice." She groaned. "And really, really hot. Maybe I can sneak backstage."

Fucking fantastic. Sneak backstage. Really hot. That was not what Emily needed right now. "Maybe you should play it cool. Call her manager for an interview next week or so."

"No, I need to get to her right here. She is very private and never gives interviews. Do you think she liked me? I tried to flirt with her, but I didn't get any vibes back."

"I don't know. She was friendly, but flirting? I think she was just being polite." Emily desperately tried to think of something that would distract Jen. "Do you want another drink?"

"No. I'm good. Let's get closer to the stage." She took Emily's hand and pulled her to the front, where a small crowd of fans gathered, complete with T-shirts with the band's name and a cardboard sign saying, *Sleep with me, Julie!*

As the guitar player strummed the opening chords of the next song, the fans screamed.

Emily moved away from them, to Jen's other side.

More and more women pressed to the front of the stage as the band played on. And there in the back was Diana, or rather Dee, sitting behind the drum set and looking right at home. At the bar, Emily had tried to avoid staring, but the darkness protected her now. Dee's shoulders were broader than the loose scrubs revealed at work, and the parts of the tattoo that wound around her biceps accentuated her muscular arms. The brown locks falling over her collarbones and the soft swell of her breasts provided a feminine contrast. Light and shadow played over the rippling muscles as Dee hit her drums. *Sexy.*

Emily bit her lip. She shouldn't think of her as sexy. Diana was her colleague, and they were in a mentoring relationship. But right now she was Dee, her drummer, the first woman Emily had ever felt a sexual stirring for.

A painful twisting behind her sternum arrested her breath. The pounding of her pulse sounded unnaturally loud in her ears, drowning out the music. She shook her head, clenched her fists, and looked at Jen to anchor herself. Maybe she should leave.

The tension in the crowd increased as the singer interacted with the fans. The hum of anticipation surrounded Emily like a swarm of buzzing insects.

Dee looked into the audience as if searching for something or someone.

One of the fangirls squealed. "Oooh, look at the hot drummer."

"Who is she looking for? Her girlfriend?" The other fan's voice was painfully high.

Emily dug a tissue out of her pants pocket and improvised a pair of earplugs. The fangirls annoyed her, but she asked herself the same question. Was Diana's girlfriend in the audience? Or in the band? Did she even have one? What did she really know about Diana? Nothing. And now she was keeping her secrets.

Jen took Emily's hand and squeezed it. "Isn't the atmosphere great? Better than sex."

Emily suppressed a groan. Sex. Not a word she should associate with Diana.

When the music started again, Jen rose on her toes. She had really found the perfect job to pursue her enthusiasm for music. Maybe she'd find another story here and wouldn't mind if Dee disappeared again after tonight. No, that was wishful thinking. Knowing Jen, she was far more likely to dig into Dee's background until she got the full story.

The smoky darkness should have hidden Emily, but Dee's gaze seemed to be directly on her. She tried to close her eyes and to lose herself in her dancing as she always did, but she was too self-conscious. Images from that night on the beach flickered through her mind, the rhythmic movement of Diana's whole body echoing the ecstatic drumming in front of the fire. When she looked at the stage again, Diana's eyes were closed and her concentration seemed to be completely on the music. It was the same expression she had seen many times in the last few weeks at work.

That was too much. Her private life and work had always been separate. The mingling of them was like a physical pain in her thorax. She had to get out of here.

Emily pretended to check her phone. "I need to go. Got a call from work." She had to shout directly into Jen's ear.

Jen only nodded and waved her off. She was used to Emily's dedication to work and seldom questioned or delayed her. She might deliver one of her famous your-work-is-not-your-life speeches tomorrow.

A text message woke Emily four hours later from an uneasy sleep. She reached for her phone on the bedside table. She always kept it close in case the hospital called. Now it was just Jen, letting her know that she had talked her way into the backstage party. And if Emily interpreted the winking smiley and abbreviations correctly, she was about to spend the night with someone. Probably Dee.

Emily tossed her phone back. *Who cares?* She punched her pillow, trying to find a comfortable position. Nothing worked. Frustrated, she threw it out of the bed and lay flat on her back. After a few minutes, she gave up the pretense of falling asleep again and stood up to get a glass of milk.

On her way back from the kitchen, she detoured to the window to retrieve the pillow. The thousands of city lights were only a weak substitute for real stars. She couldn't remember if she had ever taken the time to watch the night sky after that party on the beach. Life had flown by so fast, first college, then med school and her residency. Stargazing had never been on any curriculum. Now work left her with hardly any free time, and that was tightly scheduled. Sleeping, eating, and staying fit. The occasional extra hour with Jen or volunteer work. No vacation, no weekends at the beach or in the mountains. The only times she had been out of town had been for conferences, at sterile hotels without a trace of nature. She stood by the window, watching the flicker of the city lights until she was chilled and tired enough to return to sleep.

The next text message from Jen arrived late in the morning. She planned to spend the day with her newest conquest and to return directly home from there to write her article. She called herself inspired, and the text was again full of winking smileys. Emily didn't want to think about their meaning. She could vividly envision Jen in bed with Diana, and the image was like a slap in the face. But why? Jen was her best friend, and she had never been envious of her many affairs. No, this wasn't about Jen. Diana… The visceral pain morphed into nausea. Jealousy, pure and simple. Nothing else explained her reaction. The rational part of her wanted to dispute that idea, but it was true. Diana was Dee, and Dee was the faceless drummer she had always kept as her secret deep inside her heart. It was a childish crush that belonged in the realm of fantasy. In reality she would never have an affair with a rock star. And the rock star would never be interested in a plain and boring workaholic. So Jen could have Dee, and she would keep the memory of the beach.

Not fond of mixing work and private life anyhow, she would keep things simple. Diana was a colleague; Dee was Jen's business, and her faceless drummer was history.

Chapter 6

LURKING HALFWAY BETWEEN THE PARKING garage and the ED's back entrance, Diana resisted the urge to pace back and forth. Her stomach churned, and it had nothing to do with the too-bitter coffee she'd brought with her. At least the travel mug held enough warmth to stave off the early-morning chill. It had been raining at night, and the cold dampness crept even through her leather jacket. She'd been waiting for Emily to arrive at work for over half an hour, and with each passing minute her appreciation for her former fans rose. They had lain in wait at the stage entrance or in front of her hotel, not seeming to care about rain, snow, or scorching heat. Last year, an aspiring baby-dyke drummer had stopped her with millions of questions about a possible career path in the music industry. Hopefully, the good karma she had created by answering her patiently would help her today.

Firm steps announced Emily's arrival.

Diana hastily swallowed the sip of coffee she'd just taken, suppressed a grimace at the taste, and blocked her way. "Hi, Emily."

"Diana." Emily nodded once and stepped to the side to pass her.

"Wait, please." Diana attempted her most winning smile. "Do you have a minute before we go inside?"

Emily pulled her phone from her navy rain jacket and looked at it, presumably to check the time. "Sure. Do you have a work-related problem?"

"No." *At least not yet.* And Diana hoped she could keep it that way. "I'd like to talk about our meeting at the club." She studied her closely. The knowledge about Diana's past must have changed Emily's perception of her, but would she act differently today?

"What's there to talk about? You made your point clear, and I agreed to keep this out of the ED." Emily's voice was even and her expression unreadable.

Was it really that easy? Three days ago, Emily had been full of doubts, unsure she could keep the secret. "I'm sorry we had to cut the conversation short on Friday. Is there anything you want to know? Is everything okay with your friend?" Diana had seen Jen at the after-show party but had managed to avoid her with Mel's help.

A faint color rose to Emily's cheeks. "As I said, we should keep this out of the ED. We have an excellent reputation, and I'd like to keep it that way. That's my focus, not personal feelings. If I need to know something, I'll get back to you." She looked again at her phone, then shoved it into her pocket. "The residents' teaching starts in twenty minutes. Don't be late." Without waiting for Diana's reaction, she walked to the entrance at a brisk pace.

Diana stared after her. While she had been nervous about this conversation, a tiny part of her had been looking forward to sharing some of her past with Emily. Apparently, that wouldn't happen; Emily had made that clear. She could deal with that, but why had Emily stormed off like that? Was she annoyed? Angry? Her tone had been perfectly polite, and her words should have been reassuring; Diana just couldn't get over the feeling that she was missing something.

She sighed, chucked the rest of the disgusting coffee, and followed Emily inside. No way would she want to be late today.

✛✛✛✛✛✛✛

Emily studied the X-ray and sighed. Bilateral pneumonia, as she'd suspected.

She turned to her patient's husband. "I'm sorry, Mr. Jefferson."

He kept on stroking his wife's hand, without acknowledging that Emily had spoken.

She touched his arm to get his attention and leaned closer. "Mr. Jefferson, I'm sorry." She spoke as clear and deep as possible to overcome the failure of his almost hundred-year-old auditory system. "Our options are limited. But I promise you; we'll do our best that she feels safe and comfortable."

He nodded and beamed at her. "Thank you. She's breathing easier since you're here. She'll pull through, she's a fighter."

Emily didn't have the heart to tell him it was more the effect of the morphine than anything she could do to actually heal his wife. She'd discussed the situation with the couple's daughter on the phone, who'd told her about his mild dementia. He tended to forget his wife's widespread ovarian cancer and had called an ambulance just as the daughter had been out grocery shopping.

A sound Emily couldn't identify pulled her out of her musings. She looked at her patient, but nothing had changed in the last minute.

Mr. Jefferson had returned his attention to his wife, and Emily decided to leave them alone for now.

She looked at Tony to see if he needed anything else, but he made a shooing notion. "I'll call you when the daughter is here or…"

Emily nodded. He didn't need to speak out loud what they both knew, that the woman would probably die before they could move her to a private room or arrange a transport home.

As she left the cubicle and pulled the curtain closed behind her, Emily recognized the sound immediately. Laughter! And not just one person. The inappropriate noise drew Emily to the direction of the nurses' station. The sight of a small crowd stopped her in her tracks as she rounded the corner.

Playing rock-paper-scissors, Diana and Peter stood in the center of the laughing group.

What were the residents doing? Nothing, absolutely nothing should be decided by chance in an ED.

Peter groaned as he lost. "One more. Best four out of seven. Promise."

"No more. That's what you said the last two times." Diana took a pair of gloves and handed it to him with a flourish. Her mischievous grin made her look younger. "Congratulations. You got curtain number three: the tapeworm."

He took off, and the group of ED personnel dispersed. Diana remained with Madison, and they both leaned on the counter to study the electronic whiteboard.

"Let's see what treat we can find for the winner." Madison, the much too thin, much too blonde nurse, stood much too close to Diana and giggled.

Were they flirting? Even though she knew that hospitals were a breeding ground for friendships, affairs, and relationships, Emily didn't like when her ED turned into a soap opera. She led by example and kept her professional distance from her co-workers. Nothing good came of blurring the lines of work and personal life. And Diana should know that, but maybe she needed a reminder that she was here for work, not fun.

"Dr. Petrell. The patients are waiting." Emily didn't raise her voice, but both women flinched. Good.

"I'll just…help…" Madison bolted without finishing her excuse.

Diana looked after her for a second. When she turned to Emily, all traces of the previous elation had vanished from her expression. "Do you want me to take someone specific? I was just signing on to my next case."

"No, you weren't. You and your co-workers were disrespecting the patients by making this a game. We have rules regarding the patient assignment. If you can't take your work seriously, you should just go back to LA." *And to your band.* Emily had enough control to swallow her last thought.

A muscle in Diana's jaw twitched, and her eyes blazed a brilliant green, but she remained silent.

Emily preferred it to an insincere apology. She glanced at the whiteboard and found Diana's next patient within seconds. "Cubicle five."

Without checking the whiteboard for details, Diana nodded once and stalked off.

The triumph of having the last word wore off too soon. Emily stared at the computer as if it held the answers to her racing thoughts. Maybe it did. She picked out her next case and typed both their names in the text fields, ignoring the slight tremor of her fingers.

Diana looked at the clock on the wall. If she hurried, she could grab a sandwich for lunch before the cafeteria sold out the best selection. She could type her lengthy notes while eating.

Courtney jogged into her path. "Dr. Barnes is looking for you." She pointed over her shoulder and rolled her eyes. "I'd hurry if I were you."

Great. No lunch for her now. Diana steeled herself for another of Emily's lectures about one topic or another. Since their meeting at the club two weeks ago, Emily's behavior toward her had changed completely. She used to be a great teacher who guided her residents by asking the right questions and provided many opportunities to learn. Now she limited their conversations to commands and criticism.

Standing at the nurses' station, Emily read something on the computer and frowned. When Diana approached, her head shot up and she nodded toward the open file on the monitor. "What were you thinking? No, wait, don't tell me. I guess you weren't thinking at all."

Diana glanced over Emily's shoulder and recognized the case immediately as the one she had wanted to type up during lunch. "I can explain. I've—"

Emily raised her hand to stop Diana's answer. "She has classical symptoms and a high-risk profile for a cardiac vascular disease."

"Yes, but—" Another gesture interrupted Diana again, just as she had expected. Her stomach clenched, and she took a deep breath to ward off the rising sensation of powerlessness. It was better to let Emily get whatever lecture she had in mind off her chest before she tried to get in a word.

"You need to clear this kind of patient with me. It's not your place to decide that she doesn't need to see a specialist. I didn't expect you to be afraid of Dr. Riley, too, like all the other residents." Deep lines appeared in the artificial smoothness of Emily's makeup-covered skin.

Why didn't Emily let her explain? Diana bit her lip. Who was Dr. Riley? And why would she be afraid of someone she hadn't met yet? Another deep breath was necessary. Not that it seemed to help much.

Emily obviously mistook her attempt at restraining herself for an interruption "Don't argue with me. You know the procedures. You know I'm right." Her volume had increased with every word, and several nurses stopped working and looked at them. A stab of her finger in the air accompanied each sentence.

Something inside of Diana snapped. *Fuck Emily and her attitude!* Diana wouldn't play the meek resident anymore. She consciously stepped into Emily's personal space and lowered her voice. She had just enough self-control left to know that turning this into a shouting match would be the end of her short career in this ED.

"Dr. Barnes, listen to me. You haven't talked to the patient or her family doctor. As long as you don't know her complete history, you can't come to the same conclusions as I did. You have three options: let me explain, repeat my work and draw your own conclusions, or request a cardiologist now and embarrass yourself. It's your call." She looked straight into Emily's eyes without wavering.

Surprisingly, this seemed to shut Emily up, and Diana took a step back. She looked around and nodded toward the nurses pretending not to stare at them. "Let's take this to the lounge."

Without another word, Emily turned and stalked toward the staff lounge. She held herself very straight, and Diana guessed she was still mad at her, but now they were talking. Or at least planning to. Hopefully.

Maybe she could even broach the real problem. Diana didn't know why Emily's discovery of her secret should be the cause for the abrupt change in behavior, but the timing was no coincidence. Her chest tightened at the thought of discussing her past with Emily if she was in that contentious mood. No amount of breathing could alleviate her trepidation. She passed the ambulance entrance as two paramedics left with an empty stretcher. The open doorway seemed to call her. *Is it worth it? Just run away and leave all the stress behind.* She sighed and followed Emily to the staff lounge. It was time to prove that she had indeed grown up.

After entering behind Emily, Diana closed the door to the lounge. She didn't want an audience for their talk.

They took a seat on the same couch, and Diana turned toward Emily. "I think we need to talk about two things. About the patient first. May I explain the reasoning behind my treatment?"

Emily just nodded.

"Okay. The patient was here twice in the last month. And she saw about ten doctors in different settings with the same symptoms during the last six months. Her EKG and TropT were always normal, but because of her insistence and her high-risk profile, she received several echoes, stress tests, and even two catheters. She didn't mention any of these tests to me, but her husband listed them all—against her protest—and even showed me all the relevant results. They were all negative." Diana swallowed. In her hurry to get it all out before Emily lost her patience, she had talked much too fast.

Emily regarded her without betraying her thoughts and motioned at her to continue.

"The symptoms started right after her sister died of a massive heart attack. She was only fifty-nine; everyone thought she was in good health. I believe her problem is psychosomatic and explained it to them. While she's still in denial, her husband concedes that there might be a tiny chance of it. They are willing to talk to psych for a second opinion and to see a grief counselor." Diana hesitated and finally looked directly into Emily's eyes. "I would have told you about her after she had seen psych and before I'd let her go home."

Emily held her gaze for a few seconds. Her stiff posture relaxed slightly, and she finally said, "I'm sorry. You're right; I didn't know the whole story. But you should have completed your notes before you went off to do something else."

Diana barely kept herself from rolling her eyes. This was typical of the new Emily—she always found something to criticize, even as she was apologizing. "You're right. I'll do it immediately the next time."

"What else do you want to talk about?" The cold tone was anything but inviting.

Diana had thought of several diplomatic openings for this conversation but couldn't remember any of them. She hoped Emily valued straightforwardness. "I believe you have developed a problem with me, my work, or my attitude in the last couple of weeks. And I don't know which. Or why. What went wrong?"

"What problem are you talking about?"

"I don't know if you have a problem. I just feel like there might be one. Your behavior toward me changed. In the beginning, you challenged me with questions, and you taught me a lot. Now, you just criticize me at every opportunity."

"You think that the constructive criticism I provide is a problem? My problem?" Emily's voice rose.

"No. Yes. Wait—" Diana reached for her but stopped short of touching her arm. "Please, let me explain. I don't mind constructive criticism, but somehow the tone shifted in the last few weeks. I'd like to get back to how we worked together before. What can I do to make that happen?" That sounded too close to pleading for her taste, but she wanted to break through to the woman she sometimes glimpsed underneath the veneer of Emily's aloofness.

Emily hesitated and studied the floor for a moment. She rubbed her forearm absentmindedly and finally raised her head. For an instant Diana thought she looked hurt, but her face closed off immediately. "Diana, I think you're overreacting." She spoke slowly, as if addressing a small child. "I've criticized you, yes, but I do that with anyone else who needs it. I don't believe in coddling residents. This is not kindergarten." Emily stood and headed toward the door. Before she reached it, she turned around and added, "This is real life, not an after-show party with a couple of adulatory fans. If you can't cope with that, maybe you're in the wrong line of work." She strode out without waiting for an answer.

Diana slumped back onto the couch and hit the cushion with her fist. "Fuck!" This didn't go as planned at all. Well, the plan had been rather sketchy, but it had definitely ended with an understanding, an improvement of their current situation. She didn't believe that this talk had solved any problems. They hadn't even touched the possible trigger for the change, their meeting in the club. Did Emily think her fame as a rock star had gone straight to her head and left her unable to deal with criticism? But the real question was, was she? Did she expect too much from their work relationship? If Emily was right and this work atmosphere was normal, she had to thicken her skin. The alternative was to leave and start over somewhere else.

Like last time. Diana wanted to argue with that voice nagging in the back of her head. She hadn't run away from work; she had purposely walked toward a different career…hadn't she?

But this was neither the right time nor place to sort out her lingering doubts about her motivation for switching careers.

She stood, straightened her scrub shirt, and fingered the name tag she had received from her eldest brother, George, for graduation. The familiar lines of the engraving calmed her. D. Petrell, MD. That's who she was today. She strode to the door, intent on taking up work again. Food could wait until she got home.

Six hours later, Diana sat at the counter at the nurses' station and had just finished yet another chart when Courtney slumped onto the seat next to hers. She sighed dramatically, and when Diana didn't react, she sighed again, more loudly.

Diana kept her own sigh inward. "Hey, Courtney. What's the problem?"

Courtney swiveled her chair back and forth.

What is she, a five-year-old?

"The pedantic witch of paperwork, what else? I wish I were as good as you. She always makes me rewrite my charts. I don't know how she's doing it, but she finds something wrong or missing every time. But I heard she yelled at you today. So, you're no longer her favorite?"

Diana pretended to concentrate on her notes to gain some time. Favorite? Where had that come from? She wanted to be respected for her work and for her personality. Being called a supervisor's favorite could cause problems. First, it would be a joke; later, envy would turn it into a curse. She hated the threat of a competitive atmosphere.

"Favorite? Never felt like it to me. I guess she yells at all of us from time to time. Isn't that part of her job description?" She finished with her chart, saved it, double-checked that it had actually saved, and rose.

"Are you done for today? Do you want to come with us for a beer? A bunch of residents get together at the bar across the street and let off some steam. It's a Friday tradition." Courtney winked. "You can even throw some darts and pretend to see a certain face on the board."

Diana hesitated. She was beat and had been fantasizing about a hot bath for hours. But having a good relationship with her colleagues mattered, especially if Emily continued to give her the cold shoulder. Maybe hearing the others talk about Emily would help her put her own experience into the right perspective. "I'll be there."

Diana looked around the bar. The place was nice enough, not too modern, not too dingy, just without character. The particular draw wasn't the interior decoration or the menu, but the proximity to the hospital. She recognized several nurses, and a group of paramedics still in uniform stood at the bar.

She sneaked a glance at her phone. Only eight thirty. The hour she had spent with the other residents felt like five. They hadn't even needed five minutes of talk over burgers and beer to get to their favorite topic: the world was unfair. The residents were victims of the system, the older doctors, the nurses, and even the patients. They were all out to get them, especially Emily.

Diana could certainly understand the emotions, but she didn't share them. She liked Emily, especially the old Emily she had worked with the first few weeks. Her underlying genuine concern about her patients spoke to Diana. Emily wasn't vindictive but tried to improve the quality of care. Only her methods lacked social skills. But that was no reason to detest her.

Her phone rang, and Diana looked at the display. Mel. Perfect, she could be her ticket out of here. "Mel, hi."

"Do you have time to talk?"

"Sure, hold on a second." Diana took some money from her wallet to cover her share and laid it in the middle of the table. "Hey, everyone. I need to go." She waved her phone. "A friend has an emergency. See you next week." She slipped on her jacket and left before anyone could ask questions. Outside, she raised the phone back to her ear. "Mel, are you still on?"

Mel chuckled. "Emergency? Did I wreck my car or break my leg?"

"Both? You choose. I just had to get out of there." Diana tried to zip up her jacket with one hand. The sun had just set, and during the twenty-minute walk home the mild spring air would cool down fast. Everyone thought she was crazy for walking any chance she got, but sleeping the day away in tour buses and faceless hotels for years had given her a craving for being outdoors.

"Bad date?"

"No, just some colleagues. The usual. Whining about work: Everyone's unfair. Why me. Blah, blah, blah." She looked at the park entrance. Twilight had set in, so she'd better stay on the safe side and take the long way around. "We all work long hours and get little recognition in return. But we all knew that before we even started med school. They should pour their energy into work instead of complaining."

Mel just laughed.

"What? I don't get the joke."

"Listen to yourself," Mel said. "During your first residency that was all you did, complaining and bitching. Daily. You sounded like a broken record."

Diana tried to remember how she had felt years ago. Most of that time was a blur; only vague memories of frustration and exhaustion remained. "Well, okay. Maybe I'm a hypocrite."

"I think you grew up, like most of us did."

"I don't know about that. I had a discussion with my attending today. I tried to talk about a change in the work atmosphere, and she accused me of not being able to take constructive criticism." Diana again felt Emily's angry gaze piercing her.

"In the band, you took criticism well. We could always talk about what worked and what didn't. Not like Katie." She knew Mel's tone well enough to picture her rolling her eyes.

Diana groaned. Her ex had a not-so-little diva streak in her. Compared to Katie, everyone seemed reasonable. "Thanks. I guess, the real problem lies somewhere else. She didn't want to talk about it, but everything changed when we met at the concert two weeks ago. Emily confuses me. She behaved like a supportive mentor one day and like a heartless bitch the next."

"So, she's the one who knows."

"Yeah." Diana's steps were the only thing filling the silence. She gave her friend a moment to think about the situation. Diana valued Mel's opinion because she always tried to see both sides.

"Maybe she doesn't know how to treat you and hides her insecurities behind curtness. She wouldn't be the first. She could be as confused as you, just with less social skills. Or maybe she distrusts your motives."

Diana sighed. It all came back to communication. She had to find an opening to broach the topic again, soon. "Maybe. Thanks. But here I am, complaining about work, and you called to tell me something."

"It's okay. That's what friends are for. I wanted to give you an update about Jen."

"Jen? The music journalist?" Diana hadn't expected Mel to keep in touch with her.

"There's more to Jen than just her job."

"Probably, but that's not why she's meeting with you. She's trying to get information from you about Eos. About me. Why we gave up the band."

"Maybe in the beginning, but now she respects that I don't talk about all that. I think she put the story on ice after we went out for the second time."

"Went out? Like dating?" Diana ground her teeth. How could Mel do that to her?

"I don't know if you'd call it dating, but yeah, we're sleeping together." Mel sounded defensive. "She's fun and knows so much about music. We can talk for hours. And not about you."

Diana unclenched her jaw. Her reaction had been selfish. She could trust Mel. "I'm sorry. I'm happy for you, honestly. You just caught me by surprise. Do you think you could have something serious?"

"Too soon to tell. I'll let you know before the wedding."

"For a chance to see you in a white dress, I'd give her my story as a wedding present." Diana laughed. Talking to Mel was a much better way of unwinding after a shitty day at work than an evening at a bar. If only she and Emily could talk so effortlessly.

Chapter 7

Saturday afternoon, Diana packed the new drumsticks, small snare drums, banjos, and djembes she had bought last week at a sale and drove to the Rainbow Home.

"Diana, my song's finally finished!" She had just stepped inside the building of the LGBTQ youth center when Freddy engulfed her in a hug. Her mass of tiny black curls bobbed rhythmically as she talked nonstop about her song, her new room in a shared house, the neighbor's dog, and anything else that had happened to her over the past week.

Diana had a hard time following her as she threw in unfamiliar names and places. All the kids Diana had known years ago had grown out of going to the center, and in the past six weeks Diana had enjoyed getting to know the next generation, including Freddy.

"Wait, slow down, please. You've been bitten by the dog? The wound needs to be cleaned out. A dog bite can get nasty really fast. Did you go to the ER?" Most kids here were wary of authorities, especially if they had lived on the street, as Freddy had for the past three of her sixteen years.

"No need. We have the doc here today." Freddy pulled up the leg of her baggy jeans to show a fresh white bandage that contrasted sharply with her brown skin. "Have you met her yet? She's so cute. She tries to be all serious and businesslike, but after she finished with my wound and shots, she offered me a lollipop. Like I'm six! And when I told her what I'd rather lick, she actually blushed."

Diana laughed. She should probably answer with something grown-up and social-worker-like about respecting women, but the blue tongue peeking out betrayed Freddy. "Uh-huh. So you didn't take the lollipop?"

Freddy blushed but grinned as though she was the cocky teenager she pretended to be.

"So, she's cute? What's a doctor doing here today?"

Freddy shrugged. "She's been here a few times before. She's giving us shots, antibiotics, and stuff. You know, for..." She gestured vaguely to her crotch.

Diana nodded. She knew what Freddy meant. Too many of the kids turned toward prostitution to survive. But she wasn't here to judge. What she could contribute was to let them forget the hurt and anger for a few hours or at least help them to channel it into the music.

"Do you think you'll be able to play today?" Diana smiled to let her know she was teasing. "You can help me set up. I need someone to help me with some drums I brought in. They are just too heavy. Now that you got your vitamin-booster-doping shot, you're probably stronger than Superman."

"Wonder Woman."

Both laughed at Freddy's attempt to flex her tiny biceps. She was overflowing with energy, but *muscular* wasn't a word Diana would use to describe her.

Diana and Freddy set up the room, placing drums of various sizes in a circle, as the others trickled in one by one. Punctuality wasn't a priority for most of the kids, but Diana didn't mind. Satisfied everything was as it should be, she settled on a stool and placed the largest djembe between her knees. The goatskin was little rough, but it was warm under her fingers, almost alive. She seldom took the time to play with her hands anymore, so these sessions were as much a treat for her as they were for the kids. She started a slow rhythm, very basic, so that no one had difficulties following her.

Freddy took her guitar from her battered case and joined her. One by one the others picked up instruments.

Diana let them play in their own tempo and style for some time. Soon the circle grew as more and more kids joined them. Diana loved that most harmonized instinctively. She put her djembe down and circled the room to gently correct a grip here or show another variation there. Many of those kids had never had the chance to get a proper music lesson and had neither patience nor time to practice regularly, but that didn't matter.

When the different rhythms and melodies drifted apart, she returned to her djembe and increased the pace. As usual, the majority followed her lead and played faster and faster, directing their drive toward a common goal. As the music became almost impossibly fast, the harmony collapsed and became a cacophony.

Diana laughed, stopped playing, and used the hem of her shirt to wipe her forehead. "I'm beat. You guys will kill me one day."

The others laughed or giggled, and some high-fived each other. A few even stayed to help clean up the room.

Diana listened to them gossiping about the new doctor. Everyone agreed she was cute; some even called her hot.

"What's so special about her? Only her looks?" In Diana's experience it usually took them much longer to trust someone new. What had won the kids over so fast?

"She's not judging or preaching," answered Hailey, who worked the streets despite being a lesbian and underage.

Several others nodded.

If Diana weren't here in her role as a musician, she could imagine herself offering medical help. After the last instruments had been returned to her car, she decided to meet the new doctor.

┼┼┼┼┼┼┼┼

Diana knocked on the door.

A sound that was probably an invitation drifted through the wood, so Diana entered.

A woman in jeans and a dark blue scrub shirt had her head hidden inside a small storage closet. The dark denim fit snuggly in all the right places, just as the kids had said.

Forcing her gaze upward, Diana shook her head at herself. She wasn't here to ogle her colleague. "Hi, I'm Diana. I give music lessons."

The woman turned and offered her hand. "Hi, I'm Emily. I'm—" As she caught sight of Diana, she stopped abruptly, and they both stared at each other.

Even though her scrub shirt was the same one she wore at work, Emily looked different, more approachable. Maybe it was the strand of hair that had escaped her ponytail or the slight blush that colored her cheeks.

63

Seeing her flustered helped Diana to recover from her own shock. "We meet at the unlikeliest places. Where next?"

Emily shook her head. "There aren't many more places I go to." She grinned. "Maybe the supermarket?"

"Maybe. Can I help you with this?" Diana gestured in the direction of the closet and a table, where medical supplies lay in a disarray that probably contained some system, not that she could tell at first.

"Sure, thanks. I'm making a list of all the supplies that are here to see what I have to bring the next time. I haven't decided yet if I need to keep the older stuff. They are expired, but I can't see why we shouldn't still use most of it." Emily continued to take everything out of the closet and to inspect the packages for damages and the expiration date. Some she put in a box on the floor, but most of them went on the table. "Sort them by type and size." She pointed at the growing stack without looking at Diana.

Diana sighed inwardly. Emily was back to the friendly, but distant work relationship they had shared in the beginning. Maybe this was her chance to improve it. "The girls like you."

"I haven't scared them off with my vaccinations?" Emily chuckled. "They always pretend to be so tough when they are in here."

"Yeah, it takes a while until they let you see their softer side. You're new here, right?" Diana knew the answer but wanted to keep the conversation going.

"It's my third time, but the last time was a few months ago." Emily turned around, studied the different stacks Diana had made on the table, and added more supplies to each. "And you started recently too?"

"No, years ago in college."

Emily stopped the sorting and focused on her. "Really?"

"I took a course in music therapy, and we did a few projects around town. I liked it here and volunteered throughout college and med school. But the last ten years or so, I couldn't come back here often enough to set up anything regular. I took it up again when I moved back here six weeks ago. I plan to be here at least every other week if work doesn't get in the way." Diana knew she was babbling, but Emily's professionally neutral expression made her nervous.

"I want to return too. A friend of my best friend works here as a social worker, and she convinced me to give it a try. I like that the work is different here, more basic, without the equipment we have at the hospital. And an emphasis on prevention. I think there's need for more regular medical service." Emily smiled, and her shoulders lost some of the tension that seemed to be her constant companion.

"That's a great idea. A few years ago we had a monthly walk-in clinic, but when Tim retired, it was difficult to find someone new."

Emily regarded her critically for a moment. "Why didn't you volunteer for the position?"

Diana bit her lip and looked away. "I wasn't here too often in the last few years." She swallowed. "During that time I didn't think of myself as a doctor."

Emily nodded, as if this made sense to her, and continued working. "I think that's all." She handed Diana a checklist. "I'll put everything back in the closet now, and you take notes."

There it was again: the tone of voice that told Diana clearly who was the boss and who was the lowly resident. She lifted the corners of her mouth slightly upward. "Sure." Did her smile look as fake as it felt? It didn't matter since Emily wasn't looking at her anymore.

They worked in silence.

Diana sneaked peeks at Emily's ponytail and the faded jeans that hugged her figure. This wasn't what she had imagined an off-duty Emily would look like. Only the makeup was as thick as ever.

"Thanks. This was much faster than I could have managed on my own. I think we can lock up here."

"Okay. Do you have a car?" Diana nodded toward the box of supplies that needed to be thrown away. "Or I can take it."

Emily shook her head. "No problem. I took the bus. The stop isn't far away." Putting on a thin canvas jacket, she signaled Diana to leave the room ahead of her. She wedged the box under one arm and locked the door. "Are you coming?"

Diana grabbed her leather jacket from the music room. She retrieved her car keys from her pocket and dangled them in front of Emily. "I can drive you home if you want to. Or we could have dinner somewhere, and you can tell me more about the medical challenges here."

"No, thanks. See you Monday." Emily avoided eye contact and left.

Ouch. The message hit her like a slap in the face. Emily would rather take the bus than spend time together in her car.

Diana said goodbye to the social worker in the reception area. The weather had changed in the couple of hours she'd been inside. A few raindrops cooled her burning skin. She leaned against her car, closed her eyes, and turned her face toward the sky. The wetness was soothing. The scent of fresh rain washed the stench of the city from her mind. Too soon, the light drizzle turned into a downpour, and she fumbled with her keys to open the car. The few seconds outside had left her wet and cold. She turned the heater and defroster on.

After a minute the air warmed up, and the fog slowly disappeared from the windshield so she could start her way home. She didn't get far.

At the end of the street a figure with a big box huddled in a house entrance. Wet hair hid half her face, but the stubborn set of her shoulders was unmistakably Emily's.

Diana hadn't brushed off the brusque rejection yet, but she couldn't leave her stranded. The rain didn't look as if it would let up anytime soon. She stopped the car and opened the side window. "Emily?"

Emily hesitated for a moment but finally ran over to the car.

An icy gust of wind assaulted Diana as she got out to open the trunk. She put the wet cardboard box inside and hastened back to the front. When they were both in the front seats, she turned the heater to maximum.

Rivulets of water dripped from Emily's hair on her shoulders, drenching the thin jacket she had put on instead of her scrub shirt. The front gaped open, and the tight, white T-shirt underneath it was nearly see-through now, clinging to curves Diana hadn't noticed before.

What are you doing? Ogling a colleague was still a bad idea. Diana tore her gaze away.

Emily shivered and tried to warm her hands in the air that blasted out of the vents. "Thank you. I'm sorry I was short with you." Her voice was almost drowned out by the noise of the hot air.

Diana waited, but no other explanation was coming. She decided to let it go. "It's okay. Where can I drive you?"

"I live close to Green Lake Park. East of it."

"No problem." The wipers had cleared the windshield, and Diana put the car into gear. "I live there too."

"Really? It's a small wonder we really haven't met in the supermarket yet." Emily closed her eyes and leaned back.

They didn't talk for the rest of the short drive.

"We're nearly here."

Diana's words seemed to wake Emily. She looked around and then pointed to a street. "Take that one and then the second one on the right. I live just down the road."

The neighborhood consisted mostly of beautiful older one- and two-story houses, and Emily's building seemed to have been converted into apartments with separate entrances on both levels. Painted an inoffensive beige, it was nearly hidden behind a couple of old trees.

The rain had dwindled again as Diana retrieved the box. The cardboard was soggy, and the bottom already bent, as if it would burst any second. She wrapped both arms around it to steady it, awkwardly clutching her keys in one hand.

Emily opened her arms to take it from her, and Diana shook her head.

"Let me carry it. I'm afraid it'll give if I let go of it for a second. Can you close the trunk?" Diana pushed the lock button on her car key and strode toward the house. She hoped Emily would follow without another discussion.

Emily overtook her and led her up an outside staircase to the second floor. She unlocked the door and reached for the box. "Thank you. I can take it from here."

Diana grimaced and held it more tightly to her chest. "Just tell me where to put it. I already feel it tearing." Plus, she was curious about how Emily lived.

Emily's gaze flicked from the box to the inside of the apartment and back. Finally, she shrugged and led the way through a narrow hall, motioning to Diana to go ahead while she pulled off her shoes and jacket.

The apartment was a surprise. Diana hadn't thought about what she'd expect, but this place full of bookcases wasn't it. The hall was lined with them and blurred the border to the living room, where they concealed every wall. Only the doors and windows were left free. Some of the bookcases had glass doors, obviously to protect older books. Stacks of books and journals cluttered every surface: a big chair, part of the couch that wasn't covered with an old quilt, and all the tables. Diana looked around for a place to put the soggy cardboard, not wanting to damage the books or the hardwood floor.

Emily opened a door. "Please, put it in the kitchen. The tiles won't mind the water."

Diana passed her and entered a room that looked exactly as she'd guessed: white tiles, white walls, the minimum amount of storage in white cabinets, and work space with ridiculously clean surfaces. She put the box on the floor in a corner and turned around.

Emily stood in the doorway, watching her. "Not what you expected?" The corners of her mouth twitched upward in a rare show of humor.

Diana shook her head. She waved her hand vaguely in the direction of the stove. "You don't cook?" She smiled to avoid any hint of criticism.

The twitching corners widened into a grin. "I'm not such a stereotype of busy career woman. I cook, then I clean up. Do you want some tea?" Emily switched the water kettle on. "Or coffee?"

"Tea would be great, thanks," Diana said.

"What kind?" She opened a cupboard with dozens of neatly stacked, colorful packages. "I'm afraid collecting tea is a weakness of mine."

Diana wanted to ask about the other weaknesses but bit her tongue, afraid to test the extent of Emily's playful mood. She studied the teas and finally picked one in a vibrant orange-red box. The colors promised warmth.

Emily chose the same for herself, put them in oversized mismatched mugs that looked handmade, and poured the boiling water over the tea bags. "Five minutes. I'm going to change out of my wet clothes real fast. Do you need anything?"

"I'm fine, thanks."

"Make yourself at home." Emily gestured toward the living room. "I'll be back in a second."

Diana's wet sneakers squelched on the hardwood floor. She hesitated but finally slipped out of them and carried them to the narrow hallway. On her way back she took her time to study the books. Some were medical texts, several others nonfiction. Old textbooks in unusually large formats stood side by side with modern paperback copies of the same topic. She let her fingers glide over the spines as she slowly wandered from shelf to shelf. Did she use the Dewey Decimal Classification? Okay. That definitely exceeded her expectations, but it was cute, in a geeky way. The many nonmedical books came as a surprise as well. Entire shelves were dedicated to natural science, but nearly as many were fiction. Classics slightly outnumbered the contemporary authors. No lesbian fiction, though. Either she didn't like them, or she kept the good stuff in her bedroom. If she even was a lesbian or bi. Diana had never thought about it at work, but her gaydar had pinged at the club and today.

After a round through the living room, she moved the stack of journals to the side table so she could sit in the chair. Sticky notes peeked out from the pages of the recent editions of several major medical publications. She took the latest *Journal of Emergency Medicine* and leafed through it until a case report captured her attention.

"Here's your tea." Emily put the mug next to the stack of journals.

Diana let out an undignified shriek. She hadn't heard Emily coming back. "Uh…um…thanks."

Emily laughed and sat on the couch. She had dried her hair and touched up her makeup. "Find something interesting?" She gestured toward the various stacks of books and journals scattered around the room. "I'm sorry about the mess. I wasn't expecting company."

"No problem. You better not see my place right now." The truth was, it was cleaner than ever. She didn't have the energy to do anything that would mess up her apartment most evenings, but she didn't want to admit that. She decided to deflect the conversation back to Emily and gestured toward the bookshelves. "How long have you been collecting?"

"All my life." Emily shrugged. "My parents were both librarians. A lot of the older texts and first editions were their idea of a fun birthday or Christmas present." She pointed toward one of the glass cabinets.

"Were? Are they retired?"

"My mother is. But she is still volunteering at the town library and at the local high school." Emily stared into her tea.

"And your father?" The question popped out of Diana's mouth before she could censor herself. Before she could take it back, Emily answered, her voice so low that Diana could barely hear her.

"He's dead."

"I'm sorry." Now it was Diana's turn to stare uncomfortably into her own mug while Emily straightened a stack of journals on the side table. She waited, but nothing more was coming. Diana searched for a safe topic because by now Emily probably regretted that she had invited her up. She decided to take a leap of faith. "I've never really wanted to study medicine."

That caused Emily to look up from her tea.

"My parents are both doctors. Well, when I was growing up, my mother was more of a housewife. But my father is a family doctor. He lives and breathes medicine. Three of my brothers studied medicine as well. I just fell into it because it was easier to do what they expected. My real love was music, but I knew they would never support me. So I compromised and took all the pre-med courses at college while I did my BS in music. The fact that I got into med school despite my lack of enthusiasm is a miracle."

Emily frowned and started to say something.

Diana continued before she could interrupt. "But then I loved it. Not so much studying the basic science requirements, but learning about the different pathomechanisms. I loved the hunt for clues in the symptoms and medical history and the moment it suddenly all falls into place, when you have a diagnosis and can find a treatment."

Emily leaned forward, and her gray eyes reflected the light like steel. "But you didn't quit the music? You still played in a band? Or did that come later?"

"No. I didn't quit. I was in the same band since college with my girlfriend and my best friend, Mel."

"Did you start your residency after med school, or did you take some time off?"

Emily's tone reminded her of an interrogation, but she ignored it. At least they were talking.

"I started right away." Diana shook her head. "I was so naive. I thought I could continue just like college and med school. Do some ED shifts, practice or perform after work. Play in the clubs on the weekend. Party all night. In the beginning, it worked out great. Work was fun; I learned new things daily, and all this energy fueled my playing. But after a year or so, things changed." Diana hesitated. She had the urge to be honest with Emily, but she doubted she would be respected for it. Emily would probably kick her out and never talk to her again outside work. But there was a slight chance she'd value honesty as much as Diana did, and playing it safe hadn't helped her in the past. She took a deep breath and sat straighter. "I made some stupid choices. I didn't handle the stress or the pressure to conform well. The hierarchy in medicine got on my nerves, and I chafed at the rules and discipline. Sometimes I just called in sick to go and play in concerts. My head was not always with my work." She clenched the mug with both hands and took a sip to get rid of the tightness in her throat. The warmth soothed her, and the hint of ginger just burned enough to jolt her out of her self-reproachful thoughts.

Emily just watched her, the professional mask Diana knew so well from the hospital firmly in place.

Diana decided to get it all out in the open. "I was thinking about quitting. I'd played around with the idea for a while. And I'm sure the hospital thought about letting me go as well. Then came the offer I couldn't refuse. A record deal and not just with any label. A big label and the deal came complete with an international tour and everything. So I left my work behind, and we took our band to the next level." She chuckled. "Or we skipped a few levels."

Emily's expression softened a little. Maybe she was willing to listen to the full story. "Did you ever regret it?"

"Not at first, but... We did seven records in eight years. That was too much. The quality of the last two is... Well, I wouldn't recommend them. Not surprisingly, that job came with its own set of stress, pressure, and discipline problems. Katie—my partner—and I split but continued living and working together. At first it was okay, but then... Let's just say she made some bad choices, and I didn't handle that too well either." Diana didn't want to go into that particular mess right now. She hoped Emily would let it go.

"Is that why you quit the band? The stress? Or the personal problems?" Emily's gaze dug into her like a probe trying to reach the deeper layers of a wound.

Diana didn't mind the exploration. She had flushed out the hidden debris long ago. The tone suggested the question was not only about her past. Emily wanted to know how she would handle the inevitable pressure at work in the future. "Neither. I grew up. I learned to cope with the stress. My anger at the unfairness of the world receded. But then there was an incident, and it triggered something in me." Her throat constricted. She took a large gulp of her tea, wishing her memory of that night could be as easily washed away as the sour taste in her mouth. "I thought long and hard about what I wanted to do with the rest of my life. I asked myself where I could see myself in ten, fifteen years. And surprisingly, that wasn't on a stage but at a hospital. This time I didn't decide anything overnight. I read medical journals again, watched some lectures online, and attended a few conferences. In the end, the decision to return to medicine was an easy one."

Emily nodded at her last words. "At work, it shows that you know a lot about the latest studies."

So, she *had* noticed. Diana liked that. But then, there wasn't much Emily didn't notice at work. She just never let on that she did. Maybe now was the time to talk about their work relationship again. Or should she just let it go? Maybe things would grow organically from here on.

"Am I the first person at work you've told all this?" Emily's question startled Diana from her thoughts.

Diana shrugged. "Even if my contract wouldn't forbid me to, I wouldn't want to tell anyone. I'm not bonding so much on a personal level with the other residents. We get along fine, but we're not in the same phase of our lives. And I don't know them well enough to trust them with my story."

Emily studied her mug again.

Diana wanted to rip it from her hands to provoke a reaction. Anything was better than this protracted silence. But, of course, she didn't.

When Emily finally looked up again, her frown had disappeared. "Thank you for trusting me."

Diana offered a smile that Emily returned. It eased her trepidation about the conversation. Maybe Emily really got it.

"What you said the other day about the work atmosphere… It's possible that… I overreacted. Can we just rewind and start over?"

A mixture of hope and relief flooded Diana. She made a twirling motion with her finger as if rewinding an old-fashioned tape, and both laughed.

Diana sobered fast. She had to get it right this time. Another chance might not come again. "What I want to tell you is that I noticed a change in our interaction. In the beginning, I liked coming to work and was looking forward to being on the same shift with you. You taught me things, and I thought you gradually trusted me to take over more responsibility. Now I constantly feel as if I did something majorly wrong. But I don't know what it was. The only incident that fits the timing was our encounter at the club. Is keeping my secret putting a strain on our working relationship?"

"No, it's not the secret. I checked with Dr. Wallace, and what you said is true. He asked you to keep it quiet, and I agree with his decision. I've got to admit I judged you unfairly. I don't know if you've noticed, but I'm pretty dedicated to my work." She grimaced. "I thought you were only playing at being a doctor, and I doubted your motives without even asking you. So I amped up the pressure to see if you're taking the job seriously." She bit her lip and blushed but held Diana's gaze. "I'm sorry. That was not a good method."

Diana couldn't agree more. She decided not to dwell on it. Emily's social and leadership skills might be lacking, but her intentions were good. She tried to convey the sincerity of her next question. "I want to return to our old working relationship. What can I do?"

Emily studied her for a long time.

Diana tried hard not to fidget under her gaze. She couldn't interpret her expression.

"No, we can't return to the relationship we had," Emily finally said.

Diana struggled to hide her disappointment. She swallowed and took a sip of her tepid tea. "Okay. I'm sorry." She didn't know what she was apologizing for, but what else could she say? Standing up, she looked from Emily to the door and back. "I'll leave you to your tea. See you on Monday."

Emily reached out as if to hold her back. "Wait. That's not..." She ran her hand through her hair. "What I was trying to say is... I think we have to start anew. I can't forget what I learned about you in the last few weeks, especially not what you said today. I...I respect you for your choices. I couldn't have said that last week."

A heavy weight was lifted from Diana's chest. She collapsed into her seat. "And I respect you for the time and passion you invest in your work. Do you think we can work something out from here?"

Emily nodded. "We'll be fine at work." A subtle shift in her posture showed she had been tense. Her shoulders loosened, and she sank minimally into her seat. The transformation was simple, but it made her look younger. She raised one foot onto the seat and hugged her bent leg. "So, tell me about the concert I've seen. What's your connection to the band?"

Chapter 8

"DR. BARNES, STOP!" COURTNEY BARELY MANAGED to not crash into Emily.

Will that girl ever learn?

"My patient... Diana, I mean, Dr. Petrell—She's intubating him."

That got Emily to move. "What's the diagnosis?" She turned toward the direction Courtney had come from. Only years of practice helped her fight the urge to run.

"I don't know." Courtney hurried to catch up to her. "He seemed okay, just a little short of breath."

Emily rolled her eyes. That was a typical answer for the second-year resident. "Has Dr. Petrell asked for me?" It had been years since Emily's pulse had raced at the thought of an emergency, but the idea of Diana being in over her head did that to her.

"No, she's handling it all on her own." Courtney grimaced. "She's taken over and is giving all the orders."

Emily noted the hint of accusation. Was Courtney complaining about Diana rescuing her patient or about doing it without supervision? "And why are you here instead of helping her?"

"You needed to know."

From whining to defensive in five seconds. Courtney needed to grow up. Emily refrained from commenting on it as they had reached the treatment room. This wasn't the right time.

A quick scan of the scene provided Emily with almost everything she needed to know. No chaos, only busy and efficient movement of the team.

A couple of nurses administered medication and cleaned up the mess of sterile packages that littered the room, and the respiratory assistant adjusted some settings. The patient was intubated and connected to the respirator; a central line was delivering fluids, and the monitor displayed marginally stable parameters. His massively swollen legs with coarse, red skin suggested chronic heart failure, probably with an acute pulmonary edema as a cause for his problems. Courtney should have told her that instead of saying he was short of breath.

Diana worked at the computer terminal at the far wall, typing her notes. As the tech pushed the portable X-ray machine past her into the next room, Diana said something that made him chuckle.

The tension drained from Emily, and she had to lean against the doorway. Diana had everything under control, and she could hang back and wait to see if she would be needed.

"What have you got?" The question came from the Dr. Riley, the cardiologist. She squeezed past Emily, forcing her to step aside to make room for her baby bump. Wow, she really had grown over the last couple of weeks and looked ready to burst anytime soon.

Diana quickly recited the patient's history, vital signs, and her working diagnosis. She handed her the EKG and answered the few questions Dr. Riley fired at her.

Last week Emily would have stormed into the room and asked the same questions. The urge to take over itched like a barely healed scratch, but she made a conscious effort to stay on the fringe of the scene.

"I give a rat's ass about your fucking opinion! I want plain facts, and I want them now." Dr. Riley had never been known for patience, and the pregnancy had obviously not calmed her down.

Emily stepped forward to intervene. Nobody talked to her residents like that.

Neither Diana nor Dr. Riley seemed to notice her, staring at each other.

Diana didn't let the cardiologist's temper faze her. She replied without even raising her voice so that Emily didn't get her answer. Whatever it was, it seemed to placate Dr. Riley, who abruptly turned and stomped off the way she'd come. As she passed Emily, she mumbled, "Stupid resident," but a tiny smile played around her lips.

The queasiness from before was replaced by a warmth spreading in her middle. Emily admired Diana for de-escalating the situation. No one who observed her today would think of a rebellious rock star. Her gaze tracked Diana's hands as she completed her notes. The strength she had developed in years of drumming was obvious in the subtle play of muscles and tendons under her skin.

"Shouldn't she ask you first?" Courtney's question startled Emily, and she tore her gaze from Diana.

"She's done everything right. She's not a first-year anymore; she knows when to call for help." *Unlike you.* The need to defend Diana confused Emily. Courtney was obviously jealous and tried to subtly direct her to criticize Diana. This maneuvering for a better position in the virtual ranking of her residents irked her. Weren't they supposed to stick together? "Don't you have other patients?"

"But he's one of mine. Shouldn't I stay here?" There was the whining again.

"Dr. Petrell had to do your job, and you've decided to run to tell me instead of staying, helping, and learning. That makes him her patient. The next time you need me to come, call or send a nurse." Emily decided to end the conversation before she told her resident what she really thought: Courtney needed to get her game together, fast, or she wouldn't be able to finish her residency.

With a pointed look at Courtney, Emily called into the room: "Diana, good job! I could see that you've had everything under control here."

Diana jerked her head around, wide-eyed. Was she surprised at the compliment, or hadn't she been aware of Emily's presence? Emily couldn't tell. But the radiant smile Diana sent her way caused an answering rising of her own lips and warmth spreading from her stomach.

Who would've thought that complimenting someone evoked such a good feeling? When Diana continued to smile, the warmth threatened to turn into a blush, and Emily hastened to leave before anyone could pick up on it. She needed to stop this ridiculousness before it got out of hand. Diana was her resident, not the drummer at the beach.

The sour stench of urine, vomit, and unwashed human mixed with something sweet wafted past the drawn curtains of the exam bay. Emily struggled to keep her expression professional and took shallow breaths through her mouth.

Going by the greenish tinge of her complexion, Diana had the same problem. "I found the reason for her unconsciousness. She's septic, and the most likely cause are the multiple scratches and bites all over her body. She has some really nasty infected ones. They look like animal bites, maybe cats. The worst is on her left breast." She shook her head and shuddered. "I don't even want to know how an animal got there. I hope we can save the breast. Should I call regular surgery or plastics?"

Emily had a suspicion who that patient was, and a quick look behind the curtain confirmed it. "Call surgery. Just tell them Cat-Cat's here. They already know her."

"Cat-Cat?" Diana raised her eyebrows.

"She's a regular. Lives on the street and has half a dozen cats. She sometimes sleeps with them underneath her clothes, whether the cats want to or not. But she's harmless."

"Are you making fun of me? I can't tell right now." The corners of Diana's mouth twitched.

Emily laughed and shook her head. "No, seriously, she's known here."

"Okay." Diana drawled the word. "If you say so."

She's adorable. Wait. What? Emily squashed the thought immediately.

"Take swabs of the wounds and call surgery." Anger at the slip of her own thoughts made Emily's voice gruff.

Diana's mouth stopped its motion mid-smile. "Sure." She stepped behind the curtain.

Now she had done it again. Emily wanted to kick herself. Just because Diana unbalanced her was no reason to react harshly. The right thing would be to tell her what she really thought, that she'd done a good job. Most residents wouldn't have done a complete physical, so they might have missed the serious wound.

"Ugh, what's that smell? That's gross. People like that shouldn't be allowed in here." Courtney moved to the far side of the corridor to pass Emily.

A glare stopped her in her tracks. "Do you think these curtains are soundproof?"

"Um, no, but..." Courtney looked from Emily to the curtain and back and pinched her nose closed with thumb and finger.

Emily stepped closer to the resident and lowered her voice. "You need to learn to think before you open your mouth."

"Sorry." The apology was barely audible.

Emily kept up the glare for a moment, then nodded and turned around. As she opened the curtain, she heard Courtney gag and then fast steps retreated.

The difference between the two residents was striking. Diana talked in a soothing voice and held the patient's hand to keep her from interfering with Madison, the nurse who pressed a cotton swab into the wound. Only the faint lines around Diana's eyes gave away her discomfort. She acknowledged Emily's presence with a nod but kept her focus on the patient until the procedure was finished.

When the woman relaxed, Diana released her hand. "Thank you, Madison. Please let me know when surgery is here for the consult." She turned to Emily. "Anything else I can do?"

To Emily's surprise, the tone of the question was neither provocative nor offended.

"No, no. You're doing fine." Apologizing for her tone would be weird right now. "Just... You're doing fine."

Emily ducked out of the exam bay and hastened down the corridor. She could almost feel the confused stares of Diana and Madison piercing through the curtain like arrows, hitting her right between the shoulder blades.

Emily lingered in the staff lounge, checking charts she had checked twice before. Diana would be taking her break any minute now. Not that she waited for her to show up or anything. But the last few days they had met on their break by accident and talked. Only small talk, just checking in. That's what you did as a mentor, right?

Her personal phone vibrated in her scrub pocket, and she looked at the screen before answering. "Hi, Jen."

"Hey, best friend, did you miss me? Do you have five minutes?" The greeting was typical of Jen. They hadn't talked since the night at the club when she had met Diana, only texted.

"Yes to both. And did you miss me?" Initially, Emily had avoided a real conversation because she had been afraid Jen would want to talk about Dee Dragon, but now she enjoyed hearing her best friend's voice again. She closed her laptop and leaned back against the couch.

"Eh, no." Jen laughed. "Well, okay, maybe a little bit."

"How's work? Did you get some good stories?" Emily wanted to know how much Jen had found out. She was sure Jen wouldn't keep the secret from her if she knew that Dee Dragon worked as a doctor now, but she was reluctant to ask directly about her.

"Fantastic. The new contact I made the night of our last club adventure really helps a lot. She knows basically everyone in the scene. I've been texting and talking daily with her. I'll meet her later. For more stories."

The enthusiastic tone was familiar to Emily: Jen was falling for someone, either professionally or personally. Probably both.

It couldn't be Diana, could it? Jealousy flared like a torch dipped in gasoline, temporarily blinding her. This was ridiculous. She was no overemotional teenager; she was in full control of her emotions. Pushing the feeling behind a wall of ice, Emily fought to keep it from her voice. "Who is it?"

"Mel. Melinda Burton, the guitar player."

Emily exhaled slowly. "Okay."

Jen gushed about all the amazing bands Mel had played with so far, all the records she was on, and all the friends she had. Emily only listened with one ear, relieved it wasn't Diana, or rather Dee, Jen had set her sights on.

As if conjured up by her thoughts, Diana chose that moment to enter the room and wave to Emily.

Emily sat up straighter and held up her phone to show that she couldn't talk. She should probably go to her office for privacy, but she couldn't tear her gaze from Diana. She tracked her movement from the coffee urn to the fridge and then to the table and nearly missed that Jen mentioned Dee's name.

"Did you meet her that night, backstage?" Emily had no idea what Jen had said, but she wanted to keep her talking about Diana.

"Who, Dee Dragon?"

"Yeah. You wanted to talk to her, didn't you?" Feigning nonchalance was hard. She hoped it worked.

"No. She didn't stay long at the party. Mel is reluctant to talk about her, and her manager is blocking her completely."

Emily slumped into the couch, too weak to care about her posture. Diana hadn't fallen prey to Jen's charm. She hadn't even admitted to herself that this fear had kept her from talking to Jen. They had never competed over a woman before, and she didn't want to risk their friendship because of it. *Wait, where had that come from? We're not competing, because I'm not interested! Oh no, am I?*

"...I'm sure I'll have Mel spilling all her secrets soon."

"What? What secrets?" Emily had missed part of Jen's plan.

"The secret of Dee's absence from the music scene, for example." A voice in the background seemed to capture Jen's attention. "I need to go. Call you soon, okay?"

"Take care."

Emily's mind was whirling. She glanced at Diana, who was sitting at the table, eating her yogurt and looking relaxed and carefree. Should she go and end Diana's break with the news of a snooping journalist? Or maybe Jen was wrong, and Mel wouldn't tell her anything. But Jen was nothing if not convincing. Emily sighed. She walked to the table.

Diana looked up and smiled.

Emily couldn't help smiling back.

"Are you okay? You sounded a bit upset on the phone just now." Diana put down her yogurt and reached for Emily's arm.

The touch was short and barely noticeable, but Emily's arm warmed immediately.

She sat down next to Diana and shrugged. "I don't know if I should be worried. Do you remember Jen? My best friend, the journalist."

"Ah, yes. How could I forget? What's with her?"

"I think she is after your...after Dee's story. She met your friend Mel at the party after the concert."

Diana nodded. "Yeah, Mel told me. Why?"

"How much does Mel know?"

"Everything," Diana answered without hesitation.

"Would she...? Would she tell Jen? Not Jen, the journalist, but Jen, the cute girlfriend?"

"She wouldn't tell her without my permission." Again no hesitation. "But is your friend working that way? Entering a relationship to get information?"

"No! Maybe. I don't know." Emily was reluctant to admit that Jen would go that far, but it was a possibility. "She seems to really like Mel, but sometimes she loses sight of the boundaries between her private and professional lives."

"That doesn't sound very ethical. But Mel's a grown woman. She can keep secrets." Diana's voice conveyed no judgment, but Emily couldn't hold her gaze.

She had never understood Jen's lack of professional boundaries. Rules, even unwritten lines, usually existed for a reason. In the ED, living by the rules had never steered her wrong.

Just as Emily wanted to answer, Courtney burst into the room, threw her stethoscope on the table, and let herself fall onto the couch with a theatrical sigh. After a few seconds came another, louder sigh.

Emily looked at Diana, and they both had to bite their lips to keep from laughing.

Courtney heaved herself up with another sigh and poured herself some coffee.

Diana leaned closer and whispered directly into Emily's ear. "Do you want to ask her what's wrong, or should I?"

The warm breath tickled Emily, and that sensation slowly traveled down her neck toward her spine. She had to suppress a sigh of her own and decided she had to attempt an organized retreat as long as she was still able to walk.

"That's the privilege of an attending. We have the residents do all the dirty work for us." Emily gathered her laptop and left Diana to the complaints of her fellow resident. Just as the door was closing behind her, Courtney started to whine. She grinned. Poor Diana.

"You owe me." Four hours later, Emily had all but forgotten Courtney's performance when Diana entered the locker room just as she had been about to leave.

Emily laughed. "Was it that bad?"

Diana growled and changed out of her scrubs into jeans and T-shirt.

As no one was with them, she didn't hide her tattoos, and Emily got a full show of the dragon. The lean muscles of Diana's back made its skin move as she bent to pick up something that had fallen from her pocket. The metallic sheen on the green scales mesmerized her, and she wanted to reach out and touch it. All those years ago the image had burned itself into her memory, and the obsession had carried her through med school and residency. Diana had been literally the woman of her dreams for years.

Emily swallowed. Twice. This crush had to stop, right here, right now. *Rules, remember?* She had to get out, away from her. But other parts of her mind seemed to have a different idea. "Do you want to go grab something to eat?" *What? Why did you say that?*

"Sure." Diana tied her shoes and picked up her backpack.

"Just an apology for the," she lowered her voice, "Courtney incident." Just two colleagues and potential friends going for a quick bite, she reminded herself. Nothing more.

The evening was unseasonably warm for May, so they decided to meet at a casual restaurant with nice outside seating halfway between their homes and the hospital.

Just two colleagues. Emily repeated the mantra all the way to the restaurant and nearly missed the entrance.

Diana was already sitting on the large back patio when Emily arrived. Tables with place mats in any color of the rainbow and mismatched chairs were scattered between a handful of trees. A chain of lights enclosed the outside, but they hadn't been turned on yet. She had chosen a table in the middle, relaxing with her head tilted upward to catch the sunshine. Her eyes opened as Emily approached, and Diana greeted her with a wide grin.

Emily hesitated before sitting down and peeked at the sun to calculate its course. How long would it take until it dipped behind the roof?

Diana looked at her questioningly. "Is this table okay?"

"Actually, no." Emily hated to cause a scene. "I'm sorry. Would you mind sitting over there?" She pointed at a table that was shaded by a large tree. Dappled sunlight and shadows from leaves painted an intricate pattern on the table and chairs.

"No, sure." Diana moved her jacket from the back of the chair and followed Emily to the new table.

Their waitress came with the menus, introduced herself, and took their drink order, saving Emily from explaining her choice of tables.

They perused the menus in silence. Emily searched for a safe topic. "What are you having? The burgers are good."

Diana nodded. "I know. I'm here too often for my own good. I've little energy for cooking lately."

The waitress interrupted them with their drinks and asked for their orders, and they both decided on the burgers.

"You cook? From scratch, with real ingredients, or do you just microwave something?" Emily asked after the waitress had left.

Diana snorted. "No, with real vegetables, spices, everything made from scratch. I grew tired of fast food during my residency and the first year on tour. I had a lot of time between rehearsals and songwriting. The property where we all lived when we didn't tour used to be a farm, and Mel revived the kitchen garden for us. Someone was always around, so I experimented. After a few years, the food became edible." She grinned. "But my kitchen never looked as clean as yours."

Emily loved how easily Diana now talked about her past. "So your mother must be proud of you."

"Well, she'd be really, really surprised if she knew how much I enjoy it. She always wanted to do mother-daughter bonding with cooking and baking. And I hated it. I preferred to play outside with my brothers. She loved gardening, but that was too boring for me. I was too impatient as a kid." Diana's voice held no bitterness, merely amusement. "Did your mother give you cooking lessons too?"

Emily nodded. "And sewing, knitting, and anything else a good wife needs to know. She was very persistent." The resentment for wasting her time had faded over the years but never completely left her. She fought to leave it out of her voice. "She's very old-fashioned. Sometimes I think she got her ideals from the Victorian literature she reads."

The waitress brought their food, and they both took their time assembling their burgers without speaking.

"What do you mean, Victorian ideals? I really can't imagine what that could be."

Emily took a bite of her sweet potato fries to gain some time. "She has this image of a nice, pale, polite young lady in her mind. She always wanted to be like that and for me to be like her. She wanted me to read and study, but to keep my mouth shut when we were outside of the house. She had a never-ending list of correct things to say, to do, how to look."

Diana studied her for moment and frowned, but Emily couldn't detect the usual immediate judgment she had received before. When she had started college, everything about her had been mousy and old-fashioned. Her braid, her clothes, her way of talking. Her first roommate had made endless fun of it. In the second year she had lived with Jen, who had helped her to break out of her shell.

"Is that the reason you try so hard to cover up the cute freckles?" Diana's observation was spot-on.

"They're not cute. I look much too young and immature with them. Appearances are as important as medical skills in our job." Emily knew she sounded defensive. Heat rose in her cheeks, and she tried a big sip of the ice-cold water, hoping it would stop her blush from blooming.

Diana shrugged and finished chewing her last bite. "I'm sorry, I didn't want to make you uncomfortable. I just think you'd look great without makeup. But it's definitely not my place to tell you that." She smiled at Emily before she concentrated on her food again.

The compliment thwarted any chance of containing her blush.

Diana looked up. "I just remembered something. In the park, when we met the first time, you really meant what you said about not running in the sunshine. It was because of your freckles and not just a stupid excuse to get rid of a resident."

Emily shook her head. "No, no, it wasn't. Did you think that?" She reached out to touch Diana's hand. *Wait, what are you doing?* She detoured to her glass instead. "I'm sorry. I know intellectually that my upbringing was weird, but sometimes, especially when I'm nervous, I fall back on those habits."

And now she had admitted to being nervous about meeting Diana at the lake. She rearranged the slice of avocado that had nearly fallen off her chicken breast burger and tried to judge Diana's expression from the corner of her eye.

If Diana had noticed, she didn't let on, but then again, she had a pretty good poker face.

Emily decided to shift the focus away from herself. "I can't imagine how it was to grow up with brothers. How many do you have?"

Diana grinned. "Five."

"Five? That's... Wow." Emily had always wanted a brother or sister, but she would've been happy with one or two.

"That's probably four too many. I was the youngest and got tossed into a house full of chaos. It was loud. Dirty. Hungry. But so much fun."

She proceeded to tell funny anecdotes about all of them between bites of her burger. Sometimes she illustrated a point with her hands, and Emily tried hard not to stare too long at them.

Slowly, the sunlight faded, and several lights placed strategically in the trees around the patio started to glow. The waitress delivered a lit candle in a glass jar and refilled their drinks.

A comfortable warmth spread slowly from Emily's middle to her chest. The just-two-colleagues mantra had ceased working somewhere between her admission about the freckles and Diana's compliment. This felt dangerously close to a date, two women having a candlelight dinner and talking about their families. Since it probably was the only chance of getting one with Diana, she decided to pretend it was, in fact, a date. Nobody needed to know the truth. Her longtime fantasy of the shy girl who grew up in a library and the sexy drummer could be reality for one evening. Tomorrow they could be attending and resident again.

Chapter 9

EMILY SHRUGGED OUT OF HER protective gown, made a ball of the flimsy material, and threw it across the room into the big trash bag. Hitting the bag on her first try wasn't satisfactory. At all.

Her gloves followed with more force. They hit the wall, bounced back, and landed next to the gurney in the middle of the room.

One of the nursing assistants picked them up and looked around for the culprit.

Emily held up her hand, but her mumbled apology was drowned out by the beeping of the monitor as it came alive again. The shrill alarm hit her like a surprise attack.

"Shit, I'm sorry. Wrong button." Madison fumbled with the off switch.

In the abrupt silence, nobody moved.

Emily held her breath and took one last look at her patient. Gray pallor. Lifeless eyes. Remains of the fight for his life cluttered the gurney around him like a battlefield. Crumpled plastic wrappers, IV bags, and the now-useless defibrillator patches. Bloody footsteps led nowhere. Anger seeped into the pit in her stomach that had been caved by the futility of the last hour.

Shaking her head, Emily squared her shoulders and strode to the corner of the room, where Diana was standing next to the computer terminal.

She seemed frozen in midmotion, one hand clutching a few printouts with scribbled notes, the other hand hovering over the keyboard. As Emily came closer, she tore her gaze from the patient and looked at her instead. The hard green of her eyes softened into warm hazel as she held her gaze.

Around them the cleanup continued, but Emily paid no attention to the hushed voices. She tried to gauge if Diana was as calm as she appeared to be. She had shown professional behavior, even when it became clear that nothing they did would lead to a positive outcome. Emily knew from her own experience that sometimes the image of composure you projected was in contradiction to the warring emotions beneath the surface.

"Are you okay?" Emily put her fingers around Diana's arm without thinking first. The skin was soft to the touch and nearly distracted her from her question.

Diana smiled and covered Emily's fingers with her own. "I'm fine. Thanks for asking. I hate when we can't help anymore, but it's unfortunately not the first time that happened."

Emily acknowledged that with another quick squeeze before letting go. Immediately, her hand went cold, and she stuck it into her pocket. "I'll see if the family has arrived and tell them. Can you finish the paperwork?"

Diana nodded and closed the computer program with a few clicks. Her hand didn't shake. "I'll follow you outside so the nurses have more room to work. They need to clean him up before the family sees him."

Turning toward the door, Emily looked at her reflection in the safety glass and straighten her clothes and hair. But nothing she could do would fortify her for the talk that had to come now.

Emily scanned the waiting room with a practiced gaze and found the family immediately. A woman in her midforties and a teenage girl were holding hands without speaking. Both were elegantly dressed in evening gowns, matching the suit they had cut from their patient. The teenager stared at her smartphone and swiped hastily with her thumb over its surface, probably not seeing anything. The woman had closed her eyes and leaned her head back against the wall. But both turned toward Emily as she came closer, belying their seemingly disinterest in their surroundings. The woman looked anxious and guarded as though she suspected bad news, but the teenager's face screamed hope. Emily hated to crush her expectations.

"Are you with Michael Rennin?"

The woman rose from her seat, pulling the girl up with her. "He's my husband and this is our daughter, Chloe. Please, can you tell me what happened?"

"I'm Dr. Barnes. If you come with me, we can talk in private." Emily ushered them to a family room, where she could break the news without an audience.

On the way, the daughter started asking questions, but the mother silenced her with a barely audible "Chloe!" and a firm grip on her arm.

They all took seats around a small table, and Emily took her time to look both of them in the eyes.

"Mrs. Rennin, Chloe, I'm one of the doctors who took care of Michael when he arrived. Were you with him when he collapsed?" Emily wanted to know how much they had seen before the paramedics had taken him away.

Mrs. Rennin nodded. "We were at the restaurant. He had been silent for most of the meal and didn't eat much. He said he might have caught a stomach bug or something. And when the cake came..." She stopped and struggled not to cry. "And when the cake came, he just looked so pale and green, as if he wanted to puke, and suddenly, his eyes rolled back and he didn't speak anymore and..." Now she was crying, and Emily waited patiently. It was important for the family to share their story. After a minute Mrs. Rennin took a tissue from the box on the table, blew her nose, and then looked back at Emily.

Chloe spoke for the first time, her voice pitched unnaturally high. "The paramedics, I think they performed CPR, right? It wasn't a stomach bug, was it?" Both sets of eyes looked at Emily expectantly, the older even more anxious than before and the younger still carrying traces of hope.

Emily shook her head. "No, it wasn't a stomach bug. He had a heart attack, a major one. You're right; the paramedics performed CPR and managed to regain a pulse for a short time. When he arrived here, his heart arrested again. We did everything we could, but in the end, we couldn't help him. He never had a stable circulation, and he never regained consciousness. He died." Emily felt her words hit both women like a tidal wave.

They fell back in their seats. Mrs. Rennin only murmured, "No, no, no," between sobs and held on to her daughter's hand. Chloe stared at Emily unblinking, unbelieving, unseeing.

Emily hated that part of her job, but she had done it often enough to know what to expect. In a minute the questions would start and sometimes the accusations. She didn't know yet what would come from this family.

Right on schedule, the wife asked questions, and Emily tried to answer as best as she could. Feeling empathy was natural for her, but expressing it had taken some training.

She watched the daughter out of the corner of her eye and waited for her to catch up.

The door opened, and Diana entered, probably to tell her they were now ready to let the family see him.

Chloe turned from her to Diana and back. "It was a mistake, right? He's not dead?" Her voice got louder with each word.

Emily focused on her. "I'm sorry, Chloe. There was no mistake."

"No, no! That's impossible. He can't be... Not today. Today is my birthday, he can't be dead. It's my birthday!" Chloe jumped up and ran to the window.

Her mother followed her, but Emily didn't notice what they were doing. Her vision narrowed, and she couldn't breathe. The tidal wave was back, now a tsunami washing over her. *Today is my birthday, he can't be dead!* A rushing sound filled her ears, and the sentence repeated again and again. It wasn't Chloe's voice, but her own. She closed her eyes and tried to breathe but was afraid of drowning. Everything swirled around her; the ground beneath her slipped away, pulling her into an invisible abyss. She wanted to let herself be taken away, away from the pain, away from her own crying in her mind.

A steady hand gripped her shoulder, and a warm voice talked to her. It took her several sentences until she was able to focus on the words and not only the sounds. The voice was pulling her back to safe land, anchoring her. Diana. Diana was talking to her. Slowly, she could discern words from the white noise.

"Emily, are you okay? What happened?" Diana sounded concerned.

Emily only stared at her, unable to form a coherent sentence.

"Can you wait here for a moment? I'm taking the family to see him, and then I'll be back for you." Diana squeezed her shoulder. "Okay?"

Emily nodded, still not trusting her voice. Her gaze followed Diana as she walked to the window to introduce herself and lead mother and daughter out of the room.

On her way back, Diana detoured to the staff lounge to grab a water bottle and check if anyone else was there. Liz, the other attending tonight, had her feet up on the couch and was drinking coffee.

"Hey, Liz, can you cover for Emily and me for fifteen minutes? We need to talk about the case." Diana gestured vaguely toward the code room.

Liz nodded. "Take thirty. I'm here all night."

"Thanks."

Diana hurried back to the family room, hoping Emily was still there. What had happened to her? She had looked even paler than usual and ready to faint. At first, she had stared straight ahead and had shown no reaction to anything Diana had said.

Good, Emily was still sitting at the table. Her face showed traces of pain and maybe anger, but was no longer frozen in shock. She shivered, and Diana had to restrain her impulse to hug her.

Diana placed the water in front of her and sat next to her. "Are you okay?"

Emily looked at her with ice-cold gray eyes. "Of course. Why shouldn't I be okay? I'm okay. Everything is fine."

The aggression simmering under the surface was completely unlike Emily. What had triggered that? "If you say so. Sure."

How could she get Emily to talk about it? The ED wasn't the right place to inspire a heart-to-heart. She followed Emily's gaze to the window. A few trees and bushes were cramped between the main building and a smaller maintenance building. The area would be deserted on a Thursday night. Perfect.

Diana took a chance. "Emily, could you do me a favor and come with me for a minute?"

Emily's eyes widened, and her mouth half opened as if she wanted to say something. Instead, she followed Diana without questions, another sign that she wasn't herself.

Diana wanted to avoid other staff and led Emily through back doors and seldom-used side corridors. Soon they were hidden in the sad excuse for a park. She steered her toward a bench where the hospital employees liked to meet for smoking breaks without attracting the attention of the image-conscious administrators.

Emily looked around. "What are we doing here?"

Diana pulled her down on the bench. "Taking a break. Sitting. Talking."

"There's nothing to talk about." Emily's voice was as cold as her eyes, but both failed to intimidate Diana.

"You froze in there. I don't think the family noticed, but you were out of it for a few minutes." Emily started to answer, probably to deny it, but Diana didn't let her speak. "I'm concerned. You looked like you were about to faint."

Emily's eyes grew larger, and tears glittered on her eyelashes.

Diana took Emily's hand and softened her voice. "Did the family say something to upset you?"

"It's her birthday. Today is her fucking birthday." Emily sobbed.

Diana didn't know what she was talking about, but it didn't matter. She pulled Emily into an embrace and slowly stroked her back. The sky turned from indigo to gray as Emily's tears soaked through the shoulder of Diana's scrub shirt.

Finally, Emily pulled back and rubbed her eyes with both hands. "I'm sorry."

"Don't be." Diana burned to know what was going on but restrained herself from asking. They sat for another minute in the rapidly descending darkness.

"My father died when I was seventeen, the summer before I started college." Emily's voice was low, and Diana strained to hear her. "He went to the ED late one evening with pain in his right shoulder and thorax. They did an EKG and cardiac enzymes. In the six hours it took them to get the lab results, nobody examined him. A first-year resident asked some standard questions, but nobody really looked at him. When they returned to congratulate him on not having a heart attack, they found him nearly unconscious." Emily looked up, directly at Diana. "He had a ruptured gallbladder and died from septic shock."

They looked at each other without saying anything.

"I'm sorry. That's terrible." The words were inadequate to convey Diana's feelings. A surge of protectiveness flared, and she balled her hands into fists. Seeing Emily heartbroken but trying to put up a strong front made her want to hold her again, but she didn't know if Emily would welcome it this time.

Emily took a sip from the water bottle that rested between them on the bench. "You want some?"

"I'm good. Thanks."

Emily nodded and finished the rest of the small bottle. "What triggered all this...shit..." She gestured vaguely toward the hospital building. "It was my birthday as well. I said the same stupid sentence the daughter said. 'Today is my birthday; he can't be dead.' As if fate or God or anyone would be interested in that." She opened the plastic bottle and squeezed it until was folded several times over. She tried to close it again but used too much force, and the cap got stuck.

Diana gasped. How could that happen? And not only to one, but two young women. What were the odds? She looked at Emily, and the pain emanating from her drove all thoughts of statistics from her mind. She pried the remains of the bottle from Emily's hand, put it aside, and hugged her again.

At first, Emily was stiff, but then she relaxed into the embrace.

The shrill ring of a phone tore them apart.

Emily searched her pockets but only stared at it until it stopped ringing. It started again after a short silence.

Diana snatched it from Emily before she could answer.

"Dr. Petrell for Dr. Barnes." Diana's voice was calmer than her racing thoughts.

"Uh... This is Courtney. Where's Dr. Barnes?"

"Busy. Can I help you?" Yeah, calm and perfectly professional. Nobody needed to know they were hiding in the shrubs behind the hospital. And that Emily had been crying just a minute ago.

"I just wanted to know the dosage of amoxicillin."

What kind of question was that? "For a child?"

"No, normal adult. Strep throat."

"Look it up. Or ask a nurse." Diana would have never called her supervisor with such a stupid question. Did Courtney think Emily was her personal computer?

"So you don't know either?" Courtney sounded gleeful.

"Of course I know. Even the students know. Look it up and write it down for the next time." Diana bit her lip. This was not her normal reaction to a stupid question, but she wanted to be there for Emily and not stuck on the phone with Courtney.

"Hey, no need to get all riled up. It's just a question. I'll ask Liz." Courtney hung up before Diana could respond.

A smile tugged at the corners of Emily's mouth, and the sadness in her eyes had receded somewhat.

Looking at the phone, Diana shook her head. "That was weird. Why would Courtney ask such a simple question? It's basic knowledge."

Emily grinned. "She asks basic questions to nearly all her cases. I guess she wants to let me know she's hard at work." She shrugged. "I'm used to it by now."

Diana offered the phone back to Emily and touched her hand with her own. "I'm sorry if I overreached. You just looked as if you needed a break." She wasn't just talking about rebuking Courtney.

Around the phone that was still cradled between them, Emily squeezed Diana's hand. Her fingers had regained their usual warmth. "I did. Thank you." She put the phone away and picked up the bottle. "Thank you for listening." She played with the cap again. "I'd better get back to work." She didn't move.

"You're welcome." Diana wanted to say more. That she was glad Emily trusted her. That she cherished their moment of personal connection. That she wanted to be her friend.

All of that was inappropriate. They were still at work, and Diana doubted that Emily was even willing to call it a friendship.

Emily stepped closer, and this time she hugged Diana. Maybe she understood.

Diana tilted her head to tell her that she had needed the time outside as well.

In the same moment, Emily turned to say something. The words were lost as they touched face-to-face, lips-to-lips. Their breaths mingled, and unspoken words turned into a kiss.

Diana couldn't tell who had started it or who had deepened it, only how warm and soft Emily's lips felt. They kissed slowly, more tender caress than passionate exploration. Diana's world receded to the gentle touch that soothed away the tension of the last hour.

After a moment, surprise gave way to eagerness, and they deepened the connection. Diana raised one hand to Emily's neck and slid it along the soft hairline and softer skin to cradle her head. A few silken strands had escaped Emily's bun and sent tingles up her arms.

Emily moved her hands slowly up and down over Diana's shoulder blades and pressed closer.

Their breasts touched, and Diana gasped. The heat of Emily's body seemed to burn through their several layers of clothes and melted her like a candle in the sun.

This time it took Diana several seconds to recognize the ring of Emily's phone for what it was. She stepped back, her heart racing and her breath coming much too fast.

Her mind whirled. She'd never even thought about Emily that way, and now they had kissed? Not only kissed, but they'd practically made out like eager teenagers, something she hadn't experienced for a long time.

Emily searched for the phone in her pockets with shaking hands. "Barnes," she nearly shouted into it.

Diana straightened her clothes, trying to get a handle on things. What the fuck had just happened? Talk about inappropriate. How could her feelings switch from tentative friendship to full-blown attraction in under ten seconds?

Listening to Emily's one-syllable answers, Diana had no chance of gauging Emily's feelings or the importance of the call. Emily's voice betrayed no urgency, only her customary businesslike abruptness.

"Okay, I'll be there in a second." Emily hung up and turned to go.

"Emily..." Diana didn't know what to say but didn't want to let her leave without acknowledging what had happened between them.

Emily hesitated and looked back at her. Diana couldn't discern her features in the falling darkness. "Not now. Please." Her voice was soft, almost vulnerable.

Diana nodded, even though Emily probably couldn't see her. "Sure. Later."

With a murmured "thanks," Emily hurried toward the main building.

Diana closed her eyes and inhaled the mild evening air. The scent of rosemary and something fresh lingered. Did it grow here, or did it belong to Emily? A shampoo, a lotion? She tilted her head back and opened her eyes. She wished she could see stars, but lights polluted the sky.

A tiny dot of light in the distance grew larger and she only realized a helicopter was approaching when the noise of the rotor blades intruded. She sighed. A helicopter meant more work. And never easy cases. She'd better follow Emily inside.

Chapter 10

Despite how her visit to the Rainbow Home had ended the last time, Emily had left her car at home and walked the couple of miles to the University District. The chances of getting stranded in the rain on this Saturday afternoon were slim, and she didn't trust herself to drive.

In hope of clearing her muddled thoughts, she was on her way to talk to Diana about the incident in the hospital garden. In the day and a half since their series of night shifts had ended, she hadn't been able to switch back to her normal sleeping pattern or to concentrate on her usual chores. Nothing had helped.

If she was honest with herself, the problem wasn't the distorted circadian rhythm; she had long ago gotten used to that. She couldn't get her embarrassing meltdown out of her head. "And the kiss, don't forget the kiss."

Only when a young mother holding on to a toddler with one hand and a shopping bag with the other gave her a wide berth did she notice she'd spoken the last part aloud.

Great, here she was, roaming the streets and talking to herself. She wasn't in command of her own thoughts and actions anymore, and that was unacceptable.

She could understand why she'd had the meltdown in the first place, even if was highly unprofessional, but the part that confounded her was why she had allowed Diana to witness it, let alone to comfort her. Her mother had taught her to be self-reliant, and she'd neither needed nor wanted anyone before. When had someone last held her like that?

The memory of the hug suffused her with warmth like a summer breeze. Emily stopped walking and closed her eyes. The intensity of Diana's embrace had blown away her pain, and the silent support had filled her soul with strength. A powerful drug that had befuddled her mind and could easily become an addiction. The kiss must have been a by-product of her dazed state of mind.

That's it. Emily opened her eyes, squared her shoulders, and resumed her walk at a brisk pace. Comparing it to addiction might be too extreme, but maybe if she treated it like one, she could find a way to cope with it. Now that she'd owned to wanting it, she could remove herself from temptation by erecting boundaries and making them clear to everyone involved. Diana would need to understand there were rules, even if they were unwritten, that separated them for their own protection. Not mixing work with pleasure was a good rule to live by. They would just be colleagues from now on. And really, that shouldn't be too hard. In the midst of the emotional turmoil, she'd probably just confused Diana with the drummer from the beach who had starred in her dreams for far too long.

An explosion of color announced that she'd reached the youth center. Street art, most of it posters in all shapes and sizes, decorated the walls of the Rainbow Home. Some were half ripped off, sprayed over, or covering each other. The house looked as out of place in the quiet neighborhood as Emily felt today.

She wiped her sweaty palm on her jeans, opened the door, and stepped inside. Music—or rather a cacophony of drums and guitar sounds—drifted from the back of the building and guided her to her destination.

Unwilling to interrupt the session, she lingered at the open door to wait for Diana. The collection of instruments looked as diverse as the players, and their faces all showed a similar mixture of concentration and enchantment. With her back to the door, Diana crouched next to one of the kids and explained something.

Emily's breath caught at the sight of Diana's formfitting jeans, and the familiar heat in her cheeks told her that she was blushing. She quickly looked away. *Remember? Resist temptation.*

"Hey, Doc! Do you have a minute?"

The question startled Emily. She hadn't noticed the approach of the girl who now stood directly next to her. She tried to come up with the name.

She had seen her last time and remembered the girl's laughing brown eyes and the black, curly hair that stood up in every direction. "Freddy, right? Nice to see you again."

Freddy nodded, which made her hair fly up and down.

Emily would have laughed at the enthusiastic response if Freddy's expression hadn't been so grim. "Do you want to go to my office?"

"No, it's not about me. It's just… I have a friend who's in trouble and… She's not here today and… When will you come here again?" The way she worried her lower lip with her teeth between the words revealed the awkwardness the young teenager hid behind her usual bravado.

"The next planned appointment is in a couple of weeks." And if she remembered her work schedule correctly, there wasn't a good day to come here before that.

"Oh. Okay, then." Freddy's gaze dropped to the floor.

An unfamiliar surge of protectiveness toward the young woman surprised Emily. She squeezed Freddy's arm. "Do you have something to write on?"

Freddy went into the music room and brought a battered guitar case with her. She removed a stack of postcards and a sharpie from a pocket in the lining. "Is this okay?"

Nodding, Emily studied the cards. They were the kind of free-advertising cards you could find anywhere in the city, but someone had written a name, date, and address all over the pictures. She quickly wrote her full name and the address of her hospital on the other side. "If you want to, you can send your friend to my ER anytime during the day in the next week. I promise I won't charge her, and we can keep the visit off the record if she wants." After a glance at Freddy's doubtful expression, she added her phone number. "If they give her trouble at the admission desk, she can call or text me, and I'll come out as soon as I can."

"Thank you." Freddy took the pen and postcards back. She separated the one with the contact information from the stack and slid it carefully into the front pocket of her hoodie. "I'll go and find her." She slung her guitar case over one shoulder and left with a wave of her hand.

What have I gotten myself into now? Emily had never done anything like that before, but the desperation in Freddy's voice had left her with no other decent option.

During her conversation with Freddy, the session seemed to have ended. Emily searched for Diana again and found her lifting a large drum. She couldn't help admiring the lean but defined muscles of her arms and her formfitting T-shirt that revealed the edges of her tattoo on her biceps. Such a difference to the oversized scrub shirts she wore at work. *What are you doing? Stop it! You're here to talk, remember?*

Diana caught her looking, and a knowing grin appeared on her face.

Busted. Emily froze, unable to greet Diana, who didn't seem to have the same problem. She walked over, carrying the large wooden drum with one hand. She looked natural with it, confident.

"Hi, what a surprise to see you here. A good surprise." Diana put the drum on the floor and reached out to Emily, as if to hug her, but pulled back before they touched. "Were you looking for me?"

The almost-contact made Emily's head spin. She couldn't find the words to tell her why she had really come. "I had to do some paperwork and… um…yeah." She had to think of a diversion. "What kind of drum is this?"

Diana picked it up again. "It's a djembe. It's handmade, from Morocco."

"It's beautiful. I like the pattern." Emily pointed at the intricately knotted strings covering the side.

"The strings and knots are not only decoration, but they also keep the goatskin in place and tune it." Diana cradled it under one arm and pointed out the various features.

For once Emily wasn't sneaking sideway glances; she was actually required to look at Diana's hands, which made it hard to concentrate on the explanation.

Diana stopped speaking and looked at her expectantly.

Maybe those hands distracted Emily more than she cared to admit. She replayed the last words in her mind. Diana has asked if she wanted to play. Good idea. Maybe that would give her a reprieve to get back on track with her plan.

"Sure. But I'm not really good with rhythm and such." She had never played an instrument besides the piano, deemed the only proper choice by her mother. And that had not gone well.

"Don't worry. We'll start simple. There are no notes or rules to follow. You create your own rhythm." Diana led the way to a bench and gestured for Emily to sit beside her.

Usually, Emily thrived on rules. She took care to learn the written und unwritten ones and stuck to them. This was outside her comfort zone, but she saw no way to explain that to Diana. She took the offered drum and placed it between her legs.

"That's right. You hold it with a little pressure from your knees so your hands are free to play. Tilt it slightly. The sound comes from the bottom, not the top."

Emily turned the top away from her, and the drum slipped from her grip.

At the same time, Diana reached for it, and their hands collided.

Heat spread from her fingertips to her core like a wildfire. Emily pulled her hand away as if she'd been burned. *Concentrate!*

"Not so far." Diana gently repositioned the drum. "Hit it a few times in different places."

Letting her fingers hover over the drum skin, Emily looked for the best way to begin. She had never done this before and didn't know the right way to do it. And she didn't like being unprepared for a challenge.

Diana just smiled and gave her an encouraging nod.

She hit it with her flat hand in the middle. It was not as loud as expected. And it sounded normal, not out of tune like the other instruments she had tried before. She gave it another pat, a little harder and on one side. Diana was right; the differences became noticeable as she hit it methodically clockwise.

"Okay, you're doing great. Now try different parts of your hands, just the fingers, the palm, the side." She demonstrated with a fast sequence.

The first time Emily tried to hit it with her fingers, she miscalculated and barely produced a soft thump. She frowned. Somehow Diana's strokes sounded so much more powerful. After a few more tries, she got the hang of it and pounded a sort of rhythm by alternating different strokes on different parts.

Suddenly, other beats mingled with hers.

Diana must have taken another drum out of the storage closet and was now sitting beside her. When had she done this? Her rhythm faltered, and she stopped, embarrassed that she couldn't concentrate enough.

Diana paused her own play and leaned toward her. "Can I show you something?"

Her hands poised over Emily's drum until Emily nodded.

Diana showed her a sequence of slow-slow-fast-fast beats on various sides of the drum.

Determined to show at least a little progress, Emily tried to copy it. It was easier than expected. "Hey, I sound nearly professional now."

Diana laughed, made a go-on gesture, and resumed her playing. At first, it was almost the same rhythm, but as they played on, it subtly became more complex.

Varying her strokes, Diana hit different spots between their shared rhythm. Her hands moved faster and faster.

Emily tried to follow her example but lost her rhythm altogether and had to stop. Heat burned in her face and neck, and she didn't know if it came from the exertion of playing or her embarrassment over her failure to follow the simple instructions.

Laughing, Diana stopped playing as well. "Don't be too hard on yourself. It's about fun, not about perfection. That happens to everyone."

"But not to you." Emily didn't like to be placated.

"More often than not when we're improvising, I tend to lose myself in the rhythm and meander around the other players. Sooner or later I take a wrong turn and end up in a completely different place. Sometimes it works just fine, and sometimes I have to stop and start over. I think the journey can be as important as the destination." Diana looked at her with an intense focus.

Was she talking about more than drumming? Whatever they were really talking about, Emily liked the connection Diana's gaze provided. *Wait!* That was *not* what she had come here for.

"Thank you. For the lesson." Emily stood, taking the drum with her. "Can I put that anywhere for you?"

"You're welcome." Diana's tone was as neutral as hers had been, but a smile still softened her expression. "Just give it to me."

No, no. Smiling wasn't good. They needed to have a serious talk, and she shouldn't have let herself play the drums with Diana. She handed the djembe over.

Diana effortlessly lifted both drums and carried them to an open storage closet.

Having learned her lesson, Emily kept her gaze away from Diana's muscles that could distract her from her mission. When she heard the door lock snap close, she glanced at Diana. "I wanted to talk to you about something important."

"Sure. Now? Will it take long?" Diana pulled her phone out of her pocket, presumably to look at the time. "I'm sorry, but I'm meeting a friend for an early dinner. Should I call her and reschedule?"

Emily wanted to be selfish and say yes, but this was about her boundaries and problems, and she shouldn't keep Diana from meeting her friend. "No, it's okay. I just wanted to clear the air. Maybe we'll find time after work tomorrow."

"Why don't you join us? The dinner won't take long because she has to work tonight, and we can talk afterward."

Dinner with Diana and getting to know her friends veered the course of the evening definitely too close to personal waters for Emily's taste. But the alternative of another sleepless night wasn't appealing at all. "If you're sure I won't intrude, okay."

Despite the fun sign depicting a cat playing with a ginger root, the Vietnamese restaurant in the heart of the University District looked cheap and uninviting from the outside, and Emily would have passed it without a second look if she'd been alone. She followed Diana past tables filled with chatting college students to a staircase. The second floor was much nicer. Irregular clusters of white paper lamps cast a soft light on sturdy wooden tables decorated with ceramic bowls containing a single bloom. It seemed like the perfect place for couples on a date. Not that she had a lot of firsthand experience in the romance department.

"Over here." Diana steered Emily to a booth in the back of the room with her hand on her back.

The touch of her fingers was light, perfectly innocent, but it took all of Emily's willpower not to squirm in the heat it generated.

A dark-skinned woman in a burgundy shirt with dark gray pinstripes and matching gray slacks stood to greet them. She seemed a few years older and vaguely familiar. Who was she? Did she work in the hospital too? Whoever she was, she looked gorgeous with a very short and stylish haircut.

"Ooh, Melinda, you look great." Diana hugged her friend.

"Don't call me that, Di!" A pointed look and a punch to Diana's arm accompanied the last word.

"Okay, okay, truce." Holding up her hands in surrender, Diana took a step back and half turned toward Emily. "Emily, this is Mel. She played guitar in our band. And this is Emily, my colleague from the hospital."

This was Mel? Jen's Mel? Another rock star? The sophisticated woman in front of her was the complete opposite of the guitar player in ripped jeans and a very tight, very revealing leather vest she'd last seen on stage.

Mel's eyebrows had shot up at the introduction, but she regained her composure faster than Emily and smiled. "Hi, good to meet you."

"Hi" was all Emily managed to croak out.

Diana and Mel took their seats on opposite sides of the table, and Emily slipped onto the bench next to Diana, careful not to sit too close.

A waitress greeted them, handed out menus, and asked for their drink order.

The other two ordered Tiger Beer, but Emily was happy to find a selection of teas. Alcohol wouldn't help to keep her wits about her.

"So, seriously, Mel. Why did you dress up like that? You weren't hoping this was a date, were you?" Diana batted her eyelashes exaggeratedly.

"You wish." Mel snorted. "No, I had a meeting with an investor. Things are looking up for my studio."

"That's great. I'm so happy for you." She squeezed Mel's arm, then looked at Emily. "Mel is planning the transition from musician to producer."

"Congratulations. Do you want to stop playing too?"

"Thanks. No, not yet. I've still got some years left in me. But we're all getting older, and not everyone has such a nice alternative career in store like Diana." With a grin, she looked at Diana. "How's that working out for you, by the way?"

"About as expected. Nothing new." Diana tensed, and her tone implied the subject was closed. "So, have you found a studio space yet?"

Mel accepted the change of topic without comment and discussed the pros and cons of several locations until the waitress brought the drinks.

"What can I get you?"

Diana and Mel immediately answered with the same number without even having picked up the menu.

The waitress chuckled, tapped the order into her tablet, and looked at Emily with raised eyebrows.

Emily fumbled for the menu and scanned the tiny script. "Can you recommend anything?"

Again, both women replied with the same number, then laughed.

"Sorry," Diana said with an apologetic grin. "What we wanted to say was: pho with beef. It's delicious."

"Thanks, I love pho." Emily pushed the menu to the side. "For me too, please."

"Good choice." The waitress collected the menus and left.

Looking from one woman to the other, Emily raised her eyebrows. "So, do you come here often?"

That prompted another bout of laughter.

Emily replayed her last sentence in her head. *Oops.* "Oh, no! That's not what I meant. I just... I mean..." Since the option of hiding under the table wasn't viable, she joined them in their laughter.

After they calmed down, Diana took a big gulp of her beer. She put the bottle back on the table and traced a bead of condensation with her finger. "We used to hang out here all the time. Downstairs is open until very late, and we refueled here after rehearsal or gigs."

"Our practice and storage space wasn't far from here," Mel added. "After I moved back to Seattle, I was so happy to find out that they're still here after all those years."

"Yeah. And the menu stayed basically the same."

"Food quality too."

"Only the customers get younger every day."

"Yep. Makes you feel old."

"You're old."

Emily cradled her bowl of tea in both hands and leaned back to enjoy the way the two friends bantered. Everything was so normal, as if they didn't share a past that was so removed from Emily's life experience that they might as well have lived on the other side of the Milky Way. Wafts of lemongrass and ginger drifted up and helped her to relax further as the talk returned to the plans for Mel's studio.

The food arrived in three giant bowls filled with a fragrant broth full of noodles, thin slices of beef, and an assortment of herbs and vegetables. With apparent years of experience, Diana and Mel immediately doctored their portions with lemon and chili sauce.

Emily tasted hers first and nearly moaned in delight as the complex taste flooded her senses. "Wow. Thanks for the recommendation. This might be the best pho I've ever had."

"Yup. Diana nearly drove me crazy in LA as she tried to recreate the recipe." Mel rolled her eyes. "I mean, she's a great cook, but no one comes close to the Ginger Cat."

"It's good to be here again." Diana smiled and took a large spoonful of the soup.

"You can say that again." Mel started to eat too and exchanged a look with Diana that clearly showed they were talking about more than the food.

The moment was too private for Emily to ask about. She averted her gaze and concentrated on her meal. Pho had always been about warmth and comfort for her, something she could use now to fortify herself for the rest of the evening.

After they'd all finished, Mel pressed her hand to her stomach. "I'm so full; I've no idea how I'll be able to play." She looked at her watch. "And I need to get going."

Diana grinned. "You'll burn off those calories soon enough. Didn't you mention a date after your gig?"

"Aaand that's my cue to leave you alone with *your* date." Mel winked, stood, and pulled out her wallet.

"Don't worry, I'll pay." Diana waved her off.

Why didn't Diana correct Mel's assumption? Emily nearly choked in her haste to swallow her tea. "Oh, no. No, no. We're not on a date, not at all. We work together. Just as friends."

Mel paused in the midst of putting her wallet back and raised her hand in a conciliatory gesture. "I'm sorry if I have offended you."

"No, you didn't offend me. It's just..." If anything, she should be flattered Mel had assumed that someone like Diana would be interested in her. What could she possibly offer her? "I just didn't want there to be any misunderstandings." It was a lame justification for her outburst, but anything else hit too close to home.

"Okay." Mel accepted the explanation with a smile that removed the awkwardness from the situation. "But I still have to go. It was good meeting you."

She held out her hand and Emily shook it without hesitation. "You too."

Diana rose, but before Emily could stand to let her pass, Mel leaned over her to quickly hug Diana with one arm.

"Talk to you soon." Mel left, and Diana sat with a thud.

Neither of them said anything for a minute. Emily reached for her tea, more to have something to occupy her hands than because she wanted to drink the last dregs. The ginger had stewed too long and turned everything bitter.

"So." Diana broke the silence first. "Do you want to talk here or somewhere else?" She leaned back and smiled.

That smile wasn't fair, much too friendly, too warm. Too sexy. Emily took a sip of the tea to wet her suddenly dry mouth. The bitterness helped clear her head.

She studied her surroundings. Even though the room had filled up during their dinner, the other guests sat some distance away and the level of background noise was enough to ensure their privacy. But Diana was much too close. During the meal, her arm had brushed Emily's once, leaving her with a tickling sensation. She wished she'd chosen the other side of the table in the first place, but changing now would be too weird. "Can we talk while walking?"

"Sure." Diana waved at the waitress, who was passing the table. "Can we have the check, please?"

When she arrived with a black folder, Diana reached for it with a smile. "I've got this." She placed a few bills in it and pushed it to the side of the table.

"Wait. Let me pay my share." Emily reached for her wallet.

Diana stopped her with a hand on her arm. "You don't need too. I'd love to invite you. I dragged you here, after all."

There it was again, that tingle that ran up and down her arm. She needed to get out of here.

"I insist. This is not a date." Emily stood, removing the distracting hand from her sleeve, and placed money on the table. It was time to establish some ground rules.

The Ave was a popular destination and not conducive to serious talks. People were still strolling along the main street in the heart of the U District, chatting, and having a normal Saturday evening with friends and dates. Diana hadn't done that for so long, she wasn't sure what that even felt like. In college and med school she had spent most of her free time with her band, either practicing or playing any gig they could get.

She let Emily set the pace and waited for her to bring up the reason for their outing, but Emily didn't seem to be in a hurry to talk about it. She stopped from time to time to look at the windows of a bookstore and some of the quirky little shops.

All evening, Emily had been remarkably different than her usual confident self that Diana had come to know at work. The surfacing hints of vulnerability intrigued her. Maybe Emily would open up more during their talk, whatever it would be about. The only topic that came to mind was Emily's distress and the hug that had led to the unexpected kiss. Unexpected, but not unwelcome.

They passed a secondhand record store. The display was a wall of vinyl records and CDs, and Diana slowed automatically to check out the titles. The owner seemed to have eclectic tastes.

"I need to come back here when they're open." Diana wanted to move on, but Emily stopped and looked from Diana to the window and back.

They both studied the covers. Diana found it before Emily did. Their first live CD. She'd always had a love/hate relationship with the cover. The shot had been taken from behind the stage and showed them playing to an audience. The main focus was the colorful tattoo on Diana's back. Would Emily recognize it?

Emily stiffened for a second, then leaned closer to the glass to study the cover. Her expression reflected in the window showed an intense focus. "How long did it take for you to style your hair?"

Diana laughed. Emily was practical, as usual. The photographer had insisted on a hairstyle that left the tattoo clearly visible and had persuaded her to spike it to a faux hawk for the performance. She had hated wearing it like that but had to admit it looked good in the picture.

"Better ask how long it took to wash the stuff off after the concert." Diana groaned and shook her head. "Never again."

They continued on their way home, passing the next shops without stopping.

"Do you miss it?" Emily's question was so low that Diana nearly failed to understand it.

Diana's first impulse was to answer with a joke about her hair, but Emily's mood seemed too serious for that. "What do you mean? The concerts?"

Emily nodded. "The concerts, the fame, the fans."

She had asked herself the same question more than once during the last few weeks, especially after playing again last month. The answer was easy. "Honestly? No, not really. The feeling of belonging to a band, of being part of creating something together is wonderful. I loved the rehearsals, the improv sessions, the dynamic between the band members. At least on good days." She frowned as she remembered the fits her ex had thrown when she didn't get her way. "But the concerts were hard work. In the beginning, I got a high from being on stage, playing for an increasing audience. Later it was routine. You had to play, whether you felt like it or not." Diana looked into Emily's eyes and hoped she understood. Most people couldn't see past the supposed thrill of fame.

"Like working in the ED. It's not always about saving lives; sometimes you just have to wrap a twisted ankle." Emily glanced down and resumed their walk. "What about the fame? The fans?"

"That was complicated. Again, it started great. I mean, people are cheering for you; they adore you for something you love doing." Diana played with the zipper of her jacket. How much should she tell her? She decided to be completely open. If she wanted their relationship to lead anywhere, Emily shouldn't be the only one to make herself vulnerable. "But it messes with your head. Everyone reacts differently."

Emily hummed. Her face was hidden by moving shadows as they reached an area with less illumination.

Was she agreeing? Diana took it as a sign to continue. "Mel stayed down-to-earth. Nothing could faze her. Maybe because she's a little bit older, or just because she's just that cool. Grounded. Katie and I, we didn't do so well. Our relationship didn't survive the first year. She and I lived in our separate fantasy worlds of inflated self-importance. She made a few unhealthy choices, and I stuck my head in the sand. The band nearly split over this, but we got our act together. She cleaned up, we turned our relationship into a friendship, and everything was fine again." She snorted. "Or so we thought." The last few years blurred in her memory: concert tours, studio work, and months in between on the farm. "When we were at home, I craved solitude and concentrated on songwriting. I only emerged from my rooms to rehearse, run, or cook. Or to talk to Mel. She kept me sane."

"I like Mel, but it was weird meeting her, knowing she'll go out with Jen later. And that neither Mel nor I could tell Jen about it without revealing how we know each other." Emily's voice held a tinge of amusement. "Our best friends are going out, but we can't really talk to them. That's not complicated. At all."

Diana stopped walking. "I'm sorry about the mess and that keeping my secret prevents you from really talking to your best friend. I hate secrets. Hell, I wasn't even in the closet. I think I came out to my parents five minutes after I realized why the idea of Alissa having a date with that guy from the music store hurt so much."

Emily turned to Diana and squeezed her arm. "It's okay. I don't like secrets either, but I get it."

The touch suffused her with a warmth that spread from her fingertips all the way to her heart. After the kiss two days ago and their impromptu percussion session and dinner tonight, Diana's attraction to Emily had grown in leaps, but her mind had a difficult time keeping up. Both Emily's signals and her own reactions confused her. She'd like to hold Emily's hand while walking and get to know her better. Sometimes she thought Emily wanted the same, but then she retreated again.

As if to prove Diana's observation, Emily withdrew her hand and stuffed it into the pocket of her jeans. "So, Alissa?"

They continued down the street, and Diana accepted the redirect. "My best friend in high school. I thought she liked to hang out at the music store with me. You know, because of the music selection. And my witty company." She sighed dramatically and rolled her eyes. "I was completely oblivious to her attraction to the clerk and couldn't understand what she saw in him. I mean he was really old, at least twenty, and into grunge."

They both laughed, and the levity eased Diana's tension. Whatever Emily wanted to talk about couldn't be that bad.

The comfortable silence lasted until they'd reached Diana's car.

Diana looked around but couldn't find a good spot for an important conversation. "Why don't I drive you home and then we'll talk?" She pulled the keys from her jacket and unlocked the car with a press of the button.

"Okay." Emily opened the passenger-side door and got in.

The silence on the short drive to Emily's apartment was anything but comfortable. Diana parked in front of the building next to a streetlight and switched off the engine. "Should we go inside?"

"No, it won't take long." Emily unfastened her seat belt but kept hold of the buckle. "I want to apologize for what happened Thursday night." Her voice was as stiff as her posture.

Diana leaned forward and reached for her arm but stopped short of actually touching her. "You don't need to apologize."

"Yes, I do. My conduct was highly unprofessional, and I'll make sure it won't happen again." She swallowed several times. "I'm your mentor. You didn't need to see me breaking down. Comforting me isn't part of your duties, and I'm sorry I imposed on you."

"That wasn't about my duties, and you certainly weren't imposing on me. You were hurting. I wanted to help." The memory of the surge of warmth and affection that had accompanied their hug colored her tone, and Diana did nothing to hide it. "Is this about the kiss?"

Emily froze and stared at her, unblinking.

Mesmerized by the streetlight reflected in the gray eyes, Diana waited. They looked like dark pools of molten silver.

"I'm sorry that I kissed you." The whisper was barely audible and suffused with emotions Diana couldn't identify.

"I'm not." This time, Diana touched Emily's arm. She needed the connection, and even though the tendons and muscles were tight under her fingers as she still clutched the seat belt, Emily didn't withdraw. "But didn't I kiss you first?" She risked a little teasing to defuse the tension.

A hint of a smile softened Emily's lips, and her arm relaxed beneath Diana's fingers. "That's beside the point. It's just important that it won't happen again."

"Why?" Thursday evening, the attraction had seemed mutual.

Emily released her death grip and the seat belt shot back with a snap. "We work together. I'm your mentor. We need boundaries."

All good reasons. But the absence of the most crucial argument was noticeable. Emily hadn't said she didn't want to kiss her again. "Working together isn't ideal for dating, but I think we could find a way to handle that."

"No." Emily shook her head and pulled her arm away. "Clear lines between work and personal life are essential."

Diana didn't believe that, but she had to respect Emily's choice. The sense of loss about what might have been swirled in the pit of her stomach. "Okay, if it's that important to you, we'll do it your way." She smiled to show she wouldn't hold it against her, even though it hurt. "But if you ever want to revisit that conversation, let me know."

"Thank you." She opened the door. "See you at work."

"Wait." Diana couldn't resist pushing for a little more than polite co-workers. "What about friendship?"

One foot already outside of the car, Emily turned back to her. "What do you mean?"

"Is friendship, not hanging out and hoping for more, just friendship something we could do? Or would that interfere with work too?"

"I don't know." Emily got out and straightened her jacket. Her face wasn't visible anymore, and Diana strained to hear her reply. "But we could try." She pushed the door closed and hurried to her apartment.

Diana slumped back in her seat and closed her eyes. She needed a moment to digest the talk before she could drive.

Emily placed her empty tea mug on the wooden crate that served as a table and leaned back in the plush faux leather chair. Today she didn't mind her best friend's tendency to arrive late. She looked at her reflection in the window of the stylish coffee place to make sure her makeup still hid the dark rings under her eyes. She had barely slept last night in a futile attempt to organize her jumbled emotions and get them back under control as the talk hadn't brought her peace of mind. Jen would probably know that something was off the minute she saw her.

What had she been thinking yesterday? Not much, obviously; her actions had been guided by her feelings instead. She'd followed a sketchy plan to seek out Diana at the Rainbow Home, and then events had escalated out of her control. Their drumming session had led to an impromptu dinner, and in the end, she'd accepted the offer of friendship.

Why had she done that? She had wanted to stay away from further temptation, not invite it into her life as a friend. Her only excuse was that it had felt right. Warmth spread in her abdomen at the thought of spending more time with Diana.

She groaned. That was absurd. She was a grown woman focused on her career and not a hormonal teenager. She would overcome this silly crush. Now.

"Why do you look as if you want to kill someone? I'm not that late." Jen bent down to kiss her cheek, slipped out of her wet coat, and carefully hung it over the back of a chair.

Emily flinched. She hadn't noticed Jen approach. And when had it started to rain? She tried to hide behind a smile. "No, you're not that late. I was just thinking about something, um, at work. Nothing to do with you."

"Good. I'm starving. Did you order?" Jen focused on the menu.

Good, a change of topic. Not that it would keep them occupied for long. "No, not yet. I'm not that hungry."

Jen focused on her for a moment and then returned to studying the breakfast options.

Heat shot into Emily's face, and she hoped she could fight off the blush before Jen finished reading. She needed a distraction.

"How was your interview-slash-date thing yesterday?" Emily asked. The dark rings under Jen's eyes matched hers, but she suspected another cause for the lack of sleep. "You look…satisfied."

Jen half groaned and half laughed. "That's a terrible pun. But yes, thank you, I am."

The waitress came to take their orders.

Emily shook her head at the extensive list Jen ordered. A fruit salad was probably enough. If she wanted more, she could always steal something from her friend's plate.

"Will you see her again?" Emily hoped not. Her best friend in bed with Diana's best friend sounded like a recipe for disaster. Plus, Mel was really nice, and she didn't like the thought that Jen used her for interviews.

"Maybe." Jen doodled invisible lines with her finger on the table. "I'd like to. We had fun. And not just in the bedroom."

"That's great." Emily tried to mask her trepidation. "What did you do? Just meet for the interview, or did you go somewhere?"

"We met at a club before she played and talked about her career. After the concert, I met the rest of the band, and we went dancing together." Jen grinned and waggled her eyebrows. "And then she showed me her record collection."

Despite her reservations, Emily had to laugh. "Really? That was the best line she had?"

"It wasn't just a line. We really looked at her collection. It's huge. And we talked for hours about music, our favorite bands and songs, and everything. I think I've found my match in obscure music knowledge." She yawned and stretched her arms behind her head. "Then, of course, we had mind-blowing sex for the rest of the night."

"Of course. I wouldn't expect anything less on a Saturday night for you." Emily grinned to show she was teasing.

"And you sat alone at home and read a few thrilling articles about broken bodies, right?" Jen teased right back.

"No, I went out to dinner." Shit. Why had she said that? That was the one topic she had wanted to avoid at all costs.

"Oh, now that's something new. Alone? Or did you have a date?" Jen looked genuinely interested, and Emily couldn't lie to her.

"No, not a date. Just a friendly dinner with a colleague." Emily's lips formed an involuntary smile at the thought of the evening.

"Hey, that's fantastic. What's your not-really-a-date's name?"

"Diana. But we are just friends. She's a resident. Not my date." Emily hoped she did a better job of denying it today than yesterday.

"Mmmh. Just a friend." Jen's eyes sparkled with the same predatory gleam she had for one of her stories. "Because she is a resident."

Emily frantically searched for a distraction. It came in the form of the waitress carrying a full tray. When she had distributed the plates, Jen dug into her eggs and Emily nibbled on a piece of melon.

"Can I steal a pancake?" Emily's fork hovered over the stack.

"Sure. Appetite returned? Where did you eat yesterday?"

That question was harmless enough. "A Vietnamese restaurant."

"No romantic candlelight for the not-really-date?"

Okay. Not so harmless.

"Her best friend ate with us." *And then went on to spend the night with you.* Emily searched her fruit salad for another strawberry and avoided looking at Jen. She was afraid of what Jen would read in her eyes.

"So it's serious if you're meeting her friends already." Jen stole a grape from Emily's bowl.

"I know what you're doing. You're fishing for sordid details. There are none. We're just friends, maybe not even that. We work together. We both volunteer at the Rainbow Home. Nothing else. Stop interrogating me!" Emily tried hard to keep her tone even. If she raised her voice, Jen would know that something more was going on, but would that be so bad? She could probably offer a different perspective, with her massive experience in mixing work and pleasure. But what if she asked for more details? What if she wanted to meet her?

Emily suddenly had trouble breathing. She pulled at the collar of her shirt. Why was it so hot in here?

Jen reached over and placed her hand on Emily's arm. "Hey, don't freak out. I'm not interrogating you. I'm just being your best friend, and important parts of the job description are nosy questions and friendly teasing."

Emily let go of her collar and squeezed Jen's hand that still lingered on her arm. It reminded her of Diana's touch last night, minus the sparks and the tingling. "You're right. I'm sorry. I don't know why I'm so out of it today." Her presence was soothing as usual, and Emily slowly relaxed. She was overthinking this. Jen was her best friend, and she trusted her.

Jen took a minute to hold Emily's gaze before she withdrew her hand. "We're good?"

"Yeah, we are." Emily's mouth was dry, and she took another bite of the melon. "The truth is, I'm freaking out because of Diana, not because of your questions."

"Fair enough. Do you want to tell me why?" Jen radiated the serenity Emily lacked.

"I'm not sure what I'm feeling, exactly. I think I might be interested in her. In more than friendship. But I'm absolutely sure it isn't a good idea. She is my resident; I'm her mentor and responsible for her. It's not right. Is it?" Emily was talking too fast and too loud. She took a deep breath. It didn't help. "Oh shit. I'm a mess." She closed her eyes and massaged them with both hands.

"Why is it a problem if she's a resident? She's not a student, but a fellow doctor. You're not responsible for her grades or something like that. You're not her boss; you can't fire her. And you're both adults. Is she much younger, is that it?" Jen sounded so logical she almost convinced Emily. But things were never that easy and straightforward.

"No. She's our age. Maybe even a year or two older. She took a break after med school." This was coming too close to the part of Diana's past that should stay hidden from Jen. Emily needed to direct the focus away from Diana and back to herself. "As her mentor and supervisor, I don't have any direct influence on her residency, but things would be awkward at work if I misjudged her intentions. Or worse, if things don't work out between us." And why should they? Emily didn't have any valuable experience in sustaining a relationship.

Jen's brow wrinkled. "Are you afraid of being accused of sexual harassment?"

"No, no. Not really. It's too late for that." Emily grimaced. "I kissed her. She kissed me back. But I told her yesterday that we need to keep things platonic between us."

"Kiss?" Jen squealed like a teenager. "Why don't you give her a chance? Just see where it goes? You must be really, really interested in her to do something like that. That's not typical for you. Usually, you shove your interest behind a wall of rationalizations, lock the door, and throw away the key."

Everything Jen said was true. Diana made her nervous, but in a good way. Tingling, heat, and goose bumps appeared on various parts of her body at inconvenient times. It should have been a mortifying experience. She should have been angry at the loss of control over her physical reactions. But she wasn't. She enjoyed the anticipation and uncertainty as if she stood on the edge of a pier and the next step would show her if the water was cold or warm. Jen had read her correctly; she was simply happy whenever she thought of Diana.

Emily sighed. If only she could give in and explore the attraction. But she was an adult with responsibilities, and work had to come first. That wasn't a rationalization; that was a fact.

Chapter 11

"I HAVE MENINGITIS. I COULD have died waiting here for you!" The middle-aged man didn't even wait for Diana to introduce herself.

Diana sighed. He wasn't the first patient with a temper today and probably wouldn't be the last. The ED was swamped with people who thought they were dying, but so far she hadn't found anything more serious than the flu. She consulted the notes the nurse had taken. Headache, sore throat, stiff joints. Yep, another summer flu victim. "Okay, Mr. Derris. Could you please tell me your symptoms?"

"No need for that. I've told you, I've meningitis and I need antibiotics ASAP. And ICU treatment." The patient stabbed the air with his finger and nodded with every word that was important to him.

Diana suppressed another sigh. No one with meningitis would move their head like this. "I can reassure you that meningitis is a very rare condition and highly unlikely in your case, as you show an unrestricted movement of your head. What is your main complaint? A headache?"

"Don't you lecture me! I have a daughter your age, and I'm old enough to know my own body. I want to speak to your supervisor now, or I'll call my lawyer."

On a normal day, Diana would have tried to talk him down, but today she was out of patience. "I'll be right back." She ducked out of the cubicle to find Emily.

As she called Emily's work phone, it rang behind a curtain a few cubicles down. She hung up and went over.

"Knock, knock. Dr. Barnes?" Diana opened the curtain just enough to stick her head in. She nearly fell backward at the sight of the two figures sitting next to each other.

A sobbing woman had buried her head on Emily's shoulder so that only her lank hair was visible. Her dirt-streaked sweatshirt and jeans hung on her slight frame as if they'd belonged to a much larger person.

No sign of Emily's customary distance remained as she murmured words of comfort. She held her close without showing reluctance to touch the dirty clothes.

A wave of warmth swept over Diana. She had always suspected that Emily cared a lot about her patients, but until now she'd always hidden it behind her professionalism. Seeing her like this only raised Diana's respect for her.

Emily looked up and acknowledged Diana with a nod, then extricated herself from the embrace. "Nadia, honey, I need to go and check something." She stroked a wet cheek and carefully pushed a streak of the young woman's tangled hair behind her ear. "I'll be back. Do you want me to send Freddy in?"

The girl just nodded and wiped at her face with the too-long sleeves of her sweatshirt. She was even younger than Diana had suspected, maybe thirteen or fourteen.

Emily was wearing too much makeup, as usual, but it couldn't mask the dark rings under her eyes. Her normally pristine scrubs were crumpled and stained by the girl's tears.

The urge to wrap Emily in an embrace was strong, but Diana fought the inappropriate impulse. It wouldn't be welcome anyway. As soon as Emily's back was to her patient, her mask of aloofness slid back into place and hid her emotions.

After she'd left the cubicle, Emily stopped a passing nurse and asked her to get the girl's friend from the waiting room. By the description, she was obviously talking about the same Freddy Diana knew from the shelter.

What did Freddy have to do with the girl? And what was wrong with her? Should she offer her help? No, Emily would tell her if she needed her.

"What can I do for you?" Emily turned toward Diana with a tired smile.

Diana forced herself to focus on her own case. "I'm sorry to bother you, but I've another flu patient with dangerous semi-knowledge in room four. Dr. Internet said he has meningitis, and he insists on talking to my supervisor because I questioned his diagnosis."

Emily groaned. "That's the third one today. Was there a blog or TV show about it or something? That would explain why they're all here instead of going to urgent care. Let's tackle him together. I talk, you write, okay?"

No admonishment? No mini-lecture about successful doctor-patient communication? Maybe Emily was more shaken by the girl's tears than she'd thought.

Diana led Emily to the patient. She watched as Emily used a combination of charm and authority to get the man to talk. After the exam, he was convinced he had only the flu, and somehow she had made him believe it had been his idea all along. Diana recognized the difference between her superficial smile and the one Emily had sent her way earlier. Diana finished the notes in record time and wrote the discharge slip that Emily signed without hesitation. They were out of there in under ten minutes, and Emily returned to her young patient.

A couple of hours later they had weathered the worst of the storm, and Diana used the calm to head for the staff lounge and the much-needed coffee.

Emily was sitting on the large, sagging couch. She had closed her eyes, laid her head on the backrest, and cradled a steaming mug in her hands.

Not wanting to disturb her rest, Diana tried to pour her coffee as inconspicuously as possible. But when she tiptoed past her, Emily opened her eyes.

"What a week." Emily drank deeply from her tea and sighed.

"You can say that again." She took a seat next to her and followed her example. Her neck and shoulders were stiff from too much bending over bedsides in uncomfortable positions. "I'm sorry I bothered you with that idiot. Maybe I was not diplomatic enough in the beginning."

"Don't worry. He just wanted to be right and important. You probably could have dressed Stacy from admission in a lab coat and told him she was the chief of staff, and he would have been content."

They enjoyed their drinks in silence. Just sitting and sharing the break improved the day. In the last three days since their talk, they hadn't had a minute at work to connect beyond the professional.

Emily placed her mug on the side table and fished a postcard from the pocket of her scrub shirt. She studied both sides carefully.

"Isn't that one of Freddy's invitations? For her concert on Thursday?" She'd seen enough of them in the last weeks to recognize it. A similar one rested on her kitchen counter at home.

Emily nodded. "The girl you saw me with, she's a friend of Freddy's, and when I treated her without registration or payment, Freddy insisted on giving me something in return. She's offering to get me to the concert for free."

"Aww. That's cute." Diana couldn't help smiling.

"It really is. Don't laugh." With a mock-stern expression, Emily swatted Diana's arm with the postcard.

"Hey, my coffee!" She hadn't spilled it yet. To be on the safe side, she put it out of Emily's reach on the table. "Do you plan on going?"

"I'm not sure yet." Emily twirled the postcard between her fingers. "I'm afraid I'd stick out like a sore thumb. I'll probably be the only person over twenty."

"Not at all. Her band isn't the only one playing that evening; it's a sort of showcase for up-and-coming bands, and there'll be tons of friends and family for each of them. You'd only need to stay for her gig in the beginning and could leave any time after that."

"Mmh, maybe." Emily stuffed the card back into her pocket. "Did she invite you too?"

"Yeah, as a thank-you for my help with her song arrangement. I promised to go." Diana studied Emily, who still seemed unconvinced. "Why don't we go together? I could pick you up."

"Together? Like a…" Emily glanced around, even though they were alone in the staff lounge. "Like a date?" She whispered the last word. "I thought we'd talked about this."

"I meant to go together as friends. You said we would try, and that could be the perfect opportunity. We both want to support Freddy."

Emily played with a loose thread in the hem of her scrub shirt. She kept her gaze on it as if it were the most fascinating thread in the history of frayed cotton. "Okay." The fiber tore with a snap. "But we'll meet there."

"Sure. Do you want me to find out what time Freddy will play?" Diana didn't want to spend her evening off listening to half a dozen beginner bands, and she couldn't imagine Emily wanting that either. "I can let you know a good time to meet."

Emily nodded once, then stood. "I need to head back. A million more flu patients are waiting for us."

Diana acknowledged the redirect back to work with a groan. "Doesn't anyone just eat chicken soup and stay in bed anymore?"

Emily laughed at the exaggerated despair in Diana's voice, winked, and left.

The good mood carried Diana through the next hours of tedious work. She saw Emily only twice more in passing, but the private smiles they shared were enough to sustain her.

Who would have thought a summer flu epidemic could be fun?

Thursday evening, Emily left work on time for once. She slung her bag over one shoulder and winced as the weight settled on her stiff muscles. She definitely needed time to prepare for tonight. All day she'd vacillated between apprehensive and anticipating, and the emotional whiplash had translated into physical tension.

After a relaxing bath, Emily's muscles had loosened enough to avoid a headache. It took her longer than usual to tame her hair. She hesitated with the makeup. Diana had mentioned more than once that she didn't need any. Emily snorted. Diana wouldn't have said that if she knew just how many freckles waited underneath it. Going without makeup felt like leaving the house naked, but she would take her time to make it look as natural as possible.

Dressing was harder. She paced in front of her bed and stared at the clothes spread out on it. Boring, boring, boring.

Oh, stop it. You're going to the concert to support Freddy. You shouldn't care what Diana thinks about you. Friends, remember?

But the longer she looked at the mess, the less she was able to decide on an outfit. She took her phone and texted Jen.

Help. What to wear to a concert?

The answer came nearly immediately.

Classical concert? Rock? Jazz?

Emily was still thinking about the answer when two more texts came in rapid succession.

Date?????

Sexy resident?!? ;-)

If you looked at her texts, it was hard to believe that Jen wrote articles for a living. Emily composed her answer and nearly dropped the phone when it rang. Jen's picture flashed on the screen. Great.

"Just a concert from a band. Rock, I think. What should I wear? I'm out of practice." Emily hoped if she focused on the problem at hand, Jen would be distracted from the other questions.

"You're going on a date? It's your sexy resident you told me about, right? Congratulations!"

Emily sighed. Keeping secrets from Jen was next to impossible. "I never said she was sexy. And it's not a date; we explicitly talked about going there as friends."

"Oh, sure. You don't need help dressing for a simple outing with a friend."

"Yes, I'm nervous. Are you happy now?" Emily flopped down on the bed, ignoring the pile of rejected clothes.

"Yep. Thanks. I'm happy." Jen's voice softened. "No need to be nervous. You had a nice evening out on Saturday, so you'll have fun tonight. Why don't you go a little bit earlier and work off that nervous energy on the dance floor?"

"Maybe." She stood again and resumed pacing. "So, what do I wear? Everything looks dull."

Jen chuckled. "Your new black jeans are far from dull. Remember how the guy in the shop couldn't stop staring at your ass?"

Emily reached into the closet and stroked the soft cotton. "No. They're too—"

"Too sexy?" Jen interrupted her. "Isn't that what you want?"

"No. Maybe. I don't know."

"You'll feel confident if you look good. You don't have to fling yourself at her."

She put the phone on speaker to squeeze herself into the tight jeans. "I hope you're right. What else?"

"Combine it with one of the nicer short-sleeved blouses you own. Maybe the olive one? Trust me."

"Okay. Wait a second." Emily dressed in the blouse Jen had suggested. Looking at herself in the mirror, she picked up the phone again. Jen had been right. "Sexy, but still classy. Thanks."

"Can you send me a picture of you two?"

Emily groaned. "I'm hanging up now before you come up with more bad ideas." Like wanting to meet her. That would be a disaster.

Jen laughed. "Bye."

Emily stayed in front of the mirror and closed another button at the top. Her confidence waned as she looked at her reflection, but the alarm on her phone saved her from another change. Time to go.

Diana was running late. A patient throwing up on her had derailed her plans to leave work on time. She had only a couple of minutes at home before her date with Emily. Or rather non-date.

She grabbed her favorite top from the stack of similar black neck halter tops and threaded a black leather belt in the low-slung blue jeans. A fleeting glance in the mirror confirmed that her top was tucked in wrinkle-free, and she bent down to zip her black boots. She hesitated when she glimpsed the head of the large dragon on her shoulder and the fire circling her left biceps. Would it and what it stood for overwhelm Emily? Her past was an obstacle that still loomed between them, and she didn't want to remind Emily of it at first sight.

She opened her closet again and critically examined the other clothes. A thin gray silk shirt with long sleeves wasn't special or sexy, but it was unobtrusive. She put it on and left without another look in the mirror.

Diana greeted Tom, the bouncer at the club's main entrance, with a hug. He waved away her attempt to pay. She left her jacket at the cloak check and entered the main room with a bar at one end and a small stage on the other side that held a few instruments. A quick survey of the room showed no friends or acquaintances. Good. Diana wanted to spend her evening with Emily and not rehashing her old life. But where was she? The concert hadn't begun yet, and the middle of the room was teeming with people in little groups, drinking and talking. At the front, others were dancing to the rock song that blasted from floor-to-ceiling speakers.

The dim light hid details, but one of the dancers reminded her of Emily. She nearly dismissed the resemblance because the woman's long, brown hair was flowing unrestricted over her shoulders. Diana had never seen Emily without a bun or at least a ponytail. Even though it probably wasn't Emily, something compelled Diana to take a closer look, and she made her way through the crowd.

The woman danced with her back to Diana, apparently alone. Her hips swayed in sync to the beat, and the perfectly rounded backside in tight black jeans mesmerized Diana. As she turned gracefully, Diana gasped. It was indeed Emily who had captured her attention. Her eyes were closed, and she'd lifted her face up as if she were basking in rays of sunshine instead of flickering spotlights. She seemed completely immersed in the music. Her expression was unlike anything Diana had seen on her before, almost blissful.

Wow. Feelings that decidedly breached the boundaries of friendship rose in her and took Diana's breath away. *No, no. Don't.* She shook her head as if she could dislodge the arousal like that. *You offered friendship, nothing more. But friends can dance together, right?*

Without examining her intentions, Diana started to dance. She let the music take over. It had been a while since she had last been to a club without having to work, just to enjoy herself.

Even though Diana had been careful not to intrude into Emily's personal space, it didn't take long until Emily noticed her. Her steps faltered, and she blushed.

"Hi." Diana had to raise her voice as the song increased in volume. "Sorry, I didn't want to interrupt you."

"Hi. I was early and…" She gestured to the other dancers. "Better than just standing around."

"Definitely." Diana leaned in to speak directly into her ear. "Do you want to drink something or dance some more?"

"Dance." Emily's reply was immediate and decisive.

A subtle shift went through Emily, something Diana couldn't put her finger on. This time they danced together instead of next to each other.

Emily was a good dancer, and soon they moved closer without restricting each other. More and more people crowded around them, and she was pushed into Emily.

She reached for Emily's hip to steady herself. To her surprise, Emily didn't shy away from the touch but kept on moving in sync and close enough that Diana could breathe in her fresh herbal scent mixed with powdery makeup. Diana closed her eyes. The fabric of her jeans was warm and soft under Diana's fingers, and she used all her self-control to stop herself from exploring further.

When Emily was jostled from behind, she stumbled and ended with her right leg between Diana's thighs. Definitely not where a friend's leg should ever be.

Arousal struck Diana like lightning and knocked her out of the motion.

Breathing heavily, neither of them moved for a moment.

Slowly, Diana trailed her hand from Emily's hip to her back. She let it rest in the hollow where the jeans ended and the blouse was tucked in.

Emily answered her unspoken invitation by putting one arm around Diana's neck and starting to dance again.

Repeatedly their fronts brushed against each other as Emily's leg stayed where it was, and Diana tingled all over. She had to look at Emily.

Light and shadows chased rhythmically over Emily's features. Her eyes were closed, and the blissful smile had returned.

Diana closed her eyes too and gave herself over to the music and the sensations running through her body. Every contact with Emily made her skin long for fewer clothes. Heat spread from her middle and ran through her extremities.

Hours, or probably only minutes, later the music stopped. She stood disoriented in the stream of people surrounding them; her only anchor was Emily.

She met Emily's gaze. Her gray eyes were unusually warm and dark like the midnight sea, and Diana could willingly drown in them. Following the siren's call, she couldn't resist leaning closer until their breaths mingled. Her heartbeat soared in anticipation.

Emily sighed, and the warm air caressed Diana's lips.

Bright lights and thunder-like drums jolted her out of the spell. They both tensed and drew back at the same time, staring at each other.

Diana struggled to calm her breathing and looked at Emily.

Her chest moved as fast as her own, so Diana clearly wasn't the only one affected by that near kiss.

She quickly removed her hands and opened a few more buttons of her shirt to move it away from her sticky skin. It only helped a little, as most of the heat stemmed from a fire burning low in her middle and couldn't be doused by fresh air. How had her good intentions vanished so quickly? She hadn't behaved like a friend who respected boundaries. Should she apologize? No. It wasn't as if she had thrown herself at Emily. Whatever had happened between them had been mutual. She glanced at Emily from the corner of her eye to gauge her reaction.

Emily had turned to face the stage and stood next to Diana without touching her. Biting her lower lip, Emily absentmindedly traced a bead of sweat with her finger down her neckline.

A new wave of heat spread through Diana, and she tore her gaze back to the stage before she would evaporate in a burst of steam. She fanned herself with her shirt again.

"Take your shirt off. You must be melting." Emily spoke directly into her ear. The proximity didn't help.

Diana had half taken off her shirt when she remembered the reason for wearing it in the first place. "Some people might recognize my tattoos. Do you mind?"

Emily shook her head. "No, it's not like we're at work. Your tattoos are part of you. And they do look great."

Huh. The thought that Emily might actually like her tattoos had never crossed Diana's mind. The idea was exciting; she'd expected them to be an obstacle between them. After taking off the shirt, she knotted it around her hips.

All around them people moved to the beat of the band and looked at the stage. Emily was jostled half in front of her. Diana's world shrunk and concentrated on the small square they occupied together, like a rock in the sea. The others flowed around them as Emily lightly leaned her back against Diana's front.

Diana breathed in more of the tantalizing scent and stuck her hands into the pockets of her jeans to keep them from temptation. *Concentrate on the music. This is neither the right time nor place to take it further.*

Only she wasn't able to immerse herself fully in the show. Even her evaluation of the band mirrored her blossoming feelings for Emily. A few false beats and chords were indicators that they were relatively new; some transitions were fumbled, but all in all she liked it.

Freddy and her band ran out of songs to play all too soon. The lights flared on as the music stopped. Emily blinked a few times against the brightness. Around them people moved again, to the exit, to the bar, to meet with friends, taking with them Emily's excuse to stand so close to Diana. The loss of contact jolted her brain back to life. *What have you done?*

She turned, unsure what would happen next. Her behavior during the dance and the concert must have confused Diana. Hell, it had confused her too. She was sending out mixed signals left and right and had no idea how to rein herself in. Since the day they met, something in Diana had provoked her to act impulsively. And the worst part was that she was enjoying herself against her better judgment.

Emily searched for something to say, but her concentration was shot. Her gaze settled on Diana, who looked as flushed as she herself felt. Her top was sticking to her front like a second skin, which was definitely not a bad thing. *Stop it. Cool off and get a grip!* "Do you want something to drink?"

Diana nodded. "I'll go. What can I get you?"

"Just water." Her inhibitions were lowered enough. Emily didn't know what she would do under the influence of alcohol.

"Wait here." Diana briefly touched Emily's hand with her own and flashed her a smile.

Emily watched her weave through the crowd and took the opportunity to admire the tattoo on her back. She sighed. Even sexier than she remembered.

Someone touched her shoulder. "Emily, what are you doing here?"

Jen. Shit. Not now. Emily quickly put on a smile and turned around. "Hey. That's a surprise. Are you working?"

Jen grimaced. "My boss called and asked me to do a few lines on one of the bands. It seems his daughter has a crush on one of the band members." She looked around "Where's your resident?"

"She's not mine." Emily looked at the bar to check if Diana was returning. Jen hadn't seen them together yet, so it wasn't too late. "She's getting something to drink." How could she get rid of Jen without being too obvious?

Jen raised up on her toes to look in the same direction. "What does she look like?"

Should Emily tell her something completely misleading? But Diana could come back any moment. Emily hesitated. She didn't want to lie to her best friend, but she wasn't ready for the questions the truth would cause.

"Hey, look, there's Dee Dragon again! Maybe I can get my interview today." Jen nearly squealed. She sounded like a fangirl and not a serious journalist.

Too late. Diana was already moving toward them.

Emily tried to make eye contact, hoping she could warn her without words.

Diana froze midmotion. Her gaze darted from Jen to Emily and back, then she abruptly turned and headed back to the bar.

"I'll be back in a second. Have fun with your date." Jen hastened after Diana, or rather Dee, and stopped her.

Emily couldn't understand the conversation, but Diana shook her head.

Jen was persistent and didn't let her go.

Emily caught Diana's gaze over Jen's head and mouthed, "Bathroom," pointing to the far end of the room.

Diana gave a tiny nod.

The line was long, but she squeezed past the waiting women to go to the sink to wash her clammy hands and wipe her neck with a wet paper towel. She hated going behind Jen's back. She shook her head at her reflection. As if that was her only problem. She had to repeat her talk with Diana, and this time she wouldn't agree on pursuing a friendship outside of work. That ship had sailed. She obviously couldn't trust herself to stay on course.

The next band had started playing, and the last woman in line had come and gone, but still Diana hadn't followed her. Should Emily go back out and look for her?

Just as she wanted to give up, the door opened and Diana entered. She closed it and leaned against, holding two bottles of water.

They looked at each other.

Diana's lips twitched with mirth, and Emily giggled. She tried to stop, but the nervous energy bubbled to the surface and exploded in loud laughter. At first, Diana merely grinned, but soon she joined Emily in the near-manic laughter until both had to clutch their sides and Emily was doubled over. Wordlessly, Diana offered her one of the water bottles, and Emily gulped down half its contents. The cool liquid soothed her throat and helped her to gather her thoughts.

"How do we—?"

"Do you want—?"

Both stopped and waved for the other to go first. Another round of laughter threatened, and Emily took a sip of the water to prevent it.

"Do you want to leave? We can sneak out backstage." Diana raked her fingers through her hair. "I'm sorry, this is awkward. I've never wanted my past to intrude so much in our evening."

"It's not your fault." Emily stepped closer, her fingers hovering over the tattoo on Diana's arm. She so wanted to touch it. Would it feel different than the rest of her skin? *What are you doing?* She snatched her hand back as if the flames of the tattoo had burned her.

The talk. She had to do it now or she'd lose focus again. "We...I can't do this anymore."

"What do you mean? Go dancing? Because of Jen?" Diana leaned against the wall opposite the sink.

"Yes. No." Emily drank from the water to gain time to gather her thoughts. "We can't go out as friends. It's obviously not working. Jen has nothing to do with it."

Diana took a moment to answer, studying Emily with an intense expression. "Maybe it's not working because we're supposed to be more than friends."

She wanted to scream *yes* and throw herself into Diana's arms. It took all her rapidly dwindling willpower to remain on her side of the narrow room. The sink dug into her back, a hard and cool anchor to reason. "Nothing has changed. I'm still your mentor."

"Is this really only about work?" Diana's voice was soft now.

It was about so much more, but she had no idea how to say that. If she gave in now and then inevitably fucked up the relationship later, she would hurt both of them. Or she'd disappoint Diana when she found out she had nothing special to give. "I'm afraid," she murmured.

"I get that. I really do." Diana leaned closer, only a fraction, but her presence filled the gap between them with inviting warmth. "But don't you think it's worth it? We could be worth it? Don't you want to know where this could go?" Her eyes blazed a brilliant green in the harsh bathroom light, and her gaze was filled with emotions Emily couldn't name, but they made it impossible to look away.

An almost magnetic attraction pulled Emily to her. Unwilling to fight it anymore, Emily pushed away from the sink and took a couple of steps until she stood directly in front of her, not quite touching. Close enough to feel Diana's body heat. She swallowed, twice. "Yes."

Diana traced Emily's lips with her finger and slowly leaned in to kiss her, giving her enough time to pull back.

Instead, Emily closed the distance herself. Soft lips let her forget everything else.

Diana captured her lower lip, nipping and licking until Emily opened her mouth.

With a sigh, she welcomed the firm strokes and the delicious taste that was all Diana. Her heart raced and nearly seemed to burst as it filled with pleasure and exhilaration.

Loud music intruded into her consciousness and faded again. The door. Someone had opened it.

When Diana cupped her neck and tangled her fingers into her hair, deepening the kiss, Emily lost that thought as fast as it had appeared.

The music swelled as the someone opened the door again. It was cut off when the door slammed shut. "What the fuck, Emily? Dee?"

Jen. Emily jerked back and staggered backward, out of Diana's arms. Jen was standing at the door and stared at them with wide eyes.

"Oh, hi, Jen." What a stupid thing to say. Emily glanced at Diana.

She had spun around at Jen's voice and clutched the sink next to her with both hands, her muscles quivering with tension.

Emily yearned to tell her that everything would be okay, no matter if it was true or not, but she was paralyzed.

Jen's gaze swiveled from Diana to Emily and back. "I thought you're here with your resident?"

No, no, no, think fast. "It's not what you think." Brilliant. That line never helped anyone.

"Okay." Jen's brow furrowed as she waited for an explanation.

"It's complicated." She was resorting to clichés now. She shared a helpless look with Diana, who took a deep breath and held out her hand.

"Hi, I'm Diana. I work with Emily."

Jen fixed her gaze on Diana but didn't take her hand.

After a moment Diana lowered it to her side.

Emily reached for it. The firmness of Diana's touch gave her courage to explain. "Jen, I'm sorry. I couldn't tell you—"

"You mean you didn't want to tell me." Jen's voice became gradually louder. "Have you been laughing at me all this time? Stupid Jen and her hunt for an interview? You're my best friend, and you think you can't trust me. Great. What's our friendship to you?" Before Emily found an answer, Jen turned to Diana. "And you, Dee, Diana, or whatever you call yourself, what game are you playing? Do you think it's funny to come between friends like this?" She whirled around and slammed the door on her way out.

The door hit the frame like a slap in her face. Tears burned in Emily's eyes, and the noises around her receded to a muted buzzing. She was torn between running after Jen and crying right here, right now. Gradually, she became aware of Diana's hand in hers, her thumb moving in soothing circles. She turned to look at her.

Diana's eyes were like large, murky pools in her pale face. "Let's get out of here."

Emily nodded and followed her out of the bathroom, through the crowd, and past the bar. Jen was nowhere to be seen. They collected their jackets in silence and stepped outside.

She sucked in the cool evening air. *Get yourself together.* She clenched her fists and welcomed the pain of the nails biting into her palms. "I need to go after Jen and talk to her."

"Do you think she went home, or should we look in there for her?" Diana pointed back at the club.

Emily shook her head. "No, I'm sure she went home. I need to follow her."

"I'll go with you. It's more my fault than yours." Diana tried to take Emily's hand, but she shook it off.

She needed distance to collect herself. Her mind was useless, like a compass needle at the North Pole, tilting in every direction. She'd always relied on her plans for every contingency, but she had neglected to prepare for this. Operating in emergency mode, she could only think of the next step.

"I've got to apologize. Alone." Emily kicked an empty beer can down the street.

"Let me at least drive you to her place. I can wait outside." Diana's voice was warm and supportive, and Emily wished she could let her help.

Emily slowly backed away, shaking her head. "No." She was torn between wanting to take up Diana on her offer and wanting to turn and run away. "I need some distance. This thing between us, whatever it is, is getting too much, too soon. Nothing went as planned tonight." Everything had spiraled out of control. She stuffed her hands into her pocket so Diana wouldn't see them shaking. *That's why you don't date. Too many conflicting emotions.*

Diana slowly nodded. In the dim light of the alley, Emily couldn't be sure of her expression, but for a moment she looked hurt. "Whatever you need. You can call me anytime if you want me to come. Or if you just want someone to listen."

Emily's throat constricted, and she forced herself to swallow. She raised her hand in a vague thank-you-and-goodbye gesture and turned rapidly before Diana could see her crying. She had to concentrate on Jen now. Fast steps carried her down the crowded street. She weaved between the other people, not really seeing anyone, relying on her instincts not to run into them.

Chapter 12

Diana threw the *Journal of Emergency Medicine* onto the side table and checked her phone. No messages, no emails. She reached for the article again. *Peripartum Cardiomyopathy: A rare but life-threatening condition in the emergency department* was fascinating, but why couldn't it hold her attention? Because she hadn't heard from Emily in three days. She hadn't shown up at work since last Friday. Liz, the attending covering her shifts, said Emily had claimed a family emergency to call in several favors from the other attendings to get a week off.

She had every intention of respecting Emily's need for distance, but it still hurt to be shut out like this. In addition to her own unresolved feelings, she was worried about Emily. Was the conflict with Jen so severe that she needed a whole week to take care of it? Maybe she should call Jen herself to clear the air between them? She hadn't until now because she was afraid of pissing her off even more and pushing her to publish who Dee Dragon was, plus she didn't want to further damage Jen and Emily's friendship.

Not knowing what lay ahead was worse than facing it. She called up Mel's info. Maybe her best friend could help her with the mess she was in. "Hi, Mel. How are you?"

"I'm great, stupidly happy. Being in a new relationship does that to you."

"Congratulations." Diana was happy for her, but this would make the situation more complicated if they were in a real relationship and not just having a short fling. "I'm kinda calling to talk about Jen. Did she tell you how we met last Thursday? Not one of my finer moments."

"She's told me about the fight she had with her best friend for lying, and she was not too happy with me either." Mel chuckled. "We had some long talks, and I guess she gets why you did what you did, even if she doesn't like it. She's promised not to reveal your 'secret identity' for now. But I guess Emily told you that already."

A weight lifted from Diana's chest. She had half convinced herself she would be okay with being outed as a former rock musician at work as long as she could avoid getting fired, but in truth, she didn't want to change the status quo. "Thank you for convincing her."

"No, you can thank your girlfriend. She was quite the champion. Jen said she had never before seen her fight for something like this. If it weren't for her mother, they would probably still be arguing."

"I'm not so sure she's my girlfriend," Diana answered automatically. "Wait, what's with her mother?" Was there really a family emergency? Why hadn't Emily called her? Her stomach dropped. Why should she? It wasn't as though they were in a long-term relationship. They'd barely started anything, no matter how many sparks had been flying between them at the club.

"Oh. Didn't she tell you?" Mel's voice was hesitant.

"No, she's asked for some distance right after it happened on Thursday and hasn't come to work since. I didn't want to call and pressure her. Do you know what happened?" Diana had no idea if Emily's mother was sick or old; she had never talked about how she was doing or where she was living.

"Jen says she died suddenly," Mel said. "Emily is arranging the funeral and going through the papers now. She has refused Jen's help, but they have talked a few times on the phone."

"Oh. Okay. Thanks." Diana hadn't expected anything like that. Her predicament with Jen seemed insignificant compared to the situation Emily was going through. "Do you know if she's all right? Wait, that's a stupid question. Do you know if she's handling it okay?"

"I'm sorry, Jen didn't say. But if she were close to breaking down, Jen would go there, no matter what Emily said. So I guess she's coping for now."

It was reassuring that Jen had obviously set her anger aside to support Emily. "Oh. Okay." Diana tried to laugh, but it sounded more like a cough. "I'm repeating myself. I think I need to hang up now and call her."

"Sure. Take care."

Diana rolled the journal into a tight roll and hit her leg in an increasingly complex rhythm. She shook her head at herself. That wouldn't bring her back on track. She carefully unrolled the journal and tried to bend it back into shape. After calling up Emily's contact information on her phone, she pushed the dial button before she could find a thousand logical-seeming reasons not to do it.

"Barnes."

That wasn't very inviting. Diana hoped Emily hadn't looked at the caller ID before answering.

"Hi, Emily, it's me, Diana."

"Yes, I know. How are you?" The businesslike tone made it clear that it was merely a polite phrase, not a real question.

Don't take it personally. "I've heard what happened. I'm sorry about your mother. Can I help you with anything?"

"No. Thank you. My mother was very organized. Everything is taken care of. I'll be back in a couple of days." She could be talking about an emergency-medicine conference for all the lack of emotion in her voice.

"I was just concerned about you. If you want to talk, just call me. Anytime." It didn't feel like enough, to just offer her an ear and not a shoulder to cry on, but Emily's matter-of-fact tone precluded anything more.

"Thank you," Emily said. "Is there anything else? If not, I'll see you at work in a few days."

Emotions churned in Diana's stomach, and she fought to keep them out of her voice. Emily obviously didn't need or want to be comforted. The rejection hurt, but that was her problem, not Emily's. "No. That's all. I'll be glad to see you again. Take care." See? She could be as polite as Emily.

Emily ended the call without replying.

Diana clutched the phone harder and repressed the urge to throw it across the room. "Fuck!" *Are you really so cold, Emily, or is this part of your formidable wall?*

Emily stalled another few seconds by stowing the phone in her bag and rearranging the bag on the chair next to hers. She squared her shoulders and looked up at the man sitting on the other side of the large oak desk that was built to impress and intimidate. It failed to do both. "I'm sorry for the interruption. You were telling me about the arrangements."

"No problem, Dr. Barnes. As I was saying, your mother was meticulous. She kept her instructions and her will up-to-date." His quiet voice and demeanor were probably meant to be soothing.

It had the opposite effect, and she had to fight the urge to get up and pace the room. She stopped listening to his reading of the detailed papers that represented her mother's need to control everything, even after her death. She would get a written copy and just look at it later.

Emily tried to make a list of people to call. Only a few names came to mind. She had no relatives left, and her mother had made no real friends Emily knew of. She had many acquaintances and colleagues, members of the same charities, but she had always preferred the company of her books to real people. *Just like you.*

"Ahem." Her mother's attorney had reached the end of his papers and was obviously waiting for an appropriate reaction.

She tried to recall the last thing he had said but came up empty. "I'm sorry, I lost focus for a minute."

His features softened with what appeared to be well-practiced compassion.

Emily loathed him for it—and herself even more for the sting of tears in her eyes.

"That's understandable, Dr. Barnes. Take your time with the paperwork; there is nothing you need to do or sign now. Your mother made you part owner a few years ago." He handed her a stack of files and a set of keys. "These are for the beach house. Your mother still kept a few personal things there. Maybe you want to have a look. When you've decided if you want to keep it or sell it, I can help you with the arrangements or recommend someone trustworthy."

"Thank you. I'll sell it. I'll contact you in a couple of days." Emily stood and offered her hand.

Instead of a businesslike handshake, he held hers for a moment too long and patted her arm with what he probably considered appropriate grandfatherly concern.

Blinking back tears, she stiffened, and he withdrew his hands immediately. She took her bag, scooped up the files and keys, and left the room as fast as she could. She only slowed when she reached her car to throw the papers in the back seat. Her hands shook as she turned the keys in the ignition. Biting the inside of her cheek, she willed them to comply. She had no time for such an emotional reaction; she had things to do. Visiting the assisted-living facility where her mother had spent the last six years was the next item on her to-do list. She had already checked off the funeral home and the attorney. When she should have turned south at the next intersection, she found herself going north toward the sea.

The sunlight made her eyes tear, and she searched blindly in her bag for her sunglasses. The blaring of an angry horn returned her focus to the road just in time to steer back to her side of the road. She clenched the wheel harder and forced herself to ease up on the gas. No reason to get killed just because her mother had died.

Chapter 13

WITH THE DISTANCE TO THE town center and the lawyer's office the tension receded from Emily's shoulders. She concentrated on the narrow road. Pines loomed on both sides and cast long shadows, hiding the too-bright sun. She pushed the sunglasses up on her head, switched off the air-conditioning, and opened the windows. Warm air flooded the car, carrying pine and a hint of salt. Emily inhaled deeply. The scent brought back memories of the endless summers she had spent on the beach, reading and talking about books with her father. This time, the tears running down her cheeks weren't caused by the sun.

As she neared the small cottage her parents had bought long before her birth, she got the first glimpses of familiar buildings. At first she thought nothing had changed, but of course, it had. In some places only minor details were different, but in others new houses and even new side streets confused her sense of orientation.

Finally, she arrived at the last house on the street. The cottage looked immaculately kept up, and the parking space was free of weeds. Why had her mother spent money on maintenance of a property she didn't visit anymore? Why hadn't she just sold it?

Emily shrugged. She would have to get rid of it; she had no time for useless sentimentality.

Inside nothing had changed since the last time she'd been here twenty years ago. For that matter, nothing had changed since she could remember, probably even since the day her parents had bought the place. Beige walls, brown carpets, and décor from the seventies. She used to think of it as calming; now the lack of color suffocated her.

Emily ignored the emotions twirling deep inside her. She had work to do, and it was best to stick to the system she'd thought of on her way here. It was always better to have a solid plan, and she mentally checked her to-do list. Cleaning out the cupboards came first. She needed to remove anything personal, broken, or old that couldn't be sold. The next step would be an inventory of the furniture and finally a good deep-cleaning of the house.

With the intention to keep going until she was finished or starving, she tackled the kitchen. No surprises there. She threw away some decade-old cans but left the rest untouched. The bathroom already looked as if it were attached to a sterile hotel room, without any personal touches. The bedrooms were the same, only matching sets of bedding, no old clothes, no forgotten jewelry. It seemed as though her mother hadn't planned to ever return here after her last visit.

The living room looked as bland and empty as the other rooms—until she looked into the sideboard. Several photo albums she had never seen before stood in a neat row. The ugly green faux leather dated them in the seventies or early eighties.

Since when did they have family albums? How could she have missed something like that, growing up? She sat on the rug in front of the gas fireplace and opened one at random. It contained faded pictures of her mother and rarely her father or both at different locations. Sometimes she thought she might recognize famous landmarks like the Grand Canyon or cities like New York and London. They were obviously old holiday pictures. Both looked so young, completely different from the parents she had known. Hairstyles and clothes chronicled her mother's development from a modern, young woman to the settled and conservative librarian she had grown up with. From the style of clothes, she guessed her father's interest in taking pictures had ended in the early seventies.

Emily leafed through album after album until she came to one that was different. Her picture was on the cover. In truth, the baby in the orange-brown onesie lying on a sheepskin rug could be anyone. But her mother had neatly labeled the picture with her full name, date of birth, length, and weight. In the first year were several shots of her lying around in different clothes on various quilts. Underneath each was a date and a name. She recognized some as the names of elderly relatives who had mostly died when she was a kid; some names were completely unknown. Had they

Chris Zett

presented her parents with clothes and gotten a thank-you picture? Emily couldn't be sure. At Christmas, she lay underneath the tree, next to the presents. The next one was of her first birthday with a cake and a single candle. And so the album continued. One picture for Christmas, one for her birthday, every single year. But nothing else. Not her first steps, her first lost tooth, or her first bike.

The memory of the fight she'd had with her mother on her thirteenth birthday rose in her mind. She hadn't wanted to put on the sundress her mother had selected for her picture. In the end, her father had asked her to do it one last time, for him. The dress still showed the wrinkles her mother couldn't remove after Emily had thrown it in the corner of her room. She knew the smile was fake. She looked back at the last few pictures and recognized the same smile in many of them. Had she been happy then? She couldn't remember.

She had never rebelled before or after against the painstakingly long preparations her mother had made her sit through each year. Makeup covered her freckles, and her hair had been straightened and pulled back so the red wasn't so obvious. The clothes were old-fashioned dresses she never wore the rest of the year. After her father had died, they had stopped the tradition, so the album ended with her seventeenth birthday.

The picture captured the last moment of innocence. Her father had given her a car, nothing new or fashionable, but it was special to her. They had been looking at it when her mother had called them inside to take a picture of her with the cake.

Emily had insisted on her father posing with her, a break in the tradition that had left her mother with a pinched mouth as if she'd swallowed a lemon.

She carefully peeled the picture from the page and traced his outline, hovering over the strong hands that embraced her shoulder, his proud smile, and the neat gray hair. In the last thirty years, his features had blurred in her memory. Only his warm voice remained, reading to her at night.

After the photography, they had eaten the cake until her father had gone pale and they had all driven to the ER. Twenty-four hours later he was dead.

Emily's throat constricted, and tears welled up. She threw the album across the room. It hit the wall with a thud, and some of the pictures

140

scattered across the floor. After all these years, she still missed her dad but couldn't shed a single tear for her mother.

She shivered, suddenly feeling cold. She looked around. The room was lifeless, like a picture from an old magazine. Everything was as sterile and vacant as her mother's life had been. And what about her own life?

Finally, the tears came. She pulled her knees up to her breast, hugged them, and buried her face in the soft wool of her slacks.

Emily awoke in darkness. Her head and back hurt, and her nose was stuffed. Groaning, she stood and stretched. After a moment, her eyes got used to the moonlight shining into the cottage. She found her way to the kitchen, poured herself a glass of water, and drank it all at once. She refilled it and took it outside on the small porch. The furniture was in the storage shed, so she sat on the steps leading down to the grass. The cool evening air was a balm to her burning eyes. She was weirdly relaxed after crying and sleeping like a baby. She still missed her dad, but the pain had receded to a manageable dullness. And she was still not grieving for her mother. Her guilt over her lack of feelings lingered, though. She wished someone was here with her, sitting with her on the steps.

Not someone, Diana. The salty air reminded her of the night she had seen her for the first time, playing her drums on the beach. The drummer had been a nameless object for her to project her desire upon. Now she had met the person and missed her personality. She was quick and funny, with a strong sense of who she was and where she wanted to be. Emily wished she could borrow some of Diana's strength and security.

Fear sliced through her. What was happening to her? She had always been independent and emotionally self-reliant. For as long as she could remember, she had never wanted the support of another person. Not even from her parents.

Emily's phone vibrated once in the pocket of her pants. Diana's name glowed in the darkness.

Hesitating, Emily paused her finger over the message icon. Where had her independence led her? Did she really want to end up like her mother? Alone, only connected to books, never to people? She tapped on the message with more force than necessary.

I'm sending good thoughts your way. I hope you sleep well.

Before she could think through the consequences, Emily pressed Diana's name and the phone icon. Her pulse beat twice as fast and loud as the dial tone.

"Emily, hi." Diana's voice was warm and enveloped her like a hug.

"Diana... I... Thank you for your text." Emily stood and walked to the trees lining the property until she reached the cliffs. The old wire fence at the edge was bent and broken in multiple places.

"I know you asked for distance, but I hoped a text would be okay."

"No. I mean yes. It's more than okay. Can I take back my request for distance?" It seemed as if her voice was swallowed by the waves breaking underneath her, so she hoped Diana had understood.

"Of course. It's officially forgotten. How can I help you? What do you need?"

Emily had to lean against a tall pine as her knees turned to mush. She had not driven her away yet. "Talk to me. Tell me about your day."

Diana chuckled. "You don't really want to hear about work, do you?"

As long as I hear your voice. She couldn't say that. "I don't mind. I need to hear about something normal, about something that is not here."

"I get that. Okay, let's see, what happened today..." Diana recounted her day with funny anecdotes.

Emily tuned in and out of the narrative while the soothing voice washed over her. She walked in a wide circle along the border of the property and back to the porch. Afraid to test her newfound serenity by facing reality again, she hesitated to enter the house and sighed.

"Emily? Do you want me to tell you more?"

Emily grimaced. Diana was too perceptive. "No, thanks. I think I have to go back in."

"Can I do anything else?"

"Could you come here?" Shit, had she just said that out loud?

"Sure. Where's 'here'? How long do I need to get there?" Diana sounded as though she was ready to jump in her car immediately.

"I'm a few hours away, close to Port Townsend. What about work? You can't just stay away." Emily's protests were feeble, even to her own ears.

"I finished my night shifts this morning and have a few days off. If we need more time, I'll call in some favors. I've got free days around the Fourth of July; that's enough incentive for most to swap some shifts."

Sinking down on the porch steps, Emily had difficulty believing what she's heard. Diana would call in favors just to be with her? She quickly gave her directions before she could change her mind.

"I'll be there as soon as I can. Take care."

It was after midnight when Diana finally arrived. After an unintentional detour and a short search, she had found the right house. At least she hoped so. The car in front of it looked like Emily's.

She parked next to it, got out, and looked at the dark house for a moment. Neither movements nor sounds indicated that someone had noticed her arrival. The only noises were natural: no cars, no planes, no music. Soft rustling hinted at animals moving through the darkness, and the swishing of the trees in the soft breeze was barely audible. The mild air carried the clean scent of pines and ocean and banished the industrial stench she had encountered on her way that had forced her to close the windows.

Maybe Emily had fallen asleep. An old metal nameplate on the door confirmed it was indeed the right place. After knocking and waiting without result, Diana tried the doorknob, but the door was locked. Maybe Emily had left a door or a window open on the back of the house?

Diana grabbed her overnight bag, locked the car, and walked around the house. The first view of the ocean stopped her in her tracks. Majestic pines surrounded the house and grew nearly to the edge of what probably was the cliffs, but left enough space between them to see the horizon. The reflection of the full moon glistened on the black water, and she had to force her gaze away from the mesmerizing movement of the waves. Stairs led up to a porch.

On her way to the back door, she nearly stumbled over an obstacle in the shadows. A soft and very much alive obstacle.

Sound asleep, Emily lay next to the door beneath a large quilt.

The curled-up bundle triggered a wave of protectiveness, and Diana sat beside her. Waking her up to move inside would be the reasonable thing to do, but she was loath to disturb her rest.

Emily turned and rolled against Diana. "You really came." Her mumbling was barely understandable and followed by a soft snore. Seemingly without waking, she grabbed hold of Diana and laid her head on her thigh.

The light weight anchored her like a calm haven. As Diana's eyes adjusted to the darkness, she studied Emily's features. She'd never seen her so relaxed and vulnerable; it took years off her. Diana couldn't resist trailing her hand through Emily's hair. It was as soft as it looked, like fine silk.

She shifted a little to find a more comfortable position to sit and pulled at the quilt until it covered her legs as well as Emily's. Diana closed her eyes, rested her head against the wall of the house, and allowed the rhythmic breaking of the waves to wash the tension from the late-night drive and the last few days off her. Just five minutes, then she'd wake Emily to go inside.

The cry of some bird woke Diana. A seagull? Disoriented, she opened her eyes and took stock of the situation. Golden light sneaked through the trees and cast long shadows. The last thing she remembered was sitting with Emily on the porch of her mother's cabin. She must have fallen asleep during the night. Now she was lying on her side on the wooden floor. Her front was spooning Emily's back. It was cozy and warm under the quilt, but the arm stretched under Emily's head hurt as if it had been pricked with a thousand needles, and her face was cold and wet from the morning dew. All in all, it wasn't too bad for a night outside. Her bladder was screaming at her to get up, though. She moved slowly and slipped out of her jacket inch by inch, so as not to wake Emily. She left the soft leather as a cushion beneath Emily's head.

But when she stood, Emily turned onto her back and looked at her with big eyes.

Diana smiled. Emily was cute with tussled hair and creases from Diana's jacket lining her face. "Good morning."

An answering smile crept hesitantly over Emily's face. "Good morning."

"I wanted to wake you last night, but I must have fallen asleep. I'm sorry." Diana lifted her arms to stretch and turned a few times from right to left. Her spine popped appreciatively.

Emily blushed and jumped up. "I hadn't planned on sleeping here either." She folded the quilt over her arm, then looked at the house for a moment and bit her lip. "Do you want to go in? Or go directly to a café? I didn't think to bring anything to eat or drink, so we have to find breakfast somewhere else."

Diana looked from Emily to the house and back. While Emily's face didn't give a hint about her preferences, her babbling revealed how uncomfortable she felt. "I'm not too hungry, but I desperately need to use your bathroom."

"Just straight through, you can't miss it." She pointed in the right direction but didn't move to enter herself.

Diana grabbed her overnight bag and found the bathroom without a problem. She first took care of her urgent needs, then washed her face and brushed her teeth at the tiny sink. Her hair was plastered to one side. She needed a shower to make it presentable, but a comb and a hairband would have to do until she could find the time. She chuckled. This wasn't the first night she had woken up unplanned in unusual places. She had thought those days were long behind her.

On her way back she had a quick look around the house. Everything but the living room was pristine, like a hotel room. No clutter or personal stuff left clues about the owner. Had it always been like this, or had Emily done this yesterday? Was there something that had triggered Emily's obvious aversion to going back in, or was it just the general grief of seeing her childhood beach house without her parents? The scattered pictures from several albums all over the floor caught her eye. She carefully picked her way through the mess but hesitated to touch any of the photos. Nothing jumped out at her as unusual.

When she came back outside, Emily had a suitcase open on the porch. Had she gotten it from the car? She had changed into new clothes, a pair of jeans and a hoodie, and bound her hair in a low ponytail. It was the most casual style Diana had ever seen on her.

"Let's go to a diner and grab something to eat. Maybe take a walk afterward." Emily didn't wait for Diana's answer, closed her suitcase, and carried it down the stairs. "Leave the house open. There is nothing valuable in there."

Diana shrugged and followed Emily to her car. She was here to support her. Ignoring the problem would work for a while. "A walk would be great.

I'm still stiff after the long drive and the sleeping on the floor. I guess that's what getting old feels like." Her comment earned her a smile.

Emily had gladly accepted Diana's offer to drive. She was stiff and wrung out, but she assumed that was more due to the emotional strain of the last few days than because of her night outside. Slowly, the memory of waking several times during the night returned. She had felt warm, safe, and serene. Not that she would admit it out loud, but the presence of a warm body to snuggle with had helped her get the best sleep she'd had in ages. Not just any body. Diana.

"Where to?" Diana stopped at an intersection.

Emily quickly gave her directions. Focusing on the once-familiar roads helped her snap out of her musings. The drive into town didn't take long, and the café was empty except for a few older people who appeared to be regulars. Most tourists were probably still sleeping.

Eating in silence, Emily struggled with what to say. She owed Diana an explanation for having her drive here, but she didn't want to have that conversation at a public place. She had the same problem with the other topics such as Diana's past career and Jen's discovery of it. And the kiss. She didn't even want to think of the kiss, let alone talk about it.

She excused herself to visit the restroom. Washing her hands, she stared at herself in the mirror. Most of her makeup was gone, and only dark smudges remained beneath her eyes, enhancing her paleness. She shook her head. She looked like a drug addict. What did Diana see in her? Was this some kind of charity, like her work for the Rainbow Home? She washed her face in the cold water, scrubbing until it glowed with a pink that made her look too childlike. Why hadn't she brought any makeup with her?

Do you really want to go out like this? Her mother's voice cut into her thoughts.

Shut up! She balled up the paper towels she had used and fired them into the wastebasket. *I'm thirty-six and shouldn't care what my mother thinks. My dead mother.*

Emily squared her shoulders and marched out of the restroom without another glance at the mirror. She stopped at the counter to pay the bill. As she walked over to Diana, she had calmed enough that her voice wouldn't betray her. "I need to get out of here. Would you mind going to the beach for a walk?"

"Not at all." Diana rose and grabbed her jacket from the back of the chair.

Emily pointed out familiar landmarks from her youth until they reached the parking lot at North Beach. A couple of other cars were parked there, but they couldn't see any of the owners as they walked to the water. The tide was out, and the sand and gravel stretched for miles along the coast.

Heading east, Emily had to keep her eyes to the ground to avoid looking at the rays of the early-morning sun, but the warmth that spread slowly through her was welcome.

Every few steps Diana picked up something. Sea glass, shells, or small pieces of driftwood. "You must have had a big collection as a child."

Emily snorted. "No, not really. After every summer my mother made me bring it all back to the beach. 'Real memories need no sentimental knickknacks' was her motto. We had no souvenirs at our home. I wonder why she kept the albums." *Great, jump right in.*

"I saw the pictures." Diana hesitated. Did she want Emily to go on? "I guess it was difficult to look at your family pictures."

Difficult was an understatement. "Yes and no." Hurt, anger, and disappointment resided in a tight knot in the depths of her stomach, coated with a generous amount of self-disdain. *Why do I care about the stupid albums?* Emily kicked a piece of driftwood, and it flew a short distance until it got stuck in the sand again. "I have almost no memories connected to those pictures. Most are from a time long before I was born. One album is about me. Two pictures each year, one on Christmas, one on my birthday. That's it. Nothing else." Emily tried to keep her tone neutral.

Diana didn't say anything until she reached Emily's piece of driftwood, picked it up, and turned it around in her hands. "So they weren't into pictures. I'm sure they had other ways to remember. Stories, for example."

"Maybe." They walked for nearly half a mile as Emily considered this. She had never thought about her life as anything but ordinary. She'd had two parents, a roof, warm clothing, and regular meals. Nothing remarkable had happened in her years growing up, so why should they document it? And the most important question was why did it hurt that they hadn't? Diana mentioned stories as an alternative, but they had lacked as well. How could she explain her family to Diana? "You probably have a lot of these embarrassing stories about you growing up that are repeated at all family gatherings and that annoy you, but secretly you enjoy them."

"Sure, with five brothers... Don't we all have them?" Diana looked at her with genuine interest.

Emily kicked at another piece of driftwood, but this time it stayed stuck in the sand, and she nearly fell.

Diana reached out to steady her.

"Thanks." Emily sent her a short smile, but then she looked back down and frowned as she noted the rising heat in her cheeks. Her ears tingled. She had to get it out before the embarrassment melted her skin. "I have nearly no stories like this. One of my father's colleagues always told me about an incident when I was four. I cried through the speech my father made at the party for his sixtieth birthday because I had to wear an uncomfortable dress, but I can't remember the dress, nor do I have a picture of it. My father used to tell me stories about the books he read to me and what my first reactions to them were. My mother never told me anything like that. She never talked about her past with my father either." She tried to gauge Diana's reaction from the corner of her eye.

"It must have been difficult growing up. Where you ever close to your mother?" Diana's tone was merely curious, not judgmental as Emily had feared.

"No. Not really. She wasn't the affectionate type. Not even with my father. I just wonder..." Emily picked up a piece of sea glass. It was pale green, with an uneven, rough surface, factually nothing more than junk that polluted nature. But it caught the sunlight, and the warm glow revealed its beauty.

"What do you wonder?" Diana prompted.

Emily clenched her fist around it and concentrated on the hard sphere biting in her palm. The pain was real, tangible, not like the churning pit of emotions her abdomen had turned into. She forced herself to say it. "I don't know if she loved me, and I won't ever find out."

Diana stopped and turned to her, reaching for her hand. "I'm sorry."

Emily kept walking, away from the temptation of Diana's touch. She didn't deserve Diana's compassion. "Don't be."

With a few long strides, Diana caught up to her. She didn't say or do anything but walk beside her, so close that their arms touched lightly.

Overflowing emotions seeped through cracks in Emily's defensive walls. Diana's silent support helped to plug the leaks, but it wouldn't be enough. Maybe if she let some of it out, only a little bit, the pressure would fall to a manageable level. "My problem is that I don't really care. I don't miss her because we never had a meaningful relationship at all. She was just the woman I lived with until I went to college. I didn't love her; I didn't hate her; I didn't really notice or care if she was home or not. I didn't need her." Her throat was dry, and she had to swallow. Had she screamed?

She stopped and turned to Diana. She hadn't meant to say all of that, but now that she'd started, she couldn't seem to stop. "What's wrong with me? What kind of daughter am I? Why can't I love?" Tears misted her sight, and she wiped them away with sharp movements. She took a deep breath to stuff the rising emotions back where they belonged. But for the first time in her life, she failed to contain them as they burst through a rift in the dam.

Suddenly, Diana was there and hugged her, whispering into Emily's hair. "It's okay. I've got you. There's nothing wrong with you."

Emily shook her head and squeezed her eyes shut more tightly to keep the tears at bay. "I'm a terrible person. Cold. Uncaring. Aloof. And now I'm only crying because I'm sorry for myself. How selfish is that!"

She tried to escape from the embrace, but Diana held her tighter.

"You do care. Or you wouldn't ask yourself these questions. You do care." Diana repeated the last sentence over and over.

The explosion that ripped apart the last barrier to her feelings caused Emily to stumble. Only Diana's arms kept her standing as she cried.

The warmth of Diana's embrace slowly thawed the chill around her heart, and her steadiness grounded Emily.

Emily had lost all sense of time when her body called for attention. Her legs cramped from the stiff posture, and the sun had burned across her right arm and face. She extricated herself from Diana, who patiently waited until Emily wiped her face and blew her nose with a napkin she found in her pockets. She noticed that she still clutched the sea glass in her hand and slipped it into her jeans.

Diana lifted her hand and slowly stroked Emily's sunburned face. Without talking, she took her hand, turned, and led them back toward the car.

Emily followed without comment. Diana taking the lead was what she needed right now. A new tranquility flooded her, and she wanted to bask in the feeling without thinking or making any decisions. She gingerly touched her cheek. It was hot, but the pain was bearable. "I think this is my first sunburn ever."

Emily stuffed the last of the three boxes into the trunk of her car. It was tight, but it fit. Three cardboard boxes full of albums, a small painting, and some books were all that was left of her parents. She carefully placed two old quilts over the boxes. They looked handmade, but she had no idea who had made them. A relative who had died long before she was born, her mother, or had they just bought them somewhere? But they reminded her of summer nights spent reading on the porch, huddled in a quilt to ward off the chill. She closed the trunk with more force than necessary. The large bag with old towels and clothes they had collected from her mother's retirement home went on the back seat. She planned on dropping it off at the Rainbow Home; maybe someone would want them. What was old-fashioned today could be retro or vintage tomorrow.

Who was she kidding? It was junk. But something stopped her from just ditching her mother's clothes.

Diana had been a great help in keeping her focused. Anger, frustration, and embarrassment had threatened to overwhelm Emily. She still didn't miss her mother; she missed the idea of a mother. She needed to accept that it was something she had never had and wouldn't get in this life. She had molded herself to fit her mother's ideals of paleness and silence but had never received an acknowledgment that she'd succeeded in satisfying her. She wasn't sure if her mother had been indifferent or just hadn't been able to express her feelings. She was rapidly vacillating between contempt and compassion for her mother's emotional state and self-disgust and self-pity for her own.

All day Diana had run errands with her and subtly prompted her to share stories of her youth. The more she talked about her mother, the more she had realized how similar her life today was. She planned every detail of her day and liked to control things so that everything went according to plan. Devoting nearly every minute to work, she had no real hobbies, no close friends, no attachments. Nobody wanted to be friends with the control freak, and like her mother, she never left the role of the supervisor at work.

Except for Jen. Did Jen really count? Jen did most of the work in their friendship, and Emily sometimes wondered what Jen saw in her. Emily didn't contact her that often or suggest outings. If Jen hadn't persisted, they wouldn't have become friends in college or stayed in touch afterward, but would be a distant memory the day after graduation.

And now Diana. Diana was different. Yesterday, Emily had asked for her company. She knew she wanted more than friendship, but she was afraid to ask for it. What could she possibly offer Diana in return? She had no experience sustaining a relationship, not even with her own family. All the rational reasons she shouldn't pursue this lingered in her mind all day. Whenever Diana smiled at her, Emily's heartbeat accelerated, and every time she managed to make Diana laugh, she was proud. She was rapidly losing the will to fight against her attraction. So what did it matter that she was an attending and Diana a resident? It wasn't as if she would treat her differently at work. Or would she? She was still in control of her actions, even if her feelings had slipped from the tight reins in the last days.

Emily sighed and closed the door of her car. She had taken too much time to stow her things, and Diana would wonder what she was doing. She had to go back inside and talk to her. About the kiss at the club. And what it all meant. She'd been wrong; she wasn't ready for a relationship. She had no clue what she was doing. Especially with the complication of working together.

Her knees were suddenly too weak to support her, and she leaned against the side of the car to steady herself. Her breath came fast and fogged the window from the outside. Her fingers tingled and hurt as if she had pricked them with a thousand needles. A detached part of her seemed to watch her from afar and stated the diagnosis: hyperventilation and panic attack. She needed to slow her breathing. Her clinical knowledge didn't help her, though. *How the fuck can I control my breathing? I can't even control my thoughts or my life.* Black spots appeared in her line of sight, and a warm feeling spread from her stomach to her limbs, like cuddling in a downy bed. She closed her eyes. She was falling. Falling through clouds. Soft, soft clouds.

"Emily! Emily, don't faint!" The yelling ripped her from the soft clouds back to earth. "Emily, look at me!"

Diana. Diana was calling her, holding her up against the car from behind.

Opening her eyes, Emily tried to turn in Diana's arms.

She gave her a little room to move but stayed close enough that her arms could still support Emily.

Heat burned in her cheeks as she thought about her weakness. She'd nearly fainted. That had never happened to her before. Wasn't that something only silly girls did? She hastily stepped out of Diana's embrace. "I'm fine." That had come out harsher than planned.

Diana looked at her. Her brow was creased in concentration as her gaze wandered all over Emily.

She forced herself not to squirm.

Apparently satisfied with whatever she found, Diana nodded and her frown disappeared. "Okay, if you're sure." Stepping back, Diana softly squeezed her arm and let go.

"I just need some food. We haven't eaten since breakfast." Not that she ate more on a regular workday.

Diana nodded as though that made sense. "Just let me grab my wallet and lock the house." She pointed to the car. "Sit down. I'll be back in a minute."

When she reappeared only moments later, Emily hadn't yet found the will to move.

Diana opened the door and invited her into the passenger seat with a gesture. "Just give me your keys, and I'll deliver you to the food."

Emily thought she should protest. Nobody drove her car. Not another part of her life should be controlled by someone else. She opened her mouth and found she didn't really want to argue. She wanted to let someone else do the driving for now. Even it was only her car.

Emily asked Diana to drive to the same café. Had that been a favorite place for her in her youth, or was the proximity to the house the deciding factor?

During the ride, Emily closed her eyes, but the hard lines around her mouth and eyes showed she was awake.

While they had dinner, Diana waited for Emily to bring up the near collapse. As expected, she didn't. Halfway through their sandwiches, she decided to tackle the topic herself. "How are you feeling?"

"I'm fine." Emily accompanied the statement with a smile that was as fake as the plastic flowers decorating the table.

Diana raised her eyebrows and waited. Did Emily really think she'd believe that?

"Okay, I'm not fine." Emily folded her paper napkin into a neat square, then a series of decreasing triangles. "But I'm getting there. The food helped."

The tension in Emily's expression had softened a bit after the sandwich, but Diana still doubted hunger had been the reason for her hyperventilation. What could she do to help her?

"I'm here if you want to talk about it." Diana rescued the squished napkin from Emily's grip and squeezed her hand.

"Thanks. I know," Emily said with a smile. A real smile this time. "I just need to digest all this for a bit. Let's drive back."

Arriving at the house after another silent fifteen minutes, Diana wasn't keen on immediately hitting the road again for the next couple of hours. "I need to stretch my legs and clear my head before we leave. How close can we get to the sea?"

"Our land has only steep cliffs. Even as a child I wasn't so stupid to attempt to climb down there. But our neighbor has a natural dip and added some stairs. I hope they're still standing." Emily led the way around the house and through the trees to the cliffs.

The moonlight was barely enough to navigate the dark columns guarding the sea. Emerging from the tree line, Diana gasped and stopped to take in the panorama. Night had fallen, and the few pale clouds lingering on the dark velvety background only enhanced the beauty of the stars. The unbelievable amount of stars. The moon had just risen, and the light glinted on the waves rolling to the shore. It was insanely romantic. Resisting the urge to touch Emily, Diana stuffed her hands into her jeans pockets.

After a few minutes of silently walking westward, Emily stumbled, and Diana reached out to steady her. She was reluctant to let go, and Emily seemed to feel the same. They continued holding hands and adjusted their stride as if they'd done this a thousand times before. As promised, the cliffs lowered, and a wooden handrail signaled the beginning of the stairs.

Emily shook the handrail and tested the first step with her foot. "Seems sturdy enough. I guess the neighbors visit their place more often than my mother did." She slowly climbed down.

"Be careful." Diana followed the dark silhouette, relying more on touch than on sight. But the wood under her left hand was solid, and the steps were even enough to navigate without accident.

By unspoken agreement both turned east, toward the moon, and reached for the other's hand again at the same time. Diana enjoyed the silence that felt deliberate rather than uncomfortable and thought about the state of their relationship. Should she bring it up or wait for Emily?

They were both scheduled to work the night shift again tomorrow, and Diana wanted to at least acknowledge their tenuous bond before they returned to the clear boundaries at the hospital.

Would that be too much for Emily, who was clearly preoccupied with the death of her mother? She claimed to be unaffected, but the hyperventilation incident earlier had looked very much like a panic attack to Diana. Obviously, handling the boxes had been emotionally taxing, whatever Emily said. Was it fair to add to that stress? The answer was easy. No, it wasn't fair. She could postpone her own need to process. Her discomfort paled in comparison to the turmoil Emily must be in.

After maybe fifteen minutes, they reached a stonier part of the beach, and, still acting in silent synchrony, both turned to head back and reached for each other's hand simultaneously.

"I like it here. The fresh air, the sky, the stars. I'll miss this when we're back in the city." Diana sighed.

Emily hummed in agreement. "Me too. Waves settle me. I could watch them for hours and never grow tired of them."

"That's how I feel about the stars. At first, you think it's a static picture, but if you watch them for hours, you see the movement, every star and planet in its own course and speed, but still in perfect harmony. Like a dance."

Emily hummed again but didn't comment further. She sounded relaxed. After a few more steps, she sighed deeply. "We should talk about it."

"About your mother?" Diana appreciated that Emily made the first step to opening up.

"No. About work. About...about us, what we are to each other." Her voice was nearly a whisper, and she kept looking at the sand.

"We're friends now and on our way to more." Diana made it a statement, not a question. "And I'd like to see where this is going between us. You said you wanted that too, at the club. Is that still true?"

Emily's hand in Diana's tensed, but she didn't let go. "On our way to more." She said the words as though she had to try the taste of them. "I've never been friends...much less involved with someone from work. I'm not sure how our personal relationship will affect our work relationship."

That hadn't been the point Diana wanted to make, but she accepted that it could be difficult for Emily. "I can only guess how it'll be. In the band, I worked and lived closely with my partner and later ex. It was sometimes difficult when we disagreed on songs; we fought and said things we shouldn't have. In the end, it came all down to respect. We respected our opinions and made it work."

Emily dropped Diana's hand. "That's different. We're not in a band. We won't have time to work out our different opinions with fights or discussions. Medicine is not a democracy. In the end, you're still a resident, and I'm responsible." Emily's voice had turned cold again. She took a few steps back toward the water.

Diana couldn't make out the details of Emily's expression, but she didn't seem angry; to Diana she actually looked a little lost. "I know. That's where the respect comes in. I don't want to take advantage of our relationship to get privileges. I respect your position as my supervisor, your knowledge and experience. I wouldn't expect you to treat me differently from the other residents."

Emily moved closer to Diana as a wave swept farther inland than the others. "You'll resent my scrutiny. No matter how much I like you, I'll still have to check everything you do. I can't trust you just because we're...you know."

The water flowed over Emily's feet, leaving the sand around her wet and full of holes. It retreated before it reached her own shoes.

Working with Emily, Diana had already realized she wouldn't do anything halfway. "I know, and I wouldn't expect you to do anything different. And we can still be professional about our interaction at work. I believe I know my limits and when to ask for help. I wouldn't sacrifice my patients' health or lives for my ego. Your job is to teach me and prevent me from doing harm, and I won't resent you for it. And that leads us back to mutual respect." Diana looked directly into Emily's eyes. It was important for her that Emily saw her sincerity. "I hope you can respect my integrity and work ethic even if you can't trust my knowledge or experience yet."

Emily held her gaze and nodded. "I do respect you." She looked at Diana for a moment before she lowered her head, shrouding her face in darkness. "I can think of a million ways this won't work. I think it would be easier to just remain colleagues for now, without any further complications."

Pain stabbed Diana behind her sternum like a knife. It wouldn't be easier for her. Probably not for either of them. "I don't think it's possible. I like you and have witnessed different sides of your personality outside work. Even if you go back to treating me the way you did during my first week, I won't forget what happened between us." Desperate to connect again, Diana reached for Emily's hand and intertwined their fingers. "I don't think we can go back. And wouldn't it be better to have someone you can trust to know you, to care about you?"

Emily squeezed Diana's hand. "You're right. I can't go back. This is important to you." It wasn't a question. "And to me too." She walked on and let their joined hands swing between them.

Relief flooded Diana and swept away the pain in her chest. "I know that this is neither the right time or place, but I want you to know I'm very attracted to you. I love spending time with you, and even if we seem different on the surface, I feel we have a lot in common. I'd like to explore that attraction if you want to, whenever you're ready." Her heartbeat had picked up during her confession and drowned out the constant beating of the waves against the small rocks in the sea. She hoped that Emily wouldn't notice the sudden clamminess of her hands.

Emily stopped walking again, but this time she didn't let go of Diana. Stepping closer, she looked into Diana's eyes. Her gaze seemed searching, but Diana couldn't tell what she was looking for. Honesty? Affection? Diana hoped she conveyed both.

"I'm feeling the same attraction, but I don't know when or if I'll be ready for it."

Diana's stomach lurched, but she didn't say anything since Emily sounded as though she hadn't finished yet.

"You're right. We can't go back." Emily was so close that her breath caressed Diana's cheeks. "I'm not sure if we should go forward either. There are so many reasons we shouldn't. I'm definitely not ready for anyone at work to know about us. Being the object of gossip and speculation is unacceptable." A hint of desperation colored the last words.

Diana shared her concerns; that was the last thing she wanted too. In a closed community like a hospital, there was a distinct possibility they would end up being the talk of the week until something juicier came along. She was willing to take the risk, but she needed to accept Emily's boundaries.

She locked her gaze with Emily's. "I know what you mean. I certainly can't promise you that this won't happen, but we can minimize the chances. We're responsible adults, not hormonal teenagers. No one will know our thoughts unless we tell them. We'll just keep work separate from whatever else happens in our life."

Emily came even closer, invading Diana's personal space and bringing the already-familiar hint of rosemary with her.

Waiting for her next move, Diana deeply inhaled the soothing scent mixed with saltwater.

Emily raised their joined hands to her sternum and reached with her free hand around Diana's shoulder and tangled it into her hair.

It felt as if they were dancing to the rhythm of the waves, so Diana hugged her around the waist.

"I don't want to end up like my mother. Always afraid what others think." Emily spoke close to Diana's ear. It tickled, sending shivers down Diana's spine. "Always choosing the rational and secure options and finally dying alone."

Diana drew her closer, and Emily caught her breath. "You're not alone."

"Can we go slow?" Emily whispered.

"As slow as we need to," Diana whispered back. Her lips brushed Emily's earlobe. She pressed them together in an effort to resist kissing the soft skin.

Emily sighed and turned her head, inviting Diana closer.

Giving in to temptation, Diana placed light kisses down the slender neck and back up toward Emily's lips.

When she reached them, Emily kissed her back with rising intensity, nibbling and sucking her lips, growing bolder with every second.

Heat enveloped them and melted Diana's bones. She gave herself over to the sensation and got lost in the kiss.

Minutes or hours later both were out of breath; Diana's hair was completely mussed, and Emily's T-shirt crumpled where Diana's hand had roamed over her back.

Diana groaned. "I think we have to work on this going-slow stuff."

Laughing, Emily swatted her arm with one hand. "Maybe slow is overrated. Let's race back, okay?"

"Okay." This time, Diana let her set the pace and followed her back to the house.

Chapter 14

EMILY RUSHED INTO THE STAFF lounge and took the only seat still available between Ian, the attending currently on the day shift, and Liz, her partner for the night. Letting her gaze sway over the group of tired-looking doctors and PAs, Emily wished she belonged to the half of them that was ready to go home for the night.

Directly opposite her, Diana smiled in greeting.

The innocent gesture released a rush of adrenaline.

Don't blush! Emily pulled her notepad and pen from her pocket and turned to Ian, who had started his report. His monotonous voice relaxed her enough to focus. Using an insane amount of willpower, she kept her gaze on him. He resembled a spider with his gangly long arms and legs and his unfashionable thick glasses.

"Have a good night. See you tomorrow." Ian stood and waved to his fellow colleagues. The rest of the day shift followed him like eager ducklings. No one wanted to linger any longer than necessary.

Having survived turnover without embarrassing herself was step one. Step two would be worse.

As everyone stood to tackle the new shift, she remained rooted to her seat. The burden of doubts and worries weighed heavily on her and pressed her deeper into the cushions.

"Liz, do you have a minute?" Proud of her even tone, Emily half turned to her left.

"Is this about your family emergency? Are you okay?" Her eyes full of concern, Liz sat back down.

"No, no. Work." Emily swallowed. "It's about work."

"Sure. What can I do for you?" Liz blew on her still-full mug of coffee.

"I... You... Usually..." Emily clicked her pen between each word. Last night on the drive back to Seattle, the conversation she needed to have had been clear in her mind. Now only snippets remained in her memory like a rare glimpse of a road sign in the fog.

Her head tilted to her side, Liz slightly raised her eyebrows and waited.

Click. "We should restructure the supervision of the residents." Click. Click.

"What do you mean?" Liz sipped her coffee.

"Usually, I take on the new residents." Click. "But maybe it's time to reconsider that approach." Click. "Share the responsibility." The thought of giving up control had her breaking out in a sweat.

"Okay."

"What do you mean, okay?" Click. Emily had no idea if Liz understood her request. She barely made sense to herself. Click.

Liz reached over and gently pried the pen from Emily's hand. "We've worked together for quite some time. Six years, seven? And I never saw you do anything halfway. Always demanding mathematically impossible two hundred percent not only of your residents, but of yourself too. No one can keep this up forever. So, okay, let me take over some of your workload."

Her first instinct was to protest. Blaming the workload as the reason hadn't even occurred to Emily. She only wanted to step back as Diana's supervisor and certainly not because it was too strenuous. The problem lay in separating work from her private life and feelings, but she couldn't say that, so she nodded.

"How do you want to do that?" Liz expression was open, friendly. Not at all judging.

Asking for help had never been Emily's strength. From an early age, she had learned to solve her problems independently. But Liz's easy acceptance made it surprisingly painless. "Could you please take over as Diana's supervisor?"

"Diana? I hadn't expected it to be her." Smiling, Liz leaned back.

"W-what do you mean?" Did Liz suspect something? Emily forced herself to hold her gaze, even though she wanted to jump up and pace.

"Nothing. I'd love to help." Liz handed back Emily's pen and stood. "See you later."

┼┼┼┼┼┼┼

Diana stepped out of the hospital and blinked as the sunshine hurt her eyes. After a twelve-hour night shift surrounded by artificial lights, she wasn't up to more brightness. She searched for her sunglasses in her backpack and heard more than saw someone stepping up close behind her. "Sorry." She moved to the side of the entrance she was blocking. When the other person didn't go past her, she turned around.

"Hi." Emily had her sunglasses in place, but they couldn't completely conceal the pale purple shadows under her eyes.

Had she slept at all since yesterday? Diana hadn't.

They hadn't returned to Seattle until well after midnight and had gotten separated when Diana had stopped for gas and missed getting on the same ferry as Emily.

Keyed up from their talks and too much caffeine on the road, Diana had played drums until sunrise to clear her head.

Emily didn't look as though she'd found more rest.

They hadn't gotten to work together today, always missing each other like passing ships in the middle of the night. Diana didn't know if it was Emily's intention or something else that had paired her for the night with Liz.

"Hi." Diana searched for something meaningful to say, but her overtired brain wasn't very original this morning. "Are you driving home?"

"I'm walking. It takes me a few night shifts to get into the rhythm, and I'd rather not kill anyone on the street in the process. And you?"

Diana laughed. "I used to be a night owl, but it seems I've lost that trait over the last few years. I'm with you. Do you want to walk through the park together?"

They reached the park after a few blocks. Luckily, it was still relatively empty. Most outdoor enthusiasts would arrive later, so they nearly had the park to themselves, except for a few early-morning runners.

"Maybe I should plan to get a good run in tomorrow morning after work," Diana said as the third runner overtook them.

Emily playfully hit her on her arm. "Shush. Don't make any plans. You'll attract catastrophes to work tonight."

Diana snorted. "I can't believe it! You're superstitious."

"No, I'm not. It's not superstition; it's the law. You know that." Emily tried to remain serious, but a twitching corner of her mouth gave her away.

"Like sitting down with something to eat and wishing for a ten-minute break?"

Emily nodded. "Exactly. As soon as you say it out loud, an ambulance arrives."

They both laughed, and the tension that had been building all night lifted from Diana's shoulders. Emily hadn't retreated into her shell.

"Speaking of something to eat... Do you want to go for breakfast?" Diana wasn't hungry, but she wouldn't mind spending more time with Emily.

Emily stopped walking and turned to her. "Can I have a rain check? I'm really, really tired."

"Sure. I won't have a problem falling asleep today either." Diana smiled. It was a good sign that Emily didn't just brush her off.

They walked without talking until they reached the end of the park. The silence was comfortable and soothed her exhausted mind that had been running in overdrive all night.

When they both hesitated at the exit, Emily was the first to break the silence. "This is where I need to turn right."

Diana smiled. So she wasn't the only one too tired to be original. "I can almost hear my bed calling from here." She kissed Emily on her cheek and hugged her. "Sleep well."

"You too." Emily held on to her for a moment.

Diana breathed in the herbal scent of her hair and was reluctant to let her go, but her own bone-deep wariness and the knowledge that Emily was probably feeling the same prevented her from prolonging their conversation.

After a couple of days, Diana had found a new routine. Twelve hours of work at night, a walk back through the park with Emily, seven hours of deep sleep, a refreshing shower, and finally a meal she wasn't quite sure what to call. Breakfast? Dinner? As long as it had enough sustenance to get her through another night of work, she didn't care.

Tonight she was early and decided to catch the last rays of sunshine in the park before work. She texted Emily her plan and received an immediate reply.

I'm already here. Meet me at the lake.

Diana smiled. Emily surprised her now on a daily basis, and it had all been good so far.

Ten minutes later she found Emily sitting sideways on the wide stone border. She was barefoot, and her jeans were pushed up to her knees. One foot rested in the water, and the other leg was drawn up to her chest. She wore sunglasses and had her face angled to the sun. Diana couldn't quite put her finger on it, but something apart from her casual clothes was different.

"You look relaxed." Diana sat close to Emily's foot and mirrored her posture. "Hi."

"Hi. Good to see you." Emily smiled and turned her head slowly in Diana's direction. "Do you mind if we sit here for a while? Sometimes I think I see more daylight during the night shifts than during regular hours. Normally, we would still be at work."

Diana hummed in agreement and bent down to remove her own shoes. "We probably shouldn't think about what lives in the water." She wriggled her toes and sent small waves toward Emily's foot.

"No, definitely not. Let's just pretend we're back at the seashore." Emily closed her eyes again and tilted her head back up.

Diana used the opportunity to study her close up. The hair was the same, the smile not really different, but Emily seemed younger and more carefree. Her eyes were without shadows for the first time in the last week, and her skin had a healthy glow, dusted with freckles. *That's it, she's not wearing makeup.* Diana wondered if she should say something because it was an important change for Emily and she wanted to tell her how stunning she looked without the artificial enhancements. On the other hand, she didn't want to make her feel self-conscious. She shook her head. Now, that was overanalyzing. She closed her own eyes to soak up the sunshine.

"Everything okay?" Emily's question was tentative.

"Yes. Why?"

"You just seemed...unhappy a minute ago."

Busted. They were getting to know each other better, but Diana wasn't ready to tell her the truth. "Only about my thoughts." She pulled her foot from the water and retrieved her shoes. "Do you know what I need right now? Ice cream."

Emily picked up her shoes as well. "Great idea. And I know just the place."

Maybe that had been not such a bright idea before work, Diana thought as Emily licked her tiny spoon. The salted caramel seemed to evoke sighs and moans that sounded too close to satisfaction from another source of stimulation.

She concentrated on the refreshing tartness of her own rhubarb yogurt ice cream until she noticed that Emily had a bit of ice cream left on her cheek.

"You have something right here." She pointed it out.

Emily tried to reach it with her tongue but kept missing it.

Uh-oh. Not such a bright idea. That image sparked her imagination and led her thoughts in an inappropriate direction. They were in a public park, and Diana had to end this before she gave in to the impulse to kiss Emily.

She wiped away the ice cream and licked her finger. "Hmmm. Good." She deliberately didn't do it in a provocative or sexy way, but Emily immediately blushed.

"No, no." Emily pulled Diana's hand down. "You can't do that to me. Not here."

"What? Nothing a parent wouldn't do for her child." Diana pointed to a father who wiped his little boy's chocolate-smeared face with a paper napkin.

"Because you neither look nor feel like a parent to me." Emily laughed and started walking toward the south side of the park and their final destination of the evening.

"Okay. I'll behave. As long as you promise not to eat any more ice cream right before work."

"Deal."

Emily saw Liz leaning at the nurses' station and slowed down. Maybe she would leave and Emily could avoid another awkward conversation. Their talk the other day had opened the floodgate of social interactions.

Liz just nodded in greeting and remained focused on the computer screen.

Suppressing a sigh of relief, Emily mumbled a hello and checked the lab program at the other terminal. Still nothing. She ground her teeth. "What are they doing down there? Sleeping?" *Maybe I need to call and kick some ass.*

"They're short one lab tech tonight. Summer flu." Liz stretched her arms over her head and yawned.

Emily immediately yawned too. Four hours of sleep hadn't been enough today, but snippets of her talks with Diana at the beach house kept replaying in her mind.

"Coffee?" Liz closed the program she was working on with a few clicks.

Emily nearly jumped. She was unsure how to answer. Would sharing a cup of coffee lead to personal talks? Her old self would have refused, but she had promised herself to be more open. "I could use some caffeine."

"Let's go to the coffee shop and get some of the good stuff for everyone." Liz walked past the waiting room.

Emily followed warily. The room was eerily quiet and empty except for a couple who was waiting in the corner, probably relatives of someone. They looked up but didn't seem concerned when they just walked by. She usually avoided walking past the waiting room, afraid to be accosted with demands from patients and family members.

They entered the coffee shop on the side of the main entrance hall. It was a miniature version of a larger chain and open twenty-four/seven. Liz ordered a mixture of regular coffees, cappuccinos, and lattes for everyone.

"And a tea, please."

The young guy behind the counter grunted and pointed at the list of iced teas. Cold and sweet wasn't what she needed now. She scanned the board for the least-offensive coffee creation.

"Okay, no tea. A chai latte for me."

She searched her pockets for the few bills she kept for emergencies.

Liz lightly elbowed her away and handed over her credit card. "Next time is on you."

They sat at one of the empty tables to wait.

"So, how does it feel?" Liz said, playing with a stack of sugar packages.

Great. Now the interrogation was starting. Emily looked longingly at the door. Too bad fleeing wasn't socially acceptable. "What do you mean?"

She was stalling for time. How long could their order of a dozen fancy coffees take?

"Sharing your workload with me. Letting go of the control." Liz seemed genuinely interested and not condescending.

Emily leaned back. She'd thought for a second that Liz would ask her about Diana. Work was something Emily was willing to talk about, even if they skirted uncomfortable topics. She knew intellectually that most of the other attendings and all the residents thought she had a problem with giving up control. Which was true, she admitted to herself. Hearing it spoken out loud wasn't something she was proud of anymore. "It feels surprisingly good. I didn't know how much stress I was causing myself until recently."

Liz grimaced. "I hear you. We can be our own worst bosses. Nobody judges us as harshly as we judge ourselves."

"It's not only that. I didn't trust anyone to do a good job if I wasn't checking everything twice. I've always assumed all of you don't take the job as seriously as I do." Emily cringed. That was insulting, even though she hadn't meant it to be.

Liz only raised her eyebrows and regarded her calmly.

Emily raised her hands, palms outward. "I know, I know. That's bullshit. Why shouldn't you perform your chosen profession as good and conscientiously as you can? Why spend years and years studying and working hard if you didn't care?"

"Exactly." To Emily's relief, Liz didn't seem to take her confession personally and just continued to smile at her.

Emily wasn't sure if she should elaborate or leave it like this. Talking to Liz was easy. If she had known how helpful it was to discuss her situation at work with a colleague, she would have done it years ago. On second thought, maybe not.

Opening up had never been in her repertoire, neither with her parents nor with Jen. Her parents had never encouraged her to share her problems, and later she had been stuck in the habit and had been too proud and independent to ask anyone for support.

Now she had to figure out how to let go. She had no idea how she could implement the practical application of her newfound insights into her daily life.

"Coffee is ready!"

She jumped up and grabbed a cardboard tray full of drinks, relieved she could get out of the conversation now without further awkwardness.

"Hey, coffee! Thanks," Madison called out as they arrived at the nurses' station. She reached for one of the cups.

From every corner of the ED the staff members came and helped themselves to the drinks. Emily set the box on the counter and took her own chai latte. She would have preferred to drink it on her own in the staff lounge or her office, but it would have been impolite to leave Liz alone right now.

"Thank you. Just what I need." Peter reached past her to get one of the last cups. His hair looked a bit flat on one side, and a crease ran over his cheek as though he had rested his head on something.

"It was all Liz's idea." Taking the credit felt dishonest. Emily hadn't even though about doing something like this before.

The resident just nodded and sipped his coffee with a grateful smile.

"Hey, Peter, did you leave something for me?" Diana's voice came from directly behind her.

Emily forced herself not to spin around and waited until Diana had walked around her to the counter. She looked up to meet Diana's gaze.

She just smiled, mouthed, "Thank you," and sipped her coffee. Her conduct was completely appropriate for the work environment, but her eyes held affection that warmed and invigorated Emily more than any caffeine.

Diana was lying in wait in front of a curtained examination area. How long could Liz take to talk to a patient? She checked the clock on the wall again that stubbornly insisted that only a minute had passed. Diana hated running late.

The last few days she had always finished work before Emily and lingered in front of the entrance so that they seemed to meet by accident. They had never talked about waiting for each other, but she hoped Emily wouldn't leave without her.

As if conjured up by her thoughts, Emily turned around the corner, already wearing street clothes. She looked at the same clock and back at Diana. "Still working?"

"I'm waiting for Liz to sign off on my last patient." Diana shrugged. "No idea how long it'll take. Do you need to leave now?"

"Has Liz already seen the patient?" Emily asked.

"No need. It's just bronchitis." Liz gave her more leeway at work and let Diana decide if she needed to see the patient or not, but she still had to sign them off.

Emily hesitated. "Why didn't you ask me if Liz's busy?"

Diana hadn't wanted to bring it up at work, but maybe they had to talk about it sooner rather than later. "I'm not sure if you want me to, unless we have an emergency. You never said anything, but the recent change of work distribution between you and Liz is kind of obvious. If you want to keep your distance at work, I don't mind."

Emily blushed. "I'm sorry. I didn't want you to feel as if you couldn't come to me. I haven't figured out how to do this properly. Here. At work." She waved her hand between them and the rows of curtained cubicles. "But you shouldn't have to work overtime because of it." She reached for the chart and went to the computer terminal at the end of the room. "Anything special I need to know?"

"No. Standard case. Fifty-five-year-old male, kept on working through a cold until he couldn't stop coughing long enough to go to sleep. His wife brought him in after another sleepless night. He's stable; clinical examination, X-ray, and blood work match. I started him on antibiotics."

Emily had logged in and signed the paperwork before Diana had finished her explanation. "I'll wait outside."

Even if it was only bronchitis, it was a new development that Emily trusted anyone enough to sign off on a patient she hadn't seen herself. Was it because of their relationship, or was Emily changing?

Diana returned the chart to the nurses' station and tried to avoid looking directly at Courtney, who lingered there and talked to Tony. She'd learned the hard way that Courtney leaped on every perceived invitation to chat.

Tony jumped up from his chair and nearly pulled the chart from her hand. "Finished? Should I go and give him his papers?"

"Sure. If you've nothing else to do. Thanks."

Tony grinned and rolled his eyes in Courtney's direction. "You're welcome." He hurried off toward the examination room of her last patient.

Diana just nodded at Courtney and walked in the direction of the locker room. Her hope of a fast escape was destroyed by an overly loud and drawn-out call of "Di!"

She scowled and turned around. "Courtney. You know I don't like to be called that." She liked her mother, but she didn't know if she could forgive her for naming her after a famous member of the British royal family.

"Oooh, the princess is testy this morning. Bad night?" Courtney walked over to her. "Do you want to get some coffee and talk?"

"No, I'd better get going." Diana had just looked over the electronic whiteboard. It hadn't been full yet, but several patients showed an empty field next to their name where a physician should be assigned. "Don't you have patients to see now?"

Courtney rolled her eyes. "Nothing urgent. They can wait. Let's go to the coffee shop and catch up."

"I'm sorry, but I have to go. Someone is waiting for me." Of course, she wasn't sorry at all, but it never hurt to be polite to the department gossip.

"Ooh, a hot date?" Courtney took her arm and pulled her toward the locker room. "Come on, you can tell me all while you change."

Shit, now she had sent her on the right track. Diana had to cut this off before rumors started. She forced her features into an unconcerned smile. "Sorry to disappoint. I'm only meeting my electrician, and I'm not into middle-aged, bald guys."

Courtney let go of her. "Okay. How boring. See you tomorrow."

"No, see you in three days." Diana's laugh was genuine now. "I'm finished with nights and have a few days off before I return to the day shift."

She hurried to change and leave the hospital before anyone else could interrupt her. She couldn't stop grinning. She was free of work; the sun was shining, and a beautiful woman was waiting for her. Life was good.

Chapter 15

EMILY SHUFFLED HER CHAIR A little to the right, slipped off her shoes, and eased back the backrest. Perfect. She was pleasantly full after their breakfast of fresh fruits and a large croissant. She shifted closer to Diana's chair until she was completely in the shadow of the triangular white cloth Diana had hung between the house and a tree to ward off the sun. She studied the pattern of little holes that were left after some stitching had been removed. "Is that a sail?"

"Mmmh." Diana sounded as relaxed as Emily felt.

"Yours?" There was so much they didn't know about each other.

"No. Just something I found in a secondhand store." Diana turned onto her side to face Emily. "I never learned to sail. Do you?"

"Sail? No. My parents thought it was too dangerous. And my mother wasn't keen on being outdoors too long." *Looks like a sailor* had been one of the worst judgments her mother had to offer if someone was tanned.

She traced the tiny points of light that broke through little holes in the sail. A straight line ran from her stomach over the wooden armrests of both their chairs onto Diana's arm and swung back again in a wide arch. Maybe a *D* or a *B*. Diana's skin was soft, and goose bumps erupted in the wake of Emily's finger. She looked up.

Smiling, Diana watched the finger's movement.

To see how she would react, Emily decided to reverse the path.

Diana's smile deepened, and she closed her eyes. If she were a cat, she probably would have purred by now.

Emily traced a vein on the muscular forearm and decided to follow the tendons next. She hooked her finger under the ball of the thump and slowly turned the hand around until it rested palm up. The soft skin gave way to several rough bumps on the middle of the fingers, next to the thumb, and on Diana's palm. The skin wasn't irritated, broken, or red, so the calluses had to be older. They intrigued Emily.

"They're from playing drums." Diana's voice was barely audible, but Emily thought she detected a hint of insecurity. "I've had them for over twenty years. I guess they won't go away anytime soon." She tried to turn her hand, but Emily held it open with soft pressure.

"I like them. They're you." Emily leaned forward and placed a soft kiss on the callus next to the thumb.

Diana stroked her cheek, and different textures glided over her skin. She had to hold back from leaning in to the touch. Diana's hand tensed slightly and lifted Emily's head. Had it been too much, too soon?

Emily looked up just in time to see Diana move closer. The smile told her it hadn't been too much, and then she stopped analyzing her behavior as Diana's mouth met hers.

Her lips were softer than she remembered. After a minute of tentative pecks and licks, Diana kissed her harder, and heat shot from Emily's mouth to her core.

She tried to move closer and was stopped by something hard against her abdomen. She didn't care and pushed closer still.

Diana seemed to have the same idea and twisted in her seat to put her arms around Emily. "Ow." Diana pulled back, breathing fast. "Stupid armrest!" She rubbed her middle and laughed.

Emily fell back against the chair and joined in her laughter. "Not such a good idea."

"Oh, I liked the idea, but we have to work on the details." Diana looked from one chair to the next. "I guess both of us won't fit on one of them. I hadn't thought of that when I went furniture shopping."

"No? No rating according to style, comfort, and make-out possibilities?" Hiding her real feelings for a moment behind the banter took the pressure off Emily. The kiss had been intense, and she hadn't cared about the armrest or anything else. It wasn't like her to lose awareness of her surroundings, and that frightened her a bit.

"Mmmh. I must definitely take you with me next time." She sat up straighter and stretched.

Emily couldn't help staring at the skin revealed by her shirt riding up. *Since when are you ogling anyone? What's wrong with you?* No, she corrected herself, not anyone, but Diana. Diana who hadn't let herself be driven away and was on the verge of becoming her girlfriend. *If you only let her.* "We can do some tests now. You know, scientific research."

Diana looked at her and blinked. "You want to go furniture shopping now?"

"No." A flush spread out from Emily's neck to her cheeks. Flirting was something she'd never initiated before, but it felt natural with Diana. "I want to test your other furniture so that we have a basis for comparison."

Her furrowed brow was replaced by a sexy grin as Diana caught on. "Oh yeah. I've got a nice couch, a few armchairs, and a bed. I'm all for research."

Bed? Emily's heart skipped a beat. Heat that had nothing to do with the sun melted her brain into a useless puddle.

Diana stood and offered her hand to Emily. When she accepted, Diana pulled her to her feet and into her arms. "We can take it as slow as we want to. Proper research takes time."

Strong arms encircled her waist, and a sense of security and trust flooded through Emily. Knowing that Diana would support the pace she needed gave her the freedom to move forward.

Emily leaned in for another kiss. She couldn't get enough of those lips and the way Diana caressed her back.

Her taste and scent mingled in Emily's mouth, and she couldn't find a description that fit. Some traces of strawberry lingered after their breakfast, but mostly Diana tasted uniquely of herself. And what an intoxicating taste it was. Emily buried her hands in Diana's hair to draw her closer. She just wanted to lie down and get lost in her. They both came up for air at the same time.

"Furniture testing?" Emily asked.

"Inside, now!" Diana said at the same time.

The door to the deck wasn't wide, and they barely fit while holding hands, but neither of them seemed to want to let got. Emily bit her lips to suppress a giggle. She felt like a teenager on her way to an illicit make-out session. Not that she had ever done anything like that as a teenager.

Diana steered her to the couch, sat, drew Emily down next to her, and immediately kissed her again.

How could each kiss be better than the last? She had never understood the appeal of kissing in her previous short relationships. It always had been messy and slightly awkward. Now she knew. Each kiss was different, but they all had the most important aspect in common: Diana.

Their bodies touched along their sides, which was an improvement on the deck chairs. Emily still needed to get closer. She held on to Diana's shoulders and raised herself a little to bring their upper bodies together. *Wow. So much better.*

Diana sighed, and her hands slowly wandered down her back until they rested on her butt, half supporting Emily's position, half caressing her.

Emily didn't know where the idea came from, but she wanted to straddle Diana. She hesitated for a second and then just did it. She moaned as she slid into place. They touched all along their bodies; her legs cradled Diana's, their breasts skimmed, and Diana's arms wrapped completely around her. She had never done anything so forward before. The excitement made her light-headed, and she stopped kissing to lean her head against Diana's.

They were breathing fast, and Emily had the sudden vision of herself hyperventilating until she fainted. This time, she couldn't suppress a laugh.

Diana looked perplexed for a few seconds, but then she joined her.

"So, Dr. Barnes. What is your scientific evaluation of my couch?" Diana slid her hands lightly up and down Emily's spine over her bare skin.

When had she moved them under her shirt? Maybe it was a good idea to slow down a little to get back some control. Emily examined the back cushion with a mock-serious expression. She patted the dark gray canvas and slid her hands along the thick seams and the boxy corner. Then she pushed first one leg and then the other against the seat as if to test its firmness and noted the effect the movement had on Diana.

She groaned, and the stroke on Emily's back turned into a firm grip on her hips.

To tease her some more, she pushed down with both legs simultaneously. Heat shot to her core as her crotch connected with Diana. They both leaned in for another kiss, this time with increasing passion.

Gasping for air, Emily leaned back again. The idea to tease Diana had backfired, not that she minded much. "Well, Dr. Petrell, the couch has sufficient make-out potential, at least in one position. I guess the result is inconclusive without further studies."

"Mmmh. Further studies." Diana resumed her light stroking up and own Emily's back. "Maybe a variation of the variables could be a good idea."

Emily tried without success to concentrate on the conversation and not on Diana's fingers that had reached the edge of her jeans and slowly dipped beneath it. The touch sent shivers up her spine. The good kind of shivers. "Maybe. Do you have a suggestion?"

"I thought of a reversal of the parameters." The corners of Diana's mouth twitched, but otherwise she managed to remain serious.

Emily licked her lips; that twitch just asked to be kissed. "Reversal?" Uh, not such a clever answer.

Diana just grinned as her hands clutched Emily's hips. "Reversal."

That grin meant trouble. What was she up to?

Diana prompted Emily to lift up and guided her to lie down on the couch on her back. Slowly, she crawled over Emily, giving her enough time to stop her, and lowered herself inch by inch.

Protest was furthest thing from Emily's mind, and she lifted her head to kiss Diana again. Now their bodies were touching from head to toe. Emily moaned. Had she ever felt so good before? They fit as if they were made for each other. Emily's body seemed to move without her directions. Her hands roamed all over Diana's back and ass. One leg slid out and wrapped around the small of Diana's back to press her even closer. Where had all this passion been hiding until now? The next kiss wiped all self-analytical thoughts from her mind.

Emily didn't know how much time had passed when they both came up for air. She loved that Diana was as breathless as she was. She groaned as Diana lifted up on her arms and her leg pressed harder against her crotch. Was she as wet as Emily was? Was that even possible? The urge to find out was nearly irresistible, but she hesitated to explore further. She had never before considered herself passionate. Sex with her lovers had been more about curiosity, and satisfying herself had always been merely a fulfillment of a bodily requirement, like eating or sleeping, never this out-of-control need. Heat crept up Emily's neck. Was this the same for Diana?

Diana's lips were moving, but it took a moment for Emily to hear her over the pounding of her pulse in her ears. "We're not going slow anymore."

Slow. Why had she ever thought that slow was a good idea? Struggling to come up with an answer, she suddenly yawned. Heat shot to her face. Had Diana noticed it?

Diana rolled on her side and giggled. "I'm crashing too."

"I'm sorry. It's just the night shift and…" She unsuccessfully tried to stifle another yawn that Diana immediately mirrored. "I feel as if all my systems are overloading and shutting down. Maybe I should go home."

"Or you could stay." Diana reached for her hand. The soft strokes were hypnotic. "I'm not talking about sex. I'd rather be fully awake to enjoy it. But you could stay on the couch or in my bed, just sleeping. I'm sorry, I haven't set up the guest room yet."

Diana's offer was tempting. Sleeping in the same bed sounded very intimate, more so than sex. Now that her libido was succumbing to weariness, Emily feared she might not be ready for that. "The couch sounds like a good idea. If it's not too much trouble."

"No trouble at all." Diana's smile was brilliant as she sat up. She removed a book and a few journals from the large wooden chest that served as her couch table and opened it. Inside was a cushion, a stack of sheets, and a neatly folded blanket. "I've everything you need right here. I'll leave a new toothbrush and a T-shirt in the bathroom." She hurried away, presumably to do just that before Emily could protest.

Emily stood and stretched. Why should she protest? If she was honest with herself, she liked being here. Diana's house had an open floor plan that gave the impression of it being much larger than it was. As much as she liked her own apartment full of books, sometimes it isolated her like an ivory tower. Emily took the oversized cushions from the couch and stacked them on the floor before she spread one of the sheets. It was soft like Diana's skin, only cooler. She snorted. Not really comparable, but currently all her thoughts revolved around Diana. *And if you're honest with yourself, she's the reason you want to stay, not the house.*

Diana returned, dressed in a different T-shirt and plaid PJ bottoms, carrying a nearly identical outfit for Emily. "Do you need anything else? Tea? Water? A book?"

Emily shook her head. "I'm fine. Thank you."

Diana stepped closer and kissed her on the cheek. She smelled of a simple soap. "Sleep well. Sweet dreams."

"You too." Emily kissed her back. It was sweet and chaste compared to what they had done before, but her heart skipped a beat just the same. "See you later."

Diana turned onto her side and extended her arm to reach the alarm clock. Ugh. Only four p.m. She'd slept enough to feel relaxed and reenergized, but not enough to get her through another night shift. Turning onto the other side, she willed herself to go back to sleep, no matter what her internal clock insisted on doing instead. *Wait. The night shifts are over.* She jumped out of bed, keen to spend the rest of her day moving, preferably outside. *Emily.* The thought slowed her gait to tiptoeing. Three hours obviously weren't enough for her brain, even if her body seemed relatively awake. On her way to the bathroom, she paused to listen for a noise indicating that Emily might be up, but the regular breathing hadn't changed since she'd stepped out of the bedroom.

While she brushed her teeth, Diana contemplated what to do now. Should she wake Emily? What was her routine on a day after night shifts to reset her circadian rhythm? She knew many personal details Emily probably hadn't shared with many others but had no idea about the most mundane things. Their relationship had progressed in leaps and bounds from colleagues to friends to something more—lovers or girlfriends—all without following the usual steps that included the getting-to-know-you small talk parts. She spit and took some extra sips of the fresh water. *We need to remedy that, soon.* She smiled. Maybe they could put their days off to good use.

Back in the bedroom, Diana opened her closet to look at the clothes, still undecided. Usually, she'd go running in the park, but that option was off since she had a guest sleeping on her couch. On the bright side, that left out cleaning, washing, and doing the dishes. Reading would put her back to sleep, and then she'd have trouble adjusting to the day shifts again. That left her with only one method of acquiescing to her urge for movement.

She pulled jeans and a tank top from the closet, dressed, and tiptoed to the kitchen to fill her largest bottle and a glass with water. She left the glass on the table next to Emily, adding a note that she was in the garage and how to get there. Emily had turned her face into the cushion, and her hair spilled over the edge of the couch. Diana wanted to touch it, to stroke the silkiness, but she forced herself to leave. Emily hadn't slept much the last few days and needed any minute she could get.

Diana detoured to pick up a pair of trainers, then left the living room via the deck. She had to chuckle as she found the remains of the breakfast where they had left them. She shrugged. Her mind hadn't been on housekeeping duties, and now they could wait some more.

The two-car garage had a door in the back that she preferred. The detached building with thick walls and an unusually high ceiling had been one of the selling points for her, next to the deck and the small garden. She had renovated it completely, putting in a new floor to remove the oils stains, high-quality soundproof insulation, and a top-of-the-line alarm system. She'd left one of the side walls as it was. It was built out of frosted glass blocks that let in light but shielded the inside from view. She guessed one of the previous owners had been a car enthusiast who spent too much time inside the garage with his darlings. And now she used the room to spend it with hers.

She picked up a set of drumsticks from the shelf, placed her water bottle next to the throne, and performed a quick set of stretches. After sitting, she quickly touched every drum and cymbal with a flick of her wrist in her usual ritual. Closing her eyes, she played slowly to warm up. She ran through a few of her earlier songs that she knew in her sleep, then turned to improvising.

Every beat drew out her frustrations and conflicting emotions. Since her teenage days, the music had helped her work out her problems. Scenes from the last few days at work flickered through her consciousness. Her annoyance at her fellow residents, her helplessness when she held the hand of a dying octogenarian, and her insecurity at Emily's intentional distance. She channeled all these moments into her playing until her muscles were pleasantly weak and her mind was empty. Now it could refill with positive thoughts.

She paused to drink some water and to slow her breathing. A draught caught her, chilling her back through the sweat-soaked tank top. She swiveled her throne to look at the door.

Emily leaned against the doorframe, her hands in her jeans pockets, watching Diana with a smile. She was still wearing Diana's T-shirt. Too large, it obscured her figure, but revealed a sexy clavicle on one side. "Don't stop because of me."

"No, I'm all played out. I don't have the endurance for endless sessions anymore. Come in and meet my favorite toy." She stood to grab a fresh towel and cleaned first her drumsticks then herself from the sweat she had worked up.

When Diana had finished toweling her neck, Emily still hadn't moved, and Diana followed her gaze. Emily seemed to stare at the tattoo on her right biceps. Her head snapped up, and she blushed an adorable shade of crimson.

Diana chuckled and couldn't resist flexing her muscles to move the scaly tail of the dragon. "Come, we're not biting."

"Just smelling." Emily winked, stepped closer, and kissed her quickly on the lips. "Are these the drums you played in your band?"

"Partly. Depending on the gigs and the tours, we often used a smaller drum kit. Here, I used the maximal configuration as I have enough space and don't plan to move it anytime soon." Diana flicked a finger at a cymbal and let it ring. She gestured to the different cymbals and snare drums. "For most songs, I don't need it all, but I like to improvise and play around. It's a great feeling that I don't have to rehearse the same songs over and over and get to reclaim it as a hobby."

"And a workout." Emily pointed at the wet towel.

"Yep. Beats weight lifting in the fun department every time. And speaking of workout, I need something to eat and a shower, not necessarily in that order." Her stomach used the cue to growl. Ignoring it, Diana picked up her drumsticks and offered them to Emily. "Do you want to play?"

Emily shook her head. "Now that you mentioned shower and food, I noticed I desperately need both as well. May I have a rain check?"

The way Emily asked was more than a polite brush-off and conveyed genuine interest.

"Sure. You're welcome back anytime." Diana stowed her drumsticks, took the towel, and went to the door. After Emily had stepped outside, she switched off the light, set the alarm, and locked the door. "Do you want to shower first?"

They walked through the garden to the deck. As usual, Diana brushed her hands over the rosemary bush that had been a housewarming gift from Mel.

"How about I head home and shower there? I need some clean clothes."

"Oh. Okay." Diana stole a glance at Emily. Did that mean she didn't want to spend the rest of the day together? Her stomach clenched, and she didn't know if hunger or disappointment caused it.

On the deck, she stacked the empty plates and cups with satisfying clunks and snatched up the cutlery before Emily could reach for it. She rushed through the glass door and nearly fell over the couch cushions on her way to the kitchen. *Slow down. The plates don't need to break because you hoped for another evening with Emily.* Sorting everything into the dishwasher helped her to calm down and focus on Emily's wishes instead of her own. "If you wait a few minutes, I can drive you home. I just need to change."

"Maybe... I thought..." Emily leaned against the kitchen island, turning a spoon in her hands.

Another light blush tinted Emily's features. Diana wasn't sure what it indicated. Was she uncomfortable that Diana wanted to drive her?

Emily's color deepened. "Would you like to spend the evening together? Eat, talk, maybe watch a movie or something?" She talked faster than usual.

Diana's stomach unclenched, and she smiled in relief. "That sounds like the perfect plan."

┿┿┿┿┿┿

Emily made up the couch while she waited for Diana to shower and dress. She tried not to think of Diana in the shower. Or Diana playing drums. Watching her play had triggered memories of the night at the beach years ago. The setting had been completely different, but she remembered Diana's posture and the movement of her muscles as if it had been yesterday.

She clutched one of the cushions and buried her head in it to stifle her groan. How embarrassing was it for a thirty-six-year-old woman to swoon like a teenager? The sweat glistening on Diana's neck and shoulders had enhanced the bright colors of the tattoo as it had blurred the fine lines of ink. Caught between the impulses of running away and running her hands all over Diana, Emily had clung to the doorway, her heartbeat coming as fast and hard as Diana's music. *Get a grip.*

Emily placed the last cushion where it belonged and ran her hand over it to smooth a wrinkle. The texture reminded her of the "research" they'd done this morning. She'd completely lost control, and Diana had to slow her down. When she examined her feelings, she found no remorse. She'd been excited, aroused, and overwhelmed, but the spinning out of control hadn't fazed her. What was different?

"Is casual okay?" Diana's question interrupted her introspection.

Casual? Nothing of this felt casual to her. Oh, she was probably talking about her clothes and their plans for the evening.

Emily took the excuse to study Diana. Her dark brown hair was still wet from the shower and much curlier than usual. She'd put on a pair of faded blue jeans and a green T-shirt with a V-neck. Except for the print of a light green vine clinging to her side, it was a plain shirt, but the snug fit accentuated Diana's curves without revealing too much.

She snapped her eyes to Diana's face when she noticed where her thoughts and gaze had strayed.

Laugh lines crinkled around Diana's eyes that shone a brilliant green instead of the usual hazel and regarded her questioningly.

What had the question been? Emily blinked and replayed the last minute. "Casual is fine with me." Chewing her lip, she wondered if she should say anything about her thoughts. She wasn't used to complimenting women. Or anyone. "The color looks good on you."

"Thank you."

The brilliant smile directed at Emily set free a swarm of butterflies. They definitely needed to spend the evening in public so that she was forced to keep her hands to herself.

After Emily had showered and changed, they strolled down the street toward the same neighborhood restaurant they had visited before, holding hands. The waiter seated them at a table warmed by the late-afternoon sun. Diana started to protest.

Shaking her head, Emily squeezed Diana's hand and sat. They ordered drinks, and Emily perused the menu as if nothing had happened.

Diana put down her menu. "You don't want to sit in the shade today?"

"I'm trying to shake old habits." Emily shrugged.

"I hope you're not doing this for me." Diana wanted to be supportive, but she wasn't sure if she had crossed the fine line into being persuasive. The last thing she wanted to do was push Emily in a direction that wasn't her own.

"No, definitely for me." Emily closed the menu and traced the embossed name of the restaurant with one finger. "You might have triggered some changes recently, but it has been coming for a long time. I've been stuck in the same routine, not exactly unhappy, but something was lacking. Initially, I didn't want something different. You know, never change a winning team and all that nonsense. But my life led nowhere, and I ran myself in perpetual circles. Once I saw it, I couldn't unsee it."

The waiter returned with their drinks, and Diana glanced at the menu and chose the first thing that jumped out at her. She wasn't picky and wanted to return to their conversation.

Emily seemed to have the same idea.

Diana laid her hand on the table, silently inviting Emily to take it. A pleasant tingle spread from their joined hands up her arm. "Even if seeing it now makes you feel worse, it's probably for the best. You can't start the correct treatment if you don't have the right diagnosis."

Emily shook her head. "You can't really compare it to work. When I know a diagnosis, I have a treatment plan memorized. Or I can look it up. Here, I'm trying to find my way in the dark. At first, I thought changing up my routine would be enough. That's why I volunteer at the Rainbow Home."

"Does it help?" Diana wanted to lay her arm around her in support. The knowledge that Emily wasn't that demonstrative with her feelings kept her on her side of the table.

"Some. But it wasn't enough. I thought about cutting back on my responsibilities at work next. I just don't have an idea how to tell Dr. Wallace I'd like to have a life outside of the ED too."

A bitter taste spread in Diana's mouth. She tried to wash it down with a sip of water. "The burden of another resident came at the wrong time."

Emily grimaced. "I'm sorry. Just because I had decided to change didn't mean anyone else should suffer." She squeezed Diana's hand. "And it was my fault. I didn't communicate with Dr. Wallace that I didn't want to do this anymore. He was always a good boss to me, more like a mentor. His opinion matters to me, and I was afraid to let him down."

"No wonder you've been so short with me." Diana rolled her eyes and grinned to take the sting out of the words.

"Nah, that's just because I'm short with everyone at work." Even though Emily tried to joke about it, Diana detected the frustration about her behavior just beneath the surface.

Diana wished she could offer an easy solution; instead she intertwined their fingers. "You don't have to be."

Emily acknowledged the return from joking to serious conversation with a smile. "I'm slowly realizing that. What surprised me is that Liz helped."

"I guess accepting help isn't easy for you." Diana could relate to that.

"No." Emily laughed and shook her head emphatically. "I didn't just accept an offer when she made it; I actually asked her for it." She rolled her eyes. "And it didn't even hurt," she added in an exaggerated childlike tone.

They had to let go of each other's hands as the waiter brought large plates with their salads and a basket of artisan bread. Diana offered the bread to Emily, then grabbed a slice. It was still warm, and the delicious aroma of herbs inspired her stomach to rumble. She had to hold herself back from devouring the rest of the loaf. The drumming had left her ravenous.

Halfway through the salad, Emily laid her fork down and bit her lip. Twice she started to say something but took a sip of water instead. "Why did you decide to change your life?" Her voice nearly got lost in the backdrop of laughter and chatter from the other guests.

Diana had switched directions too often to answer this question easily. She focused on the last time. "You mean, why did I return to medicine?"

Emily nodded. "You mentioned an incident that triggered the change."

Blue lights flashing in the distance filled her vision, leaving her stranded in the middle of the night with only her guilt and helplessness. She shook her head and blinked several times to clear the images from her mind. "I haven't talked to anyone about it."

"You don't have to talk about it." Emily picked up the fork again and searched her salad until she speared a cherry tomato.

Diana looked around. Nobody seemed to be listening. "Only a handful of people know the story. Mel, Katie, and our managers. And they just know parts of it. I'd like to tell you, but I can't do it here, in public."

Emily reached for Diana's hand. "It can wait."

Warmth spread from their joined hands, and the affection in Emily's tone helped her focus on the positive consequences that had come from that night. "The short version is, there was…a medical emergency, and I was the only one who could help. Having all this knowledge and training, but no equipment, made me feel so useless. I think that feeling triggered the change. I kept asking myself if I had more experience or anything else to work with other than my hands, would it have led to a different outcome?"

Emily squeezed her hand, seemingly not caring about the sweat covering Diana's palm. "So you quit the band to help others?"

"No, not really. I left the band to do what I've always wanted to do. I just had been too stupid to admit the truth to myself years ago that I had been too afraid to want it." Diana paused, mentally replaying what she had just said. Why was it so difficult to say what she really meant? "Does that make sense?"

Emily tilted her head to the side, her brows wrinkled in concentration. "A little. You want to say you'd been afraid during your first residency."

"Exactly. The idea of responsibility freaked me out." Diana hesitated. Should she tell her the rest? Honesty was important to her, and she wasn't the person anymore who avoided serious discussions. "I wasn't a great student, and the holes in my knowledge started to show. Instead of focusing on my residency and studying to catch up, I quit. I took the easy way out, without thinking if it was what I wanted to do with my life."

Emily only shrugged and didn't show signs of contempt as Diana had feared. "I think most of us were at that point once, wanting to quit and start over with something else. Only most of us didn't have a really good alternative, so we stayed and worked through it. At least I know I did."

Wow. Diana had never considered that her running away could have been a normal reaction. A weight she hadn't been aware of carrying until now lifted from her shoulders. Smiling with relief, she squeezed Emily's hand before letting it go to pick up her glass. The cold water helped her retrieve her voice. "Thank you for admitting this."

They continued eating, and Diana appreciated the silence as she was able to disentangle her jumbled thoughts and emotions. The new perspective that she hadn't been unique in her struggle to grow into the role of a doctor alleviated some of her guilty conscience. She had tried telling herself for years that she had left the residency because of the great opportunity of a professional record deal. But deep inside, she had always feared she wouldn't have been a good doctor, even if she had finished her residency. She would never know now how she would have evolved if she'd stayed. She only knew she wouldn't waste her second chance.

Diana swallowed the last piece of chicken and looked at Emily. While she had been busy with her introspection, Emily had finished her salad and seemed content to wait her out. She leaned back in her chair, her eyes closed and her face angled slightly to the side to catch the last rays of the setting sun that broke through a space between the buildings. She was looking more relaxed than Diana had seen her so far. Her freckles had multiplied in the last few days and coated her nose and cheekbones like cinnamon dust. Diana wanted to kiss every single one of them, but here wasn't the right place. "How about we watch that movie now?"

Emily opened her eyes and smiled. "We can go to my place. Jen gave me a DVD a few weeks ago that she thought I'd like."

They paid, both reaching for the bill at the same time. Diana relented after Emily pointed out that she had invited her. Not that it mattered who paid, but it was a nice feeling that she wasn't with someone who wanted her for the supposed fame or money people expected to come with a record deal.

━━━━━━

Emily poured boiling water in two large cups with tea bags, choosing the ginger-orange-honey mix because Diana had picked it last time. While she waited for the tea to steep, she put away the clean plates stacked next to the sink and wiped the already-clean counter. She was nervous, but not like the first time Diana had visited. So much had changed in the last month. Anticipation had replaced anxiety. She no longer resented the intrusion into her private sanctuary but enjoyed sharing her space with Diana.

Diana had already made herself comfortable on the couch that looked much smaller than usual. The butterflies that seemed to have taken up permanent residence inside her fluttered at the thought of sitting close together. The only light came from the small lamp on the windowsill and the TV, setting the atmosphere for a romantic evening.

She left the tea to cool on the side table and sat next to Diana. Their legs were barely touching, but the heat seemed to sear through their clothing. Emily reached for the remote and started the movie.

"*The Secret Life of Walter Mitty*," Emily read as the title was revealed on subway signs. "Did you read the back cover? I forgot what it's about." In the first scenes, the setting in a depressive concrete urban desert was filmed in haunting beauty and underlined the loneliness of the main character trying to date online. Had Jen wanted her to watch it to remind Emily to go out and date?

"I just skimmed it. I think it is about changing your life." Diana put her hand on Emily's thigh and squeezed. "Do you think this is too much for today?"

Emily put her own hand on Diana's and intertwined their fingers. "No, I guess I should accept that the universe is putting up neon signs for me instead of giving subtle hints."

Diana softly bumped her shoulder against Emily's and relaxed into the backrest. Now their bodies were touching from shoulder to toe, and her butterflies swarmed again. She forced her gaze to the TV to avoid burying her face into Diana's shoulder.

The movie was a good distraction, and Emily concentrated on the journey of the protagonist, whose search for the lost negative of an important photograph led him to several exotic places and freed his suppressed creativity and hidden talents. In the end, he became more himself than he had ever been and won the love of the colleague he had admired for a long time. Jen's message for her was obvious.

As the credits rolled, Emily reached for her cold tea to soothe her dry throat. She'd nearly cried during the film, which was completely unusual for her, and she was afraid her voice would show it now. "Jen's right. This was a good film for me."

Diana half turned in her seat toward Emily, pulling one leg underneath her. "Not only for you. Change has been on my mind a lot too. Even though I have reached my goal of working as a doctor again, I'm not at the end of my journey. Personal development is a process."

Diana hadn't let go of her hand, and Emily clung to it like a lifeline. She needed the warm touch to ground herself. "I want to change so much, but I feel overwhelmed. I don't know where to begin. My work? My love life? My personality? I have conflicted feelings about my mother. On the one hand, I think she barely touched my life because she was so absent emotionally; on the other hand, I ingrained a lot of things that were important to her to…I don't know…to please her or to be seen by her. And I need to go back now to find out which of my beliefs and convictions and habits are me and which are her and what I want to keep." Emily was babbling and knew it. What was Diana thinking? Her face was shrouded in darkness now that the DVD had stopped.

"I think you're doing a great job so far. You don't have to do it all at once." Diana's voice warmed and soothed her more than the ginger-orange-honey tea could. "I didn't change my life overnight. I made plans and communicated them with everyone important. The second time I didn't want to just quit and run away; I wanted to be sure of my motives. Talking to a therapist helped me gain some perspective."

Fear sliced through her. *Only the broken and weak need therapists*, her mother's voice hissed. But that wasn't true. This was just another prejudice she had picked up from her. "Do you think therapy helped? Was it necessary?"

"Not necessary, but definitely helpful. I think I could have done it without, but why should I? If I broke my leg, I'd use crutches as long as I wore my cast."

Emily giggled; she couldn't help it. That argument was so simple, it sneaked through all her barriers, erected by years of listening to her mother's judgmental monologues. "Thanks. I needed to hear that."

"Anytime." Diana's smile was evident in her tone. "I'm not tired yet, are you? Do you want to watch another movie?"

Good, the serious conversation hadn't driven Diana away. Emily leaned back against the couch. "I'm not tired either. Let's watch another one, but I have to warn you. I don't have Netflix and my DVD collection isn't that big either. Usually Jen lends me new stuff."

Diana squeezed Emily's hand, then stood and went to the entertainment unit and removed the disc from the DVD player. "Are they in here?" By the movement of the dark silhouette, Emily guessed Diana pointed to the drawers.

"Yes." Emily switched on the lamp on the side table. The light was bright, and she had to close her eyes for a second. "Why don't you pick one, and I'll make us another tea? Or do you want anything else? Water? Wine?"

"Tea is great. Surprise me with a new flavor, and I'll surprise you with the movie."

"Deal."

When Emily returned with two caramel-and-vanilla-flavored rooibos teas, Diana was already back on the couch. She sat in one corner, leaning against the side with her legs stretched out over all the seats.

Emily hesitated. Did Diana want her to sit on the armchair?

"I thought we could try another position for the next film. You know, just for scientific purposes." Diana looked up at her, patted the couch between her legs, and smiled.

That smile brought back the butterflies, and Emily relaxed. Laughing, she shut off the light and snuggled between Diana's legs. She carefully lay back until she was completely wrapped in Diana's arms.

"Okay?" Diana whispered, her warm breath tickling the sensitive skin behind her ear.

Emily sighed. "More than okay."

Diana pushed play. She'd chosen *Sense and Sensibility*.

"Oh, great. I love Jane Austen." Emily reached for her tea and blew across the surface to cool it.

Diana chuckled. "I love Emma Thompson." She reached around Emily to take her cup and took a sip. "And I love your tea. It tastes like dessert."

They watched the movie in comfortable silence. When Emily shivered at the sight of a drenched and ice-cold Marianne Dashwood, Diana pulled the large quilt from the backrest of the couch and spread it over them both.

Emily had never felt so safe and secure. Closing her eyes, she relished the slow and rhythmic movement of Diana's chest beneath her head and the hand tangled in her hair. The familiar banter of the Dashwood sisters washed over her. She'd open her eyes again, soon. In another minute.

Chapter 16

THE LAST THING DIANA REMEMBERED was that Emily had fallen asleep on her, and she had wanted to wait until the movie was over to wake her. Now the room was dark and silent. The TV must have shut off automatically, and they both lay on the much-too-small couch. Emily had shifted in her sleep, and now one leg pressed unromantically directly on her bladder. No way could she go back to sleep like this. Carefully, she tried to extricate herself without waking Emily, but she moved immediately.

"What...? Diana?" Emily mumbled.

"Ouch! Wait..." Diana wriggled back until the immediate threat of losing control was gone. "We must have fallen asleep. I just need to use the bathroom, then I'd better leave."

"No." Emily held on to her arm to keep her from leaving.

Diana rubbed her eyes. "No bathroom?"

"No!" Emily laughed. "Don't go home. Stay with me tonight? But not on the couch. My bed is much more comfortable."

The idea of spending the night with Emily jolted Diana awake. Lacking a witty answer, she leaned forward and kissed Emily instead. She tasted of caramel, vanilla, and something uniquely her. Delicious. Soon she was breathing faster and had to stop for air. Yesterday Emily had hesitated to stay with her; was she ready for this?

Emily traced a finger along Diana's jaw. "Bathroom break? Then I'll meet you in my bedroom."

The invitation swept away Diana's doubts.

She tried to stand at the same time Emily moved. Their legs were tangled, and they nearly fell off the couch.

Diana groaned. "I'm sorry. I'm usually not such a clumsy teenager." She stood first and offered a hand to help Emily.

Emily didn't let go of her hand as she led Diana through the dark apartment to the guest bathroom. "See you soon."

The warm glow of a light guided Diana to the bedroom after she finished in the bathroom. Emily waited beneath the plain sage-green cover, her bare shoulders gleaming creamy white with just a hint of golden dust. Following Emily's example, Diana undressed and placed the folded clothes on the dresser next to the door. She left on her panties, not wanting to appear too presumptuous.

Emily held up the cover, and Diana slipped underneath. Both lay on their sides, so close they were almost touching.

"Hi." Emily's warm breath tickled Diana's skin as she exhaled.

Leaning forward, Diana brushed Emily's nose with her own a few times before retreating slightly. "Hi back."

Emily swallowed several times but didn't say anything as a blush spread over her cheeks. Her eyes flickered rapidly from side to side as though she couldn't decide where to focus.

To see her nervous and without the usual confidence prompted Diana to take the lead for now. Maybe reverting to their code language would help. "Have you scientifically tested the comfort level of this bed yet?"

"Ah, you want to expand our study to a multicenter setting." Emily's smile was grateful.

Diana wriggled her legs and stretched her toes, exaggerating the movements. "This furniture has the best legroom of all the test subjects so far."

Emily grinned and patted her pillow. "And a comfortable headrest."

"Maybe we should take it for a test drive."

"Test drive?" Emily poked her ribs. "Are you mixing metaphors right now?"

"Shut up and kiss me."

Both of them laughed, and Diana relaxed. Her shoulders loosened. She hadn't been aware of the tension that receded now. Sex, even sex with relative strangers, had never made her nervous before, but being with Emily was different.

Emily's hand on her hip followed the contours down and backward to her ass before she kissed her. That was unexpected, and she leaned into her hand to enjoy it more. Emily's touch grew bolder, and Diana groaned as Emily's hand wandered up and down her spine.

Diana traced the delicious freckles on Emily's shoulder with a finger, following with her lips along her clavicle via the rapidly pulsing carotid to her jaw, savoring the journey. When she reached her mouth, she reveled in the passion they both poured into the kiss. For a while, she focused only on the sensation of soft lips nibbling and biting and tongues stroking until they were breathless. Catching her breath, she buried her head in Emily's neck. Her skin was flushed, and the pulse raced as fast as her own.

Her awareness of the rest of her body returned. While kissing, they had moved closer, and their naked breasts touched in pools of warmth. Her fingers had tangled in Emily's hair. It was beautiful, smooth, and cascading downward over her shoulders like a cape made from brown silk. She tried to turn Emily onto her back to explore more of her.

"Nuh-uh" Emily stopped her movement with a hand on her shoulder, a soft but unmistakable push that slowly pressed her down on the bed.

The sheets were cool against her overheated skin.

Emily traced the tattoo that reached over Diana's shoulder and wrapped around her biceps. The touch melted her skin as if the dragon's fire were real.

Hovering above her, face flushed, pupils dilated, and lips swollen, Emily was so beautiful it nearly hurt.

She pulled Emily's head down to kiss her again. Those lips drove her crazy. Diana couldn't resist sneaking a hand to Emily's side and the swell of her breast. So soft. Emily lifted slightly, and Diana took the chance to caress more of the warm, round flesh. Her thumb passed over one nipple, and she admired the rose-colored skin as it puckered and tightened into an inviting point. Another pass of her thumb elicited a moan of pleasure. Diana wanted to hear that sound again and again. She moved to kiss her breast and worked her way from one side to the middle. She traced the uneven surface with her tongue, taking her time to explore the difference in texture.

Emily pressed closer and moved as though to direct Diana back to her nipple.

Diana obliged and kissed her there. And licked her. And sucked her. She loved the feeling of Emily twisting above her. When the squirming had turned into a decidedly rhythmic movement, she left the nipple to slow down again. She placed light kisses on the soft skin between Emily's breasts and moved upward, again following an irresistible path of freckles like a gold digger searching for glimpses of the rare nuggets in a stream.

"Don't stop now," Emily whispered.

"I'm not stopping. I'm just exploring." Diana grinned and returned to kissing a line from her breasts to one shoulder. "Where do you want me to go next?" She'd reached Emily's neck and got lost in the scent of her.

"Uh, what do you mean? Is this not okay?" Emily leaned back and looked at Diana with wide eyes.

The sudden loss of contact hit her like an icy shower. Goose bumps erupted all over. What had happened? "It's very okay. I was just... you know...asking. What you want. What you like."

Emily traced the tattoo with the opening chord of her first recorded song that covered the thin scar of Diana's appendectomy and looked at it as if it were the most fascinating piece of skin she had ever seen. "Oh. Okay, then. I'm sorry." She slowly made eye contact again, almost shy. "So, where were we?"

Maybe some humor would relax Emily. "I was admiring your neck. Do vampires usually go for the jugular or the carotid?"

This seemed to help. Emily playfully slapped her shoulder and laughed. "Let's find out."

Emily's nibbling on her throat drove all thoughts of anatomy out of Diana's mind. She mimicked the route Diana had taken a moment ago. When she reached Diana's breast and sucked her nipple into her mouth, the pleasure shot directly to her clit.

Diana reached with both hands for Emily's hips to anchor herself. The friction of Emily's leg pressing into her groin was driving her crazy. She needed more, needed to get closer. When Emily lifted up, Diana groaned. Where was she going? But then Emily pulled Diana's panties down. When they got stuck on her ankles, Diana kicked them the rest of the way off.

Finally, firm, warm fingers touched her where she needed her the most. Emily stroked her slowly at first. Was she hesitating? Exploring? Every time she brushed against her clit, Diana strained to get closer to the fingers.

She couldn't take it anymore. "Emily, don't play. I need you now."

Emily stopped and looked up at her. She was beautiful; her skin glowed, and her gray eyes sparkled with passion. Her answer was a kiss, soft lips and a hot tongue taking Diana's breath away. Emily's fingers returned to their torture, but now they moved with an intentional rhythm. They slipped into Diana's opening, and her thumb slid over her clit, faster and faster.

"Don't stop." The crescendo of her arousal reached almost painful heights. Everything else ceased to exist. Diana lived only for Emily's mouth on hers and the movement of her hand. The climax hit her like a surprising drum stroke, leaving her with ringing ears, deaf to the world for a moment.

Emily snuggled into Diana's shoulder but left her fingers in her. "I can still feel you," she whispered in awe.

Too breathless to answer, Diana hugged Emily and placed a grateful kiss on her forehead instead.

After a minute, Emily carefully slipped out of Diana and pulled up the covers. She used the time to gather herself and to study Diana. Her face was flushed; she was breathing heavily, and her pupils were still dilated. The diagnosis was easy. Arousal. To know that she had been the one to affect Diana this way made her heart beat even faster.

Until now, she had considered the point of having sex to be her own climax. As she achieved that more easily on her own, she had never searched for a partner to repeat her few boring encounters.

What an egoistic idiot she'd been. To see Diana give up control, to see her react to each touch and stroke, to hear her call her name, to feel her arousal coating her fingers, satisfied her on a deeper level.

"Thank you."

Diana chuckled. "I think I should thank you." She brushed her hand slowly up and down Emily's side, never quite touching her breast. With soft pushes, she encouraged Emily to turn onto her back, which she quite willingly did.

Diana started kissing her again all over her shoulder, neck, and cleavage. Those kisses had nearly robbed her of her sanity earlier.

Emily reached for Diana's shoulders to ground herself. Her gaze locked on the red flames snaking across Diana's left biceps. Her fingers followed their path. It was the same image that had lived in her fantasies for so long, but the touch made it real and bound it to Diana.

"You do like my tattoo," Diana mumbled against her neck.

Emily blurted out the first thing that popped into her mind. "I think it's sexy." Heat rose to her cheeks, but she did nothing to fight it. She'd probably blush a lot more before the night was over.

"I—think—you're—sexy." Diana accentuated each word with a kiss.

Emily's skin burned with the truth behind her touch. She believed her.

Diana proceeded to kiss her all over as if she wanted to map every centimeter of her skin. Slowly, her path led her downward. Her hot breath burned like the dragon's breath as she blew over Emily's hair at the apex of her legs.

Emily flinched. Would she...? Her breathing escalated, and her abdominal muscles tensed. She didn't know if she wanted her to continue or to stop.

Diana quickly kissed her way back up in a direct line and only paused after she'd touched her lips softly. Her gaze searched for Emily's. "Relax. I won't do anything you're uncomfortable with."

Her blood pounded in her ears, making it nearly impossible to think. She was so far outside her comfort zone that past experiences wouldn't help her. Perhaps the familiar touch of fingers would be easier to enjoy. "I know. Maybe we could come back to it later?"

Diana's smile flooded her with warmth, releasing her tension. "We have all the time in the world." Slowly, she trailed her hand down to where her mouth had been. "Is this okay?"

The words caught in Emily's throat, and she could only nod. Vigorously.

Diana caressed the inside of her legs, moved over, parting her hair, and finally dipped into the waiting wetness. That was more than okay.

Her last conscious thought was that *familiar* was such a wrong description for Diana's touch. Heat concentrated inside her, like molten lava trying to break free. She tried to contain it, to prolong the pleasure, but much too soon she exploded.

Emily found herself wrapped in Diana's arms, lying half over her with the covers back in place around them. She had no recollection how she had ended up here, but now she never wanted to move. Lassitude sank over her, and she struggled to keep her eyes open. She wanted to say something, anything, but speech eluded her.

"Sleep now," Diana whispered.

That was a perfect idea.

++++++

Sunlight and chirping birds pulled Emily from a deep sleep and infused her with energy. Her head was once again resting on Diana's shoulder, and she had wrapped a leg over her. The rhythmic movement of Diana's chest suggested she was still asleep. But when Emily opened her eyes and turned her head to look at Diana, she found she was already awake. The hazel eyes sparkled more green than brown this morning, and the few fine lines around her eyes deepened in amusement.

"Good morning, sleeping beauty."

Heat rose to Emily's cheeks, but after last night her tendency to blush didn't faze her anymore. "Morning."

Emily trailed her hand along Diana's abdomen to the soft swell of her hip and back. She relished the sensation of skin against skin as she listened to the birds outside her window chatting excitedly. Were they as happy as she was, or was she just anthropomorphizing and projecting her emotions? For the first, time she understood the sights and sounds of spring as a symbol of new life and love. Love? Her heartbeat soared. She froze. Was it too soon to call this new and exhilarating feeling love?

"Are you okay?" Diana laid her hand over Emily's.

She had dug her fingers into Diana's side and now loosened her grip. Was she okay? She scrutinized herself and searched for doubts or regrets. She couldn't find any, only this slightly frightening feeling of bliss. Unable to put her thoughts into words, she rose on her forearm and kissed Diana, pouring everything into the touch.

When her liquefied muscles couldn't support her anymore, Emily let herself fall onto her back. Judging by Diana's response, the kiss that had lasted quite some time had been the right way of conveying her emotions.

Diana rolled on her side, cupped Emily's jaw, and stroked her lips with her thumb. Her smile was different now, more intense. Her gaze seemed to echo Emily's emotions and burned into her until Diana closed her eyes to kiss her.

Emily stopped overthinking and analyzing. Her world was only filled with sensations as they made love again.

Diana fought her heavy eyelids. *Don't fall asleep again!* She placed one last kiss next to Emily's navel before she rose and stretched her spine. "As tempting as it is, I don't think it's the best idea to stay in bed all day."

"Afraid of bedsores? Let me see." Emily made a show of inspecting her backside. Her soft kisses tingled. "Nope, skin is still intact." She sat up against the headboard and grinned.

Diana laughed. *Who would've believed that Emily hid a wicked sense of humor?* "No, but I'm afraid of wasting away if we don't have breakfast soon."

Emily looked at the alarm clock on her bedside table and shook her head. "Closer to lunch than breakfast. I can't remember the last time I spent so much time in bed. You're a bad influence."

"I don't think you can blame the last hour on me." Diana hadn't gotten over the surprise yet that Emily had taken the initiative and had shown so much passion. For a moment she'd looked as though she wanted to bolt, and Diana's heart had clenched painfully, afraid Emily would end the relationship before it had really begun.

"Maybe it's all the dragon's fault." Emily placed a kiss on the dragon's tail on Diana's right biceps before she scrambled out of bed. "I'll just take a quick shower, and then I'll see what I can find to eat. I'm afraid shopping wasn't my top priority last week. Eggs? Maybe toast?"

"Anything is fine. Can I help?"

"No, relax. You can take a shower after I'm done if you want to. I'll leave out fresh towels."

In the shower, Diana discovered Emily's source of the faint rosemary scent, her shampoo.

Breakfast passed much too fast, and neither tried to address topics more serious than the plans for the day. They both needed to catch up with errands around their respective houses before starting a busy series of six workdays tomorrow. Diana wanted to prolong the feeling of belonging again, but she had to find some breathing time to process the rapid escalation of their relationship.

"I should go and get some work done at home." The idea of not seeing Emily again until they assumed their professional masks at work was depressing. "Come for dinner. I'll cook for you."

Emily smiled. "I'll be there."

Diana had rushed through her routine for her days off. Washing, cleaning, paying bills, grocery shopping, and an absolute minimum of yard work to keep her backyard from turning into a wilderness. She was left with just enough free time to prepare dinner. The vegetables were cut; the chicken was marinated in Indian spices, and the saffron rice warmed in the rice cooker. A romantic playlist streamed from her computer to the hidden speakers on the first floor. She turned to the table. Should they sit on opposite sides or at the corner, closer to each other? Exchange the candle for a few tea lights?

The doorbell interrupted her fussing over the table setting. Since when had decorating become important to her? Shaking her head at her silliness, she went to answer the door.

Emily held out a bottle of wine with a shy smile. "I didn't know if you wanted me to bring something."

"Only you." Diana took the bottle with one hand and pulled her in with the other. Her cheeks glowed a bright red, either from the chill drizzle or from seeing Diana again...or both. She couldn't resist kissing Emily immediately.

Emily's hands roamed her back, and when the cold fingers reached her neck, Diana was reminded that they were still standing in the doorway, letting in the evening air. She took her jacket, hung it near the door to dry, and led her to the high stools at her kitchen island.

"We could have some wine while I finish cooking. Do you want a glass? Or tea? I bought some of your favorites today." *Very smooth.* She shut her mouth and peeked at Emily out of the corner of her eye as she searched for the bottle opener.

Emily's lips twitched as she obviously tried not to laugh. "Wine would be great. Thanks."

Diana opened the bottle and poured the dark red liquid into two glasses. She handed one to Emily and raised hers. "We probably should let it breathe, but let's toast."

"To what?" Emily's gaze locked with hers, and Diana nearly forgot to answer.

"To our date?"

"To our date." Emily leaned her glass toward Diana's, and they met with a bright clink, the high note lingering nearly as long as their gazes.

The wine was rich and smooth, and Diana could immediately feel it going to her head. Or maybe Emily's smile made her dizzy. Laughing at herself, she put down her glass next to Emily's and turned to the stove. "Do you like Indian food?"

"I love it. But I've never had it outside of a restaurant before. Isn't it difficult to make?"

Concentrating on cooking relieved some of the nervousness. "Not really. You need a lot of different spices, and it takes some time to get comfortable mixing them, but you can't really make many mistakes. I suppose there are as many variations as there are families in India. I used to follow recipes, but now I just season until it tastes good." She fried onions with the spices she had powdered in her large granite mortar.

Emily stepped closer and wiggled her nose in an adorable way. "It smells authentic."

"I probably have westernized the recipes over the years. But it still beats the stuff you get in a supermarket." She added the chicken strips and vegetables to the pan and finally poured chopped tomatoes over the rest to let it simmer under a lid.

"I hope it's spicy?"

"Not too spicy. I didn't want to use chilies." She grinned.

Emily frowned. "Why?"

"I don't want to have traces on my hands." She exaggeratedly waggled her eyebrows. "Or my tongue."

The immediate blush covering her cheeks told Diana that Emily got it now. To give her a moment to cool down, she checked that the rice was still warm and removed a few papadums from the package. Microwaving the thin disks only took a minute, and she piled a few on an oval plate and added a small silver bowl with mango chutney next to them.

She carried the starter to Emily. Her cheeks were still glowing, and Diana leaned in to kiss them.

Emily turned her head at the last second and captured Diana's mouth in a searing kiss that left them breathless.

Seating herself next to Emily, Diana noticed she had barely touched the wine. "You want some water?"

Emily placed a hand on Diana's forearm and smiled. "Stop fussing. I'm fine."

"Okay. We can just sit here for a while and relax while the chicken jalfrezi is cooking. What did you do today?"

They snacked on the papadums and exchanged details of their day. Diana enjoyed the warmth spreading from her middle. It could have been the spicy chutney or the wine, but she guessed it had more to do with the woman sitting next to her. Soon the fragrant scent of cardamom, cumin, and tomato filled the kitchen, and Diana's stomach growled. When she rose to check on the sauce, it had reduced to the perfect thickness. She piled the plates with yellow rice, red chicken, and tomato sauce and sprinkled fresh coriander over it.

The table was set with colorful woven mats she'd bought at an Indian shop in London. The thick, white candle was burning, and the window next to the large table reflected its light. Raindrops broke on the surface, ran down in irregular rivulets, and obscured the view to the garden. The bleak weather outside only enhanced the coziness she felt inside with Emily.

Emily had followed her with their wineglasses. "It looks great."

"Thanks. Where do you want to sit?"

When Emily turned to the left side, Diana pulled the chair for her.

Emily concentrated on the food, making appreciative noises. "It tastes even better than it looks and smells. Thank you. Not only for the food. No one has ever done something so beautiful for me." She gestured to the candle and the decoration.

"I'd love to do it again." Emily's content smile was certainly worth the effort.

When they had finished and Emily had refused another helping, Diana topped off their wine and carried the glasses to the couch.

They gravitated close to each other, entwining their fingers. Where did that longing for physical closeness come from? Diana had never considered herself a snuggler in her previous relationship and short affairs. And no one who knew the formidable front Emily presented at work would recognize her now. The reminder of work sobered Diana. They needed to talk about their relationship before they returned to the day shift tomorrow.

Diana took a deep breath. Better to get it over with now, like ripping off a Band-Aid. "What do you think will happen at work?"

Emily stiffened next to her. "You mean because of our relationship?"

"I know it's not forbidden, but I'm thinking of the reactions. We'll have to endure some teasing, or in the worst case someone will accuse me of sleeping with you for preferred treatment." That thought was so absurd that she had to chuckle.

Emily's jaws clenched, and she closed her eyes for a moment. When she opened them again, the warm gray had turned into cold steel. "I've never given anyone reason to doubt my judgment, and I don't intend to start now. But I've always been very private. I don't believe it's anyone's business what I…we do outside of work."

Privacy was important to Diana too. After their first album had reached the top ten, her love life had been under constant scrutiny. "So we just pretend we're not together?"

"We don't have to pretend anything." Emily shrugged. "We just keep on doing what we did before: behave professionally at work."

Diana took a moment to examine the emotions whirling in the depth of her stomach. "I don't feel like I did before, and I'm not sure I can act that well. I'm torn between telling everyone how happy I am and keeping you all to myself at the same time."

A straight line had appeared between Emily's brows at the mention of telling everyone.

Before she could say anything, Diana continued. "Don't get me wrong, I'm all for professional conduct at work. Katie always loved to play with people's expectations and used our relationship as a marketing tool without consulting me, even after we separated."

"There's nothing to gain by making our relationship public knowledge at the hospital. We don't work in a TV show with all that drama. Our conduct reflects on the reputation of the ED and the hospital. This should be our top priority." Emily's voice had hardened.

It cut Diana like a knife. Shouldn't their relationship be the top priority? The thought of keeping another secret stung like a melody played slightly off beat. Something she could ignore for a few chords, but not for a whole concert—or the fucking rest of her life.

She drew her hand back, but Emily wouldn't let go.

"It's just... You're important to me. I don't want to deny you. But... this is new for me." Emily's lips trembled, and a hint of wetness glinted in her eyes.

Diana's irritation evaporated as fast as it had come. She squeezed the hand that was still holding on to her. "You're important to me too. We'll figure it out."

Emily's rigid posture softened, and the warmth return to her gaze. "I want to do this right, but there's no rule book."

"I think we'll do fine, as long as we keep talking about it." Diana already felt lighter after seeing Emily's honest reaction. "We can continue at work like we did before. Liz will help us. I'm pretty sure she already knows about us, by the way. Do you think that will be a problem?"

"With Liz acting as your primary supervisor we can minimize our interaction. That'll make it easier. And I think you're right. I believe she has at least her suspicions about my interest in you." Emily grinned and rolled her eyes. "But she's been discreet about it."

Diana nodded. "Clever woman. I knew I liked her for a reason. Working with her is easy. But I don't mind reporting to you again, if we need to. I trust you not to mix business with pleasure."

"We're no teenagers. We should be capable of acting professional and keeping our hands off each other."

"At work." Diana decided to return some levity to the discussion. "I don't think I can keep my hands off you today." Wriggling her fingers, she aimed for Emily's sides.

"You." Laughing, Emily tried to push her hands away. When it wouldn't work, she retaliated with her own tickling attack.

They squirmed and wrestled on the couch until Diana was gasping for breath. "Truce, please." Her sides hurt from laughing.

Resting against her, Emily stroked Diana's thigh. The warm tingling following her fingers mesmerized Diana and didn't help in getting her breath back.

"So, Dr. Petrell, are you up for more scientific research in your spare time? I believe we haven't finished evaluating all the possibilities at your place yet."

Chapter 17

EMILY CLOSED HER EYES, INHALING the aroma of her extra large, extra strong mocha that was only palatable with lots of sugar, as the rest of the day shift arrived one by one. Usually, she was watching the clock like a hawk, but today she couldn't be bothered. If the others only knew why, her fierce reputation would be gone in a second. A smile tugged at her lips.

"Great, coffee! I could kill for one." Diana's face lit up as she swept into the staff lounge with barely a minute to spare. She reached for one of the to-go cups in the middle of the table and sat between Courtney and Liz on the sofa.

Torn between the impulse to grin madly at the sight of her lover and to admonish her for almost being late, Emily drank deeply from her own cup. *Definitely a coffee morning.*

The colleagues from the night shift started the turnover as soon as the last one had arrived, eager to be done with their work. Normally, the ritual helped her focus, but today she had trouble concentrating.

John paused and looked at her expectantly. Had she missed a question? She took a large sip to gain some time and mentally replayed the conversation. No, no questions. He had made a succinct report.

"Okay, if you have nothing to add, I'm off now." He grabbed one of the cups from the table and waved. "Thanks for the coffee, Liz."

"I didn't bring it today. Thank Dr. Sleepy here." Liz nodded in Emily's direction.

All gazes moved to her.

Emily forced herself not to squirm and attempted a nonchalant shrug. "It was my turn." Not that she had ever cared before about the unwritten social rules at work.

To be honest, if she hadn't been so sleep-deprived this morning, it wouldn't have occurred to her. But waking up one hour early to get from Diana's place to hers to shower and change, after getting only half her usual hours of sleep, she had needed more help to wake up than her usual cup of Darjeeling. In the coffee shop, she had wanted to bring something for Diana, but she couldn't single her out.

Concentrate! Emily shook her head to clear it and reached for her notes. She quickly distributed the patients between the three residents and repeated what John had already listed for them to do this morning. "Courtney, Alec, you're with me. Diana, you're with Liz. I'll be in my office."

Emily rose and left to go directly to her room, where she could wake up properly without the constant temptation of staring at Diana like a fool. Halfway down the corridor the caffeine had finally reached her brain, and she remembered she wanted to talk to Liz about the resident teaching next week. She'd better get it over now before the patient influx left them no time.

Laughter drifted through the half-open door of the lounge. Maybe she should get coffee more often if it lifted the mood like this.

"I wonder who tamed the witch? I wouldn't get close to her with a ten-foot pole. Poor guy. Or girl?"

Emily froze. The coffee in her stomach turned to lead, and the weight held her in place.

"Alec! Don't say that."

Wow, Courtney was taking her side?

"What? It's true."

"Yeah, it is." Courtney giggled. "But she's probably bugged the room. You know she doesn't trust us. Paranoid nutcase."

"Stop it!" Liz said at the same time as Diana said, "Shut up!"

Emily held her breath. She should leave now. It was nothing she hadn't heard and dismissed before. Only today it hurt like a knife twisting deep inside her.

"Stop acting like high-school students." That was Ian. Emily had forgotten that the other attending of the night shift was still in the room. "I know that she's usually very reserved—"

"You mean stuck-up," Alec said.

"I mean what I said; she's reserved. But that's no reason to talk about her like that. You were happy enough to drink her coffee ten minutes ago. So she's obviously had a nice weekend and translated that into doing something nice for all of us. Instead of saying thank you, and keeping your thoughts to yourself like any civilized adult, you spout spiteful crap."

Warmth flooded Emily's cheeks, and she bit her lip to suppress a groan. Her state of mind had been obvious to everyone. Maybe not so surprising, considering she had probably grinned during the whole turnover. What surprised her, though, was that the usual quiet Ian had stood up for her. Not that she needed anyone to be her shining knight. She could very well defend herself. She stepped toward the room to do just that, but the sound of moving chairs stopped her.

"I'd better go and get some work done before I say something I regret." Diana's voice was full of contempt.

Footsteps indicated Diana would leave the room any second now.

Emily fled around the corner and into the first storage room she passed.

It must have been difficult for Diana too. Maybe even more so, because she was right in the middle of the mess. Emily couldn't blame her for only speaking up a little; she didn't know what she would have done in her place.

"Ouch, Liz. Thank you for holding me back, but did you have to dig in your nails like this?" Diana's voice was still tense.

Emily's heart beat so loud in her ears that she nearly missed Liz's answer.

"I thought you'd explode any minute. I'm sorry I hurt you, but I guessed that wasn't how you wanted everyone to find out." Liz chuckled.

Their footsteps faded as they passed Emily's hiding place. Slowly, her tension subsided, and she rubbed her burning eyes. Here she was, hiding in a storage closet, as if her life were a soap opera masquerading as a medical drama. She didn't know if she should laugh or cry.

Emily stretched her legs under her desk. She had just returned to her office after a day of gleefully picking the worst cases for Alec and Courtney.

Maybe it was petty, but someone had to take care of the chronically constipated four-hundred-pound woman and the smelly guy with the perianal abscess, right? The downside of this strategy was that she had to supervise them doing it, but she had long experience in switching off her sense of smell on demand.

A knock on the door made her sit up straight. "Come in."

Diana stepped in and raised her eyebrows. "Bad day?"

Emily slumped in the seat again. "Not too bad, just the usual. But today I'd rather not be here at all."

Diana sat in the visitor's chair and stretched her legs as well. "I could think of something better to do right now." Her tone had lowered to the sexy teasing that made Emily feel warm and tingly all over.

"No, no, don't go there. I thought we would keep this professional at work." Her protest was only feeble, and judging by Diana's smile, she knew it. Having Diana here in her office, alone, was the highlight of her shift, but she couldn't give in to the temptation of touching her. She clutched the armrest to keep from walking to the other side of the desk. She wanted to pull her from the visitor's chair and drag her over to the sofa in the corner that she sometimes used to sleep at work. Not that she was sleepy now.

"I was only talking about dinner; what did you think?" She playfully tapped her foot against Emily's under the desk. "But now that you mentioned it..."

Laughing, Emily loosened the death grip on her chair. "Do you want to grab something quick on our way out?"

"Or maybe we can pick up some takeout and eat at your place." Diana twirled the drawstring of her scrub pants around her finger.

This small sign of nervousness relaxed Emily. She wasn't the only one invested in their relationship. "I'd love to. Meet me at my car?"

"Great. I need to return. Lab results should be back by now." Diana stood and looked at the closed door, then back at Emily. Shaking her head, she turned to go.

"Wait." Emily jumped up, following an impulse she didn't want to examine too closely. She stepped around the desk and quickly pecked Diana on the lips.

Diana grinned and left the room with a wink.

Leaning with her back against the closed door, Emily pressed a hand against her tingling lips. Professional conduct, right. She hadn't even lasted one shift despite her good intentions.

Sunday afternoon Diana fought to keep her eyes open as she attempted to read the newest *Journal of Emergency Medicine*. Not that it wasn't interesting, but no amount of coffee could help her concentrate after a week of too much work combined with too little sleep. Putting her feet up on the couch at work probably hadn't helped either. A few minutes of rest now that the ED was quiet just felt good.

"What are you thinking?" Emily looked up from her own journal. She sat on the couch opposite, leaning her head back und stretching her legs in front of her. Anyone who knew her at work would be surprised to see her that relaxed, but Diana thought it looked good on her.

"Karma is a bitch." Diana sat up and stretched. "If Courtney had been here yesterday, my feet wouldn't hurt from running around that much."

Courtney had called in sick two days ago after her request for a few days off had been declined. Her new boyfriend wanted to take her away for the weekend, and she apparently didn't care that they couldn't find anyone else on short notice.

"And what has karma to do with that?" Emily asked.

Diana kept her gaze on Emily. She wasn't proud of what she'd done, but she wouldn't hide it from her. "I did this more than once to my colleagues during my first residency. Now I know why I wasn't anyone's favorite."

Emily's lips narrowed to the firm line Diana had seen so often during the first weeks. "I need to talk to Courtney again when she returns to work."

Diana shook her head. "Not on my account. I don't know what happened. Maybe she's really sick."

"Yeah, right." Emily rolled her eyes. "Don't worry, it's not because of what you said. This isn't the first time she has pulled a stunt like this. We can never prove it, though. Her overall attitude isn't exactly motivated."

A sharp line furrowed Emily's brow, and Diana wanted to smooth it out with her fingers. Or kiss it. But she couldn't do that at work.

"Forget about her. Let's talk about our plans for our day off tomorrow. I vote for sleeping in."

A rosy glow tinted Emily's cheeks. "I wish I could. But tomorrow is Monday, and I am presenting the lecture to the residents."

Diana groaned. "I nearly forgot about that. I guess I have to show up too. My boss is kinda strict, you know?" She winked, delighted to see the hard lines disappear as Emily laughed.

"How about we go out for breakfast after the lecture and then see what we want to do with the rest of the day?"

Diana lay down on the couch again. "Good plan. But then I need some rest now. Wake me if something happens."

"Lazy resident." Emily chuckled and returned to her reading.

Diana studied her through half-closed eyes. A small smile remained on Emily's lips, even though her concentration had shifted back to the journal. Her hair was curly, giving her a softer look, and Diana warmed as she remembered what had kept Emily from her usual morning routine of straightening it. The lack of sleep might kill her soon, but it was worth it.

Chapter 18

EMILY SAT ON THE SAGGING couch in the staff lounge, cradled her new travel mug in both hands, and inhaled the warm fragrance. Her favorite Darjeeling. Diana had to switch to nights three days ago and had given her the burgundy metal cup so Emily would think of her. Not that she needed a reminder.

Today she had come in an hour earlier than usual under the pretense of working on an article. She had come up with this plan when she was lying sleepless in bed, missing Diana like crazy. She had lived all her adult life alone, and now three days were too long. Saying hello and goodbye at turnovers in the morning and evening just wasn't enough. Hoping to catch her in the hour before shift change, she had been disappointed when Diana was too busy to talk. The summer flu still held Seattle in its grasp, clogging the ED. Every bed in the hospital was occupied, and some of the patients stayed days in the ED until they could either go home or move up to another floor. The virus had spread among the overworked staff too. Several nurses, residents, PAs, and an attending had called in sick, and now Diana was stuck on the night shift with double the workload and half the staff.

The door opened, and Liz and Diana entered together. Both looked like they were awake and moving on willpower alone.

Diana fell on the couch next to her with a thud and unsuccessfully tried to suppress a yawn. "Hi, good to see you." She pressed Emily's hand in what could have been a platonic gesture, but her eyes told a different story. Her hazel irises were a murky brown today, and dark shadows contrasted with her too-pale complexion, but the spark in them shot directly to Emily's heart.

"Hi." Emily wished she could hold and kiss her or at least hug her.

"I'll just go over there, get some coffee, and stare at the wall for at least thirty seconds. Don't do anything I wouldn't do." Liz grinned, stood, and did what she had just announced.

Immediately, heat suffused Emily's cheeks. Were her thoughts written all over her face?

"Hi." Diana leaned closer. Her tone was more intimate now, and Emily shivered in anticipation.

"Hi," Emily whispered. She dug her hands into the seat cushion, but the pain didn't curb her desire to reconnect with Diana.

Stupid rules! She kissed Diana before she could lose her nerve. Her lips were warm and so, so soft. They touched slowly, reacquainting and reassuring themselves of their connection.

Separating felt like the hardest thing Emily had ever done. She leaned back and growled with frustration.

Liz chuckled. "You two are so cute. You should have seen this one here moping around last night."

Diana threw her pen at Liz. "Shut up!"

Laughing, Liz caught it with one hand and threw it back.

As the first colleague of the day shift arrived, Emily reached for her tea again, hoping the others would think the hot beverage had caused her cheeks to flush.

The door flew open, and Tony stuck his head in. "I need a doc, stat. Ambulance just brought in an unresponsive woman. Overdose, they say. Idiots didn't call first."

Diana stood before Emily could decide if the night shift was still responsible or the day shift should take the case. "I'll go. Bail me out after turnover."

Emily wanted to protest. The last three nights had taken a toll on Diana, and she looked beat. But Emily wasn't known for coddling residents and wouldn't start now.

Adrenaline swept away Diana's bone-deep weariness. Overdose, the magic word to wake her up, better than a double shot of espresso.

Diana hurried past the open doors of the ambulance bay to treatment room one. For a second, the flashing blue lights catapulted her to the cold night that had changed her life. She shook her head. *Get a grip! That was over a year ago.*

She stepped into the room and consciously left her past outside as she donned the protective clothing and gloves. "What have we got?"

One of the paramedics stepped closer, snapping off her soiled gloves. "Female, midthirties, found unconscious in a hotel room when she didn't meet with her driver. GCS five, BP ninety over sixty, heart rate one hundred and forty. We gave her a bag of saline without improvement. We couldn't get a reliable sats, best was ninety-one. She puked just now when we moved her. Possible aspiration." She shook her head with a disgusted expression. "Probable overdose. We found an empty container of oxycodone on the bedside table."

Diana thanked her and hurried over to the gurney, where the nurses were busy attaching the patient to the monitor and cutting her out of her soiled clothes.

Tony suctioned her mouth, cursing. "Diana, I think you need to intubate. No gag reflex."

A quick glance to the monitor confirmed they couldn't get a reliable reading on the sats either. The gray color of the woman's face and the too-few and shallow breaths with gurgling sounds were a sure sign that oxygen supply was lacking. "Tony, get everything ready."

Diana stepped to the head of the table. The sour stench of vomit made her stomach heave. She swept the black sweaty hair out of the woman's face and opened the eyes with soft pressure. No resistance, not a good sign. The pupils were tiny black specks in a sea of pale blue, adding plausibility to the theory of an overdose. Diana looked up at Madison, the other nurse. "Give her 0.4 naloxone." Maybe the antidote would be enough to wake her up, and Diana wouldn't need to intubate her. "I'll bag her until it's taking effect."

Tony handed her the bag connected to a plastic mask on one side and the oxygen on the other end.

With one hand Diana adjusted the patient's jaw to prevent the tongue from blocking the airway and pushed the plastic mask snuggly over nose and mouth with the other. She pressed the bag regularly, but the woman's cheeks didn't lose their ashen complexion. For the first time since she had entered the room, Diana had a moment to really look at her patient. She was young, maybe Diana's age, and the cut of the eyes reminded her of someone.

Oh fuck, Katie! The mask and bag slipped from her hands with a squeaking sound.

She quickly readjusted her grip. Was she imagining things after twelve hours of nonstop working? She studied her again. The color of her hair was all wrong; she was even thinner than before, and the lines around her eyes were more pronounced than the last time Diana had seen her, but it was Katie. Diana's heartbeat accelerated, nearly matching the frantic beeping of the monitor. Sharp pain shot through her hand with every move as it cramped from the effort to keep the mask in place and to stop herself from trembling. *She promised. What happened?*

The shrill alarm of the monitor interrupted her. It had finally gotten a signal of the oxygen saturation, and it wasn't good. Sixty-five percent and rapidly falling.

Diana pushed everything from her mind and let her training take over. "Intubation, now." She put the useless mask aside.

While Diana pulled Katie's mouth wide open with her right hand, she blindly held out her left for the laryngoscope, trusting Tony to hand it to her. She inserted it and pulled to get a good view, again reaching for the tube without taking her eyes off her goal. She pushed the tube between the vocal cords with a slight twist, relieved when she got it on the first try. "Inflate the cuff."

Diana switched the bag from the mask to the tube and handed it to Tony to press it. She fumbled with her stethoscope, nearly dropping it, before she placed it correctly in her ears. "Sounds good. Secure the tube."

She looked from Katie to the monitor and back. The color slowly returned to her cheeks with each squeeze of the bag, and the oxygen levels climbed steadily. Both Katie's and her heart rate decelerated somewhat, now that the immediate life-threatening situation was under control. *What have you done, Katie?*

"Excuse me." Someone pushed past her, and Diana took a step back, realizing she stood in the way of the respiratory tech who wanted to hook Katie up to the respirator.

She should examine her now, give instructions, make calls, but she was stuck in a bubble of slow motion, with the rest of the team rushing through their routine. Her hands were trembling, and she peeled off her gloves. Katie's saliva was clinging to them. Clenching her fists until her nails bit into her flesh, she fought to regain control. The pain helped to pierce the bubble surrounding her, and she grabbed a fresh pair of gloves and jumped back into the fray.

She continued working as if Katie were any other patient until Stacy from registration stuck her head in and asked for a name. Diana froze.

"She didn't have an ID on her. Call the hotel." Tony handed her the papers the paramedics had left them.

"Katie...Kathrine Dawn, date of birth January twenty-fifth, 1979," Diana heard herself say.

Great, there goes my chance at handling this discreetly. Diana shrugged. She couldn't take it back now; she'd deal with it later. She looked around the room. It seemed as if everyone had stopped in midmotion to stare at her. She flinched when she saw Emily leaning at the wall next to the door.

Her lips formed a silent question. "Your Katie?"

Diana winced and nodded. Katie hadn't been *hers* for a long time.

Emily's expression hardened. "Everyone, you have to be careful who you talk to. The press might call or try to get in. Nothing leaves this room." Her voice softened as she addressed Diana. "Does she have immediate family?"

"Only her mother. I'll call her, and she'll bring an ID with her." Diana didn't look forward to that call, but at least the bad news would be coming from her instead of a stranger. Katie's mom had suffered through enough of those notifications.

"Okay, everyone. Get her ready for transport." Emily stepped closer and led Diana to the corner of the room.

The touch of her hand warmed Diana even through the layers of protective clothes.

"Are you okay? I would have never guessed you knew her from the way you did your job."

"I don't know. I'm too numb; I think it'll hit me later." Diana couldn't talk about it now or she'd break down.

"You call her mother, and I'll take care of her, okay? You're off the clock now." Emily's voice soothed her like a hug, not the usual impersonal tone she used at work.

"Okay, thank you." Diana ripped off her gloves and the protective gown and balled them together. Too tired to even try to throw them accurately, she dragged herself to the wastebasket on the other side of the room.

She pulled her phone from the pocket of her scrubs. Luckily, she had never cleaned up her contact list as she had started her new life.

Diana tried not to squirm when one of the younger nurses stared at her until Tony elbowed her and pointed out something for her to do.

So, that's how it will be from now on. She sighed and left to find some privacy for the difficult call. The second code room next door was empty.

Katie's mother answered on the first ring.

"Olivia? It's Diana."

"Hi, honey. Good to hear from you. How are you?" Her tone was genuinely happy. Diana hated that she had to change that.

"I'm fine. You know that I work in a hospital again? In Seattle?"

"Katie told me that, but she didn't know where exactly. You don't talk much anymore, do you?" Olivia sighed.

"No, not recently. I think we both needed our distance. But I'm calling because of her. Did you know she is in Seattle right now?"

"Yes, we met the day before yesterday, but she wanted to fly back to LA today. Have you met?"

"No, well, yes. But not like I wanted to meet her again. I'm actually calling from the hospital I work at, the Seattle General."

Olivia didn't answer. Different scenarios must be going through her mind now, each worse than the one before. And the truth wouldn't hurt any less.

"She was unconscious when the paramedics brought her in."

Olivia gasped. "Is she okay?"

"She is stable now, but still unconscious. She'll go to the ICU any minute now."

"But she'll be okay? Diana? Please?"

Diana swallowed the lump in her throat. Her medical experience told her it was too early to tell. Anything could have happened to Katie's brain during her oxygen deprivation, and her fight against addiction was far from over. But she was talking to her former almost mother-in-law, who had always treated her as a family member, even in the years Katie and she had only been colleagues and barely friends.

"I hope she'll be okay. They...we're doing everything we can. But it would be good if you were here when she wakes up."

"I'll be there as fast as I can."

"Olivia, don't drive. Get a cab."

"Good idea. Thanks, honey. Will you be there?"

"Yeah, I'll go with her to the ICU and wait for you."

After she had disconnected, Diana leaned against the wall and closed her eyes. Chaotic thoughts swirled through her mind, and she struggled to make a plan. What should she do first? Go back in and face the stares and maybe even questions of the others? Talk to Emily? Call Katie's manager, her ex-manager?

A soft touch to her face startled her. Diana opened her eyes and looked directly into Emily's. They were dark gray and full of concern. Only when Emily brushed her fingers over Diana's cheekbones did she realize she was crying. Emily swept her hair back and pulled Diana closer. Her hug grounded Diana, and calm spread from her embrace to Diana's center. It was short, but the reaffirmation of their connection gave her strength.

"Thank you. I really needed that."

"I just wanted to let you know she's on her way to the ICU. Before she left, she grimaced a little and even struggled against the respirator."

These were good signs, showing the effects of the drugs were wearing off. Only time could tell if any brain damage remained and to what extent.

"I promised her mother I would meet her in the ICU. She is a good woman, genuinely caring. Katie's drug problems broke her heart."

"And yours too?" Emily's eyes swept over her, her gaze searching.

"It was one of the reasons we broke up, but not the only one." Diana shrugged. At the time, her heart had been broken, but now the pain was only a faint memory. "We have been separated for nearly more years than we were together, and I'm over it. But she's still my friend, and it hurts to see her like this."

"What can I do for you?" The support in Emily's tone soothed her like a hot bath at the end of a long day.

"You're already doing it. You're here, with me. I wish I could hold you or…rather, you could hold me tonight." Diana knew she sounded needy, but she trusted that Emily would understand why.

"I'll come by your place after work. I'm going to make a few arrangements so you're off tonight."

"No, you can't do that. We said no special treatment, remember?"

"I hope I'd do it for any of my residents. You're overworked as it is, and you won't be fit to come back to the night shift after spending all day in the ICU."

Diana's mind was racing. Emily's suggestion was reasonable, but she didn't want to appear as though she couldn't cope with the stress. "But—"

"No buts. Please. I don't want to fight with you. Go and meet her mother, see that she wakes up, then go home and sleep. Doctor's orders. I'll make a house visit tonight and check up on you. If you want, you can come back to the day shift tomorrow." Emily's tone conveyed her usual no-nonsense attitude, but she smiled and the warmth never left her eyes.

Diana didn't have it in her to argue. "Okay, Dr. Barnes. I don't want to fight either. See you later."

"Call me anytime you need me. See you tonight." Emily looked around and hugged her again. All too soon, she stepped back.

┼┼┼┼┼┼┼

"Diana," a female voice whispered.

Diana opened her eyes and sat up. Shit, she'd fallen asleep in the visitor's chair in Katie's room. She wouldn't have thought it possible to relax enough on the hard plastic.

Olivia, Katie's mom, stood in the doorway, waving her over. Hadn't she left just a second ago to get something to eat?

Diana tiptoed out of the room and glanced at Katie before she softly closed the door behind her. Nothing in the serene features of the sleeping woman showed what she had been through over last several hours. Olivia, however, seemed to have aged ten years today.

"You need to go home now." Olivia used her best mom voice, a mixture of caring and scolding.

Diana had secretly always loved it, even if it sometimes triggered adolescent impulses to protest. "I'm fine. I want to be here for you." That

215

was the truth. At this point in her life she cared more for Olivia's well-being than Katie's.

"You helped a lot today. Seeing Katie going from unconscious to crazy in a second was terrifying. I was glad you were here. It must have been hard on you too." She hugged Diana.

Diana held her for a moment. Katie had been delirious and in withdrawal when she woke up, ripping out her breathing tube before Diana could stop her, so she had to be restrained. Diana had held her hands down until a nurse could give her a sedative and had gotten a kick in her side as thanks. She was sure Katie hadn't even recognized her. Strangely, that hadn't affected Diana as much as she thought it would. She had felt sad for Katie but nothing else. The anger and hurt she remembered feeling during Katie's previous fights with addiction had vanished like the love they had shared.

Olivia kissed her cheek and stepped out of their embrace. "Diana, honey, you look like shit. Go home and sleep and try to forget about us for a while." The mom voice was back, but the smile softened her words.

"Thanks for the compliment." Diana rolled her eyes and kissed her back. "Let me know if you need anything, okay?"

Diana snuck into the locker room via the corridor that led to the staircase in the back of the building. She wasn't up to answering questions, and she was afraid if she met Emily, she might do something inappropriate, like hug her. Luck was on her side, and she was alone until she passed the administration desk to get to the front door.

"Dr. Petrell, wait," Stacy called after her.

Diana didn't stop, pretending she hadn't heard her. Not very nice, but she'd apologize tomorrow.

Stepping through the front door, she searched her backpack for her sunglasses. Instead of glaring sunlight several camera flashes blinded her. *Fuck!* She held up a hand to cover her face and ran. She didn't stop until she had reached the park.

Panting for breath, she turned around to study the way she had come. No one followed her on foot, and no car was going suspiciously slow. Good. Maybe they hadn't recognized her. Maybe they just took pictures of anyone leaving the hospital, hoping to score. She leaned against a tree, catching her breath, waiting for her heart rate to decelerate.

People passed her without a second glance on their way to and from the park. Mothers with children, a group of students, several runners and skaters. Everyone looked happy to be out on a sunny June day; everyone looked so fucking normal.

Why couldn't she have this? Last week she thought she had made a good start. Her work was going well, and she was happy in a new relationship. She didn't need this drama in her life.

Diana pulled her sunglasses from the still-open backpack and closed it. The brown glasses tinted her surroundings in warm and happy colors that didn't reflect her mood at all.

She straightened and shouldered her backpack. *Suck it up! You chose the life you had, and now you have to deal with the consequences.*

Shifting the takeout bag to the other hand, Emily pressed the doorbell again and waited for movement from inside. Nothing. She fished her phone from her pocket and thumbed through her contacts until she found Diana. She should really mark her as her favorite. The call went directly to voice mail. Maybe she was in the garage, playing drums? Or outside?

Emily went to the garage first. It was locked and the tiny red light of the alarm was on. The garden was empty, but the back door was open. Should she knock again? The house was quiet and dark, so she decided against it and let herself in. She placed the bag on the kitchen island and went directly to the bedroom.

Diana lay on her stomach on the bed, her naked curves only half-covered by a bath towel. The soft glow from the hall illuminated her, highlighting her shoulder blades and the dragon. Her dark hair was mussed and still damp.

Emily's breath caught. Diana was so effortlessly sexy. Sleeping deeply, she didn't even react when Emily sat beside her. Should she let her sleep? Being in her house without Diana's knowledge made her feel like a stalker. Plus, waking her up would be the sensible thing to do. Emily guessed Diana hadn't taken the time to eat anything all day, and if she continued sleeping, she would most likely wake up during the night, unable to go back to sleep. The recent night shifts had probably switched her circadian rhythm again.

"Diana." No reaction. She tried again, louder. "Diana, wake up."

A protesting growl was the answer, but Diana didn't move.

Emily just wanted to poke her lightly, but the warm skin under her fingers was too tempting. She stroked her arm, tracing the flames around her biceps over her shoulder to her back, until she encountered hard knots under the skin. Kneading them softly, Emily was delighted when the growl changed into content sighs.

After a few minutes, Diana turned around, captured Emily's hand, and kissed it. "Thank you. What a perfect way to wake up."

"You're welcome." Emily kissed Diana lightly on the lips and stood immediately to avoid the temptation of deepening the kiss. She wanted nothing more than to crawl into bed with her, but then they wouldn't get up anymore and would definitely not spend the time talking. And that probably wasn't what Diana needed right now. "Come to the kitchen. I brought dinner."

"I don't know if I can eat anything." Diana's stomach growled, and she laughed. "Okay. My body agrees with you." She sat up, completely ignoring the towel that slipped down.

Emily took a step back to the bed. She stopped in midmotion and swallowed. *Food first, then talk.* She turned and fled to the kitchen, where she busied herself with distributing rice noodles, thin slices of beef, vegetables, and fresh herbs from the plastic takeaway bowls into real ones.

"That smells delicious." Diana had put on sweats and an old T-shirt. She had obviously tried and failed to tame her sleep-tousled hair.

"Pho is my go-to comfort food on my grumpy days." Emily poured the still-hot broth over the other ingredients and carried the bowls to the table.

Diana followed with chopsticks and spoons. "Grumpy days? Is that a euphemism for your period?"

Laughing, Emily shook her head. "That's what I call the first day after a series of night shifts."

"That's a good one. I might steal it." Diana took a mouthful of broth and sighed. "Ooh, did you go to the Ginger Cat? Thank you!"

"Mmmh." She was too busy chewing to reply. Emily hadn't been able to eat anything at work today.

She still worried about Diana. Some of the lines around her eyes had disappeared while sleeping, but the shadows under them persisted.

Diana played with the last rice noodle in her bowl. "My brain is finally waking up now. How did you get in here?"

"The back door was open. Maybe not the best idea if you're sleeping." Emily smiled to show she was teasing. She didn't want to start a discussion on security now.

"I didn't plan to sleep. I just wanted to rest and collect my thoughts for a minute before I called my manager—Fuck! I didn't call Vic!" Diana jumped up and left the room.

Seconds later, she returned with her phone and plugged it into the charger in the kitchen. "Come on, charge."

Emily took the bowls and cutlery and carried them into the kitchen. Placing them into the dishwasher, she waited for an explanation. When none came, she went over to Diana. "Why do you need to talk to your manager? And why do you still have a manager?"

Diana put down the phone and rubbed her eyes with both hands. "He's mostly the contact person for anyone who wants to reach Dee Dragon. He also collects the royalties from the old records for me. I need to warn him." She looked up at Emily, and a muscle twitched in her cheek.

Why was she so focused on her manager right now? Her gaze held an emotion Emily hadn't seen on her before, something akin to despair. She hadn't looked so shaken directly after treating Katie. "What else happened?"

"I did something stupid. When I left the hospital, I didn't think and just went through the front door. Someone was taking pictures. I don't know if they recognized me or not." Diana picked up her phone again as the logo appeared on the black screen.

Emily's thoughts swirled like a maelstrom. The hospital's management would be furious if Diana dragged their good name through the mud. They'd fire her without a second thought.

What would happen to their relationship if Diana had to leave the ED? To many variables were at play here to formulate a plan. She wouldn't get another job in Seattle, that was sure. Would she just pack and leave? The last thought hurt like a punch in the stomach and took her breath away.

But maybe they hadn't recognized her. Or even if someone did, would the presence of a former bandmate be newsworthy? A tiny spark of hope flickered deep within her.

The phone sprang back to life with a rapid sequence of beeps. With each one, the flame of hope got doused with cold water until it died out and the last hope of controlling the situation scattered like the ashes. The amount of missed calls and messages left no doubt that her picture had been published.

Diana grimaced as she opened her messages. "They sold the picture to several internet tabloid sites. Vic tried to do some damage control when he couldn't reach me." She frowned as she listened to a call, presumably from her manager.

Finally, she put her phone down with trembling hands. "Vic said they don't know yet that I work there. That's good. But the shit they write…" She shook her head. "They guessed correctly that Katie got admitted with an overdose and then spun the tale that I was doing drugs with her. One site even writes I fought with her and that she tried to kill herself because of a lovers' quarrel. And to prove all of that, they pointed out that I look like death warmed over in the fucking photograph."

Emily was torn between going around the counter to hug her and staying on her side to keep the distance she needed for rational thought. "You have to be careful tomorrow morning and go in through the back entrance. We need to protect the ED."

"I don't want to be careful; I just want to do my job. Fuck it." Diana hit the counter with her fist. "Ouch. Anyone on staff can see the picture on the internet and make the connection, and then they earn their fifteen minutes of fame and some easy money by telling on me. I don't know if it even makes sense to go back at all. Dr. Wallace made it clear I'd be history if I draw negative attention to the hospital."

Emily swallowed several angry replies. Did Diana want to give up on them? Did she want to start over again? Somewhere else? She pushed her churning emotions into the back of her mind. The numbness that filled her instead must be better than the pain. She reached for that place within her that allowed her to face human tragedies at work without outward displays of emotion. "If you want to take the easy way out, stay at home. Or run away; that's what you did before. If not, I'll see you tomorrow, seven a.m., sharp."

Grabbing her bag on her way out, Emily fought her rising tears. This wasn't like a work situation at all. She had no control, and she was too invested already. That frightened and angered her at the same time. She didn't know if she was angry at Diana or herself. Slamming the door helped a little, but it only lasted until she had reached the corner of the street.

Diana wasn't sure what had just happened. One minute she was voicing her frustration with the situation; the next minute Emily had turned ice-cold. That tone reminded Diana of the first weeks at work after Emily had met her at the club, before they had become friends. Was it so easy for her to shrug off their connection as if it were a dirty lab coat? For her, it wasn't possible to switch off the love she felt.

Love? Her heart skipped a beat as she examined the idea. The realization of being in love again should have been a joyful thought, not this tangled mess of frustration and confusion. But she had no doubt it was true.

With a sigh, she walked to the back door and locked it. Pacing in her living room, she picked up stray journals, books, and knickknacks that had migrated from their designated places.

No matter what Emily believed of her, it had never been her intention to quit and run. That accusation hurt. Whatever happened to her residency, Diana had no intention of giving up on their relationship.

The doorbell rang just as she put her sneakers in the closet next to the door. Had Emily come back? A peek through the peephole confirmed that she had. Hope blossomed like desert flowers after a rainstorm.

Diana immediately opened the door.

"Can we talk?" Emily bit her lip. She clutched the strap of her bag with one hand so tightly that her knuckled had turned white, but her expression was too restrained to give away what was going on beyond the surface.

"Now you want to talk? I thought that was what we were doing ten minutes ago." Diana clenched her jaws shut.

Emily flinched at her words or maybe at the harsh tone. "Please…"

The real hurt and regret in her voice deflated Diana's anger. She took a step back and waved her in. "Come in."

Emily left her bag and shoes at the door and went to the living room. Her neck was a lovely shade of pink.

She knew that Emily hated her propensity to easily blush, but right now Diana was grateful. The blush admitted louder than words that Emily was as affected as she was by their argument, no matter how well she controlled her features.

They both sat on the couch, not quite touching, but closer than strangers.

"I want to apologize." The words rushed out of Emily as though she was short of breath. "Please."

"Okay." Diana waited for her to continue.

Emily's expression softened enough to allow Diana to see the real woman again. "I ran because I panicked. I thought you'd tell me that you'd rather quit work than face the consequences." She looked down at her hands that were digging into the seat cushion. "I'm sorry I made stupid assumptions and didn't give you a chance. That was my fear speaking. Once I slowed down for a second, I knew that's not like you at all. You always want to talk about things, and I'm the one running from my feelings."

Diana gently peeled the cushion out of Emily's grip and offered her own hand to hold instead. "I accept your apology. It hurt that you didn't trust me." She smoothed out the wrinkles in the cushion. "To be honest, with my history, your assumption wasn't that far off. Ten or maybe even five years ago, that might have been my reaction. I used to take the easy way out."

"But you changed." It wasn't a question. "I thought I did too. But I just fell back into my old habit of not trusting anyone." Emily still didn't meet her gaze, and her blush hadn't receded.

"Don't drive yourself crazy. No one changes in a day or even a month. Just the decision to do so doesn't make it work. Only resolve, patience, and repetitions." She touched Emily's shoulder with her own. "And you came back when you realized what had happened. That's what is important."

"Thank you, but I still think I should have stayed and talked." She leaned into the touch. "So, what can we do to keep you at Seattle General?"

Diana lifted a corner of her mouth in a teasing half-smile. "We're clever and independent women who know what we want and how to get it, at least most of the time. Imagine what we could accomplish if we worked as a team?"

"A team." Emily's smile was brilliant. "I could get used to that idea. So, what's the next step?"

Diana thought about it for a moment. Helplessness dug a hollow in her middle, growing every second. "I need to take back the control of my story. I don't want to live with the fear that I could be outed as a former rock musician any minute. But the problem is selling that strategy to Dr. Wallace."

Emily nodded thoughtfully. "I can see why he wouldn't like that. I think we should concentrate on finding a way to protect the hospital's good name. If they aren't linked with your story, then they won't need to fire you." She let go of Diana's hand to pull out her phone. "Let's make a list of ideas."

"The chances of completely leaving the hospital out of it are slim. I'd rather work on a plan to convince them that having a former drummer working for them isn't the end of the world. The contract only states that I have to avoid negative PR, and it's not the same, no matter what Dr. Wallace says."

"I don't think that's going to work out for you. What do you think of lying low for a while? Maybe going to an outpatient clinic in the outskirts? Or doing research for a few months at the university? I'm sure Dr. Wallace can arrange something like that. If you're out of sight, we can contain the damage to the ED."

Despair filled the hollow, and Diana didn't see a way out. If the hospital perceived her as a threat to its reputation, she'd be kicked out in a heartbeat. Emily's lack of support for her plan, vague as it was, hurt and threatened her more than the idea of being jobless.

Chapter 19

DIANA SNEAKED INTO THE HOSPITAL through the delivery entrance and shot furtive glances in the direction of the ED area. Lead in her stomach weighed her down and slowed her steps. It wasn't as though she had to hurry. The plan they had come up with yesterday was for her to stay out of the paparazzi's view and to talk to Dr. Wallace. Emily had offered to arrange a meeting with the chief of staff.

Arriving before sunrise at five a.m. had helped her stay undetected but left her with two hours of nothing to do but avoiding co-workers and their questions.

Suck it up. Even if they know, you're still the same person as yesterday. Diana straightened her shoulders and held her head high as she entered the ED through the staircase from the basement. The corridor was only dimly lit and empty. The familiar background of voices chatting at the nurses' station sounded around the corner. Diana had to walk past them to reach the locker room, so she mentally steeled herself.

The easy banter stopped immediately. "Oh, um, hi, Diana. Didn't expect you here today." Courtney, lacking diplomatic skills as always.

"I'm back on day shifts. I just helped with the night shifts while you were out sick." *Or while you were enjoying a vacation over Memorial Day weekend with your boyfriend.* She didn't add what she really thought.

"I meant because of the drug scandal." Courtney's grin was wide. What had Diana done to her that she enjoyed this?

Madison gasped. She looked from Courtney to Diana and back with wide eyes and an open mouth as though she couldn't believe that Courtney had the audacity, or maybe courage, depending on your point of view, to mention it.

Diana called up a smile of her own, hoping she could leave defensiveness out of her voice. "I'm not involved in a drug scandal. A patient who came into the ED, who has every right to confidentiality, by the way, happened to be my ex. And the usual suspects construed a story as clickbait to sell advertising online. I'm just surprised they didn't insinuate I was abducted by aliens or was worked to death by greedy slave drivers, after the way I looked in those pictures."

Madison laughed at the last part, and Diana took this as a mini victory. She was probably going to have to fight many more of these skirmishes today, but it was a step in the right direction. She decided to leave while she was ahead. "I'm going to go and get changed. See you soon."

After changing, Diana went straight to the staff lounge. Liz sat on the couch, looking as tired after her fourth night shift as Diana had been yesterday morning. She typed rapidly on a laptop, probably notes.

"Good morning, Liz. How was your night?" Diana sat on the same couch but left a distance between them in case Liz didn't want to talk to her.

"Hi. Missed you. Courtney's constant chatting got on my nerves." Liz rolled her eyes. "I shouldn't say that, but it's true."

The normalcy of the comment alleviated part of Diana's tension. Or hadn't Liz heard?

Liz lightly punched Diana's shoulder with her fist. "So, that's what you were hiding. I'm actually relieved. I imagined something much more sinister."

"What do you mean? Sinister?"

"Maybe I read too many crime novels, but when you showed up with the nine-year gap, always wearing the long sleeves underneath your scrubs, never changing in front of others, I thought you were hiding scars. Either from an accident or abuse." Liz shrugged. "I would never have guessed you were hiding beautiful tattoos. And all of that fascinating history."

Wow. That anyone would think that hadn't even occurred to her, but Liz had a point. She hadn't been as inconspicuous as she'd thought. "Beautiful, huh? Did you google me?"

Liz laughed. "No, but Courtney did. And I'm afraid she had shown everyone before I had a little talk with her about professional conduct. Not that I think it worked."

"I expected as much. And I don't really mind that everyone knows about my past. I'm not ashamed or anything. It's just that Dr. Wallace made it clear I won't work here for long if I bring negative attention to the ED."

"Really? Stuffy, old-fashioned idiot. He shouldn't have hired you if he wasn't prepared to stand behind you. Don't worry, he's usually more bark than bite."

Diana didn't believe the last statement, but Liz's indignation on her behalf eased her tension a little and brought the other doubts nagging at her to the foreground. "Do you think our co-workers will take me less seriously? Or the patients?"

Liz's brows wrinkled, and she didn't answer immediately.

In the quiet room, Diana's heartbeat sounded unnaturally loud to herself. She tapped a rhythm on her thigh to redirect her focus.

"I can't speak for everyone here, but I think your work will stand for itself. Hospitals are always full of exaggerated rumors and scandals, as if to prove the TV shows right. For a few days or maybe weeks, you'll be the focus of those, but then something else will come along, perhaps an affair or a pregnancy, and then they'll forget about you. The good news is, they'll defend you against outsiders. Some might think of you as a disgrace, but you're *our* disgrace, and we won't let others bad-mouth you. I sincerely doubt the patients will even notice." Liz had reached for her with the last sentence and squeezed her arm affectionately.

Diana grimaced. The last bit was reassuring, but it was still out of her control. She hated waiting. "So, provided I'll still have a job tomorrow, I just let it blow over? I wish I could do something."

"Be yourself. You're friendly, respectful, and a hard worker. That's what the others, especially the nurses, notice about you."

Groaning, Diana let her head fall back. "Thanks. That helps, even if I wish you had a magic wand that could make everything go away."

"And I could cure cancer while I'm at it." Liz laughed.

Diana chuckled, and it lifted her spirits a little. But the fact remained that their boss would probably not find any humor in it. "If you could only change Dr. Wallace's attitude. But thank you for the pep talk."

Liz turned serious immediately and nodded. "Anytime. Just let me know what else I can do for you."

"That means a lot." Diana stood. "I think I'll start my shift early and see if I can find something useful to do."

At the nurses' station, Diana hurried to complete her file before the shift change at seven. When a shadow fell on the screen, she turned around.

Tony was watching her. His expression was serious, devoid of the usual cordiality.

Diana wiped her suddenly damp hand on her scrubs. "Good morning, Tony."

He looked her up and down. "Why are you here?"

"What do you mean, here? Now? I'm completing a file."

"No, I mean here." He moved his arm in a wide arc, a gesture that encompassed the whole department. "Is this a joke for you? Something to check off your to-do list before you go back to being a star?"

Diana shook her head. "No, definitely not. This work is what I want to do. Preferably for the rest of my life."

"Good, work it is, then. But I'll reserve my final judgment." He smiled, not as openly as he used too, but it was good enough for now. "You better hurry to make it to the turnover on time. Today is not a good day to piss off Dr. Barnes."

"Thanks." Diana hesitated for a moment. She wanted to thank him for more than reminding her of the time but couldn't find the words.

Tony nodded as if he got it and winked.

She had never thought she would not only got used to his constant winking but actually appreciate it.

She slipped into the staff lounge a minute after seven. Everyone stopped talking and stared at her. That was getting tedious. Emily wasn't here yet, so she let herself flop down on the end of the couch, wondering what had delayed her.

Alec leaned closer and slapped her on the shoulder. "A rock star? Wow! I bet you scored tons of cool chicks."

Resisting the temptation to stand and sit somewhere else, Diana rubbed her shoulder. She didn't know what to say to that absurd statement.

"Alec, shut up. Just ignore him. He grew up in a cave." Peter flashed her a quick grin and ran a hand through his short, dark curls. "Is there anything we can do to help?"

"Thanks. Not talking about it would probably be best, but I hope someone will do something crass soon and create new rumors."

"Maybe Alec can help you with that," Peter said.

Diana laughed, and the others joined in. After a moment, Alec chuckled too.

The sound of a door closing with more force than necessary stopped the laughter. Emily strode to the short side of the table and sat, looking only at Liz. "Start your report."

She was wearing too much makeup again, covering each freckle and line as if they'd never existed. Diana hoped it was more armor than mask and that the real Emily wouldn't disappear beneath it.

After Liz had finished, Emily turned to Diana. Her expression was unreadable, but her gray eyes were a shade darker than usual and bored into Diana like laser beams, reaching all the way into her heart.

"Dr. Petrell, we have an appointment with Dr. Wallace at eight." Emily's tone was carefully neutral.

"We? I don't want you to get into trouble because of me." Diana wanted to reach out and touch her hand to reassure herself that everything would be okay, but, of course, she didn't. "Can we talk about this?" The last thing she wanted to do was pull Emily down with her on her sinking ship.

"No time." Emily jumped up. "Liz, I need you to come with me." She strode to the door without waiting for Liz.

Liz looked from Emily to Diana and back. She gave an apologetic shrug to Diana before she stood and followed her.

Diana closed her eyes, slowly exhaled, and slumped back against the couch. Was that a good sign? It certainly didn't feel like one.

Emily had just finished her talk with Liz as her phone rang. The caller ID immediately made her heart race. What did Dr. Wallace's assistant want? To postpone the meeting? She accepted the call. "Barnes."

"Dr. Barnes, Brian speaking. Dr. Wallace asked me to set up an additional meeting. Do you have time now?" The professional politeness didn't reveal the intention behind the summons.

The question was rhetorical, so she agreed and hung up.

Oh shit! Has he found out about Diana and me? How?

"Emily, are you okay?" Liz caught Emily's shaking hand in her own.

"I don't know." Emily mentally rearranged her timetable. "I need to go up to Dr. Wallace now. Could you take care of everything?"

"Don't worry, I've got this. Don't let the old buzzard get to you." With an encouraging smile, Liz left.

During the ride in the elevator, Emily tried to find an alternative explanation for the imminent meeting but came up blank. She checked if her scrubs were still wrinkle-free and knocked on Dr. Wallace's office door.

Brian called her in immediately and waved her through. His bright expression was as welcoming as every other time she'd been here, and it helped to assuage her nervousness.

She had countless talks with Dr. Wallace in the past, all of them friendly. Since he'd been promoted to chief of staff and she'd taken over the day-to-day matters of the ED, they'd conferred regularly, and she'd come to enjoy their conversations. She'd learned a lot from him and appreciated the informal mentorship. But today was different.

"Dr. Barnes, good morning. How are you?" Dr. Wallace looked up from the document he had been studying and pointed to the couple of chairs in front of his mahogany desk that dominated one side of his large corner office.

"I'm fine, sir." That was a complete lie, but politeness was deeply ingrained in her. Emily took a seat and restrained herself from stroking the gleaming surface that reminded her of her father's desk. As Brian placed a cup of tea in front of her, she thanked him. *See, no reason to worry. Everything's as always.* But she didn't dare to reach for the tea as her stomach was in knots, and no amount of denial could wash away the nausea.

"Dr. Barnes, I wanted to talk to you privately before…the other matter. I have a proposal for you. As you know, I highly value the good work you do in our ED, and I think it is past time to honor that officially." He beamed with a proud smile as he handed over the papers in front of him.

Emily blinked. What was that about? A raise?

A few words popped out from the paper. Her name. *Employment contract. Head of Emergency Department.* Her vision tunneled on the last one, and everything else swam out of focus. Head of Emergency Department. A wave of heat raced through her body like an out-of-control rocket and took her breath away. A dim voice filtered through the blood pounding in her ears, and she looked up to see Dr. Wallace's mouth moving. Emily shook her head to clear her senses and took a deep breath.

"Dr. Barnes? Everything okay?" The concern in his voice calmed her.

"I'm just…overwhelmed. I hadn't expected this." Her hands shook as she quickly scanned the pages of the contract until she came to the figures that would be her new salary. Wow. She put the contract on the desk to concentrate on Dr. Wallace.

He chuckled. "You've earned it, no question. We've always been on the same wavelength, and I know I can trust you to have the same priorities. I can guarantee you, you won't find a better offer. Take a couple of days to read the contract and think about it."

"Thank you, I will." That crazy rocket had catapulted her onto a cloud of happiness, and she couldn't stop grinning. He didn't know about their relationship, and now she'd be in the perfect position to help Diana.

The phone rang, and Dr. Wallace grimaced. "I'm sorry to cut this short, but I have to take this. I'll see you at eight. I hope I can count on you."

Emily clutched the contract to her chest and nodded. "Of course, sir, see you soon." Her steps lighter than before, she left the office in search of Liz. Everything would work out fine now.

┼┼┼┼┼┼┼

Five minutes to eight, Diana hesitated to enter the chief of staff's office, trying to decide if she should face the lion's den alone or wait for Emily. She adjusted the collar of her immaculate white lab coat, one she had never worn at work before, squared her shoulders, and stood straight. Just as she raised her hand to knock, a soft touch to her back distracted her, and she turned around.

Emily, wearing the same unfamiliar uniform they had no use for in the ED, stood directly behind her. Her gaze was confident and shining with a passion that reminded Diana of a cat about to pounce on her prey. She seemed at home in a lion's den. Emily quickly squeezed her hand.

The touch was warm and firm, and it melted the cold dread residing in her stomach.

"Trust me," Emily whispered. "Everything will be fine."

Diana nodded. She did trust her.

Emily held her gaze for a moment, and a small smile played around her lips. They lost their perpetual hard line, and Diana wanted to kiss them, even though they were tinted in a fake rose color that covered up their natural beauty.

Emily let go of her hand and stepped around Diana to knock on the office door. An assistant answered and ushered them to Dr. Wallace's office. The chief of staff sat behind his enormous desk that had nearly the same color as his skin. With his wide shoulders in a navy suit, he looked fit for his age. Diana guessed him to be in his midfifties.

"Dr. Barnes, Dr. Petrell, welcome. Let's sit over here." He pointed to a large round table. Windows completely covered one side of the room. The view from the top floor of the building over Seattle was stunning. Diana could look past the Space Needle to Mount Rainier looming in the background. At least the parts that were still visible. Clouds as somber as her mood obscured the sky, leaving only tiny slivers of blue.

She chose a seat with her back to the windows to avoid distraction. And maybe a little bit of sunshine would break through and divert Dr. Wallace.

Emily took the chair directly next to her, flanking her like a bodyguard and leaving some space between them and Dr. Wallace on the far side of the table.

His assistant had followed them in, offering water, coffee, and tea. He handed Dr. Wallace a thin file, no doubt Diana's, and a stack of printouts. The one on top showed quite clearly the fucking picture.

Dr. Wallace moved the file until it was perfectly aligned with the other papers and the edge of the table. "Dr. Petrell, I'm sure you remember our last conversation quite well, but let me recap it for the other participant in this meeting. You informed me of your previous occupation and assured me this part of your life was over. I gave you this spot in the residency program as a second chance, counting on you not to endanger the reputation of this hospital."

Emily sat up straighter. "Dr. Wallace, she didn't—"

"Dr. Barnes, let me finish, please." He interrupted without anger and swept his gaze over the two of them as though to see if another comment would come.

Diana swallowed, fighting to keep her expression as neutral as Emily's. *Like a bunch of fucking robots.* She suppressed an inappropriate giggling, born more of desperation than humor.

When everyone stayed quiet, he continued. "As I was saying, you violated the trust I placed in you. The reputation of this hospital is at stake, and I'm sure Dr. Barnes would agree we have to do everything to avoid negative PR. You broke that part of your contract. I should have fired you immediately, but because of Dr. Barnes's request, we're having this meeting now."

Diana swallowed, preparing to answer.

Emily's hand beneath the table stopped her. She squeezed Diana's thigh, but her gaze never left Dr. Wallace. "Sir, let me explain to you the circumstances that led to this picture. You might not know that Dr. Petrell filled in for the night shift on her days off. And on this particular day, she took on a patient around turnover, voluntarily staying longer to support the understaffed ED. After she realized she had a personal connection to the patient, she still performed her work, staying professional throughout the incident. I have signed reports of this incident and Dr. Petrell's excellent performance from Mr. Rodriguez, the day shift nurse in charge, and myself."

Emily took several pages from a folder Diana hadn't even noticed her carrying and slid them over to Dr. Wallace. Before he could read them, she continued. "After the patient was stable, Dr. Petrell stayed on, contacting the family and supporting her friend. When she finally left the building after being awake for more than twenty-four hours under extremely stressful circumstances, this picture was taken. In no way did Dr. Petrell speak to the press about her involvement in the situation. Not only are these articles pure fantasy, but they also don't mention her working here as a resident. Correct me if I'm wrong, but only her stage name was published. Right now, we don't even have a public scandal involving a member of this hospital." She leaned back and patiently regarded Dr. Wallace.

His jaws were working, and a muscle in his left cheek twitched. "Yet."

Emily conceded this with a nod.

Diana's heart raced as she looked from him to Emily and back. When was the right time to say something for herself? Her right hand tapped on her thigh until Emily covered it with her own beneath the table. It was only a quick touch, but the warmth of the contact coursed through her system like an anxiolytic and strengthened her resolve.

Emily leaned forward in her chair. "Dr. Wallace, for a good part of the last two months I've been Dr. Petrell's mentor, not that she needed much support. She is a hard worker, very conscientious, and more mature than most residents. She is, of course, more mature because she has life experience that exceeds college and med school. She is an excellent fit for our ED, not only professionally, but personally as well." She handed Dr. Wallace several pages from her folder. "Here we have signed statements from every attending who has worked with Dr. Petrell so far and the majority of the rest of the staff I could reach in such a short time. They all support a continuation of Dr. Petrell's employment."

This was the first time Diana had heard about these statements. Emily must have collected them this morning, and the support from her colleagues let Diana sit a bit straighter.

His thick brows formed a menacing line as Dr. Wallace skimmed through the pages. "This is all very nice, but I never doubted Dr. Petrell's qualification as a physician or her work ethics. Dr. Barnes, I thought we had the same priorities. This doesn't help the hospital's reputation." He flung the papers on the table and looked directly at Diana. His dark brown eyes held no mercy.

Diana pulled her shoulders back. "Sir, I'm sorry a picture of me leaving the hospital was taken and published. You're right; some tabloid will probably find out soon that I work here. But I don't think it will automatically turn into a scandal or damage the hospital's reputation. Maybe we can discuss our options and find a compromise—"

"No. No discussion. No compromise." His voice boomed and drowned out the rest of her argument. "You're fired."

That blunt statement knocked the air out of her lungs as if she'd been hit over her head with her own cymbals. The ringing in her ears nearly drowned out her racing thoughts. *That's it.* Her dream was over, at least for now. She'd wait until the stir created by the press had blown over and then search for another residency. But as soon as she got on the short list, they'd call her former employer, and Dr. Wallace would tell them exactly why they had fired her. Maybe she'd get a third chance in a few years, somewhere remote they were so desperate that they'd take anyone, like Alaska.

Tears stung her eyes, and she had to swallow a few times before she could speak without crying. Only her dignity was left, and she wanted to take that with her. "I understand, sir. Thank you for the opportunity of working here. Goodbye."

Emily clenched her fists on her lap until her knuckles whitened. The pain of her nails digging into her palms was nothing compared to the searing agony raging in her chest. Dr. Wallace's words rolled through her like thunder until the meaning hit her like lightning.

He'd mentioned shared priorities twice, now and during their earlier conversation. She hadn't understood the relevance then, but it was obvious now. The offer to become head of Emergency Department was tied to her support in firing Diana.

No, no, no. Leading her own department had always been her goal, but the choice between getting the promotion and fighting for Diana was no choice at all.

He hadn't even listened to Diana's offer of discussing other options and shut her down without a second thought. Anger at the unfairness of it all blazed like a wildfire, burning away her restraint. "No!"

Diana and Dr. Wallace froze in midmotion. She had walked around the table with an outstretched hand, and he had half risen from his seat.

"Bullshit!" Emily hit the table with her fist. "We don't even know what will happen. And you want to ruin her career, her life over a possibility? Without the decency of listening?"

Both stared at her, mouths agape.

Dr. Wallace recovered first. "Dr. Barnes, there's no need for you to become involved. Dr. Petrell seems to understand the situation and—"

"No! This is as much my ED as it is yours; you admitted that earlier. I worked extra shifts without payment, handled the schedule, smoothed over every minor and major incident, without complaint, without asking for favors. For years and years I've given my life for the ED. I'm already involved. If you fire her, you'll lose me too." Emily's voice broke at the last word.

What had she done? Would she really leave her job?

Yes. The furnace in her heart had tempered her determination to steel. She unclenched her fist that still rested on the table and reached for a water bottle with trembling fingers. The cool liquid soothed her raw throat. Had she been yelling? And when had she stood?

Diana looked at her with wide eyes and shook her head, taking a step back into her direction.

With deliberate calm, Emily put the bottle back on the table and sat again. "Dr. Wallace, please, let's start this conversation over. I can't support this decision. It's not right, and it's not what's best for this hospital and our patients."

He fell into his chair with a thud. "What are you suggesting?" He waved a hand at Diana. "Dr. Petrell, take a seat."

Diana hurried back to Emily's side, still shaking her head. "You don't need to go because of me. I know how much the ED means to you." The faint lines around her eyes crinkled in concern.

You mean more to me. Emily couldn't say it here, but she hoped Diana could read it in her eyes. The thought that as the head of the ED she'd truly be Diana's boss flashed through her mind. Suddenly, the position lost its appeal.

She turned back to Dr. Wallace and hardened her gaze. "I think we can agree the picture and the publicity around it are a problem. Why don't we talk about actions we can take to avoid a scandal other than firing an accomplished resident who has neither done anything wrong nor violated her contract? Maybe we could even turn the situation around so we actually gain positive PR."

Dr. Wallace returned her gaze with a severity she'd never seen in him before. After a minute, the deep lines between his brows evened out. He nodded thoughtfully as he arranged the papers he had thrown on the table into a neat pile. "How can we put a positive spin on things?"

Finally! He was listening. Emily held back a sigh as she turned in her seat to her left. "Dr. Petrell, do you have any experience with this kind of media attention?"

Diana raised one eyebrow as she obviously recognized the talking points she'd suggested and Emily had rejected the night before. "Not personally, but yes, it happened to the band."

"Perfect. What did you do in the past?" Emily squeezed her leg again, longer this time. She had no other way to apologize in front of her boss for her dismissal of Diana's ideas yesterday.

"We usually used a publicist who specialized in damage control. Often the media only want to print a story that's interesting and pushes sales. They prefer getting a better version from a publicist to the half-truths attached to a sketchy picture."

Dr. Wallace studied Diana for a moment as his expression came around from suspicious to curious. "And do you know of such a publicist? And could you contact them?"

Emily could feel the tension leaving Diana's thigh beneath her hand. Their plan had worked. No, Diana's plan had worked. She should have listened to her from the start.

The first genuine smile of the day appeared on Diana's lips. "That's a good idea. I can get in touch with my manager. I'm sure he has someone excellent on speed dial. Do you want to talk to them, sir?"

"No, no, you talk to them, and you hire and pay them. If you can squeeze some positive PR for our hospital out of this mess, you can stay here, even if your name comes out. That's the only deal you'll get. Take it or leave it." Dr. Wallace rose, putting an end to the discussion.

Diana walked over to him and shook his hand. "I'll take it. Thank you, Dr. Wallace."

Half afraid her legs wouldn't carry her, Emily followed. Dr. Wallace's concession wasn't much, but at least it was a chance. She walked around the table and held out her hand, surprised it wasn't trembling anymore.

He hesitated for what felt like an eternity before squeezing it. "Keep me informed of your plans."

What plans? Did he really still consider her for the promotion? She nodded and left the room in a haze, barely aware of Diana at her side.

Chapter 20

EMILY HEADED FOR THE ELEVATOR, but before they reached it, Diana opened the door to the staircase. She tugged on Emily's hand and led her down the stairs.

They hadn't said a word since they had left Dr. Wallace office. Emily guessed Diana's mind was reeling as much as her own with her one-hundred-eighty-degree turn.

At the first landing, Diana stopped. "What—"

"Let's talk in my office." Emily's voice was still shaking.

Diana nodded, and Emily hurried down the stairs before she could say anything else.

Liz waited in front of Emily's office. "Are you okay? How did it go?"

"It was surprisingly okay." Diana shrugged. "I'm not fired yet, but I've some work to do to make sure it stays that way."

"I'm glad." Liz hugged her.

Seeing them close together was confusing. Emily probed the feeling the way she would explore a wound. It wasn't jealousy, no, more envy for the easy friendship they had developed, something she always struggled with.

Liz stepped back from Diana. "I'm going home now. Call me anytime you need me, okay?" She looked from Diana to Emily and back until both nodded.

To her surprise, Liz hugged her too. Emily had never been a hugger in any friendship, not even with Jen, but she had to admit it felt good. She tentatively squeezed her in return.

"Don't worry so much," Liz whispered before she let go.

That was easy for her to say, but Emily nodded anyway. She'd at least try.

They entered the office, and Emily locked the door behind Diana. No sense in taking the risk of anyone barging in on their conversation.

She took off her lab coat and hung it on a peg on the door. "I hate these things. Do you want to sit here?" She gestured to the sofa. She didn't want to have barriers between them, neither real ones like her desk nor invisible ones like their work hierarchy.

Diana regarded her for a moment with an inscrutable expression, but then a smile played around her lips. She took off her coat, placed it over the back of the chair, and sat on the sofa. She wasn't as relaxed as Emily was used to seeing, but not as tense as she'd been in Dr. Wallace office as she turned toward Emily and angled her leg.

"That went well, don't you think?" Emily cringed at the false cheeriness in her voice as she sat.

"Yeah. I can't believe he took it so calmly. After the first part of the conversation I really thought it was over." Diana reached for her left hand and intertwined their fingers. "Thank you. But I meant what I said. You don't need to risk your career because of me."

"But I want to," Emily blurted out. "I don't want to work where you don't even get a fair chance. I don't want to be the head of the ED if it means losing you."

"Head of the ED? What do you mean?" Diana's gaze bored into hers, searching for answers.

"Nothing." Emily looked down.

"Em." Diana tilted Emily's chin upward with a finger. "What do you mean?"

"He offered me the position if I help him get rid of you. Well, he didn't say it quite like that, but that's what it comes down to. But I won't do it. I can't." In her haste to get it all out, Emily hadn't taken a breath. Now she gulped in oxygen and clung to Diana's hand like a drowning person.

Diana's eyes darkened to a warm hazel, and she inched closer. The touch at her chin turned into a caress along the side of Emily's neck.

That was so not appropriate at work, but she didn't want Diana to stop. Emily shivered.

As she leaned closer, Diana radiated warmth. "Thank you." Her kiss was soft and almost chaste, but it promised more, passion and love, if Emily wanted it.

"I love you." Emily froze. Had she just said it out loud? Here? Now? Her heart raced, but before she could panic, Diana kissed her again. This time the underlying passion broke through and drove all doubts from her mind.

Diana drew back and fought to catch her breath. "I love you too." She grinned. "But your timing sucks, because here and now I can't show you how much."

A million butterflies broke free. Emily grinned back. "Tonight?"

"Tonight. I better get back to work before I do something stupid." Diana winked, stood, and reached for her lab coat.

"Wait. What is the next step?" Emily smoothed her scrubs, not looking at Diana. She was afraid she'd lose her self-control if she saw her smile.

"You mean with the PR? I have to call Vic and set up a meeting with a publicist. Finding a trustworthy journalist is the second step." Diana groaned. "I hate interviews."

An idea flashed through Emily's mind. She jumped up. "What about Jen? She could do the interview."

"That could work. Good idea." Diana squeezed her shoulder. "And, Emily, let's talk about that job offer later."

"No need. Even if the blackmail didn't taint the offer, I wouldn't want to be your boss. And I don't think it would be healthy for me to be in control of the ED. I'd never go home anymore." With each reason she listed, another link of the chain that shackled her to her own expectations popped open.

"Sure?" Diana ran her hands through her hair.

Emily had never been so sure of anything in her life. She nodded and kissed Diana quickly on the lips again. That tousled look was just irresistible. "Stay here and make your calls. I'll go and see that the work gets done and we can get out of here as soon as possible. Oh, and I'll call Jen right now and tell her to expect your call. I'll text you her number."

Before the temptation to stay grew too strong, she rushed out the door and struggled to suppress her smile. By the time she reached the staff lounge, she had managed a halfway convincing scowl. She had a reputation to uphold, after all.

The doorbell rang as Diana was straining the pasta. She tossed it into the saucepan, ignoring the splashes of hot, salty water on her slate kitchen countertop, and hastened to open the door.

Twenty-four hours after her last visit, Emily was here again, this time with a bag for the weekend in one hand. She looked gorgeous in a taupe long-sleeved blouse and blue jeans.

"Sorry to keep you waiting." Diana took the duffel from her.

As soon as she was inside, Emily pressed her against the closed door. She had showered, and the hair that fell onto Diana's face was still wet. The faint scent of her herbal shampoo enveloped her.

Diana returned the kiss and dropped her bag. It landed with a loud thud on the wooden floor. "Oops, sorry again." She laughed, picked it up, and deposited it next to the bedroom door. "Do you mind joining me in the kitchen?"

"No, it smells heavenly." Emily inhaled deeply through her nose, and her stomach growled.

"Do you want something to drink?" Diana opened the cabinet that held her glasses. "Water? Wine? I opened a red for the sauce, but I didn't drink any yet."

"Both? I'd love a glass of wine with dinner, but I need to rehydrate first, or I'll be drunk in no time."

Diana filled a water glass from the pitcher resting on the counter and rose on her toes to reach the upper shelf to pick two wineglasses. As she turned to offer the water, Emily's gaze snapped back up, but it was too late.

After years in the music industry, Diana was used to being the focus of sexual attention. But never before it had turned her on. "Checking me out?"

Emily grabbed the water glass and nearly emptied it in one gulp. It didn't seem to cool her, though, and her cheeks flamed an adorable scarlet.

Diana laughed and refilled the glass. "I'll be over here, stirring the sauce until you can talk again." She turned to the stove and raised on her toes again.

"You're a tease." Judging by Emily's playful tone, she didn't mind. "Can I help you with anything?"

"No, it's almost ready." She stirred the sauce and put a lid on it. "It only needs to simmer a little bit."

"Do you want to eat or talk first?" Emily took a sponge from the sink and wiped away the spilled water.

Diana shrugged. She'd rather get the potentially uncomfortable part of the evening out of the way. "Everything is going as planned. I talked to Vic and the publicist, and they agree an article could be a good way to go. Jen was nice on the phone. She even offered to help me find another journalist if I didn't trust her because of how we met first."

"Oh, I never thought about that. Did you choose anyone else?" She returned the sponge to the sink and washed her hands.

Diana handed her a clean towel, smiling to herself. No wonder Emily's kitchen looked as though she never used it. "No, I think it's a good idea to get to know each other better. We're meeting tomorrow morning at the Rainbow Home. I had a session scheduled, and she wanted to see it. Do you want to join us?"

"I'd love to." Emily stepped closer and took Diana's hand. Her fingers were cool, but the grip was warm and reassuring.

Diana raised their joined hands and kissed Emily's knuckles before letting go. She turned back to the stove to stir the sauce and to mix it with the pasta. Thyme and rosemary filled the air with scents of home. The quiet domesticity of Emily helping in her kitchen had flooded her with the same warmth. She wished she could share that sense of belonging with her.

Oh, but she could. She switched off the gas, covered the pan, and opened her kitchen drawer. It was full of stuff that didn't fit elsewhere, like a ball of rubber bands, wooden barbecue skewers, and the ugly Christmas tree bottle opener. She'd bet her drum kit that Emily's fingers itched right now to sort it by function, size, and maybe even color.

Here it was. Before she lost the courage, Diana took one of Emily's hands and pressed the cold metal into her palm.

Emily's eyes widened as she opened her hand to reveal the key. "Is that...?"

"I don't want you to break in or wait for me anymore. Come in whenever you want to, whether I'm here or not. Stay as long as you want to. I'll show you how to set the alarm later." After growing up with five brothers and later sharing a house with Mel, Katie, and whatever lover Katie had picked up, Diana hadn't thought she'd give up her newfound solitude so soon, but Emily's presence wasn't an intrusion.

Emily still hadn't said anything.

"Too much too soon?" The last thing Diana wanted to do was to push her into something she wasn't ready for.

A smile slowly softened Emily's stunned expression. Instead of answering, she wrapped her arms around her and buried her face in her neck. After a minute, she mumbled into Diana's hair, "No, it's perfect. Thank you."

Her warm breath tickled Diana, but soon her giggles turned into moans as Emily nuzzled her neck and followed the contours of the tank top down to the swell of her breasts. Her hands roamed Diana's back downward until she squeezed her butt.

The key hit the slate floor with a high metallic sound. Emily immediately let go of Diana and bent down to retrieve it.

Laughing, Diana stepped aside to give her more room. "I'll get you a key chain if you want."

Emily shook her head, went to her bag, and retrieved the simple ring that held her keys. She pushed them to one side one by one, then hesitated at the last one with a wistful expression.

Diana recognized the key to the beach house, but before she could bring it up, Emily fastened Diana's key to the ring and stowed it away.

Instead of joining her again, Emily extended her hand and wriggled her fingers in invitation. The spark in her eyes left no doubt that she had no intention of getting back to the kitchen and dinner anytime soon.

Suddenly, Diana wasn't hungry anymore, at least not for food.

The ravenous gleam in Diana's eyes mesmerized Emily. She walked backward until the backs of her legs bumped into the bed. She hooked a finger through a belt loop to pull Diana closer for the last inches. The scent of vanilla, almonds, and Diana made her weak in the knees. With a deep sigh, she sat on the mattress.

Goose bumps erupted on Diana's skin as Emily blew along the line between her tank top and her faded blue jeans. She skimmed her fingers underneath the hem of the forest-green cotton to widen the gap and then placed openmouthed kisses on the soft, soft skin.

Diana moaned and leaned into the touch. Her hands came to rest on Emily's shoulders, a light contact that turned into a solid grip as Emily opened the button of her jeans and slowly pulled down the zipper.

The power that came with the knowledge she was responsible for Diana's sighs and squirming, signs of her pleasure, shot directly to Emily's head and nearly made her dizzy.

The jeans had to go, as much as Emily had enjoyed the way they showcased Diana's tight ass. She pulled them down, taking the panties with them to the floor. On her way back up, she kissed the inside of Diana's left leg, mirroring the path on the other side with a fingertip. Just before she reached the apex, she moved outward, toward the curve of the hip bone.

The hold on Emily's shoulder tightened as Diana quickly stepped out of her clothes that pooled on the floor. A gentle push and Emily toppled onto her back with her feet still on the floor.

Just as fast, Diana crawled up to straddle her.

Perfect, just where Emily wanted her: Every part of her easy to reach.

In a teasing slow motion, Diana pulled up her tank top to reveal perfectly shaped breasts.

Emily's gaze immediately fixated on her nipples, which had already hardened in expectation. She wasn't wearing a bra, and Emily sat up and kissed first one, then the other, enjoying the curves between them and the moans she elicited from Diana. Her abdominal muscles quivered, but the strain was worth it.

Diana untucked her blouse at her back and slid both hands beneath it. The contrast between the soft fingertips and the calluses on her palms sent shivers up and down her spine.

Moaning, Emily pressed her face closer to Diana's soft flesh. She could get lost in her scent and the rapidly beating heart under her lips.

Still supporting her with one hand on her back, Diana sneaked the other between them to open the buttons of Emily's blouse from the top.

Every light touch tingled and made her yearn for more—more skin, more contact, more Diana. Emily leaned back to give her room to work with, enjoying the sense of security that resting in her strong embrace brought.

As if she sensed her need, Diana let go of the buttons and pulled up the hem of the blouse instead, over her head and down both arms.

But the inside-out garment wouldn't slip over her wrists. Emily tried to reverse the movement to pull the cuffs free so Diana could unbutton them. A strong grip clutched her closer to Diana, trapping her arms and the blouse between them.

"Oh, no," Diana whispered directly into her ear, her voice husky. "Why don't we leave it like that for a while?"

Adrenaline spiked, and Emily thought her heart would explode. She trusted Diana; she really did, but giving up control like that had never been a fantasy of hers. Fear of the unknown froze her insides, and she couldn't reply.

Diana nuzzled her earlobe, then whispered, "Is this okay?"

Her gaze fell on the flames licking across Diana's shoulder and winding around her biceps. Instantly, her reluctance melted as red-hot desire scorched her brain.

Unable to speak, Emily nodded and was rewarded with featherlight kisses along her chin to her mouth.

Their lips met in a deep kiss, and Emily tried to convey her arousal. Diana answered in kind, and each stroke of her tongue sent tendrils of fire through her blood.

When they came up for air, Diana was panting as much as she was. After a moment, Diana slowly leaned forward and lowered Emily to the bed. She nudged her to lift her legs and scoot up toward the headboard. Her gaze locked with Emily's, and without blinking she slid her hands to the front, following the contours of the bra Emily was still wearing and down to the hands captured in the wrinkled blouse.

Emily's heartbeat kicked up another notch as she realized her intentions. She didn't protest.

Diana encircled both wrists, lifted her arms and the entrapping blouse, and laid them on the pillow behind her head. "Can you stay like this?"

Her mouth was dry, and she needed two tries to answer. "Yes." All the moisture in her body seemed to have pooled between her legs. How on earth hadn't she known that something like that would be so hot?

The permission broke the spell of Diana's gaze, and she kissed her on the mouth again. This time, she didn't linger but followed a path down her neck to her breasts, accompanied by strong hands stroking every inch of Emily they could reach.

From Emily's point of view, she could only see the dark, tousled hair and glimpses of the brilliant green and red ink. Her fingers ached with the need to guide and encourage her, but she forced herself to stay still and enjoy the sensual exploration.

Diana didn't remove her bra, lavishing her breasts and taut nipples through the thin silk instead.

Every touch ran directly from her nipples to her clit like an electric current. Emily feared she might come from this stimulation alone, so she was grateful for the wet fabric soothing and protecting her skin.

The pop of the button and release of the zipper of her jeans was a relief. Cool air caressed her as Diana pulled her jeans and panties down and tossed them aside. As Emily had done, she kissed up one leg while stroking the other. Only she didn't move outward as she reached the apex of her thighs, but hovered over her, her warm breath tickling her curls.

Emily raised her head with difficulty and met Diana's gaze. A small circle of brilliant green surrounded her dilated pupils. The mixture of tenderness and desire reflected in them flooded her with a warmth she'd never felt before. Any insecurity was swept away by her trust in Diana. Closing her eyes, she spread her legs and lay down again.

Emily was so tense with excitement that the first touch of Diana's tongue almost didn't register, but with each stroke and swirl, her focus narrowed on the elating sensations. At first, she tried to discern the different stimulations, then the tide of pleasure reduced her to a moaning and shuddering mess. She no longer thought about what Diana did or how she was doing it. Her body was Diana's to play with like an instrument, and Diana's performance drew her to heights she'd never dreamed of before. The climax completely overwhelmed and surprised her, and Emily came with a yell, almost crushing Diana between her thighs.

After a while, Diana removed her fingers and crawled up to her. She licked them clean with an impish grin, wriggling her eyebrows. "I don't want to stain your blouse." She untangled the garment, opened the cuffs, and kissed each wrist as it was freed.

Finally, Emily could bury her hands in Diana's hair. "It was torture not to touch you. I love your hair." She massaged her scalp and elicited tiny moans. Her muscles had turned to mush, and she wasn't yet ready for more, but she wanted to keep Diana close.

"Mmmh. Likewise." Diana rested her head on her shoulder and twirled a strand of Emily's hair around a finger. "Why do you color it?"

"What? How did you know?" She'd done it for so long that she almost thought of brown as her natural color.

"Well, it doesn't match your other body hair. Your natural color is red, right?" Diana tickled her chin with the tip of the strand.

Heat that had nothing to do with arousal rose to her cheeks. "I always thought... I've been told it looks unprofessional. Nobody would take me seriously." She didn't want to bring her mother into the bedroom, but she supposed Diana knew her well enough to guess.

Diana shook her head. "I wouldn't think so. But it is your hair to do whatever you want with." She pushed up on her elbow to look into Emily's eyes. "No matter what you do to your hair, I think you're sexy and professional and beautiful and serious and perfect." She accentuated each word with a kiss, working her way up from Emily's collarbone to her mouth.

She was far from perfect, but right here and now she almost believed Diana. The kiss roused her enough to collect her strength and push Diana onto her back. It was her time to play.

Diana studied Jen as she set up a recording app on her phone and then placed it on the wooden crate between their deck chairs. With her straight blond hair in a ponytail and wearing jeans and a T-shirt from a band so obscure that even Diana didn't know them, she looked deceptively young and innocent. Maybe that helped with snooping out the stories. *Stop it.* The few questions Jen had asked so far had all been professional and respectful. And Diana had promised Emily and Mel to give Jen the benefit of the doubt and trust her. Jen had shadowed Diana on her visit to the Rainbow Home but had suggested more privacy for the interview.

Emily arrived with a large pitcher of iced tea she had made in a surprising show of domesticity. Maybe it was her way of coping with the tension between the three of them.

Diana sighed. Sitting in her garden with her lover and her lover's best friend on a warm June afternoon should have been a fun social event. Instead, it filled her with trepidation.

Jen took the glass Emily offered and sipped from it. "Thanks, that's great." She smiled at Emily, then turned to Diana with a far more serious expression. "Before we start the official part, I'd like to say something."

"Sure." All day Diana had waited for a glance behind the friendly girl-next-door facade.

"We have gotten off on the wrong foot. You probably thought I was an unprofessional hussy who tried to sleep her way to a story after our first meeting. And after our second encounter, I definitely thought you were a player who wanted to take advantage of Emily's limited experience with women." Jen held up her hand to stave off the protest from Emily and Diana. "I know, I know. I'm sorry."

She held out her hand, and Diana shook it. "I'm sorry too. Mel assured me that I could trust you."

"Great. Let's do this interview. Now, what I suggest is not my normal journalistic behavior, but I think unique circumstances allow for unique measures. Don't hold anything back. Don't censor every word and just talk to me. Trust me to extract the story that needs to be told without compromising your reputation as a physician. I'll let you read and approve the articles. That's something I've never offered to anyone before."

Did she really mean that? This contradicted everything Diana had learned about working with the press during her music career. She wanted to trust her because Emily did, but a small grain of doubt remained. "What are you getting out of it?"

Jen smiled and didn't seem to be offended by the question. "An exclusive story?"

Diana raised her eyebrows and waited. That answer only scratched the surface.

"I'm doing it for Emily. She always supported me and kept me grounded, even during my wild party years at the university." Jen reached for Emily's hand and squeezed it.

The genuine caring for her best friend showed in Jen's expression, and Diana believed her, but this wasn't just about her. Her life story was intertwined with Katie and Katie's drug addiction. "What about Katie?"

"I could probably make a lot of money selling the backstory now that she's back in rehab, but then I'd lose two friends and a lover. Believe me, that's not worth it."

Diana could only detect honesty in Jen's gaze. "Okay. Let's do it your way. Where do we begin?"

Jen started the recording.

━━━━━━

Night had fallen while they had talked. Emily lit a few candles and replaced the iced tea with pizza and beer. Diana's growling stomach was grateful for the attentiveness. She munched on the pizza without tasting it. Her thoughts swirled around her past, and Emily and Jen's quiet conversation became white noise.

Jen opened a second beer and placed it in front of Diana. "Do you want to call it a day?"

Diana shook her head. She wanted to get it over with, and the sooner Jen had all the information, the faster she could write the articles. She took a large sip of her beer, enjoying the refreshing bitterness. "What's next?"

Jen restarted the recorder. "Why did you leave the band?"

The question wasn't a surprise, but the emotional turmoil the memories still evoked caught Diana off guard. "Short story: someone nearly died, and I resuscitated them. I realized then that I wanted to go back to medicine."

"Okay, if you think that's enough, we can leave it like this." Jen's voice was calm, and Diana couldn't make out her features in the semidarkness to see if her expression matched.

If Diana was honest with herself, it wasn't enough. She wanted to tell the story, especially to Emily. Jen had proven to be an attentive listener, asking insightful questions. She took another sip of beer to wet her dry throat, then pushed it away. She didn't need any more alcohol to make her more light-headed tonight. "It was February, Katie's birthday, and we had a party at our place. Not that she needed an excuse to celebrate, but there were more guests than usual. I didn't want to mingle and tried to hide in my room, but Mel brought me out to socialize. I wasn't in the mood for small talk and putting on a happy facade."

Diana closed her eyes and concentrated on the state of mind she'd been in. She wanted Jen and Emily to understand she'd hovered on the edge of change, even before the trigger had pushed her over the precipice. "I wasn't exactly unhappy with the band and my life, but I didn't like the direction I was going anymore. Not so much going as staying stagnant, repeating the same cycle every year. We wrote songs, recorded them, went on a tour, became stressed and unhappy, returned to the farm to recharge, and then did it all over again. Mix in a few parties and award ceremonies, that's it. Nothing meaningful. Not even writing music held any meaning anymore, because we tailored our songs to appeal to our fans rather than to express our feelings. Nothing worthwhile happened that we could honestly write about."

Despite her intentions, Diana took a large sip of her beer. It had warmed and tasted stale. "That evening, I saw Katie with a new lover. I didn't mind, but they shared drugs, and that pissed me off. We had nearly lost our first contract because of it, and I thought Katie had changed. Instead of facing her, I crept back to my room and ignored the party." She peeled the label from the bottle with her fingernails and took a few calming breaths before continuing. "In the middle of the night, Katie ran naked into my room and woke me up. At first, I thought she was having a bad trip, then I realized something was wrong. I followed her and found her lover unconscious in her bed. She'd obviously vomited and probably aspirated some of it. I did everything by the book, called 911, started resuscitation when her breathing stopped. Only I couldn't do much without equipment. It felt like ages until the paramedics arrived. They intubated her and got her back, but it was too late." Diana's voice wavered. "I never learned the details because the family kept her hidden, but I know she's got severe brain damage. I should have been faster." The guilt remaining from the night lingered, and now it rose. Fighting to keep it from swallowing her, she dug her nails into her palm. The pain kept her in the here and now.

Emily opened Diana's fist and took her hand. She had moved to sit on Diana's armrest while she talked, not that Diana had noticed anything. "You can't know how long she was in this state before Katie got you. And even if you'd been superhumanly fast, the odds of resuscitation always remain incalculable."

"I know. Thank you." Setting the beer bottle with the shredded label on the table, Diana turned to look at Jen. "That night changed something. I couldn't go back to my life as a drummer and seriously contemplated returning to medicine."

"You did it because you feel guilty," Jen said.

"There's nothing to feel guilty about!" Emily's voice was sharp.

Diana considered both statements for a moment. "Guilt might have sent me on that road again, but it didn't keep me there. What I learned from the resuscitation was that I had grown enough to take on the responsibility for another life. During my first residency, I had always feared my reaction in such a situation and had avoided critical patients whenever possible. Playing in a band wasn't just more fun; it was emotionally easier. Nobody died if I played a wrong beat. I think I have finally grown enough to be a good physician. I might not have needed a detour of nine years; maybe a good kick in the ass would have brought me to the same result."

Emily linked their fingers. "You're right. You have that sense of responsibility now. I see it more in you than in the other residents. I always thought it was because of your age, but that's only part of it."

"And Katie? If the rumors are true, she overdosed. I know you can't break patient confidentiality. Can you tell me how it was for you to see her again, as her physician?"

"At first I didn't recognize her. I just did what had to be done, but it reminded me of the scene with her lover. I struggled with that, but it was a relief that I was able to do all the things I wanted to do last year." Diana looked from Emily to Jen. Both nodded, and it helped to see the understanding in their expressions. "When I realized who she was, it hit me like a meteorite, but it didn't immobilize me. It hurt to see her like this. Intellectually, I knew she'll always struggle with addiction. No matter what her mother, her friends, what I did, no one could help her stay clean for long. But I thought after what happened last year she'd come around, but obviously, I was wrong." To her surprise, the hurt was only a faint memory now. Diana was tired of thinking about Katie and the emotional roller coaster she'd been through in the last nine years. She massaged her neck with one hand. The tension threatened to evolve into a headache.

"I've one final question. Did you ever take drugs? Serious stuff like Katie, not a just some weed?" Jen looked at her with a steady gaze, and her tone was nonjudgmental.

"Jen!" Emily's voice rose to a painful height.

Diana had expected the question, and her respect for Jen rose. She asked what everyone wanted to know: was she safe around prescription drugs? Diana hesitated. Did she trust Jen enough? Holding Jen's gaze, she decided honesty was the only way to go. "Yes. I tried most of it. I don't know where my upbringing or genetic makeup differed from Katie's, but I was lucky and never got addicted. I was curious, gave it a try once or twice, and that's it. I never even touched a joint after college." She shrugged and grinned. "I'd prefer it if that didn't make it into the article."

Jen nodded and grinned back. "It won't. Thanks for your honesty."

Diana turned to Emily, afraid of her judgment. She couldn't read her expression in the darkness, but the clasp of her hand never wavered.

Emily bent down and kissed her on the lips. "I love you."

Chapter 21

DIANA'S ONLY CONSOLATION WAS THAT the drunk student who had been stupid enough to try to run through a glass door probably felt worse.

She was dead tired, and it was only the beginning of her first night shift. She'd been relegated to nights in an attempt to minimize exposure to the public as a compromise for keeping her job. Not too bad as compromises go.

The upside was that she'd had time to spend the day outside in her small garden, taking advantage of the late June weather to plant a few flowers and shrubs. Mel had surprised her with a visit to take her mind of her current situation. The day had been great, but the downside was that she hurt all over now.

A check of the electronic whiteboard at the nurses' station showed that finally every patient was covered for now. Time enough for a quick coffee run. Without it, the night would be endless. She hadn't even taken three steps in the direction of the coffee shop beyond the waiting room when someone called her name.

Diana turned around.

Stacy had left the admissions desk to jog after her. "Dr. Petrell, wait!"

Diana had to smile as the giant bun on top of Stacy's head wobbled with each step. "What can I do for you, Stacy? And I've told you to call me Diana."

"I wouldn't go through there if I were you. Another couple of fans pretending to be sick are waiting. Peter volunteered to see them. They asked me if you have a girlfriend." Stacy blushed and avoided her gaze.

"I'm so sorry you have to deal with them. Thanks for warning me." Diana sighed. "I hoped to get some coffee."

Stacy perked up. "I can get you one. How do you like it?"

"No, but thank you. I'll be fine with the brew from the staff lounge." Not that Diana didn't appreciate the offer, but since her outing as a former rock star two weeks ago, Stacy's usual friendliness had turned into starstruck adoration. She didn't want to give her wrong signals and encourage that behavior.

On her way to the staff lounge, angry yelling caught her attention. A female voice was scolding someone, probably one of her colleagues by the words she could make out. "Brainless resident" was repeated several times.

The door to treatment room two swung open and nearly hit her.

Dr. Riley, the cardiologist, stormed out, and Diana jumped back, but it was too late. She hit Diana directly in the middle like a medicine ball. Both swayed, and Diana fought to keep on her feet, trying to steady the very pregnant woman at the same time.

"Keep your hands off me. What are you doing here, standing in the way?" Dr. Riley fixated her with cold blue eyes.

Diana raised her hands in what she hoped was a conciliatory manner and took a step to the side. The cardiologist's temper was legendary, and she didn't want to get into a discussion with her.

Dr. Riley brushed by her without another word, but after a couple of steps she stopped and clutched her belly with both hands. Her breath came in short bursts.

Had Diana hurt her? Or was she having contractions?

"Dr. Riley, are you okay? Can I help you?" Diana didn't like the woman, but ignoring her obvious discomfort wasn't an option.

"Okay? I haven't been okay for nine fucking months." Her voice shook, and she clutched her belly again. "I don't have time for this today."

"Do you want to lie down? Should I call your obstetrician?" Diana looked around for anyone who could help, but for once, the hallway was empty.

Dr. Riley shook her head. "Just Braxton Hicks. No need to call anyone. I've still got work to do." She had regained control of her voice, and it was as cold as her eyes. Only the sweat beading on her temples and the tight set of her mouth betrayed her discomfort.

Diana doubted the contractions were just false labor judging by their force. The real question was should she interfere? Dr. Riley was a colleague and could interpret the signs as well as she could. If she wanted to ignore them, it wasn't really dangerous to let her go off to another part of the hospital. Wherever she went, she'd be surrounded by medical personnel, and as soon as the pain became unmanageable or her water broke, Dr. Riley could get help. She'd give it one try to convince her, then she'd let her go. "We could check you out real quick without signing you in. If you're right, you can return to work anytime."

"You're the rock chick, right?" Dr. Riley pointed her finger at Diana. "What do you know?"

Diana suppressed a wince. She'd heard something along those lines from a couple of patients in the last week, but not until now had a colleague doubted her. Diana watched her leave, too frustrated to reply. And what should she say?

Wait, where was Dr. Riley going? That wasn't the way to the cardiology department. That way was only the back entrance to the small garden. Should she follow her and risk another confrontation? She shouldn't be alone in her condition. Diana squared her shoulders and hastened after her.

She caught up with Dr. Riley at the bench where she and Emily had shared their first kiss. It seemed as if it had been another life, but was only two months ago. "Dr. Riley, I'm sorry to disturb you out here, but I think you shouldn't be alone right now."

Dr. Riley turned around with a frown. She opened her mouth, but the scalding reply Diana expected didn't come. Instead, Dr. Riley paled, and her eyes rolled upward. Swaying, she reached out to steady herself. It was too late. She tumbled to the ground like an overripe pear falling from a tree.

"Dr. Riley?" Diana kneeled next to her and tried to rouse her. When shaking didn't help, she rubbed her knuckles over the upper part of Dr. Riley's sternum peeking out from her scrubs. No reaction. She checked her pulse at her neck. Irregular and racing, but strong enough. She reached for her phone but then remembered she had left it in the locker today because someone from a so-called news website had found out her number and bombarded her with messages. She patted Dr. Riley's pockets until she found her phone, but it was locked. Great. Should she call 911?

A soft moan came from Dr. Riley. "What...what happened? Why am I on the ground?" She clutched her belly and moaned. After a moment, the pain seemed to have passed, and she slowly looked from one side to the other until her gaze fixated on Diana. "You, Rock Chick! I said I didn't need help!"

Diana had enough. "That was before you fainted. Now shut up and let me help. And that's Dr. Rock Chick to you."

To Diana's surprise, Dr. Riley did as she was told. Diana didn't know if she reacted to her words or the authoritative tone or if she was too weak to protest, but it worked. "Can you sit up?"

"I didn't faint," Dr. Riley mumbled. She lifted a hand to push her sweaty hair out of her eyes and sat.

"Fainted, collapsed, call it what you want. You had a syncope and an irregular tachycardia." Diana pulled gloves and her stethoscope from her pocket and worked through a physical examination before Dr. Riley could complain again. When Diana touched her belly, it hardened with a contraction, running from left to right.

Dr. Riley gripped her hand, and Diana nearly groaned along with her as she squeezed it. When the contraction had passed, she extricated her fingers.

The green scrubs pants were now stained and wet. Her water must have just broken.

Shit. "If I help, can you move to the bench?"

It wasn't easy, but she managed to heave Dr. Riley up. Both gulped for air when she had finally settled.

"No way you can walk back now."

"Just give me ten minutes, Rock Chick, I'll be fine."

"In what kind of denial are you? You're in labor, and I don't know if we have ten minutes. Could you unlock your phone so I can call for a stretcher?" She called the nurses' station and quickly explained where she was and what had happened. Madison promised to come with help. Diana turned back to the woman on the bench.

She was still pale around her mouth and eyes, but red splotches colored her cheeks. Breathing much too fast, she was clutching her belly again.

"Dr. Riley, I need to get you undressed to see how far you are."

She let her head fall back and nodded.

Diana took the silent compliance as a bad sign. Removing the wet scrub pants was awkward, but with some help from Dr. Riley, Diana managed to pull them down to her ankles. They were swollen and judging by the discoloration of the skin had been like this for a while. *No wonder she's so bad-tempered. That must hurt like hell.* She carefully peeled the pants and her underwear off the rest of the way.

Another contraction started. Dr. Riley pulled up her legs and moaned.

Diana glanced at the hospital building. *Where are the others?* When she looked back down, she could already see the baby's head. Oh shit. "You need to push."

"I can't. Not now. That's not the plan." Dr. Riley's eyes were large and filled with fear.

Why was she so stubborn? "Are you kidding me? Fuck your plan. We don't have time for this. The head is crowning, and you need to push—now!" Diana carefully pulled her legs apart, holding eye contact with Dr. Riley, who didn't resist but still didn't look as though she realized the importance of the situation. "Listen, I'm sorry the birth is not going as you planned, but your child seems to be as stubborn as you are. We can do this, but only with your help. So when the next contraction comes, you push. Okay?"

"Fuck!" Dr. Riley screamed and pushed.

"Yeah, fuck." Diana couldn't agree more.

Emily needed a minute to make sense of what Madison was trying to tell her. Diana was delivering Dr. Riley's baby in the garden? Was this a joke? But the nurse wasn't such a good actress to pull off the mixture of excitement and incredulity.

Hastening around the last bend in the garden, Emily couldn't believe her eyes. She stopped abruptly, and Madison, Tony, and Courtney nearly barreled into her.

Dr. Riley lay on the bench with a tiny baby wrapped in dark blue cotton that looked suspiciously like a scrub shirt, grinning in the deliriously happy way only new mothers with the rush of endorphins could. It was the first time Emily had seen her without a frown.

"There's the cavalry." Dr. Riley pointed at Emily.

Diana turned around. She looked stupefied but echoed Dr. Riley's wide grin. Blood covered her gloved hands, and she wasn't wearing anything but scrub pants, a stethoscope around her neck, and a black sports bra. The contents of her shirt pockets were scattered on the ground. She must have just tossed everything when she'd used her shirt as an improvised wrap for the baby.

Emily opened her mouth, closed it, and opened it again. She didn't know what to say.

"Oh my God!" Madison didn't have the same problem.

Diana peeled off her gloves, turned them inside out, and stuffed them into a pocket of her pants. She exchanged a glance with Dr. Riley and both started laughing like maniacs.

Emily shook her head but couldn't help smiling. She waved at the others to push the gurney forward. "Let's get them inside before a visitor finds us and thinks they stepped into the shooting of a new soap opera."

Tony and Madison shook out of their trance and moved to help Dr. Riley sit up, while Courtney hung back. She was probably already formulating the story that she wanted to spread as soon as possible.

After she was transferred to the gurney, Dr. Riley reached for Diana's hand. "Thank you, Rock Chick. Sorry, I mean *Dr.* Rock Chick."

Diana rolled her eyes. "No, I have to thank you. I guess my story won't be number one on the gossip charts of the hospital any longer."

"Yeah, me giving birth like an animal in the wilderness might top a former rock star." Beneath the veneer of a foul temper, Dr. Riley had a surprising sense of humor.

Emily wasn't so sure about that, especially considering Diana's state of undress, but at least she would no longer be the sole focus of the gossip. She stepped up to Diana and put her hand on the small of her back to offer silent support.

Dr. Riley looked at Emily's hand and raised her eyebrows. "Or maybe you two will head up the charts next."

Emily froze as her words registered, and Diana stiffened underneath her hand. *Oh, shit.* She hadn't realized what her automatic gesture would broadcast. Heat rising to her cheeks, she took a step to the side.

What happened then would be anyone's guess. Multiple scenarios from indifference to outrage flashed through her mind.

Diana's gaze locked on Emily's eyes, searching for an answer to the unspoken question. There might still be time to deny it.

Her heartbeat echoed painfully loud in her ears. No, she couldn't lie about this. Diana's story had taught her that you could never control what others were thinking and doing. You could only try to stay true to yourself.

Determined to follow her heart for once, she moved back to Diana. "Let them talk."

Warmth spread through Emily at Diana's beaming smile. If anyone had any doubts before, the adoration in Diana's eyes cried out her love louder than any speech could.

"I guess today will stretch the capacity of the gossip network. Does anyone want to take a bet what story will spread first?" Tony stepped to the head of the gurney and pushed.

Madison nearly stumbled as she jogged to the other end to pull. Courtney followed them but glanced back to Emily and Diana every few steps.

When the procession had disappeared around the corner, Diana held out her arms and Emily willingly stepped into them. "Are you okay?"

"Shouldn't I ask you that? You just played midwife on a park bench." Emily buried her nose in Diana's neck. The faint scent of sweat, almonds, and something that was purely Diana reassured her their decision to admit their relationship was the right one. They had nothing to be ashamed of.

"I can't believe I did that. Good that Dr. Riley and I were alone. We both cursed and swore like sailors. And all the fluid and blood..." She shook herself. "You're lucky neither of us is a man. A close-up of a birth is a powerful contraceptive method."

"So, I don't need to be worried I left you alone for ten minutes and already another woman undressed you?" Emily kissed her neck to show she was teasing.

"Hardly. And for the record, I undressed her first." Diana tilted Emily's face up and cupped her jaw.

Emily closed the last inch herself to kiss Diana. As always, the world retreated until only the sensation of warm lips remained. Diana softly nibbled at her lower lip until Emily opened her mouth. The gliding of Diana's tongue against hers caused a tingling that quickly spread through her body. Emily couldn't get enough of the exciting sensation of belonging together. She'd buried her hands in Diana's hair to deepen the kiss when a shrill cry tore them apart.

The baby didn't seem to like the last part of the transport, or maybe he or she was hungry. Emily leaned her forehead against Diana's to catch her breath. It was good the little one had reminded her of her surroundings. They were still at work, even if Diana didn't look and feel like it in her arms.

Diana stepped out of the embrace with a happy sigh. "I know we didn't plan it like this, but I think it's better to have it out in the open. I hate secrets."

Emily couldn't agree more. "Throwing plans overboard seems to be the theme today."

And not only today, she added mentally. Diana had completely derailed Emily's plans for her life. Not that they had been the best of plans, but she had felt safe and secure. Only now she knew they had lacked the most important factor for happiness. With the love they shared, any path they chose for their future together would be the right one.

Epilogue

EMILY EMPTIED THE BAG OF marshmallows into the large bowl her mother had only ever used to serve salad.

The door to the kitchen opened, and the smell of campfire and the sound of laughter preceded Jen. "Are you ready? I'm starving."

As she reached for one of the soft sugary treats, Emily swatted her hand away. "You're always starving. We just had giant burgers."

"Who knew that Mel could grill like a pro?" Jen's voice was dreamy.

"Next to a chef, she's probably the best match you could ever find. I like her." Mel's quiet humor was a good foil to Jen's exuberance.

Emily effortlessly got along with Diana's best friend too. The four of them had spent the last weekend renovating and painting her parents' beach house. The kitchen was now bright red, and little pieces of driftwood had replaced the cabinet handles. Emily couldn't believe it was the same room her mother had reigned in. She pressed another bottle of wine into Jen's hand and grabbed the bowl to return outside.

On the porch, she had to smile at the collection of shells and sea glass on the wooden railing. Diana never returned from their walks with empty pockets.

Diana and Mel sat on the log of the old tree they had spent the morning lugging across the plot to the new fire pit. A tall drum stood to one side, next to Mel's guitar case. The open fire colored the scene in golden light and cast long shadows. Emily's heart clenched at the sight of Diana's back, the emerald dragon dancing on her skin with each movement. Unlike the drummer in her recurring dream, Diana turned around, and her bright smile invited her into their circle, close to the fire.

Mel reached for the bowl and pierced a marshmallow with one of the sticks she had carved this afternoon. Liz, who had joined them to celebrate the Fourth of July, took the bottle of wine and topped off their glasses, then relaxed back into the deck chair she had dragged to the fire earlier.

"Come here." Diana pulled her onto the cushion she had placed on the ground in front of the log.

Emily sat and leaned back, safely ensconced between Diana's warm legs. "Don't you want to play your drum? What's it called again?"

"Djembe. And I can always play later." Diana ruffled Emily's hair and massaged her scalp. "I love your new haircut."

"I'm still getting used to it." Sighing, Emily relaxed into the mesmerizing movement of Diana's fingertips. Last week, she had the hairdresser cut it radically short because it was the only way to grow out the mousy brown color she had hidden behind for too long. She planned to let it grow back to her old length, but for now, she could enjoy Diana's fascination with touching the short strands.

The flames flickered, shooting up sparks now and then. The roar of the ocean interwove with the soft voices of Jen and Liz talking on the other side of the fire and the melody Mel played on her guitar. Happiness filled her, a new feeling of belonging to a family. Emily tilted her head back, and her heart swelled at the sight of Diana smiling at her.

She immediately bowed down to fulfill Emily's unspoken request to kiss her. She tasted like home.

About Chris Zett

Chris Zett lives in Berlin, Germany, with her wife. TV inspired her to study medicine, but she found out soon enough that real life in a hospital consists more of working long hours than performing heroic rescues. The part about finding a workplace romance turned out to be true, though.

She uses any opportunity to escape the routine by reading, writing, or traveling. Her favorite destinations include penguin colonies in Patagonia and stone circles in Scotland.

CONNECT WITH CHRIS
Website: www.chris-zett.com
Facebook: www.facebook.com/ChrisZettAuthor
Instagram: ChrisZettAuthor
Twitter: @ChrisZettAuthor
E-Mail: chris-zett@web.de

Other Books from Ylva Publishing

www.ylva-publishing.com

L.A. Metro
(The L.A. Metro Series – Book 1)
second edition

RJ Nolan

ISBN: 978-3-95533-041-5
Length: 349 pages (97,000 words)

Dr. Kimberly Donovan's life is in shambles. After her medical ethics are questioned, first her family, then her closeted lover, the Chief of the ER, betray her. Determined to make a fresh start, she flees to California and L.A. Metropolitan Hospital. When she meets Jess McKenna, L.A. Metro's Chief of the ER the attraction is immediate. Can either woman overcome her past to make a future together?

All the Little Moments
G Benson

ISBN: 978-3-95533-341-6
Length: 350 pages (132,000 words)

Anna is focused on her career as an anaesthetist. When a tragic accident leaves her responsible for her young niece and nephew, her life changes abruptly. Completely overwhelmed, Anna barely has time to brush her teeth in the morning let alone date a woman. But then she collides with a long-legged stranger…

Falling Hard

Jae

ISBN: 978-3-95533-829-9 (paperback)
Length: 346 pages (122,000 words)

Dr. Jordan Williams devotes her life to saving patients in the OR and pleasuring women in the bedroom.

Jordan's new neighbor, single mom Emma, is the polar opposite. Family and fidelity mean everything to her.

When Emma helps Jordan recover after a bad fall, they quickly grow closer.

But neither counted on falling hard—for each other.

Heart Trouble

Jae

ISBN: 978-3-95533-732-2
Length: 312 pages (109,000 words)

Dr. Hope Finlay learned early in life not to get attached to anyone because it never lasts.

Laleh Samadi, who comes from a big, boisterous family, is the exact opposite.

When Laleh ends up in the ER with heart trouble, Hope saves her life. Afterwards, strange things begin to occur until they can no longer deny the mysterious connection between them.

Are they losing their minds…or their hearts?

Irregular Heartbeat
© 2018 by Chris Zett

ISBN: 978-3-95533-996-8

Also available as e-book.

Published by Ylva Publishing, legal entity of Ylva Verlag, e.Kfr.

Ylva Verlag, e.Kfr.
Owner: Astrid Ohletz
Am Kirschgarten 2
65830 Kriftel
Germany

www.ylva-publishing.com

First edition: 2018

Credits
Edited by Sandra Gerth and JoSelle
Cover Design and Print Layout by Streetlight Graphics

Printed in Great Britain
by Amazon